FLASH POINT

JASON TRAPP - BOOK 3

JACK SLATER

1

His name was Alexy Sokolov. *Professor* Alexy Sokolov. And he was a dead man.

Alexy knew this was true because in Russia, you did not see the things that he had seen, or steal the things that he had stolen without either being very, very powerful–or very, very dead. He had stumbled into this mess by accident, but that wouldn't save him.

He was a loose end.

They knew who he was.

And it was only a matter of time.

The professor was sitting in the St. Petersburg lounge at Moscow Sheremetyevo Airport, on the very edge of a deep, leather-backed armchair, clutching his briefcase. His knees were close together, and if someone had looked closely, they might have seen them shaking. His back was ramrod straight.

"*Nervnyy letchik?*"

Alexy flinched at the sound of the woman's voice. His head snapped to the left, toward its source, and found only an apologetic glance flashing back in his direction. He gulped, attempting to remember what she had said.

Nervous flyer?

He fished a handkerchief from the inside pocket of his corduroy blazer and wiped a bead of sweat from his forehead.

"*Izvineniya*," he said. *I'm sorry.* "I don't fly very often."

It was a lie.

Alexy was a practiced flyer, although ordinarily it was for business, and the jets were both far smaller and significantly more opulent than he expected even his business class Aeroflot seat to be. But it was a useful excuse.

He knew that he needed to relax, to avoid drawing attention, but it was difficult. His heart was growling in his chest, adrenaline flowing through his system forcing sweat from his pores in an endless stream. His handkerchief was already damp through. It was a feeble attempt, like trying to dam the Moskva River with a tampon.

The woman chuckled. She was wearing elegant attire–a sleek, black catsuit that was just restrained enough to indicate that its purpose was for a business setting and not the catwalk, her neck accented by a single diamond, glittering on a simple gold chain.

She leaned toward him, from an armchair a couple of yards opposite, and even amidst the depths of his panic, Alexy found it impossible to ignore her tightly-toned frame, or the alluring scent that wafted into his nostrils, as if on cue. "Can I let you in on a secret?"

"Please." Alexy coughed, adjusting his glasses, quickly looking away. He shot her a smile, then worried that it seemed forced. He needed to calm down. But it was almost impossible, knowing that the next few minutes would determine whether he would either cheat death or succumb to its clutches.

"Me too. I hate everything about it." The woman smiled. She reached out her hand, as if to offer it for a shake, and then caught herself, realizing the distance was too far to bridge. "What am I doing?"

Alexy let out a strangled laugh. Even through his own ears, it sounded strangled and high-pitched. He wasn't good at interacting with women at the best of times–it was why he was still a bachelor in his 40s, unlike the well-heeled Russian men in this city who adopted that position by choice–and this was far from the best of times.

"I'm Elena, by the way." She smiled. "Can I tell you how I conquered my fear of flying?"

He swallowed hard, attempting to master himself. "Please, yes."

Elena winked. "Alcohol."

"I'll bear that in mind," Alexy said, his voice cracking as he attempted a half smile.

"Just a suggestion..."

Elena busied herself in work, opening a laptop and tapping away at the keyboard. The nervous professor just sat there, clutching his briefcase, impotent in the face of a tidal wave of anxiety battering his mind, worrying thoughts hammering for his attention like driftwood thudding against the hull of a rudderless fishing boat caught in the swell. He could no more resist them than turn back time.

Why was she talking to him?

Alexy was used to being invisible. He had been a hardworking, bookish child. Never friends with the athletic set at school or college. He was never bullied, just...

Ignored.

Women like Elena did not talk to him. At least, not in his experience–and he had enough years under his belt to be pretty certain by now.

So, what then?

The rational part of Alexy's mind chided him, sure he was overreacting. Before, in the oligarch's retinue, he was just an employee. A servant whose only purpose in life was to attend to his master's whims. And so, when he came face to face with those higher up the social ladder, it was no surprise they treated him as though he simply didn't exist. To them, he was just furniture, and you didn't thank your armchair, after all.

But this was different. In the side-pocket of his briefcase was a business class ticket to London, purchased with a credit card set aside precisely for emergencies like this. In this airport lounge, he was just like everyone else–an equal, not an underling.

But as waves of fear batted Alexy's mind, cortisol and adrenaline flooding through his veins, raising his heart rate, causing his pupils to narrow and his palms to sweat, it wasn't the rational part of his mind he was listening to.

No, instead the primal core of his brain spoke up, like a stone digging into a heel at the start of a long hike. It would not be ignored.

She's with the FSB, it murmured. *She's watching you.*

An announcement came over the lounge's speakers. "Passengers for British Airways flight BA233 to London should proceed to gate 72. The flight is now boarding."

The unexpected sound made Alexy jump. He waited half a beat as the announcement ended, listening for his own name with his left ear cocked. But the echo died away, replaced by the chinking of glasses, the rustle of confectionery wrappers, and the low murmur of businessmen in small huddles discussing last-minute changes to the strategy for their upcoming meetings.

Elena looked up from her laptop, shook her head as a wry smile played on her lips, and said, "It'll be fine. There's nothing to worry about," before returning to her work.

Alexy stood without replying, clutching his briefcase, and made to leave. As he walked through the marble-floored, luxurious yet slightly too warm lounge, he cast an anxious glance backward, to check if he was being followed.

But why would the men in dark suits play coy? If the

Federal Security Service, the successor to the KGB, wanted him, they would simply snatch him in broad daylight and frog-march him to a cell in the bowels of the Lubyanka.

If he was lucky.

It was as likely that he would be taken in the trunk of a sedan into the forests outside of Moscow, where he would be dispatched with a single bullet to the head and buried in a deep grave, where even the bears and wolves would never find him.

So perhaps he was safe after all. Perhaps the false passport sitting in his briefcase, with which he had bought his ticket, had done the job for which he had kept it safe for so long.

Alexy shivered.

The air conditioning was now blasting out freezing air, but that was not the reason. These thoughts were doing him no good–either he would make it on to the plane and into the air or he would not. But constantly second-guessing his situation would only put him at increased risk.

Pull yourself together.

He walked among a small gaggle of fellow travelers, mostly dressed in business attire, all heading for the flight to London, and attempted to lose himself within their ranks. It was easily done. Most were lost in the glow of cell phones held in their hands, or their attention was consumed by a pair of earbuds. A few chatted excitedly–these mostly seemed to be vacationers, not business travelers.

The walk to gate 72 felt to Alexy like the green mile, like he was walking to his own execution chamber. It was not uncommon in Moscow Sheremetyevo Airport to encounter paramilitary police officers from the Interior Ministry strolling in pairs, armed with AEK-971 assault rifles – a weapon which bore some similarities to the venerable AK-47.

Alexy passed one such patrol and felt the heavy weight of a bulldog-like policeman's stare linger over him. He forced himself to keep walking, without looking to either side, checking the watch on his left wrist as though in a hurry to get to his destination. At any moment, he expected to feel an iron grip closing on his shoulder, to hear the man inform him that he was under arrest.

But the moment did not come.

Alexy Sokolov was allowed to pass unhindered through the airport terminal by virtue of the fact that his pursuers did not yet know where he was. The name in his flawless counterfeit passport, Grigori Trubetskoy, was not yet flagged on any system, though it would be soon.

Alexy made it to the gate, presented his passport and his ticket, and was ushered on to the jet with a welcoming smile. At his seat, he accepted the offer of champagne–presented in a real glass flute–gratefully, and downed it down in one gulp to settle his nerves. The flight attendant, accustomed to the uncultured manners of the Russian nouveau riche, scarcely blinked as she took his flute for a refill.

A few minutes passed as the final remaining passengers settled into their seats, and then the captain addressed the cabin in a clipped English accent as the jet began to pull onto the taxiway. "Ladies and gentlemen, thank you for flying with British Airways today. The local time in London is two minutes before noon, and with the wind at our back, we should be landing a little before four in the afternoon. I do hope you enjoy your flight, and I will give you an update on our progress when we're in the air."

There was a short pause before the plane's massive engines began spooling up, causing Alexy's padded leather seat to vibrate. He was clutching the armrests with white knuckles, his left leg juddering up and down furiously as he counted down the seconds until British Airways flight BA233 was finally in the air.

And he was safe.

At any moment, Alexy expected the captain to return to the gate, and for plain-clothed FSB agents to enter the plane, weapons drawn. The people of Moscow, long accustomed to the vicissitudes of the state, knew better than to pull out a cell phone and record the arrest, unlike their counterparts across the globe. At least when the men in dark suits were involved. And after that moment, Alexy Sokolov would simply cease to exist.

And the secret he had discovered would die with him.

The loudspeaker crackled, and the anxious professor's heart plummeted, as though the Airbus jet was already in the air, engines blown out, falling helplessly to the ground. The captain's calm, unruffled voice spoke once again. "Cabin crew, take seats for takeoff."

Fewer than sixty seconds later, the jet engines powered up to a bone-chattering roar, and the jet tore down the runway, before leaping into the air.

Alexy finally sagged back into his comfortable seat, a deep sigh of relief escaping his lips in a low hiss. He wiped a single bead of sweat from his left temple and closed his eyes, offering up a prayer of thanks. In under thirty minutes, BA 233 would cross the border from the Russian Federation into Belarus. Three hours after that, he would land in London—safe at last.

He had done it.

2

G overnment Communications Headquarters (GCHQ) Cheltenham, England

THE MOMENT BRITISH AIRWAYS flight 233's passenger itinerary was finalized, the information was fed directly from the airline's mainframe into a computer system at GCHQ, the British government's version of Fort Meade.

The name Grigori Trubetskoy meant nothing to the analysts in Cheltenham, nor to either MI6 or MI5, the two British espionage agencies. Even so, the name was flagged, as was the number on the passport in Alexy's briefcase. The CIA wanted to be informed immediately if this individual appeared on their systems, and as dutiful members of the Five Eyes Alliance, the British government would obey that request.

A young analyst, munching on a ham and cheese sandwich he'd just purchased for lunch, scrolled through a list of alerts generated by the computer system. He often considered that his job might as well be carried out by the system itself. He didn't know who the targets were, or why they were being tracked.

But protocol dictated that intelligence information could not be shared with a foreign government without the involvement of a human eye with a British passport. So the analyst, a young man in possession of both, reviewed the slim file, concluded that informing his counterparts in American intelligence could not harm Her Majesty's interests, and cleared the information for release.

He picked up the phone, dialed the number for the CIA liaison at the US Embassy in Vauxhall, London, and set in train a sequence of events that would shake the world.

"WHAT THE FUCK IS HE DOING?" Director of Central Intelligence George Lawrence growled.

It was barely six in the morning in Langley, and yet he was already sitting in a small, secure conference room in the CIA's New Headquarters Building. The glass was frosted, and several screens hung on the opposite wall.

Lawrence was used to both early starts and late nights. He had been appointed by President Nash as the new DCI only a few weeks before, but he'd cut his teeth on the Agency's European desk, so he was accustomed to the time difference. What he wasn't accustomed to was being informed by an urgent phone call, while he was in bed, that the Agency's foremost, highest prized asset in Russia had just cut and run, and that the only reason they knew anything was even wrong was because the Brits had told them.

FRANCIS GERBER, head of the Russian desk, glanced at his new boss apologetically. "We don't know, sir."

Lawrence ground his teeth and spoke from between pursed lips. "What do you mean, you don't know?"

"His handler has been out of commission for the past week. Appendicitis. We're getting him out of his hospital bed now, but if Sokolov attempted to check in over the past few days, we don't know what he wanted."

"That much, Francis, is *abundantly* clear," Lawrence grunted. He ground his fist into his palm, clenching his jaw with frustration. "Fuck."

"Director, we have to assume that Sokolov's cover was blown. He would not have attempted to flee the country unless he had no other choice. He knows the risks."

Lawrence chose to ignore Gerber's statement of the obvious. "Where is he now?"

Gerber pointed at the screen on the wall and pressed the button on a small black remote. "About eighty kilometers from the Belarusian border, on a British Airways flight to London."

Lawrence did the math in his head. The plane would be out of Russian airspace in under ten minutes. "I want our people there when it lands at Heathrow, understood?"

"Already on it, sir."

The DCI glanced up at the map of Europe on the wall screen. BA 233's projected route was overlaid over it, a thick line indicating the journey already travelled, a sequence of dots denoting the path that lay ahead. He didn't like what he saw. "Scratch that, contact the pilot. Get him to divert over Lithuania–discreetly. If you have to, get them on the ground. Call it a technical emergency, I don't care. Just get it done."

Gerber nodded, and communicated the instructions to one of his aides.

Lawrence leaned back, closed his eyes and rubbed his hands against his face. Belarus was little more than a client state of the Russian Federation. If the FSB figured out what was going on, then he had no doubt they would compel the Belarusian government to order the British Airways flight to land. And if that happened, then Sokolov would be on a one-way trip back to Lubyanka Square.

Lithuania, by contrast, was a NATO state. Hell, unless Lawrence was very much mistaken, there were several thousand US troops in the country at that very moment, participating in an exercise with the Lithuanian military. It was an oasis of freedom in a dark corner of the globe.

One of Gerber's aides cleared his throat nervously, immediately judging the DCI from his reverie. "Sir," he said, signaling for his boss. "We've got a problem."

"What is it?" Lawrence snapped, glancing back up at the screen. The icon representing BA 233 jumped half an inch, and now sat directly on the Russian border with Belarus.

"We contacted our counterparts in Six, and they're working with British Airways to change the route. But I think the Russians have figured out what's going on."

"Why?"

"They just instructed BA 233 to return to Moscow airport."

"Stop them."

Lawrence snapped his fingers at one of Gerber's analysts. His heart was racing. This was the first big crisis that had occurred under his watch, and it was going sideways–fast. "Can you get air traffic control on that thing?"

"On it."

A second later, the crackle of a radio filled the room. The world's aviation language was English, so although Lawrence had an excellent, if recently unused, grasp of Russian, there was no need to tangle with translation.

"– Say again, Moscow Tower?"

"I repeat, BA 233, we have evidence that an explosive package is on board. You are instructed to land immediately, on the following heading–"

Lawrence turned to Gerber. "That plane cannot be allowed

to return to Russia. Understood? Do whatever you have to, twist whatever arm has to be twisted, but get the Brits to get that fucking plane into friendly airspace *immediately*."

Gerber's analyst, a kid who barely looked out of college, spoke into the phone in a hushed yet urgent tone, relaying the DCI's instructions. Lawrence knew that all he could do right now was wait, but nevertheless adrenaline swept through his body like a relentless tidal wave–a primal instinct designed to provoke a fight or flight response in the face of danger, but not well adapted to a crisis that was unfolding thousands of miles away.

And yet one that was no less critical for the distance.

The green icon that indicated BA 233's present location twitched, and the plane made a lazy turn in mid-air, back toward Russia. Lawrence studied the track intently, barely able to tear his eyes away from the image on-screen. The next few seconds were critical. In legal terms, the British Airways pilot was required to follow the instructions of the Russian air traffic control network.

But practically speaking, when it came to a pissing contest between his own government and that of the Russians, Lawrence was pretty sure which one the man would choose. He would face no repercussions for acting in what he believed to be the safety of the passengers in his charge.

"Francis?" Lawrence asked, the tension in his voice over-riding any attempt to hide it.

Gerber glanced at his analyst, who held a finger in the air to preempt the interruption, and pressed his phone against his ear. Finally, the kid flashed a thumbs up, and Lawrence let out a breath he didn't even know he was holding.

"It's over the border," the analyst said. "The pilot knows not to turn back to Russia."

Lawrence shook his head and felt the stress draining from

his body. "That was a close call. Too close. Get that plane on the ground, and find out why the hell Sokolov ran."

3

Jason Trapp woke at dawn, just as the first tendrils of another baking hot day's sunshine began to creep through the country retreat's wooden shutters. His eyes quickly adjusted to a now familiar sight – an enormous bedroom with rustic, exposed stone walls, and complete with a fourposter bed that had probably rested in the same spot for hundreds of years.

For almost two millennia, in various guises, Castello Romagno had sat on this very spot, high in the hills overlooking the old Roman road that ran north to south through the mountainous region of Tuscany. Even before the Roman Empire, the Etruscans had held this very piece of high ground and used it to project power.

These days, however, it was more of a country mansion than a functioning castle. A century before, the battlements were stripped away, the arrow slits widened into windows, the defensive fortifications turned into pleasure gardens. There was still a tunnel that led to the plateau hundreds of feet below, though the owner claimed that its full extent hadn't been explored in decades. To Trapp, that wasn't a throwaway comment – it was practically an invitation, and one he intended to honor.

Through the thick oak door that defended his slumber, his ears pricked up as he heard the creak of a wooden floorboard. Instantly, his instincts jumped into action, his sense of smell honed, picking up on the dusty warmth of the old building, his ears embracing the sound of cicadas growling in the hills, and the lonely caw of a bird of prey circling overhead.

And something else. Someone was moving. And they weren't supposed to be.

Trapp leapt out of bed, landing in a graceful crouch. He was naked – the old building didn't come equipped with air-conditioning, so he pulled on a pair of light gray exercise shorts that clung to his muscled body. His lean, scarred torso remained unclothed, and though his wraithlike eyes passed across a loaded Beretta 9 mm on an old mahogany writing desk on the other side of the room, he made no move for it. The prey he was hunting required a much firmer treatment – and he knew the cold metal of the pistol would do nothing to spook it.

She would require a more personal touch.

Trapp prowled through the old Italian castle, his feet making no sound as they grazed the wooden floorboards. Through no conscious effort, he remembered those which protested loudest, and avoided them as though they were landmines. For the experienced CIA operative, this behavior was natural, instinctual – he knew no other way. Although he was entering his fourth week of idyllic bliss in the Tuscan countryside, that did not mean he could simply switch off.

Jason Trapp did not work a desk job. He wasn't a man who climbed into his sedan at eight in the morning and clocked out by six. He worked a government job, sure, but not the kind that came with a comfortable pension and early retirement. Trapp's only safety net was his own wits, and the skills he had honed over many long years of visiting the places that ordinary Americans dared not, of doing business with people who would kill him as soon as shake his hand. Constant vigilance, perfect reflexes, and a very short fuse had kept him alive for almost two decades in the field.

They hadn't failed him this morning. As he took his place at the top of a spiral wooden staircase that hung suspended on metal cables – a model in addition to the old building – his eyes flared as he zeroed in on his target.

Bingo.

"Just where the hell do you think you're going?" he said.

Eliza Ikeda froze, her own slate-gray eyes flashing guiltily as they met his. She held her pose: standing on her tip toes, running sneakers held in her left hand, a slim water bottle in her right. Her shoulders were shrugged, catlike, in the same position as they had been during her abortive attempt to sneak out of the old castle without being seen.

But the five foot ten, lean, competitive distance-swimmer had never knowingly backed down from a fight. Her tone was accusing when she said, "You're supposed to be asleep."

"And *you*," Trapp said, emphasizing the word, "are sure as shit not supposed to be running. Doctor's orders. That's why I'm here. To make sure you behave yourself."

Ikeda's sneakers dropped to the floor, with the sound of two fleshy palms smacking together. The water bottle followed, with a duller thud, and she placed her arms on her hips, kinking a challenging eyebrow.

"That's why you're here, huh?" she said, in a tone that indicated she didn't believe a word of it.

"Scout's honor." Trapp grinned.

They'd been playing this game for a week now, maybe a little more. It was still only a month and a half since the operation in Macau that had seen a corrupt defense contractor killed and Ikeda kidnapped by a twisted North Korean army officer who'd intended to remake the Korean Peninsula in his own image – but not before moving both the United States and China off the chessboard.

Permanently.

The operation was blown all to hell, and it was two weeks before Ikeda was given the green light to escape quarantine. But it wasn't the effects of the genetically-altered Marburg virus that were the problem, at least not for the female CIA operative. Ikeda had been beaten and tortured by colonel Kim and his men, starved, neglected, and subjected to psychological pressure that might have broken a lesser operative.

But it didn't break Eliza Ikeda.

She was made of sterner stuff than that. Her hobby was to inflict physical torment on her own body of a kind that few people could understand, and to do so on a regular basis. But it was the emotional strain that bothered Trapp.

It was why he had taken leave from the Agency, and called in a favor with an Italian businessman for the use of Castello Romagno. The Italian, Gabrielle Agnelli, owed Trapp not just his life, but that of his wife and children, as well as the survival of a multi-billion dollar business that had been handed down through sixteen generations of his family.

"Something tells me you don't concern yourself very much with the doctor's orders," Ikeda continued, changing tack. She cast an appraising eye over Trapp's scarred upper body. "It looks like you sewed some of those up yourself."

"Maybe I did." Trapp shrugged. "But that doesn't change the facts. You're still an Agency employee, and you're under orders to recuperate. You're no good to your country if you push yourself too hard, too fast."

"Is it my country you're worried about?" Ikeda retorted. "Or me?"

Trapp paused before replying. In truth, he had needed this break every bit as much as Ikeda. The past few weeks of almost total isolation from the world's problems had offered him a rare opportunity to unwind. For the first time in what felt like years, he wasn't keyed up, waiting for the next crisis to arise, or the next trouble zone to pop up which required the application of his very specific skill set. The relaxation time felt good. He was fitter than he could remember, and some niggling aches and pains had faded into the background – and not just the physical ones.

But he had been offered plenty of opportunities to take vacation time over the past two decades, and he very seldom had. The reality was, he wasn't here for himself. At least, not entirely.

"Touché," he said. "But that doesn't change the facts. You're barely supposed to be eating solid food yet," he exaggerated, "let alone going out for an early morning run."

Ikeda fixed Trapp with a determined stare that plainly suggested she thought he should tread carefully. "What are you going to do about it?"

He didn't know. He wasn't Ikeda's babysitter, after all. She was a grown woman, a highly-trained espionage operative, a killer, and more pertinently, someone who had survived more acute pain than almost anyone else in the vast American intelligence machine ever had. If she wanted to ignore the edicts of a white-coated doc who was thousands of miles away, and didn't know who Ikeda was or where she had come from, then who was he to stand in the way?

On the other hand, as he looked down at the tanned, beautiful operative, he still saw the lingering after-effects of the torment she had survived. The stark red lines of fresh scar tissue against her olive skin, sickly patches of bruises that were even now only just beginning to fade.

Trapp tried one last time. "Why don't you give it a week? Let yourself heal up a bit longer."

Ikeda grimaced, her nostrils flaring with irritation. She almost stamped her foot. "I am going fucking stir-crazy in here,

Jason. There's only so much expensive red wine and sheep's cheese a girl can stomach, you know? And I'm just about at my limits."

The cool wood beneath Trapp's feet, varnished by centuries of footsteps, kissed his soles as he bounced from one to the other in indecision. He put himself in Ikeda's shoes, and that made his mind up more effectively than anything else he could have done. She was just like him: a creature of action, of forward movement, someone who was only happy when she was achieving a goal. Heck, he wasn't sure he would've stuck it out for so long.

Then again, he thought, cocking his head and glancing at the faint shimmer of dust that marked the sides of Ikeda's sneakers, perhaps she hadn't waited either.

"Fine," Trapp muttered, knowing this was a fight he simply would not win. "But I'm coming with you."

4

T rapp had already suspected that this wasn't the first time Ikeda had snuck out of the castle before he was awake, and that suspicion was soon confirmed.

He ran a couple of yards behind, to allow Ikeda to set a pace with which she was comfortable. After swimming in the balmy waters of Hong Kong with her some weeks prior, Trapp was more than aware that in peak condition, Eliza Ikeda was easily his physical equal. And although on this occasion she didn't run flat out, neither did the punishing hills seem to tax her too greatly. Certainly, Trapp thought wryly, she didn't seem challenged by the effort a first run in almost two months should pose, especially in this unforgiving terrain.

Still, he knew better than to confront her on the topic. Clearly she was healthy enough to run, and to do so fast. And besides, Trapp knew that he was no paragon of virtue. As with many from US military's elite special forces and intelligence agencies, he was a man from the 'do as I say, not as I do' mold – loath to take anyone's advice, unless it was his own.

Ikeda was cut from the same cloth.

And more than that, he was enjoying the view. Not just the

olive groves, or the sweet-smelling vines that stretched in neat rows up the dusty hillsides, but the sight of Ikeda's lithe, tanned body eating up the dirt road ahead of them with ease. At thirty-three years old, Eliza Ikeda was in the prime of her life. Though she hadn't had the opportunity to take to the water in weeks – as far as Trapp knew – she still had the lean, muscular frame of a distance swimmer. There was scarcely an ounce of fat on her body, in spite of Trapp's best efforts to remedy that fact over the past few weeks. Presently, she was wearing an almost neon orange vest that exposed powerful yet feminine arms, and tight running shorts accented with yet more orange.

So all things considered, Trapp had no intention of ruining a good thing.

It was coming toward the start of September in the hilly Tuscan country, and though the days were still long and hot, the mornings were marked by a chill. It was perfect running weather, and the two runners ate up the miles in a comfortable silence, working up a sweat – and an appetite.

After they passed what Trapp judged to be the five-mile mark, at the crest of a hill not too far from their adopted home, he gestured at a dusty, rustic farming village about a mile below them. It had probably been there, in one form or another, for several thousand years, and it would doubtless be there long after both he and Ikeda were gone.

About eight minutes later, they came to a halt in the center of the village, next to a small water fountain, and gratefully splashed water on their faces. Though the sun was already beginning to kiss the tops of the hills, and would before long bestow its punishing heat on the vineyards and olive groves, there was still a bite to the air, and it didn't take long for the two of them to cool off.

Once they were done, Trapp glanced down the street, at one of the village's only meeting spot. Because this was the depths of rural Italy, the café was closed on Sundays, Mondays, and seemingly at random, whenever the owner didn't want to come into work.

Thankfully, today they were in luck. "Breakfast?"

Ikeda grinned. "Thought you'd never ask."

Trapp spoke a little Italian, and while a month ago Ikeda hadn't known a word, she was a natural language scholar, and had picked up more than her fair share. She strode into the small café, a bright smile on her face, which was matched immediately by the elderly gentleman behind the counter. He was short, deeply tanned, and wore a white apron that matched the color of his hair.

"Gianni," Ikeda said. *"Come estai, questa mattina?"* *How are you this morning?*

"Ciao bella," came the smiling reply. *Good morning, beautiful.*

They commandeered two seats and a table on the street just outside of the café, and within a couple of minutes Gianni arrived carrying two tiny espresso cups, which he set down on the rustic wooden table with a beatific smile. It was the Italian way.

The first time Trapp had ever visited the country, some years before, he'd ordered a coffee, expecting thirty ounces of hot, black liquid. When he received a quarter-ounce of jet-fuel strong espresso, he assumed it was a practical joke. It wasn't. It was just the way the Italians did things – and over time, Trapp had grown to appreciate it. Unlike back home, here they appreciated quality over quantity. There were pros and cons to both approaches, of course. Trapp kind of liked being able to turn up to a coffee shop on a Monday morning and simply assume it would be open. That wasn't always possible here, but strangely enough, that was what he liked. The pace of life was slower, and somehow better.

Gianni returned a few minutes later with a selection of local hams and cheeses, along with olive oil and freshly-baked focaccia bread from a nearby bakery. He spirited away the espresso cups with a clink, and shortly after returned with two more. Ikeda thanked him, and the old man beamed with satisfaction.

"What's the plan today, then?" Ikeda asked.

Trapp chewed thoughtfully on a hunk of the Italian bread, savoring the freshly-pressed local olive oil. It was simple, and yet the richness of the oil meant that it needed nothing more. After a short pause, he shrugged and said, "I don't know. I was thinking we chill by the pool, maybe open a bottle of wine, grill some steaks on the barbecue for dinner. How does that sound?"

Ikeda arched her eyebrow. A ray of sunshine broke over the terracotta roof of one of the rickety, hundreds-of-years old buildings at the head of the street, painting it a rich, deep orange, and Trapp's attention was briefly stolen from his companion's beauty to its natural counterpart overhead.

"That sounds," Ikeda said, a little tartly, "a lot like what we've been doing for the last month."

Trapp recognized the tone in her voice. It was one he had deployed himself on many occasions. Like Ikeda, he was a predator. A jungle cat, used to his freedom, accustomed to roaming across huge swathes of land, with no pack to constrain him, no boss to watch over him – not even a friend to watch his back. Neither he nor Ikeda was good at spending so much time in such close proximity to another human being. For both, operatives who were trained to conceal their identities, their emotions, even their own thoughts, this was something new entirely.

Exactly what relationship he and Eliza Ikeda had was still unclear, and it seemed that issue was coming to a head. Since they'd shacked up together – in a manner of speaking – in the luxurious Italian country home some weeks earlier, Trapp had been the perfect gentleman. A month before, Ikeda had been a battered, damaged individual. Trapp had heard her screams in the darkness of the night as nightmares stole her sleep, as a terror the likes of which few can imagine robbed her of precious, irreplaceable mental peace. He had held her as a friend as her body thrashed with fear, as cold sweat dripped off her brow. And after the nightmares faded, he retreated every night to his own bedroom, to give the healing operative her own space.

But over the past week, something had changed. Ikeda's nightmares had faded. Where once they came like clockwork, twice, even three times a night, for the last four nights there had been none.

Something else, however, had taken their place. A looming question that would need to be answered: what exactly was there between the two of them?

Trapp cleared his throat awkwardly, dismissing the thought. "So what do you suggest?"

Ikeda shrugged. "Something fun."

"How about skydiving?"

"You find a plane you didn't tell me about?" she asked skeptically. The excitement in her eyes, however, was impossible to miss.

A long time ago, Trapp had earned his jump wings as a shit-scared, wet-nosed kid straight out of boot camp. Ikeda had never served in the military, but the Agency threw you out of enough planes to teach you the basics. Operatives like her weren't expected to parachute onto a target from a dark sky, and rain down hell on America's enemies.

That wasn't the point.

There is something about jumping from the side door of a plane moving hundreds of miles an hour through the air that demonstrates what kind of resilience and character a person possesses. You can either do it, or you can't.

If you can't, you're probably not the kind of individual the Agency wants on its books anyway.

"There's a jump school about twenty miles down the road." Trapp grinned. "I booked us a plane."

Ikeda sprung to her feet. "Well what the hell are we waiting for?" she demanded with the childlike exuberance of a spaniel puppy.

Trapp chuckled and threw a couple of crumpled ten euro notes down onto the table, placing a saucer over them so they didn't blow away in the morning breeze. "Hold your horses, okay? It's not till this afternoon. We've got plenty of time."

"You have plenty of time," Ikeda corrected, pointing at her head. "This hair won't wash itself." She started walking back up the hill before turning, a quizzical expression on her face as she questioned why he wasn't following. "You coming?"

"I'll meet you up there. The Internet café is about open. I just want to check my email, okay?"

She shrugged. "Suit yourself."

5

Lieutenant Colonel Andrey Petrov was a drunk.

This was not unusual in Russia, a nation with among the highest rates of alcohol consumption – and addiction – in the civilized world. As a child, Lt. Col. Petrov's parents were stationed in a military city in the deepest reaches of Siberia, and while their service in the then Soviet Union's Armed Forces fast-tracked their son into a successful military career, there was little to do in the region once the long nights had drawn in but drink. Andrey picked up the habit from his father, who picked it up from his own, and so on and so on down a dozen generations of the man's family tree.

He knew some of this, but not all. The precise causal pathway that had led him to a lifetime of steadily worsening – though still just about functional – alcoholism wasn't a matter that interested him very much. A therapist might come to exactly the opposite conclusion, but Petrov had never cared for those quacks. In that moment, as he reached out with trembling fingers for a bottle of cheap vodka to salve his aches, he just wished he hadn't drunk so goddamn much last night.

The red phone on Petrov's desk rang. The harsh sound was

loud and discordant, and cut through his hangover like the buzzing of an electric drill. He winced, his hand freezing in midair on its journey to the bottle.

A battle raged in his mind. He should just ignore the call. It would go away, eventually, and then he would be left in peace. Left to focus on his one true love. But as it kept ringing, the insistent clatter contributing to a building headache, he broke.

"Petrov. What do you want?"

The voice that came through the phone was cultured, yet carried with it an unmistakable sense of menace. "Lieutenant Colonel Petrov. My name is Yuri Zharkov. Listen very closely, because I do not intend to repeat myself. Is that understood?"

Petrov frowned. His alcohol-addled mind was operating at half its usual speed, and in truth, even those who knew him well would be hard-pressed to declare him a genius. Was this a practical joke? "Zharkov? I don't recognize that name. How did you get this number?"

"That was not an answer, Andrey, it was a question," the menacing voice replied. "Very shortly, a colleague of mine will enter your office. He is a very dangerous individual, and he does not like it when I am disappointed. Perhaps you understand *that*, Lt. Col.?"

"Who...who are you?"

"*Better*, Andrey. But I'm afraid I must cut the pleasantries short. We do not have much time."

Petrov gulped and gazed longingly at the half-empty bottle of clear liquid on his desk. Just one swig would calm his nerves, he thought. Yes, just a small drink, and then he would be able to think clearly. It was the hangover. That was the problem. His hands crept toward the bottle.

"*Andrey*," the cold voice chided. "I need you sober."

"What –?" Petrov choked, the words escaping his lips before he could pull them back. Was this strange man watching him, somehow? "How did you know?"

"I know everything about you, Andrey. Remember that."

The man did not knock as he entered Petrov's cramped, cluttered cabin. He was a bull, a brute, with flat, cauliflower ears and a rounded forehead that seemed to extend a full inch over his eyes. He wore a padded winter coat in forest camouflage, but as far as Andrey could tell, there was no visible marking of either rank or unit.

Petrov spun to meet this new surprise. "Who the hell are you?" he croaked, his throat suddenly devoid of all moisture.

The brute didn't say a word. He stood with his hands clasped in front of him for a few seconds, eyeing Petrov with a look of grim distaste, like he'd just stepped in dogshit. Then he raised one hand and pointed it at the phone still clutched in the now terrified officer's palm.

It was slowly beginning to dawn on Lt. Col. Andrey Petrov that he was in serious trouble. He gulped, glanced back down at the red phone in his sweaty palms, and pressed it with trembling fingers to his ear. He found himself unable to say even a single word.

"Are you ready to talk, Lt. Col. Petrov?"

Petrov's voice was shaky and uneven. "What do you want from me?"

The reply was crisp and emotionless. "Give my colleague your service weapon."

"Why?"

"Consider it an order, Andrey."

"But I don't even know who you are!" Petrov moaned. He could barely take his eyes off the pistol holstered at the brute's right hip. Somehow he knew that this man had come to take his life. He was the angel of death, the grim reaper, sent to end his time on earth. He just didn't know why.

And there was nothing he could do to resist it.

"I'm with the FSB, Andrey."

The FSB was the modern-day successor to the KGB, the

Soviet-era secret police – an unholy amalgamation of the CIA and the Gestapo. Former KGB officials populated the highest ranks of the Russian government, including the president himself, along with a raft of billionaire oligarchs in the president's inner circle. In short, they were the kind of people you seriously did not want knocking at your front door.

"The FSB?" Petrov repeated dumbly, a note of shrill fear infecting his voice. "What do you want with me? I swear, I've done nothing!"

"Relax. We have a task for you. One that is vital to national security. But first, my comrade needs your service weapon."

The 9 mm MP-443 Grach, the military's standard side arm, sat in the locked top drawer of Petrov's desk. He rarely wore it, and probably fired fewer than twenty rounds a year – just enough to re-qualify. He was a terrible shot, but a bottle of vodka spirited into the right hands usually did the trick.

Now he was regretting that decision. It wasn't the first time that his fondness for alcohol had caused such a reaction, but he feared it might well be his last. He briefly considered his options. Adrenaline was now coursing through his veins, momentarily masking the most pernicious effects of his lingering hangover, but it had only redoubled the trembling in his fingers. Even if he managed to retrieve the weapon, he doubted if he would be able to aim it and fire before the muscle reacted.

Besides, he had no idea if the damn thing was even loaded.

And there was one other reason he made no attempt to go for his weapon. The same reason forced him into the cold oblivion of the bottle every night. He was a coward. It was easier to hide from his problems than face them head on. Perhaps this was for the best, after all.

"What for?"

"Your own safety, Andrey. Besides, it was an order, not a

suggestion. For your own good, I advise you to follow it quickly."

A chill spread through Petrov's body. He watched as the brute placed one hand on the weapon at his hip and fixed the Russian officer with a cold, dead stare.

He growled a single, staccato word. "Easy."

Petrov knew he was screwed. His keychain was on the metal desk in front of him, and clinked as he reached for it with his free hand. The keys jangled as he searched for the correct one, and it was as though his eyes were glazing over, like he was seeing underwater.

The voice on the phone spoke, startling him. He'd almost forgotten the FSB officer was there. "Quickly, Andrey, we don't have much time."

Finally, Petrov found the correct key, inserted it into the top drawer's lock, and turned it. The brute moved with surprising speed for a man that size, never drawing his weapon, nor taking his eyes off Petrov either. He pushed the officer back into his chair, roughly pulled the drawer open, and removed the weapon, which he stashed in one of the pockets of his coat.

"Good," he grunted.

Petrov's head slumped forward, chin kissing his chest as he prepared to meet his fate. The phone was still pressed up against his ear, but to him the hard plastic felt like the barrel of a gun.

"Well done, Andrey," Zharkov said. "I have a task for you. As I am sure you have gathered, your successful completion of that task will determine whether you live or die…"

Though Petrov didn't really believe there was any chance he was making it out of this alive, he reached for the offer of mercy like a drowning man in search of rope. "I'll do it," he moaned. "Whatever you want."

"Good. Because I need you to shoot down a plane…"

THE RUSSIAN-BUILT S-400 Triumph is perhaps the most advanced surface-to-air missile defense system ever designed. With a range of over 400 km, four times that of the US PATRIOT missile-defense technology, the air defense missile regiment stationed in Russia's Western Military District had the ability to defend the nation's capital from bombers, stealth fighters, even ballistic missiles capable of traveling many times faster than the speed of sound, and pulling G forces that would crush a human pilot into jelly.

Today's target would pose much less of a challenge.

Lieutenant Colonel Andrey Petrov's unit, the 428th Zvenigorod Guards Missile Regiment, was one of the first to be equipped with the new 40N6 long-range missile. Designed to take out high-value targets such as airborne intelligence and reconnaissance planes equipped with electronic jamming equipment, chaff and flares, its purpose today was child's play.

As the officer entered the missile system's command suite, the technicians on duty snapped to attention. They were enlisted men, but unlike most in the Russian military, they were volunteers, not conscripts. After all, the S-400 was one of the motherland's most prestigious new weapons systems. Its operation could not be trusted to farmhands from Siberia.

"We have a target," Petrov croaked. He glanced back at the FSB enforcer who had followed him into the control suite. "This is not a drill. Terrorists have seized control of a British Airways jet, and are planning to use it as a missile. We cannot allow that to happen. We have orders to shoot it down. Sgt. Yevgeny – here are the details."

The command suite, a long, cramped trailer filled with equipment that pumped out heat, was deathly silent as he handed the coordinates to the sergeant, who fed it into the missile system's targeting system.

Yevgeny's pockmarked face snapped up, his expression quizzical. "Sir, this is outside of our airspace. We have no legal authority –"

"The orders are from the highest authority," the nameless FSB enforcer interjected, perhaps sensing that Petrov was beginning to waver. "It is your duty to carry them out. It is your duty to follow the orders of your superior officer. Do you understand your responsibility, Sergeant?"

Yevgeny's gaze danced from Petrov to the new man and back again. He seemed torn by the gravity of what he was being asked to do.

"It is an order, Sergeant," Petrov said, wishing that he had a drink in his hand. "We will carry it out as instructed. We have no choice."

"Yes sir," the NCO replied softly.

"Do you have a firing solution?" Petrov asked, numbly acting out the routine that he had trained to do a hundred times.

"Yes, Lt. Col. She's –"

"She's what?" the FSB man asked harshly.

"She's flying low and slow," Yevgeny answered, guilt already etched onto his marked face. "We can't miss."

"See that you don't," he growled.

Yevgeny looked to his commanding officer for permission, his finger poised over the launch button. "Sir," he said, as if pleading Petrov to reconsider, "the plane will be out of range in nine minutes."

Petrov dropped his eyes to the floor. He couldn't bring himself to deliver the death sentence out loud. For that was what it was. "Sgt. Yevgeny. You have your orders."

The sergeant obeyed them, his eyes closed as if in silent prayer. His finger stabbed the button. The occupants of the control trailer did not feel the mechanism groaning into action, because the launch tube was installed in a separate location.

But they heard the roar of the rocket engine as it exploded out of the tube.

The maximum speed of the missile fired from the S-400 missile system was almost 17,000 km per hour. On this occasion, it did not exceed twelve thousand, closing the 300 km distance to the British Airways jet in just eighty seconds, and blotting the passenger jet out of the sky.

After it was done, the trailer was filled with a disbelieving silence, punctuated only by a harsh, electronic chime that signaled that the radar contact had been lost.

"Lt. Col. Petrov," the FSB enforcer said, punctuating the quiet. "Let us return to your office. Moscow must be informed of the success of our operation."

"IT IS LOADED?" the FSB enforcer asked, removing Petrov's service weapon from his jacket pocket as he closed the officer's door behind him. The brute's face showed no emotion, no recognition of the fact that he had just been a part of a heinous, unforgivable crime.

Petrov reached out, his hand trembling with shock. He clenched his fingers into a fist, allowing the nails to bite into his skin and deliver a jolt of pain to his system in a hopeless attempt to wash away the guilt. Opening them, though, proved the effort fruitless. His outstretched palm shook.

"Why did you make me do that?" he moaned, allowing his trembling hand to drop, before he clutched his shoulders, shaking back and forth. "Hundreds of people... dead."

For the first time, the enforcer's face cracked with feeling – but not one that Petrov expected. He smiled, cold and broad.

"I didn't make you do anything, Andrey," he chuckled, ejecting the pistol's clip, checking it, and slamming it back into the weapon. "You did that all yourself. I ask myself, what kind of man could do such a thing?"

"I didn't!" Petrov protested. "I wouldn't..."

The FSB man shrugged. "And yet you did."

Petrov hung his head in shame. Acid burned in his gut at the memory of giving the order to shoot. He had fired the anti-aircraft missile system dozens of times in training, and thousands more in simulations, owing to the great cost of the missiles. But in all his years of service, Lt. Col. Andrey Petrov had never fired on a live target. He had never been responsible for the death of an enemy.

He still hadn't.

No, Petrov knew that what he had done was a thousand times worse. It wasn't an enemy aircraft that he'd shut down. It was a passenger jet, full not of enemies of his country, but women, babies, tourists. Why in God's name did they have to die?

"I need a drink," he croaked.

The enforcer's face split in a smile, a genuine one this time. "Perfect! A toast. You have done the rodina a great service today. It will not be forgotten."

Petrov turned, eyes filling with tears as his mind spun with imagined pictures of the men, women and children he had slaughtered. He stumbled toward his desk, grabbing the bottle of vodka that still sat on top of it, pulling out the cork, and bringing it to his lips.

"Fuck the motherland," he spat, closing his eyes and drinking deep. The alcohol hit his system hard, dopamine receptors in his brain firing just at the taste of the burning liquid.

Andrey Petrov didn't hear the man step toward him. He didn't hear the click as the slide of his own pistol ratcheted back. He didn't know he was dead until it was already too late to do anything about it. As the cold chill of realization flooded through him, his eyes snapped open, flickering left, his vision flooded with the image of death.

The cold barrel of the MP-443 Grach kissed his temple, and the FSB enforcer pulled the trigger. A single shot rang out, deafening in Petrov's cramped office. The lieutenant colonel's lifeless corpse slumped to the ground, carrying with it the glass bottle of vodka, which duly smashed, the colorless liquor inside mixing with the blood now beginning to seep from the officer's skull.

"Enjoy your retirement, comrade," the man grinned, a sociopathic lack of remorse evident in his cold eyes as he stepped over Petrov's shattered body. "You have earned it."

He threw the pistol onto the ground, kicking it toward Petrov's still twitching fingers, unconcerned with the prospect of leaving forensic evidence on the weapon. After all, when the time came to investigate this tragic, unforgivable incident, it would be the FSB who would carry it out.

The incident would be recorded as a horrible mistake. An over-eager missile officer, who, when confronted with the gravity of his error, chose to take his own life rather than live with the guilt.

The West would cry out in rage, demand action. It always did. But after a while, they would forget.

They always did.

And anyway, the man responsible was already dead.

6

The Sikorsky S-92 is a twin-engine medium-lift helicopter, a variant of which is currently under consideration to replace Marine One – the preferred ride of the US president. It has a range of almost eight hundred miles, although on this occasion, as it flew low over the hazy waters of the Russian Black Sea in late summer, it would be travelling only a fraction of that distance. This particular Sikorsky was owned by a Russian billionaire, one of many such aircraft in his possession, and was primarily used to ferry its owner from an enormous, gold-hulled super yacht that currently sat on the surface of the calm inland sea, a monument both to his extraordinary wealth, and his equally extraordinary poor taste.

"Touchdown in three minutes, Mr. Kholodov," the pilot said over the intercom into the luxuriously appointed cabin.

Roman Kholodov merely grunted, the effort wobbling his ever-growing belly and said, "Try not to get us shot down."

The man, perhaps unwilling to provoke his boss's famously mercurial temper, wisely did not reply. The pitch of the helicopter's powerful engines changed slightly as the aircraft lost altitude and came in for landing.

On this occasion, however, Kholodov's mind was too occupied by relief to turn to anger. He'd just received word from his man in the FSB that the spy was confirmed dead. It had been a close call, a matter of minutes from disaster. If that disaster had struck, Kholodov reflected, perhaps it would be better to die in a ball of flames. His master's wrath would certainly prove more painful than that.

Being plucked from the sky was, in truth, a real concern. Kholodov's destination that afternoon was a large private villa fifteen miles down the coast from the town of Sochi, the Black Sea resort that was the home of the 2014 Winter Olympics. Strangely enough, the villa was – legally speaking – owned by Kholodov himself, at least in the sense that his name was on the deed. In truth, though, the property was controlled by its current occupant, the most powerful man in Russia.

President Dmitry Murov.

The source of the billionaire's worry lay in the presence of dozens of troops from the Presidential Security Service, Russia's answer to the US Secret Service. PSS agents were known for their undying loyalty to President Murov, a loyalty that was rewarded handsomely in wealth, land and power after their service. They were also known for a fierce brutality, and an institutionally itchy trigger finger that had left many a Moscow commuter forced off the road as the presidential motorcade chewed through the city's streets.

Kholodov stared out of one of the helicopter's small, porthole-like windows, notionally studying the wooded hills of Krasnodar province, though his thoughts were far away. He owed everything to his president – his power, his fortune, even the five hundred foot long super yacht that sat just off the coast. He knew better than to refuse his patron, no matter what the request. Dmitry

Murov was not a man who often heard the word 'no.' Kholodov didn't even know whether the man still understood what it meant. Even so, the proposal he was here to discuss today was dramatic enough to give even Roman Kholodov cause for thought.

The landing pad quickly approached beneath the Sikorsky helicopter, but the pilot landed it expertly, without so much as a jolt to startle its passenger from his thoughts.

"Mr. Kholodov," the pilot said, flicking switches as he powered down the engines, "we have arrived."

Murov's bodyguards wore black polo shirts and tan cargo slacks paired with wraparound dark sunglasses, as opposed to the black suits they wore in the Russian capital. It was still a uniform, but one that was less overt than their ordinary attire, and more suited to the informal surroundings of the president's unofficial seaside retreat. Except for the slightly ominous color of their shirts, and the pistols holstered at their waists, they might have been guests. But Kholodov knew better. For over a decade, he had been one of those men, at the president's side wherever he went. And he had been rewarded for that service, granted wealth beyond his wildest dreams.

One of them greeted Roman as he exited the helicopter. The man's broad Slavic face was expressionless, as his own would have been, Kholodov noted with professional interest. He led the guest in silence to his charge.

The Russian president was sitting on a stone deck facing out to sea, with a collection of Russian and international newspapers stacked neatly on the wrought iron table in front of him. Slightly to his left sat a silver tray, on top of which was a cup of black coffee, a selection of fresh fruits, and several thickly-cut slices of toast that hadn't been touched.

Murov spoke without turning, dismissing his current bodyguard before turning to his old one. "Boris, thank you. You are dismissed. Roman, you are late."

Kholodov knew that he wasn't, but didn't dispute his

master's statement. "My apologies, Mr. President. It won't happen again."

Murov rose, dusting his front as he stood, and turned to face Kholodov with a broad smile. "Please, Roman, call me Dmitry. How long have we known each other?"

"Long enough," Kholodov admitted, returning Murov's smile. "That's why it's so difficult. I was your bodyguard long before I was your friend, Dmitry."

As he spoke, Kholodov could not help but wonder how accurate his words were. Was he truly Murov's friend? Did the man even have any real friends, or simply people who were useful to him?

The billionaire knew better than to overestimate himself. Everything he had in life was at the behest of this man, and it could all be taken away as easily as it had been given.

The two men clasped hands, and Murov indicated that his guest should sit. "Would you like anything to eat?"

Kholodov glanced up and noticed a white-jacketed butler standing discreetly out of sight. "Just a cup of coffee. I ate on the boat."

Murov glanced up. "One for me as well," he said.

Once both men were suitably equipped and the butler dismissed, Murov turned to his guest. "And how is the new yacht, my friend?" He grinned. "Is she everything you hoped she would be?"

Kholodov smiled ruefully. "And more. Even with the... *complications*."

The complications he referenced were the latest round of American sanctions against the many oligarchs in President Murov's circle. It was a list which had the name Roman Kholodov at the very top. It was well known in Western intelligence circles that Kholodov was a firm favorite of the Russian president – a confidante, as well as a front man behind whom Murov hid a small fraction of his enormous, stolen fortune, and as a result he was continually a target of the attempts of their Treasury Department to humble the great country of Russia.

Though Kholodov's latest and largest yacht, the *Hermione*, had been built in a South Korean shipyard to an Italian design, using German engines and British control systems, the Americans had still done their best to bring his project to an unceremonious halt. In the end, the billionaire was forced to create a network of shell corporations to hide the true ownership of the vessel, just so that the South Koreans and the Italians and the Germans and the British would take his money, instead of crying to him about American pressure.

The remark brought a thunderous expression to President Murov's face. "Those fucking Americans," he said. "Forever inserting themselves into places they do not belong."

"But not for much longer," Kholodov replied.

Murov's expression brightened. "How go our preparations?"

Kholodov inclined his head. He better than anyone knew that Russia was not like America, where politicians demanded plausible deniability, where they left covert operations in the hands of the bureaucrats in the CIA. Dmitry Murov had once been a senior officer in the KGB, before he assumed power in Russia after the chaotic breakup of the Soviet Union. His entire career had been dedicated to regaining the might that Russia had lost in that terrible decade – by whatever means necessary.

This was another step on that relentless march. One that was pivotal, if not final.

"At pace," he said, not sparing the details. "The virus has been deployed, and we believe that it is currently installed in approximately 3% of target systems, as well as tens of millions more, which we can use to amplify our strength. That number will rise faster and faster the more nodes are deployed on the network. There was, of course, a minor complication this morning."

Murov fixed his guest with a crocodilian, unblinking stare

that left Kholodov with no doubts that he knew exactly what had happened on the Belarusian border. That was the president's modus operandi – he knew more than anyone else, faster than anyone else, about more than *everyone* else. He was no tinpot African dictator, liable to fly off the handle at the slightest hint of bad news. Though he ruled with fear, unafraid to deploy the sharp end of the Russian state to silence his critics and those who had failed him, Murov hated more than anything being lied to, shielded from the truth.

That was a road that led powerful men to their political – and actual – deaths, and Murov was too skillful an operator to allow that outcome to arise. He demanded the absolute truth from those who served him, and Kholodov knew better than to test his master on that score.

"A minor complication," Murov repeated, an ambiguous smile playing on his lips. "I suppose you could call it that. Although that's not what the British Prime Minister said when he called me. After all, three hundred dead is no small matter."

Kholodov waved his hand dismissively. "It had to be done. And besides, by the time this is over, many more lives will be lost."

"That is true enough," Murov allowed. "But Roman, do not mistake our friendship for patience. Shooting down that jet has attracted a lot of unwanted attention from the international press, the CIA, MI6. They will be sniffing around."

"As I said, Dmitry, it had to be done. There was a leak. I plugged it."

"And I thank you for that, Roman." Murov smiled thinly. "But perhaps next time you could attempt to do it with a little more discretion?"

Kholodov leaned back against the wrought iron chair, attempting to find comfort where none was possible. His pudgy frame hung over the sides of the seat a few more inches than he was entirely happy with.

"We got lucky on this one, boss," he admitted. "We didn't know about the mole until he was on the plane. The British would have picked him up at Heathrow and handed him straight to the Americans. If I hadn't arranged for his neutralization, everything would have gone up in smoke. That couldn't be allowed to happen, so I didn't allow it to."

Murov smiled again, but this time with considerably more warmth. "Good. You have done well, Roman. My thanks." His gaze narrowed, and he spoke again. "Are you sure the Americans know nothing?"

"There is one loose end," Kholodov admitted. "The spy contacted someone shortly before boarding the plane."

Murov brought his fist down on the table, causing his coffee cup to overturn, and splattering Roman's pants with the hot black liquid. "Dammit, Kholodov! This puts everything at risk. Who did he reach out to?"

"We only have a location, not a name. A small village in Italy."

The billionaire knew better than to react to his president's anger – or to the pain that was now flashing across his thighs from the caffeinated lava spilling over his legs. He opened his palms in a conciliatory gesture. "But Dmitry, the message contained nothing incriminating. Still, just to be sure, whoever it was sent to will be dead by sunset."

President Murov grimaced. "Be sure," he growled, "that they are."

7

J ason Trapp knew that something was wrong. And yet, in a move that he was profoundly unaccustomed to, he was sitting on his hands doing nothing about it. Instead of acting, he was stacking sun-dried firewood for the barbecue, worrying about a problem, as he'd been doing now for a day and a half, ever since he'd logged onto the internet and read that fateful message.

The message from the Russian asset was a blast from the past. He had neither heard from, nor thought about the man he had once recruited in at least five years. Trapp had done the man a service, and in return, Alexy Sokolov had provided high quality intelligence about the Russian government's moves and motives for the past half-decade.

At least, that's what Trapp assumed had happened. He hadn't given any thought to Sokolov's continued service with the Central Intelligence Agency for the simple reason that he was not an intelligence officer. It wasn't his job to recruit intelligence sources, let alone develop and handle them. His skills lay in a more kinetic direction – he identified problems and fixed them.

No matter what that fix entailed.

The message from the Russian had been simple. It was a coded reference to the dead drop location Trapp had first set up for him. A location that Sokolov's eventual handler would not have known about.

One question lingered in Trapp's mind. Why the hell was Sokolov contacting him – and why now? That was two questions, he conceded, but in his mind they were linked inextricably.

In truth, there was a third: what, if anything, was he going to do about it?

Trapp watched the barbecue idly, chewing the inside of his cheek as the flames began to lick the tinder-dry wood that he had spent the early part of the afternoon collecting from the hillsides near the old Tuscan castello. He'd barely needed more than a couple of thin sheets of newspaper and a Zippo lighter to get the small blaze going.

Instinctively, he wanted to drop everything and head for Moscow. The Hangman was not an individual who liked surprises, and this certainly qualified. There must have been a reason that Sokolov had contacted him instead of his usual handler, which was a significant breach of protocol. Intelligence assets – especially ones as senior as Alexy Sokolov – knew better than to break with procedure. It's what got them killed. So for Sokolov to have done so meant that whatever he had was important. Important enough to risk his life for.

But Jason Trapp wasn't the Hangman anymore.

At least, he was trying not to be. With Emmanuel Alstyne dead, the last traces of the conspiracy that had wiped out his former partner were now eliminated. He had made a promise to himself – and to Price's memory – to get out of the intelligence game before it got him killed, or else corroded his soul so irrevocably that it was impossible to reverse the damage.

The barbecue crackled, sending up a thin whisper of dark

smoke into the cloudless blue sky. The darkness would fall quickly up here in the hills, and with no major cities around for miles the stars would glisten in the heavens like diamonds, but that was still an hour away at least. For now the day's dying winds chased a few stray birds and fanned the flames in front of him.

"How you doing?" Ikeda asked.

Trapp's head cracked around, and for the briefest of seconds, his heartrate skyrocketed. He still hadn't quite come to terms with the fact that Ikeda was good. Damn good. She'd approached him without making even a hint of a sound, and gotten within touching distance.

Close enough to kill.

She closed the last few inches and clasped her arms around his waist, hugging him from behind. The unexpected action startled the experienced CIA operative, and for a few seconds his posture remained as stiff as a board, his pulse still racing from the shock.

Finally, he mustered the ability to talk. "Fine," he grunted.

But he wasn't. Not really. The truth was that he didn't know where he stood with this beautiful, exotic woman. He was experienced, sure, but not like this. He could disassemble any rifle in the US armory – or that of any other country, for that matter – with a blindfold on and the light switch turned off, then reassemble it again after someone had scrambled the components. He could do so with loudspeakers blaring and instructors firing water hoses into his face, or soaked to the skin in a commercial refrigerator.

Jason Trapp could kill a man at two thousand yards, or get close enough to his target to slit his throat without ever being noticed.

But he had no experience of relationships. If that's what this even was – for how in truth could he know? For almost two decades, he had subsumed that side of his personality. To open himself up to another person was to purposefully create a vulnerability. That vulnerability could get him killed, or worse, it could endanger his mission, even innocent lives.

And so he had steered away from love. Lust was another matter entirely, and there were women on as many continents as Trapp had digits on one hand who could attest to that. But not love. And now in his late-30s, Trapp was learning what boys two decades younger had to contend with. It wasn't as easy as he thought.

Ikeda grasped his left hip with her right hand, and lazily spun him around so that the two of them were face to face. A sly smile curled on her lips, and her slate gray eyes twinkled with amusement.

"The thing is, Jason"—she grinned—"you don't *sound* fine. Something's on your mind. And the sooner you spit it out, the sooner you'll lose that sour look on your face." She stuck out her tongue. "And believe me, you look a lot hotter when you're not grimacing."

Trapp grimaced. And then he caught what he was doing, which only made him want to do it all over again. He shrugged out of Ikeda's grasp and aimed a slow playful blow at her shoulder. She dodged it easily and came up in a fighting stance.

"Come on." She beckoned, like Neo in the Matrix films. "The sooner the better, honey."

Trapp considered his options. Holding out on the woman in front of him wasn't one of them. She was too persistent. She would get it out of him eventually, and the more he made her work, the worse it would be for him. He was quickly learning what husbands across the globe had known for generations. He just had a whole lot less practice at it than they did.

"It's classified," he offered weakly.

Ikeda rolled her eyes. "Everything we do is classified, Jason. You'll have to do better than that."

"Touché," he replied.

"I'm guessing this has something to do with you checking your email yesterday morning?" Ikeda said, dropping her hands to her hips and popping her pelvis out in a stance that screamed 'attitude.' "You've been wrapped up in yourself ever since."

"You're too perceptive for your own good," he replied wryly. He was a little annoyed with himself for being so easy to read. Sure, Eliza Ikeda was trained to observe the subtle tells in speech and body language that indicated what a subject was truly thinking and feeling.

But he'd been through the same damn training – and he had a few more years' experience in the field than the woman opposite him. He should be better than her at it, if all that was required to acquire a skill was time served, but he was quickly coming to learn that there were few things that Ikeda could not master if she put her mind to it. He wasn't on that rarefied list.

She rolled her eyes. "That's still not an answer."

Trapp knew that for people like him – operators—the classification system didn't work as it did for the bureaucrats back in Washington. The system was designed to prevent paper pushers and politicians from damaging America's vital interests, and consequently getting the men and women at the sharp end of the spear killed. Men and women like him, and like Ikeda herself. What the system wasn't designed to do – at least the way Trapp saw it—was to stop operators from getting the job done, however they saw fit. In his view, and though he would never brag about it, or profit from what he had done in service of his country, he had kept America safe by doing whatever it was that needed to be done, however it needed to happen.

And right now, Trapp decided, was one of those situations. Alexy Sokolov had clearly gone outside of the normal channels for a reason. He could have escalated his issue through his handler, or even directly to Langley. There were channels for that sort of thing. That Sokolov hadn't used them was telling.

"I got contacted by an asset," Trapp said. "Someone I recruited on a job in Moscow five years ago."

Ikeda frowned. "About what?"

Trapp ground his teeth together. A part of him still didn't want to have this conversation, because he knew what Ikeda was like. She was like him. Once he vocalized the issue, she would want to deal with it, and that would mean leaving this idyllic sanctuary, breaking the spell that both had been living under for the past month.

He didn't want it to end. And yet he knew there was no other choice.

"That's the problem. I have no idea."

"I don't get it."

"Neither do I. He sent a code word, a phrase I used when I set up the dead drop location all those years ago. I almost forgot. I guess he didn't."

Ikeda didn't say anything, but Trapp could see her quick mind turning the problem over in silence. She blinked a couple of times, her thick, dark eyelashes closing like palm fronds swaying in a tropical wind, then her eyes flicked upward and met his. "So he has a message for you. Something that had to be said in person?"

Trapp nodded. "That's what I figure."

"What's your plan?"

Ikeda began to bounce, almost imperceptibly, from the ball of one foot to the other. Trapp couldn't help but notice the action. It mirrored his own behavior when the nervous energy ahead of a mission was flooding through him too powerfully to ignore.

"Send it up the chain," Trapp lied. "Let Langley deal with it."

The beautiful woman opposite him frowned and threw him a disbelieving look. "Bullshit."

"Huh?"

"You heard me. I don't believe you. Not for a second. If your asset didn't trust this to normal channels, then he sure as shit didn't want some bureaucrat in Washington to deal with it. He wanted you. Doesn't that tell you something?"

It told Trapp a hell of a lot. One thing it said was that Ikeda's mind was on exactly the same track as his. The second was that he had a problem. The problem's name was Alexy Sokolov, and getting to the bottom of it would mean traveling to Moscow.

Trapp shook his head. "I'm not that guy anymore. It's someone else's problem."

Ikeda tilted her head back and laughed out loud. After a brief flash of irritation, Trapp decided that he kind of liked the sound. He kind of liked the fact that she wasn't afraid to rib him.

Kind of.

"What?" he said, throwing his hands up in an almost defensive fashion. One of the chunks of firewood on the brick barbecue crackled like a suppressed gunshot, briefly drawing his attention before it flicked back to Ikeda. "Something I said?"

"You're full of crap, Jason. That's what."

"How so?"

She half rolled her eyes, and half gave him an 'I can't believe I'm really having to say this out loud' kind of look. She shook her head. "You'll always be that guy, Jason. Don't try and pretend to yourself that you could be anything else."

Trapp remained silent for a few seconds, and his face assumed a contemplative, almost plaintive expression. "So what does that mean for us?"

For a second time, Ikeda laughed, though on this occasion it was a softer, tinkling sound – amusement, not mockery.

"That's a very good question," she said with a smile on her

face. "But I'm not a white picket fence kind of girl, Jason. I don't want to settle down and cook you dinner when you get home from the office. I don't want kids, I don't see myself changing a diaper anytime soon, and I sure as hell don't want to change my job. Psychopathic North Koreans aside, it's the best gig I've ever had, and I have no intention of stopping doing what I love. You do you, Jason, and I will do me, and whatever happens in the middle, we'll make it work."

She shrugged. "Or we won't – and you know what, that'll be all right with me, too. Just as long as we do it the right way. I don't want to change you, and I sure as hell don't want you to change me. So why don't you tell me more about this asset of yours, and we can figure out where to take it from there."

Trapp was processing what Ikeda had said – and realizing that a weight had lifted from his shoulders – when he froze, cocking his head like a dog. Ikeda looked at him quizzically and turned her own head, searching for whatever it was that Trapp had heard. Evidently, she couldn't detect a thing.

In truth, he wasn't sure what his instincts were telling him – but they were definitely screaming something, and they had been right more often than they were wrong, saving his life more times in the process than he could count. His eyes flickered back and forth as he scanned the horizon, searching for the threat. And then he heard the sound for a second time. It was almost imperceptible, the scrape of a man's boot against the gravel driveway. But it was enough, and it sent a shiver of premonition down the back of his spine.

He spoke in a low voice. "I think we have company."

8

The two men left their Mercedes 4 x 4 at the top of the hill leading to Castello Romagno, about half a mile from the old stone house. They did so because the cast-iron gates at the bottom of the long, tree-lined driveway that led to the house were chained together, and save from shooting the chain free, they didn't have the tools to open them up.

Simply driving through the obstacle was an option, but one they dismissed quickly, realizing that as effective a method it might prove, it would also give their quarry warning of their arrival. So they slipped out of the vehicle, walked through the small, unlocked side gate in the wall that surrounded the property, and began walking up the road to the castello. One of the two mercenaries held a bottle of cheap local red wine, purchased in the village below for precisely this purpose. The exact vintage didn't matter, merely the use of the bottle as a prop, a tool to get close enough to their targets to execute the operation.

The men were Italian. Hired guns who had both served in the Italian Army for several years with some distinction, before being recruited by a private security firm after they were discharged from the armed forces.

This was the first time they had done a job on Italian soil. For most of their time in private employment, they had jumped from one Middle Eastern shithole to another, fighting for one side and then the next for a couple of hundred euros a day in cash. They were supposed to be catching some rest and relaxation back home, but the lure of an easy job proved too difficult to resist, and so they had driven directly from Rome that morning.

"What's the plan?" the taller and wirier of the two asked. He was in his mid-30s, and had a climber's frame. His name was Bernardo, and he had once been a sergeant in the elite Italian Alpini Corps, the oldest specialized mountain infantry unit in the world. Recruited solely from small, isolated mountain villages, they were tough men, and Bernardo was no different.

The other man, Fredo, merely shrugged. Like Bernardo, he had a 9mm pistol shoved down the back of his pants, but he wasn't expecting to need it. He would prefer to kill the two Americans quietly, without firing a shot.

Up here in the hills, it was more than likely that no one would hear the sound of gunfire – and if they did, it was equally likely they would merely attribute it to hunters searching for the wild boar that were so prevalent in the region, but he didn't want to leave it to chance if it could be avoided. It was getting a little late for a hunting party to be out, after all.

Their employer hadn't told them precisely who or what they were looking for, just that the target was likely to be American or British, and that they needed to die. Quickly.

In addition, they had been given the name of the village in which their target had logged on to the Internet – San Casciano. It was a small, wealthy village about a six-hour drive from Rome, but one that few foreign tourists visited, instead frequented mainly by wealthy families from nearby Florence or Siena.

It proved easy to ask around for the foreigners, and thereafter to be pointed to the old Castello Romagno, the large house on the hill. The local shopkeepers and restaurant owners had nothing but good words to say about the American couple, and had emphasized several times that the two visitors did their best to speak in Italian, unlike most tourists. The woman was better, they said.

Finally, Fredo spoke his mind. "The Americans don't know we are coming. We'll introduce ourselves, confirm they are both present, get them to drop their guard, and then we take them out."

Bernardo laughed, cracking his knuckles as he walked. "You make it sound so easy, Fredo. I'll let you do the talking."

Unfortunately for the two Italian hitmen, they didn't know what they were coming up against. More accurately, they didn't know *who* they were coming up against.

TRAPP'S BERETTA pistol was burning a hole in the small of his back. The late afternoon sun had been on it, and it felt almost hot enough to start cooking off rounds. He knew that wasn't possible – at least, not without the propellant getting a hell of a lot hotter than it currently was – but it sure as heck felt that way.

He watched the two men stride up the long driveway from a window to the side of the heavy iron-studded front door of the castello. The small windowpanes were almost as old as the castle itself, and were held in with thick, uneven channels of lead. It was just one of the small details of the beautiful old house that he had come to appreciate during his stay. Between the message from Alexy Sokolov and the unexpected arrival of these two men, he somehow figured he wouldn't be here to appreciate it for very much longer. He didn't know if the two events were connected, but if it was just a coincidence, then it was a big one.

He suspected otherwise.

The window was narrow, shaped like an arrow slit, and was recessed deeply, so Trapp wasn't worried about being seen. As he watched, he inhaled through his nose and drank in the cool air that the stone of this old building seemed to breathe out, even when the sun was beating down overhead. It would be a shame to leave this place and the oasis of calm it had represented, but it seemed he didn't have any other choice.

The two men outside reached the imposing front door, and Trapp drew back slightly, in case either of them was to glance in his direction. A second later, he heard the report of the iron knocker bang out sharply three times.

He let the sound fall silent, until the ticking of an old grandfather clock returned to dominate the empty hallway of the castello. He pulled his shirt up and tucked it between his pistol and his skin, partly to protect himself from its burning heat, but mostly in case he needed to access it quickly. He swung the heavy door open halfway, shielding his body with the thick, weathered oak in a way that suggested he was leaning against it for support.

"Ciao." Trapp smiled.

He kept his posture natural, but his eyes danced from one man to the other, checking them from head to toe for any sign of a weapon. He saw nothing, but he couldn't help but notice the fact that both men wore closely-cropped military haircuts, or the way that the shorter, squatter of the two men stood several paces back from his companion, in a way that created a clear field of fire. The taller of the men held a bottle of red wine, as though he was a new neighbor coming over with a housewarming gift, and smiled warmly. The expression, the

American couldn't help but notice, failed to reach his eyes as he responded to the greeting.

"My apologies, gentlemen," Trapp said, deliberately layering on his American accent so that he sounded like a big, dumb tourist. He briefly wondered whether he had tipped over the dividing line into full-on redneck, but decided from the olive complexion of the two men facing him that they probably wouldn't know any better. "You'll have to forgive me – my Italian ain't so hot."

"English is fine. Is your wife here?" the shorter man asked brusquely.

Trapp frowned with exaggerated surprise. "My wife?" he said, chuckling. "Oh – you mean Anna, my girlfriend?"

"Yes," the squat man replied with a forced smile. "My apologies."

Trapp matched his conversation partner's faux enthusiasm and laughed heartily. "Don't want to be giving her any ideas, now, do we?"

The man grimaced, and shook his head. "Your girlfriend?" he prompted.

Trapp narrowed his expression, adopting a suspicious tone. With his actions shielded by the door, he reached slowly for the pistol concealed behind his back. He was careful to make no sudden movement, and inched his fingers forward until they closed around the weapon's butt. "Who did you say you were again?"

The two men glanced at each other, and Trapp noticed as the rearmost, taller man copied his own actions, his hand creeping around his body for what he could only assume was a weapon stashed exactly where Trapp's was.

"My name is Fredo," the squat man said with a conciliatory smile. "My family owns a property at the bottom of the hill. My brother and I"—he jerked the hand holding the wine bottle back toward the man behind him—"came to welcome you to the neighborhood and to invite you to dinner."

Trapp smiled broadly to put the two men at ease. The lie was delivered well, but he had no doubt that they were killers, sent here either to capture or eliminate him and Ikeda, though he didn't know why.

It was also clear that they were professionals, not local mobsters – they were both fit, had a military bearing, and hadn't simply rushed into an unknown situation with all guns blazing. In Trapp's limited experience, gangsters were different. Mostly lacking formal training, they were their own worst enemy. Unlike action heroes in the movies, Jason Trapp didn't like fighting fair. He preferred killing amateurs, not trained operatives, because unlike in the movies, specialists were much harder to kill.

"Oh," he said, "how kind. Let me get her down, I'm sure she'll be delighted to meet the two of you." He turned, still shielding the hand now grasping his weapon, and called out for Ikeda, using the name he had used earlier.

"Anna, honey," he sang out, elongating the words in a singsong fashion. "There are some guys I want you to meet."

He turned back and grinned. "She'll be down in a second. You know how women are..."

The two Italians relaxed, though Trapp noticed that both were beginning to assume a firing stance, with their feet shoulder width apart, hands hanging loosely at their sides, ready to reach for the weapons no doubt concealed behind their backs. When this went down, he would need to move fast, and hope he was better than they were.

Fredo shrugged ruefully, but the geniality he was attempting to convey wasn't matched by the cold expression in his dark eyes. Trapp had seen it before, the signs of a man hardening his heart for the violence to come. "My wife is just the same."

Trapp heard a whispered crunch from behind the two killers. It was the slightest of sounds, but the taller man flinched and appeared ready to turn around and search for the source of the noise. Trapp acted fast.

"Say," he said, pulling back the front door with his left hand, then reaching out with it for the bottle of wine in Fredo's hand. "Is that for us?"

The Italian glanced down at the bottle, and the taller man fixed his attention back on Trapp. Fredo's left hand began to rise as he handed the bottle over to Trapp, and as he did so, in one swift movement, the CIA operative's right hand twisted around his body, clutching his Beretta. The Italian looked up to see a barrel pointing unwaveringly at the spot between his two eyes.

"Don't fucking move," Trapp hissed, his voice low and deadly, leaving the squat man under no illusions as to what would happen if he disobeyed the order.

The second man, whose head had been turning to the left the second before, snapped his attention back on Trapp. The second he saw the pistol in the CIA man's hands, he reached for his own, and began to bring it around his body and up into a firing position.

The Hangman didn't flinch. He didn't need to flinch, because he knew he had the world's best backup on his side – and she was armed to the teeth.

"*No lo farei*," Ikeda whispered in a husky, almost seductive voice. The warning was delivered in Italian, but to Trapp it was as clear as day. *I wouldn't do that.*

The second man froze, his weapon halfway up. His eyes flashed with surprise as the situation threw a wrench of cognitive dissonance into the gears in his head. Trapp figured the two men had expected this to be an easy job – waste a couple of American tourists, asking no questions and expecting no answers. They hadn't known who or what they were coming up against, and so the shock would be almost crippling.

"Fuck you," Fredo spat.

He reached for his weapon, and before he could get anywhere close, the pistol in Trapp's steady fingers barked twice, and the squat man fell to the ground, his head carved open by the two lead jacketed rounds. The wine bottle smashed against the ground, splitting open and soaking the stones a dark purple that spread like a bloodstain.

Before the body hit the gravel, Trapp had switched his aim, fixing the taller man in his sights. The man's eyes now widened even further as he struggled to process the sight of his dead comrade in front of him.

"Don't do anything stupid," Ikeda muttered calmly, in English this time.

She was barefoot, in the same light sundress she'd been wearing when she had come up behind Trapp only a few minutes before. But she had an MP5 submachine gun in her hands, the stock extended and pressed tightly against her shoulder. She looked like the goddess of death. Trapp knew that the weapon could carve the Italian apart in a matter of seconds, leaving so little of him in one piece at this range that his body would be difficult to identify.

"I suggest you do what the lady says," he said, a cold smile creeping across his face. "Before she turns out your lights permanently."

The Italian's pistol was in his hands, but aimed at the ground, at a spot a couple of yards to the left of Trapp's toes. It was the position he'd been in when the shooting started, but he seemed smart enough to know that his best option right now wasn't to make any sudden movements.

"Who are you guys?" he muttered.

His Italian was thickly accented, and though Trapp had spent relatively little time in Italy throughout his career, he had enough experience in Europe as a whole to pick up on the signs of a man who had grown up far from his country's capital.

"We'll ask the questions," Trapp replied, taking a step forward without his aim wavering for even an instant. He paused for a second to ascertain whether the Italian was going to do anything stupid, and decided he wasn't.

"Drop the weapon and kick it away," he said.

The hitman's eyes flashed with anger. But he did as he was instructed. The pistol clattered to the gravel surface of the driveway. He straightened his posture slightly, and his leg opened up to kick the weapon away.

And at that precise moment, a gunshot rang out. The round impacted the Italian hitman's chest and sent him spinning, a splatter of blood joining the wine and bodily fluids already pooling at Trapp's feet.

"Contact!" Trapp yelled, his brain immediately snapping into a sniper drill before his conscious mind could process what the hell had just happened. "Get down!"

9

T rapp threw himself backward, behind the protective stone walls of the old Tuscan Castello. At the same moment, Ikeda flung herself to the ground and took cover behind the bright red Fiat rental car they had picked up upon landing in Florence several weeks earlier.

Like many European cars, it was small, but she pressed herself against the front, hiding behind the engine block.

"What do you see?" Trapp yelled, crouching behind a pillar of stone, his pistol feeling like dead weight. Depending on what the marksman was packing, and how far away he was, he might as well be holding a BB gun for all the good it would do him.

Ikeda took a second to reply. She studied the body of the second man to die and called out, "Definitely a sniper. Looks like heavy caliber."

"Shit," Trapp muttered.

His mind moved fast. He couldn't figure out what the hell was going on here. Who were these two men, and why had they just tried to kill him? Because that was clearly their intention, even if they haven't been able to carry out the plan. He cursed himself for not capturing one of them alive, even though it hadn't really been a decision that was left in his hands.

"Maybe a cleanup team," he said. "A backstop, in case something went wrong?"

"I figured that," Ikeda replied dryly, though her voice was tight from the unexpected stress. "The question is – do you think they'll stick around and finish the job?"

"Hell if I know," Trapp grunted.

A dusky gloom was already beginning to kiss the canopies of the trees that hemmed the old Castello in on all sides. He knew that in under an hour, true night would fall, and unless the sniper was damn good, his advantage would fade away. He killed the castello's lights, interior and exterior, to hasten that moment.

In any case, though, Trapp suspected that the shooter would already be bugging out. The fact that he'd killed the second hitman without even a second's hesitation suggested that he wasn't part of the Italian's crew. He was a third-party operator, sent to terminate the two men after the job was completed. He was there to clean up loose ends.

But testing his hypothesis was a hell of a gamble to take. And there was another pressing issue. If the sniper called in the failure of the operation, for all Trapp knew there were other units on the way. If the unknown shooter was able to pin them down until those units arrived, then their options would quickly narrow from bad to worse.

"You have the shooter's position?" Trapp called out.

In truth, there were few good roosts for a marksman to hole up in the surrounding area. Castello Romagno was at the top of the tallest hill in the immediate area, and a chest-high stone wall surrounded the courtyard around its imposing entrance-way. The only spot that Trapp could think of was the roof of an abandoned monastery about a third of a mile down the road. Between the Castello and the monastery lay only a few fields of gnarled, low olive trees, which wouldn't obscure their line of sight.

"The bell tower," Ikeda replied. "Has to be."

"I concur."

"What are you thinking?"

Trapp breathed out heavily. None of the options they had were good. In American terms, the Fiat 500 was basically a toy car. Any competent shooter would be able to carve up its unarmored chassis in a matter of seconds, especially with the fifty caliber rounds that Trapp suspected he was using, judging by the mess one of them had made of the Italian hitman's chest. The winding road that led down to the bottom of the valley, if he remembered correctly, kinked hard three times on the journey down. Each time, it passed through a fifty yard section of cleared forest, through which long-distance electricity cables were run in a direct line of sight to the abandoned monastery's belltower.

And so, each time – and worse, for a *predictable* length of time – the little Italian car would be exposed to enemy fire. Trapp was a good driver, and had been trained by the best. But because the gaps opened up just before the turns in the road, there was only so fast he could cross them. Three times, for precious, endless seconds, the Fiat 500 would open itself up to be shredded by the sniper, and there would be nothing they could do about it.

Instead of directly answering Ikeda's question, Trapp asked, "Where's the other MP5?"

She didn't reply for a long few seconds, long enough to make Trapp wonder if she was okay. When she finally spoke, her voice was strangled, and it took Trapp a couple of seconds to figure out why.

"In my bedroom," she said with an awkward cough. "Underneath my underwear."

Trapp flushed red. The two of them hadn't even kissed yet –

if that was even on the agenda – and yet he was going to be rifling through the deadly female operative's underwear drawer like some kind of pervert.

"Oh," he croaked, his own voice matching Ikeda's embarrassment.

The emotion quickly cleared in her professional mind, and she asked the obvious question. "Why?"

"In about thirty seconds, I'm going to lay down fire on the belltower. A second after I start shooting, I need you to cross into the house. Got it?"

"You won't hit a barn door at that range," Ikeda replied doubtfully.

"But he won't know that," Trapp said with more confidence than he felt.

Ikeda's point was a good one. The MP5 model in their possession had an effective firing range of just over 600 feet. The belltower lay about three times that far. Trapp would be lucky to have even a handful of the thirty rounds in the magazine even impact the tower, let alone kill the shooter. He cursed himself for not picking up a weapon with a heavier caliber than the 9 mm Heckler & Koch submachine gun upstairs, but then again, he hadn't really expected anyone to come after him out here in the idyllic Tuscan countryside.

It was a lesson learned. Hopefully they would live long enough to make use of it.

"And what then? We'll just be stuck in the Castello, waiting for someone to come hunt us down."

"Do you trust me?"

The answer came quickly, and carried no hesitation. "Of course."

"Then run with me on this. If the shooter's still out there, he'll take cover, even if only for a couple of seconds. It'll give you the time you need." He paused. "You ready?"

"As I'll ever be."

Trapp grinned. "Atta girl."

With that, he spun around and sprinted for the stairs. He took them three at a time and seconds later reached the landing. He turned left, shoulder-barging Ikeda's bedroom door. It wasn't exactly how he anticipated entering the room for the first time. But in his experience, events rarely turned out the way you planned.

He turned on his heel with indecision, searching for Ikeda's underwear drawer – another outcome he hadn't foreseen. He spotted a large oak chest of drawers that looked as though it might have been standing there since the old Castello was built, and pulled the top drawer open roughly. He knocked it back, seeing only workout gear, and reached for the next one.

Jackpot.

Trapp grabbed the weapon, brushing aside a lacy thong that had attached itself to the barrel like a limpet. He checked that the weapon was loaded, knowing it would be, and then made for the tallest point in the building, a tower that was once a defensive fortification, but now only hosted a large sandstone sundial on each of its outer faces, and a small terrace from which guests could savor the last of the evening sun.

An ancient, spiral wooden staircase ran from the Castello's top floor up the center of the stone tower. Thin arrow slits were cut on all sides, and Trapp made a judgment call that his movement wouldn't be visible from outside as he hurtled upward, his thighs straining from the unexpected activity. The wooden structure creaked as he ran, and then tendrils of dust fell downwards, both beneath and above him, tickling his nostrils.

The experienced operative kept himself low as he exited the stairwell into the day's fading heat, just in case the shooter had anticipated someone making a play for the high ground. He pressed the stock of the submachine gun to his shoulder and rested the barrel against one of the decorative battlements.

The old stone monastery was clearly visible from this

height, a huge, crumbling structure that had for hundreds of years housed a community of monks. Thankfully, they were long gone, since Trapp had no great desire to provoke the wrath of God by firing on an active place of worship.

"Here goes nothing," he muttered to himself as he made the appropriate adjustments for windage and elevation out of muscle memory, given the weapon's inherent limitations, and iron sights.

In truth, firing on the belltower with the weapon in his hands was a fool's errand. If more than a couple of the rounds impacted anywhere close to where he wanted – especially on full automatic – then he would count himself lucky. But he wasn't expecting to kill or even wound the shooter, just buy Ikeda enough time to get to cover. This would be more art than science, but Trapp had done his time in the trenches, apprenticed under the best, and if anyone had a chance of making these shots count, it would be him.

He forced his heartrate to slow, gently moved his index finger from the side of the stock to caress the trigger, and then squeezed. The submachine gun spat half the magazine – fifteen rounds – in under three seconds, and Trapp watched as half a dozen plumes of dust blossomed near the base of the old belltower. He paused for half a second, to allow the shooter time to react, then squeezed the trigger again. When he was done, the submachine gun clicked, and he immediately ducked down beneath the battlements, just in case the shooter was bold enough to return fire.

Trapp slumped against the stone, a sudden wave of exhaustion overcoming him as he clutched the empty weapon to his chest. He didn't bother peeking over the battlements to see if his actions had come to anything concrete. Actually killing the sniper at this range would be a one in a million, maybe a one in a billion shot, and he didn't believe in getting lucky. At least, not *that* lucky.

Besides, there was more pressing business to attend to.

He crawled back to the entrance to the stairwell, ignoring the bullet casings strewn all around his knees. They were clean – he'd loaded each magazine in this place personally, wearing cotton gloves to avoid leaving fingerprints – but even if they weren't, there was enough forensic evidence in this place to incriminate both him and Ikeda a hundred times over.

Trapp took the stairwell down a little more slowly than he had on the way up, but no less urgently. He hadn't heard any return gunfire, so he was pretty sure that Ikeda would have made it into the house unscathed, but the Hangman knew as well as anyone that combat in general – and firing a weapon on full automatic in particular – has a way of inducing tunnel vision that blocks out peripheral information intake. It was entirely possible that the sniper had been able to pick out a shot and take it, and he simply hadn't noticed.

But as he emerged from the tower stairwell, coming out onto the landing at the top of the main set of stairs in the Castello, he breathed a sigh of relief and allowed his pounding heart rate to settle.

"You made it," he said, grinning with relief.

Ikeda was standing over the body of the taller of the two Italian hitmen – the one who had been taken out by the sniper. Her submachine gun was resting against the stone wall just inside of the thick oak front door, which was itself bolted shut. She was looking down at him with an expression of disgust on her face. A reaction to the body and not him, he hoped.

"Good call," Trapp said, nodding to himself with approval as he walked down the main stairwell to join her and her distasteful package. If they wanted to get to the bottom of who had sent hitmen to kill them, then they needed evidence. As usual, Ikeda's quick thinking obviated the need to expose themselves to potential gunfire for a second time.

Ikeda merely winced, glanced down at her bloody hands,

and wiped them on her blue sundress, irreversibly staining it. It was a good thing, Trapp thought, that she wasn't a girly girl. The blood would never come out. At least, not that much.

"I figured we could use a lead," she replied.

A flicker of emotion crossed her face, like a shadow scuttling along the ground as clouds passed by in the skies overhead. Trapp wondered how she was handling the reminder of violence after everything she had been through in North Korea just a couple of months before, but knew better than to broach the topic. At least, not now. There would be a time for that once they had survived this present crisis.

Hell, Trapp didn't know how he felt about it either. For all of Eliza's fighting talk about his true nature just a few minutes before, he wasn't entirely certain that he could simply go on killing men forever. And worse still, as the afternoon's events had just proved, if he kept on making enemies at the rate he had acquired them throughout his long career, then it was only a matter of time before someone came for the king—and didn't miss.

"So," Ikeda said glibly. "What do we do now?"

10

I keda shot Trapp a doubtful look as they reached the bottom of a flight of stairs and emerged into darkess.

They had both changed into more appropriate gear – jeans, boots, nondescript summer jackets and matching cargo rucksacks that contained several sets of travel documents, thick wads of cash, credit cards, weapons and ammunition. The bug-out bags were second nature to the two operatives, but it was yet another reminder that their holiday in Tuscany had come to a sudden, unexpected, and crashing halt.

"I thought you said you had a plan," she said.

"I do," Trapp replied confidently. "Trust me."

"I figured it was something a little more fleshed out than simply hiding away in the basement to make our last stand..."

"It is." He grinned, flicking on a flashlight as he strode ever deeper into the bowels of the enormous basements beneath the old castello. In centuries past, he imagined, they would have stored huge barrels of wine down here, and aging wheels of Italian cheese, legs of ham hanging from the ceilings, and all the other sundries that would be required by the Italian nobility to host dinner parties for a wide circle of friends and hangers-on.

Now they stood empty.

When the old building was renovated to turn it into the luxurious villa in which they had stayed for the past several weeks, the builders hadn't bothered to run electrical lighting this deep into the basement. Though the dark space, cut into the bedrock of the hill beneath the Castello, was certainly cool enough to store food – especially compared with the baking heat of a Tuscan summer's day – it also smelled of damp. The advent of modern refrigeration and grocery stores diminished the need for such enormous storage spaces.

"Here we go," Trapp said with satisfaction, the beam of his flashlight playing across a bolted wooden door that adorned a section of roughly cut rock that made up the basement's far wall. Its hinges had long ago rusted. The wooden door itself was almost black with age and mildew.

"What is it?"

"Remember when I told you about those tunnels? The ones that lead down to the plateau?"

"Yeah, but–" The pitch of her voice changed. "Oh..."

"Told you I had a plan," Trapp said, grinning and turning to wink at Ikeda.

She eyed him with a look of concern. "Didn't you also say no one had explored them in decades? They're probably tumbling down."

"Probably longer," he said, throwing her another wink. "But if worst comes to worst, we have enough food and batteries to hole up down here for a couple of days at least. If anyone's waiting for us up top, they'll figure we must've made it out somehow without them noticing."

"And if the police show up?" she asked sceptically. "We weren't exactly subtle up there, and there's still a body lying in the courtyard."

Trapp winced. As much because he wished they could have risked snapping a few pictures and retrieving samples from the other hitman as for any real worries about the actions of the rural Italian police, who he suspected were not exactly known for their forensic attention to detail.

"We'll cross that bridge when we come to it." He shrugged, handed Ikeda the flashlight, and indicated the wooden door. "Hold that."

Ikeda kept the flashlight trained on the door, giving Trapp enough light to work with. He explored the bolt, wondering whether it would be irretrievably rusted, and thus effectively locked in place. It certainly was corroded, but as his fingers brushed the mechanism, he had another idea.

He retrieved the pistol from the small of his back, grabbed it by the barrel, and held it in the air just above the bolt. Using all his strength, he brought it directly down and smashed it into the ancient mechanism, which practically disintegrated, clinking as it fell to the basement's stone floor.

"That went better than expected," he muttered, grasping the door and giving it an almighty yank. Its hinges, equally fragile, protested then fell away as he levered the door open.

He turned back to Ikeda, retrieving his flashlight and shining its beam into the endless, inky depths of the long tunnel. It stretched away into the distance, the beam dying long before it reached any endpoint. "Ready for an adventure?"

She rolled her eyes. "It's always an adventure with you, Jason. I'm getting used to it."

"Crap," Trapp grunted as he made an experimental first step into the tunnel. "It's like a coffin in here."

"Maybe for you." Ikeda grinned, patting him gently on the shoulder. "I'm all right."

Trapp spoke the truth. The tunnel was a little shy of six feet tall, and a couple of feet wide, carved roughly out of rock. As they proceeded further down, it looked almost as though sections of the tunnel might be natural – larger caverns that bulged like sections of a balloon animal, making Trapp wonder if there were other such tunnels and caves dotted throughout the hill. A little further on, it became clear that a natural passage had been widened, and Trapp marveled at the effort it must have taken – years, and thousands of man hours, especially using the limited technology available when it was built.

"Watch your head," he grunted, indicating a stalactite that plunged from the roof of the tunnel. He leaned forward, his back aching from the strain of hunching over to fit through.

"So where does this come out?" Ikeda asked.

"That," he mused, "is a very good question."

"And the answer is?"

"I guess we'll find out." He grinned. "Hey – did I ever tell you what happened to me last time I was in a tunnel like this?"

"I'm sure you're about to tell me," Ikeda replied dryly. Trapp could almost feel the weight of her eyes rolling behind him.

"Guilty as charged."

"Go on then…"

"Someone dropped a two thousand pound bomb on my head."

Ikeda laughed. "Some guys have all the luck."

THE TUNNEL, thankfully, emerged behind a boulder almost three quarters of the way down to the bottom of the valley, near the bed of a small river that had been reduced by the heat of the summer to little more than a trickle. The exit was so fouled by years of vegetation growth it took the combined efforts of both Trapp and Ikeda almost half an hour to break through. By the time they were done, both were soaked with sweat, and it was long past dark.

An hour later, they were sitting on the back of an old Vespa scooter that Trapp purchased from a delighted farmer with a thick bundle of euro notes – far more than the vehicle was truly worth, except to them. The farmer threw in a pair of musty full-face helmets and walked away thanking his lucky stars for the dumb, wealthy Americans. Trapp eyed them doubtfully, wondering how much good they would do in the event of a crash, but decided that the benefits of hiding their appearance were worth it.

Two hours after that, with the dark of night firmly upon them, they came upon the outskirts of the Italian city of Florence. Trapp guided the scooter to a halt in a quiet suburban area, and Ikeda unhooked her arms around Trapp's waist and gratefully stepped off the bike. He quickly wiped any surfaces that might harbor his prints, and left the keys in the bike's ignition. Whoever came across it next could keep it. He was surprised it had made it this far.

Ikeda looked around. "So what are we doing here?"

"We need answers," Trapp grunted as he worked some of the knots out of his back and shoulders. "And I think I know a guy who can help."

11

C harles Nash was a Marine.

Retired, sure, but once a Marine, always a Marine. He was on the ground when the United States beat back the Iraqi Armed Forces from Kuwait in the first Gulf War. And like many young boys with their first steady paycheck and not a lot of opportunity to spend it, except on drink and women, the recently graduated second Lieutenant C. Nash had chosen to invest in a car. A muscle car, to be precise: a 1985 Chevrolet Camaro painted in fire engine red.

He was still driving that same car two decades later, when he first ran for the House. He'd restored it twice, upgrading the engine, putting in new leather seats, and did all the maintenance himself.

But since assuming the presidency almost a year earlier, the Secret Service had not allowed their new president behind the wheel of any vehicle more substantial than the golf cart he was currently driving, as a warm late summer breeze ruffled his now thinning hair. The agents on his protective detail hadn't liked the prospect of their charge taking even that minor liberty, but on this matter at least, he was prepared to overrule them. Two agents were following him at a respectful distance in a cart of their own – close enough to reach him instantly in case of trouble, but far enough away to allow him at least the illusion that he was alone in the presidential country retreat.

Camp David, he reflected, was a prison.

A gilded prison, to be sure, but still a prison, like the White House, Air Force One, and all of the other trappings of the US presidency. There wasn't a moment in which he was truly alone, without bodyguards and aides and the concerns of an entire globe resting on his shoulders. It was the best job he had ever had, and yet the rapidly graying mane atop his head spoke to the strains it was placing upon him.

The Main Lodge with its sloping gray roof and airy, light-filled interiors came into view around a curving paved lane that swung around a field of yellow wildflowers. A man appeared in the distance too, short, bearded, and dressed like a college professor. He was standing underneath the awning of a large porch that ran right around the edge of the building. Nash recognized him immediately as his new director of the Central Intelligence Agency, George Lawrence.

The president slowed the golf cart fractionally and sucked in a deep breath of fresh mountain air, laced with the scent of summer pollen. He knew why the new DCI was here, and what the man's presence heralded – the inevitable loss of his weekend away.

He brought the cart to a halt next to Lawrence and stepped off it with his hand outstretched.

"George," he said with a broad smile that covered the minor hint of frustration he felt at being disturbed, as was so often the case, by a matter of national security. "Sorry to take you away from your family this weekend."

"Of course, Mr. President. You –"

The DCI trailed off awkwardly, realizing his mistake at

mentioning Nash's absent family. What was left of it, anyway. "I'm sorry for interrupting yours," he finished lamely.

"So, George," Nash said to fill an awkwardness he did not share, "why don't you fill me in? I take it you're here about the British Airways flight the Russians shot down yesterday?"

"That is correct, sir," he said, looking relieved to be able to steer the conversation away from such a sensitive topic.

Nash found that fact faintly amusing, but hid the reaction, knowing that he wasn't yet sufficiently well acquainted with Lawrence to treat the man as a friend, knowing him instead only by reputation. There were only three or four men alive who had more experience of occupying the presidency as Charles Nash, which was little enough. But in the short few months during which he'd led his country, he'd found it was necessary to learn precisely what it was that motivated a man.

Some, including members of his own cabinet, needed to be loved. They demanded not just Nash's attention, but his affection. It was the proximity to power, and that power's subsequent reflection on them which drove the best out of them.

Others needed to be treated like working dogs – not starved of affection, but certainly kept at arm's length. They needed to observe the fondness that Nash bestowed on others and ask themselves why it was that they did not receive such kindness. Only then would they strive to their fullest extent.

And which one are you, George?

"Come." Nash smiled, gesturing toward the lodge. "Let's head inside."

Once inside, and suitably refreshed, the President circled back to the topic at hand. "So which was it, Director – a fuck up, or a fuck you?"

Lawrence's bushy, graying eyebrows briefly arched with surprise at Nash's coarse language, but he otherwise hid his reaction well.

"Neither, sir," he said, sliding a file across the coffee table that sat between the couches occupied by the two men. "We believe that it was a targeted assassination."

Nash said nothing, but opened the file to find a single sheet of paper. It was a redacted personnel file. "And this was the target?"

"Correct, Mr. President. His real name is Alexy Sokolov, though his ticket was purchased in the name of Grigori Trubetskoy."

"So, this Alexy?" Nash grimaced. "Who *was* he?"

Lawrence looked pained as he replied. "Until yesterday morning, Mr. President, he was the Agency's top human intelligence source inside Russia."

"And why has it taken you twenty-four hours to inform me of this fact?" Nash replied, his voice hard. He raised his hand to forestall Lawrence's reply. "President Murov phoned me last night, assuring me that it was all a horrible accident – a commander of a missile battery misunderstanding his orders. It would have been useful to know that he was lying to me, George."

Nash didn't mention the fact that when he spoke to Murov, he generally assumed that the president of the Russian Federation was being economical with the truth of the best of times, and positively fraudulent for most of the rest. The man was a snake – megalomaniacal, avaricious, and a hatful more ten-dollar words to boot, none of them pleasant.

"Yes sir," Lawrence said in a reply that wasn't exactly an apology. "We had to ensure that he truly was on that plane. It could have been an attempt by their security services to blow the asset's cover. If that was the case, then they would have been watching for our response."

Nash glanced up dubiously. "Wouldn't they just arrest him? Even just kill him?"

"Probably," Lawrence admitted, "but this is how the game

works. We've done it to them, they do it to us. Until I knew for sure, I judged it better not to do anything that might tip our hand either way."

"So this"—Nash checked the file in his hands—"this Alexy Sokolov. He's dead? How did this happen, and what does it mean? In that order."

Lawrence squirmed in place, understanding correctly that Nash was putting him under the spotlight, and that his answers would guide his boss's understanding of his competence not just in the present, but perhaps long into the future.

"Sir," he prevaricated, "I'd like to start, if I may, with a little background on my experience inside the Agency..."

Nash gestured at him to go on, though a grimace carried with it the suggestion that Lawrence should keep it short.

"Mr. President, in my opinion, the Agency has shifted its focus since 9/11, and as a result lost or bastardized many of its core competencies."

"Go on..." Nash said, intrigued despite his earlier reservation.

"Sir, the modern Central Intelligence Agency is swiftly becoming little more than an extension of the armed forces. Many of the officers under my command have spent their entire careers dedicated to finding, tracking, and then eliminating terrorists."

Nash's eyebrow arched. "Isn't that a worthy goal?"

"It is," Lawrence allowed. "And we have become extraordinarily good at it. My worry is that this creeping militarization of CIA, this focus on killing misguided goat herders who accidentally stumble across the Pakistani border, has distracted us from the real threats to this nation. With respect, sir, one suicide bomber isn't going to destroy the Republic. Hell, a hundred, even a thousand wouldn't. But one Russian ICBM could wipe out our way of life."

The president's mind jumped to a time, not many months ago, when a supposed servant of the very Republic that Lawrence mentioned had been the one who tried to bring it down. Was he not a terrorist, too?

Not an Islamic one, that's for sure. Twisted, but through greed, not faith.

"So what are you suggesting, Director?"

"Sir, I want your permission to focus the Agency back on the basics. We need to trim down the Special Activities Division, and leave most of the shooting to Delta and the SEALs. I want to go back to recruiting men and women like Alexy Sokolov. Running assets, getting real intelligence on the nations who would do us harm. Not wasting time, not to mention billions of dollars, on murdering low-rent warlords thousands of miles away."

Nash said nothing, but noted the almost messianic zeal in director Lawrence's eyes as he spoke. It was evident that the man truly believed what he was saying. That was a good thing. In the president's experience, too many powerful people rose to their positions without real conviction, simply jumping from one popular policy to the next. Lawrence's proposal was the exact opposite – the natural corollary of what he was asking was for his Agency to *lose* budget dollars, not gain them.

After all, it was easy enough to excite the old graybeards on the Senate Intelligence Committee with tales of CIA operatives busting down doors and killing terrorists. Not so much the slow, methodical, frankly boring business of recruiting human intelligence sources.

On the other hand, Nash had seen firsthand the value of exactly the kind of operators that Lawrence was disparaging. Men like Jason Trapp, whose deeds could never be publicly admitted, but were as vital to the health of democracy as any election.

"It seems to me, Director," Nash mused, "that losing your best source in Russia without even knowing why doesn't exactly fill me with confidence about your ability to pull off the kind of change you're arguing for."

"That's what I'm talking about!" Lawrence said, almost rising with excitement. "Sokolov is dead, and we have no idea why. Two decades ago, we would have had half a dozen sources in Russia just like him. At least one of them would have been able to confirm what was going on. Instead we wasted billions recruiting trigger-pullers. What the hell is some knuckle-dragging special forces gorilla going to do in the face of the Russian threat?"

"Watch your tongue, Director," Nash chided firmly.

Lawrence gulped, realizing he'd overstepped. "I apologize, Mr. President. I –"

"Believe in what you're saying," Nash said, finishing the sentence. "That much is obvious, Director. And I agree with you – perhaps we need to reassess the role of human intelligence –"

"Thank you, sir," Lawrence interrupted.

Nash shot him a black look in response.

"As I was saying," he said, receiving a flushed look of apology. "I'm willing to *reassess*, not reorder the whole damn system on a whim. When you sit behind my desk, Director, you quickly learn the value of having a few knuckle-dragging special forces gorilla types just a phone call away."

"Yes, sir," Lawrence muttered, looking equal parts embarrassed and as though he wanted to argue.

That was the problem with zealots, Nash reflected to himself. They were convinced that their way was the *only* way.

"George, I want you to find out what's going on in Russia. And draw up a proposal for what you want to do with the Agency. But," he said, raising a finger to drive home the point, "you're not to make any changes without my approval. Understood?"

Lawrence nodded, looking as though he wanted to say something, but visibly mastering the urge. "Yes, Mr. President."

Nash smiled. "Good."

12

The morning dawned bright and hot in Florence, the mercury reaching seventy-five degrees before eight in the morning. Trapp and Ikeda had stayed in a suite at the Four Seasons, checking in under assumed names, and paying with pre-paid credit cards that would lead even a determined investigator nowhere – and do so slowly, at that. They worked out together in the hotel gym and breakfasted before getting ready for the day.

"So who is he?" Ikeda asked, pushing the remnants of an omelette around her plate. "This contact of yours."

"His name is Alessandro Lombardi. He's with the Italian AISE."

Ikeda raised an eyebrow. "What's that when it's at home?"

"The Italian intelligence service, the *Agenzia Informazioni e Sicurezza Esterna.*"

"Say that five times..." she added dryly. "So what's he doing in a place like Florence? It's not exactly the center of the universe when it comes to our line of work."

Trapp glanced around out of habit. They had chosen an isolated table in a distant corner of the restaurant, and were up well before most holidaymakers dared brave the day. Assured that no one was listening, he smiled. "Alessandro is... He's an interesting kind of guy. Kind of a throwback to the old world of intelligence, when agencies recruited you with a tap on the shoulder."

Ikeda didn't look impressed. "I've met that type before, back at Langley. Mostly dinosaurs."

Trapp shrugged. "No arguments there. But Alessandro isn't like that. He's a bit of a maverick. I've worked with him once before, and he's good. Besides, he's the only person I know in this part of the world who owes me a favor."

"For what?"

"I saved his daughter's life."

Ikeda didn't react to the minor revelation. Trapp briefly wondered whether they would ever have ordinary conversations together, like couples who didn't work in their most unusual field. In any other scenario, a comment like that would have deserved at least a raised eyebrow, if not a follow-up – but not in this one. But he put the thought out of his mind.

"So what are we waiting for?" Ikeda asked as she finished her coffee. Trapp glanced up and noticed that she was practically vibrating with nervous energy.

Trapp laughed.

"Alessandro is from what you might call a noble family, and he's real old school. He works at the Banca Monte dei Paschi di Siena, and he doesn't turn up at the office before ten in the morning even on his best days. It's Friday, which means he was at the opera last night, so he'll have a sore head. I doubt he'll be in before eleven."

"Sounds like a nice life. What does he do?"

"He's a banker, primarily, but during the Cold War he was the guy the Italians turned to when they needed to hunt down a Soviet spy. These days he mostly concentrates on terrorist financing networks. You could call this his... retirement. It allows him to stay plugged into the game without being forced to work on a civil servant's salary." Trapp grinned. "Not that he needs the money…"

Ikeda leaned back in her chair. "And how far can we trust him?"

"Like I said," Trapp replied earnestly, "he owes me."

They spent the next two hours like any other tourist couple, looking like newlyweds as they walked arm in arm through a city that had once been one of the wealthiest of the medieval era – and was pockmarked with examples of beautiful architecture that attested to that fact. Florence, known as Firenze to the locals, was the birthplace of the Renaissance, then the first capital of the Kingdom of Italy.

A careful observer might have noticed the slight bulge of a weapon on Trapp's person, or the way Ikeda's eyes darted left and right, never settling on a single spot for very long, constantly canvassing the relentless flow of both locals and tourists. Neither had forgotten, of course, the third shooter from the day before. They darted through the Piazza della Signoria, the main square in front of the Vecchio Palace, with its battlements and tower, and drank an espresso in the Italian style – standing up, at a bar that offered a perfect viewpoint of the whole forum.

Only when they were entirely certain that they had not been followed did they make for the local headquarters of the Banca Montei dei Paschi di Siena, which looked out onto the Piazza della Signoria itself, taking pride of place in a building that dated back hundreds of years. The first floor was constructed out of huge granite blocks, and the floor above painted in a watercolor yellow, accented with beautifully decorated archways over openings containing windows. A discreet bronze sign was the only marker of what lay within.

Trapp flashed a smile at the receptionist. "I'm here to see Signore Lombardi," he said.

She was in her early 40s, with the nicotine stained finger-tips of a heavy smoker. The scent of that habit was covered by thick, floral perfume that hung off her in waves. "Do you have an appointment?" she wheezed.

He shook his head. "I'm an old friend."

At this, the receptionist looked doubtful. She studied Trapp, then Ikeda, her eyes moving up and down, left to right. Eventually, she said, "The signore is busy today. Perhaps you could return at a later date. With an *appointment*."

Trapp chuckled out loud, and almost imperceptibly shook his head. "I'm afraid that won't be possible. My wife and I"—he glanced at Ikeda, who smiled dutifully and didn't register even a hint of surprise at his surprise proposal—"are only in Florence for the rest of the day. It's imperative that we see Signore Lombardi."

The receptionist was already shaking her head with typical Italian frustration when Trapp added, "Tell him I saw Alessa last week. She's looking beautiful."

She frowned, her fingertips drumming the glass desk in front of her as she made up her mind. Eventually she sighed without bothering to conceal her irritation and gestured with a flick of her fingers at a waiting area. "I will inquire. Sit there."

The two of them settled into comfortable leather armchairs, and Ikeda leaned over and whispered under her breath, "Well, she's a real breath of fresh air..."

"Like I said," Trapp replied. "Alessandro is what you could call an acquired taste. She's perfect for him."

"Who's Alessa?"

"His daughter's middle name."

Ikeda rolled her eyes. "Real subtle."

A minute passed, then two, then ten. Trapp glanced up and noticed Ikeda studying the room intently. She elbowed him in the ribs and spoke quietly, indicating a high resolution CCTV camera set on a gimbal that was slowly focusing on their position. "We're being watched."

Trapp rolled his eyes. "He's playing games," he said.

He stood up, stretched out his arm and tapped the face of his watch three times, staring directly at the camera and ignoring the reproving gaze of the receptionist. Barely thirty seconds later, he heard a barrel laugh, and the sound of a not inconsiderable bulk thundering down stone stairs, moccasin soles slapping as they struggled valiantly to keep their wearer upright.

"Jason!" a hearty voice bellowed as its owner entered the reception room, arms outstretched.

He was a little shy of five foot eight, with a thick salt and pepper beard, a shaved, tanned head, and wearing an ocean-blue suit. The overall look wouldn't have looked out of place if he was a designer on the catwalk of Milan Fashion Week.

Trapp didn't have to be able to see Ikeda to know that her eyes would doubtlessly be widening at the almost comical sight of the irrepressible Italian spy.

"Alessandro." He smiled, shaking his head and saying in a lower voice, "still no good at using my cover name, I see..."

"Bah," Alessandro replied, gesturing immediately at the empty reception room. "Who is here to listen?"

Trapp raised his eyebrow and glanced over at the receptionist, who was pretending not to stare.

Alessandro shook his head with mock disappointment. "Martina has been with me for decades. Her discretion is without question!"

Then his eyes lit up as they took in Ikeda's form, now standing a couple of paces behind Trapp. He almost knocked the Hangman aside in his eagerness to reach out for her hand. "But who is this? Don't tell me that you have settled down, my friend?"

"Perhaps we could take this somewhere quiet?" Trapp interjected firmly, before Ikeda was prompted for her name. He knew Alessandro well enough to remember that his Old World charm and boundless optimism sometimes overrode his good sense.

The Italian looked wounded at the suggestion, but instantly flashed a smile to indicate that he was joking. "But of course."

They followed Alessandro up into his private office, a large, mahogany-paneled room that looked much as it might have hundreds of years ago– except for the more modern addition of a glass wall and a fingerprint-activated door lock that regulated access.

"So." Alessandro winked as the door closed behind them. "Who is this lovely lady?"

Ikeda grinned, clearly not thrown by the Italian's relentless energy. "Eliza Ikeda. Pleased to meet you."

Alessandro reached for her hand and brought it gently to his mouth, kissing the tips of her fingers. "The pressure is all mine, my dear. I am Alessandro Lombardi. Pleased to meet you."

"The *pleasure* is all mine," she replied, correcting him.

Before the words were done escaping her mouth, Alessandro shook his head, looking aghast. "Believe me, when a beautiful young lady like yourself visits an old man like me, that is never the case."

Trapp cleared his throat, grinning as she flashed him a confused look.

"Men!" Alessandro groaned, winking at Ikeda. "Always with business on their minds. Very well," he said, wandering around his desk, and relaxing into the thick leather chair behind it with a heavy sigh. "How might I help you, my old friend?"

Trapp removed a small rucksack from his shoulders and sat down on the other side of the desk. Ikeda followed his lead. He glanced around the office, taking in the leather-bound first editions stacked on shelves behind the spy's desk and the expensive artwork that adorned the walls – paintings that he was quite sure that neither the Italian's legitimate employer, or the other one, had provided him. "I see business is treating you well?"

Alessandro spread his hands wide. "As well as can be expected at my age..."

Trapp snorted. "You're sixty-five, Alessandro, not ninety. And this hardly seems like an unpleasant place to retire."

"I suppose you're right. But I also imagine that you didn't come all this way to inquire after my health?" the Italian asked, raising an eyebrow in invitation.

"Correct," Trapp conceded. "Yesterday evening, two men attempted to kill me and–" He glanced over at Ikeda, trying to work out how to describe her, and finished lamely, "my friend."

"Your friend," Alessandro repeated knowingly with a single, sharp nod.

He leaned forward and placed his elbows on his desk, the sleeves of his blue suit hiking up and revealing white shirt sleeves underneath, finished with a flash of pink cufflinks. "These men – what did they want?"

Trapp grimaced. "We didn't exactly get that far."

"I understand by that that they are dead?"

"Indeed."

"So what exactly is it that I can do for you?" the Italian spy inquired. His gaze crossed from Trapp to Ikeda, and then back again. "I take it you're not looking for protection."

"We can handle that ourselves. It's information we need, and you're about as well plugged-in as anyone this side of the Atlantic."

Alessandro's right eyebrow undulated. It was thick, stuffed with wiry hair that protruded at all angles, and Trapp could barely take his attention away from it. "And is there a reason," he said, "that you have not spoken to my colleagues in Langley about this?"

Ikeda and Trapp glanced at each other, communicating silently.

Before either could reply, Alessandro clicked his tongue. "I see. You aren't certain whether they were in on it?"

Though the idea that his country might have sold him out struck Trapp as unlikely, neither could he entirely rule it out. The Agency had a new director, a changing of the guard. And Trapp was no neophyte. He knew that every shift in political power put heads on the chopping block and left loose ends that needed to be tied up. It was possible – not likely, but possible – that Trapp now found himself in that position. To the new director, he might be a liability, a political landmine just waiting to blow up. Even in a post-9/11 world of more muscular US foreign policy, the revelation of the existence of an intelligence operative with Trapp's portfolio of kills would be hard for Congress to accept, and the news media to resist. Lawrence had a reputation as a straight shooter, focused on human intelligence, not covert action. Maybe he was making an exception to that rule. Cleaning house, and getting rid of the old guard.

"The problem is," Trapp grunted, "no one else knew where we were. We traveled in-country on fresh passports, and we didn't leave a paper trail."

This, naturally enough, pointed the finger at the CIA. But Trapp wasn't convinced. The main evidence to the contrary was the fact that whoever had tried to kill him had hired locals. If the Agency really wanted him dead, they'd surely have sent a team of pros – special forces, or SOG operatives, and briefed them that he'd been turned. They wouldn't have rushed, but acted with speed, surprise, and overwhelming force.

Alessandro leaned back in his golden brown, patinaed leather executive chair, and steepled his fingers. It squeaked and popped to accommodate his bulk. He narrowed his eyes. "You brought something for me to go on?"

It was a statement more than a question. Trapp plucked

three items from the rucksack: a memory card, a pistol in a translucent plastic bag, and a small jam jar which contained a scrap of bloody cloth, and set the items on Alessandro's desk one after another. The pistol and the jar clinked as he set them down.

"Pictures, fingerprints and DNA," Trapp added. "If there's any record of this guy, that should be enough to nail him."

Alessandro was completely unfazed by the presence of any of the items. "What did you do with the body?"

Trapp flushed. "We left them."

Alessandro's caterpillar eyebrow flickered once again. "Them?"

"There were two shooters," Ikeda interjected. "A sniper got the second before we had the chance to ask him any questions."

"Interesting," Alessandro murmured. "You never fail to disappoint, Jason…"

"So you'll help?" Trapp asked. "It needs to be done discreetly. And *carefully*," he said with a firm nod. "The third shooter is still out there. I don't want you putting yourself at any risk, Alessandro."

The old spy leaned forward, gathered the evidence, and locked it in a safe on a shelf behind his desk. He spun back around on his chair.

"It is done," he said succinctly.

"There was one other thing…" Trapp added.

Alessandro nodded. "I thought there might be. The bodies?"

"Precisely. We didn't have time to clean the place."

"Give me the address, and I'll send a team. I haven't seen anything on the news about the shooting, but then again, the plane story is sucking all the oxygen out of the room."

Trapp squinted. "The plane?"

Alessandro looked surprised. "You haven't heard? The Russians shot down a British Airways jet yesterday morning."

"Shit..." Trapp breathed.

His sharp mind quickly turned into a higher gear, though his face betrayed no sign that Russian involvement meant anything to him. Inside, though, his head was spinning. It couldn't be a coincidence that Sokolov had reached out to him, only for the Russians to shoot down a passenger jet hours later. The question was – why?

"Anyway," Alessandro said, clapping his hands and snapping Trapp out his contemplation. "Leave it with me. If I can, I will get you a name."

"How long will it take?"

The old Italian spy smiled. "Let's meet for dinner. Shall we say 8:30? You're buying."

Trapp chuckled when he saw the old man's lascivious wink. He stood up, stretched out his hand, and pumped Alessandro's twice. "It's a deal."

13

Ikeda and Trapp's suite at the Florence Four Seasons Hotel wasn't the largest available, nor the fanciest, but it wasn't the smallest, either.

It contained one double bedroom, a living room with thick, plush sofas, and a small kitchen area. The previous night, they had shared a bed for the first time, after Ikeda had laughed point blank when he picked up a pillow and blanket, and without speaking intimated he would sleep on the couch to spare her modesty. They lay side by side in an enormous bed, beneath the covers, both staring at the ceiling, neither making a move until both fell asleep, the opportunity lost.

In the Ritz-Carlton in Macau he had seen his CIA colleague wearing a shimmering black silk cocktail dress that left little to the imagination. In the warm seas off Hong Kong, he'd seen her lithe, toned body cutting through the water in a bikini. On the military base deep inside North Korea, he had seen Ikeda stripped almost naked, bearing the greatest humiliation imaginable without so much as a tremor of emotion.

Yet perhaps it was for that last reason that Trapp now treated Ikeda – without meaning to – with kid gloves, as though she was composed of the most delicate china, and not the hardened, effective operator she truly was. He was a man with a savior complex. He had seen Ikeda at her very worst, and now could perceive nothing else. Although he was besotted with her, he didn't know how to make the next step. Nothing in his life experience so far equipped him to take on this challenge.

After all, Jason Trapp was the Hangman.

He was a product of a broken home, of abusive parents, and an eventual act of patricide. He had no childhood, yet was raised by the US Army, first a raw recruit, then a Green Beret, then the Combat Applications group, better known to the public as Delta Force, before being plucked from uniform by the CIA's Special Activities Division. For a very good reason, none of those organizations set out to produce emotionally well-adjusted individuals. They aim to create men, and sometimes women, who achieve their objectives, each and every time.

Other considerations are considered secondary. As distractions that only serve to reduce combat effectiveness. Perhaps a more rounded approach would produce more rounded individuals, men who aren't simply outstanding operators, but also well-adjusted individuals.

But that route was not taken with Jason Trapp. So when Eliza Ikeda entered the room, wearing a floral summer dress in a thin, body-hugging silk that broke just before the knee, he felt like a teenager for the first time.

"You look..." Trapp began, his voice falling away.

"Beautiful." She winked. "I know. You don't look half bad yourself."

Knowing that Alessandro dined only at the best restaurants in town, Trapp had taken the time to acquire a tailored midnight blue suit from Liverano & Liverano, the city's finest tailor – and paid double for the privilege of the quick turn-around. As he felt the weight of Ikeda's gaze pass over his body, however, Trapp decided it was worth every last cent.

He had, of course, insisted that the jacket was cut in a suitable style so as to disguise the presence of a small pistol, and the hunched-over, balding Italian grandfather who'd measured the cloth had done a fantastic job, without asking why. Even looking at himself critically in the mirror, Trapp could barely make out the telltale bulge of the weapon. Never a man who was happy wearing a tie, he wore his collar open, exposing a tiny tuft of chest hair. A thin scar, barely visible through the summer's tan, circled his neck. Often self-conscious about the scar, Trapp had mellowed somewhat, down in no small part to Ikeda's insistence that she liked it.

"Thanks." Trapp grinned. He stood up and offered his arm. "Ready?"

"You bet. I'm starving."

They made their way to the center of town, walking through cobbled streets and chased by a warm evening breeze. Ikeda had sensibly foregone the option of heels, unlike most Italian women, who wobbled through the medieval city like newborn giraffes. Though at her height, she scarcely needed them.

They arrived at the restaurant Alessandro had selected, Borgo San Jacapo, at a little after eight and Trapp was unsurprised to notice the small bronze plaque that indicated it was the recipient of a Michelin star. He wasn't worried about the price. The Agency was meeting all the costs of his trip at the president's insistence. Though Trapp was not ordinarily a man who enjoyed the finer things in life, in a place like this, with a companion as beautiful as the one clutching his arm, he was prepared to make certain sacrifices.

The restaurant was nestled by the river Arno that ran through the center of Florence, and as night began to fall, lights blossomed across the city, dancing in the reflection of the water.

"It's beautiful," Ikeda murmured.

They were led to a table on the terrace outside, by the water. It was set for three, though Alessandro had not yet arrived. If history was any guide, then Trapp expected him to be at least half an hour late. It was why he'd left the hotel with time to spare. The prospect of a cold glass of champagne by the river sounded like exactly the right medicine to decompress after the events of the past two days.

Ikeda and Trapp both took the seats that backed onto the river wall. The waiter squinted with confusion, and said, "Are you sure? The view is beautiful…"

"This is just fine, thanks." Ikeda smiled.

The waiter departed with their drinks order, and a shake of the head that signaled he would never understand the Americans – but that if they were willing to pay then who was he to question. He couldn't know that his guests that evening were highly trained intelligence operatives – assassins, really – nor that months spent at the CIA training facility known as the Farm, and years of service in the field made full situational awareness as much a necessity for them as the availability of oxygen for their lungs.

The drinks arrived, the waiter departed with another uncertain frown, barely disguised, as was the Italian manner, and Trapp toasted his beautiful companion. Their champagne flutes clinked together.

"I'm sorry about all this," he said.

"About what?" Ikeda replied, reclining. Her purse, larger than local fashion trends demanded in order to accommodate a pistol, hung off the back of her chair, its chain clinking as she moved.

"Oh, I don't know." Trapp shrugged. "The whole unknown psychos trying to take us out thing, I guess…"

Alessandro arrived late, though only fractionally so, to Trapp's great surprise, and interrupted them. The color of his eveningwear matched Trapp's own suit, and his dark brown oxfords wore such a shine that Trapp doubted very much whether their wearer had polished them himself. He carried a thin black leather attaché case, which he set down next to the river wall.

"You started without me," he said in a booming voice, casting his old friend a reproachful look.

Trapp signaled for the nearest waiter, who anticipated the order, filled a glass, and had it in Alessandro's hand before the man had a chance to sit down.

"Better?" Trapp asked with a raised eyebrow.

He was curious about the contents of the case that Alessandro had brought with him, but knew better than to ask. In Italy in general, and with Alessandro Lombardi in particular, an inventive course of foreplay was considered just as important as the main event. The Italian spy would give up his information at the death, but not without a little back and forth. It was all part of the game.

"Somewhat," the Italian replied in a playful growl. He leaned toward Ikeda. "My dear, you look ravishing this evening."

"Thank you." She smiled.

"This place is very good," Alessandro boomed for a second time, clapping his hands together. He looked over his shoulder, clicked his fingers, and signaled for the waiter to bring a menu. The man only brought one, which he set before the Italian, along with the wine list.

The spy looked up. "Red or white?"

"Red," Trapp said.

At the same instant, Ikeda said, "White."

"Both, then," Alessandro said with satisfaction, his finger tracing the list. Trapp couldn't help but notice that it plunged unerringly to the bottom of the list. "I presume your company is paying?"

"Naturally," Trapp replied.

"Perfect," Alessandro said, selecting two bottles and sending the waiter off with a smile as he no doubt started mentally calculating the size of his tip.

A second waiter arrived to take the food order, without Alessandro allowing either Trapp or Ikeda even a sliver of an opportunity to survey the menu. She threw him a questioning glance, but he merely shrugged. Alessandro was Alessandro, and he would do as he pleased. The Italian banker-cum-spy chose a selection of dishes, from a sea urchin risotto to veal cheek, and oysters to what Trapp was suspiciously worried was half a suckling pig. He wondered exactly how far his CIA expense account would take him, and decided that since he didn't have a choice in the matter either way, he might as well enjoy the culinary journey.

They drank, and gossiped about many things but nothing in particular, and after the first course was cleared away, Alessandro took a long, thoughtful sip of his red, a 1992 Chianti Classico, and said, apropos of nothing in particular, "I do not think the Agency was behind the attempt on your lives."

Trapp glanced around, checking that they were not in any danger of being overheard. When he was sure they were in the clear, he said, "And why is that?"

Alessandro shrugged contemptuously. "These men who were sent to kill you, they were not exactly tier one. If your people are behind it, then it was an insult, not a real attempt to take you out of the game."

Trapp squinted. "You identified both of them?"

"I sent a team to the Castello. The crime scene hadn't been touched, though by all accounts the bodies were a little worse for wear."

Trapp grimaced at the thought of what the hot Tuscan

summer sun would have done to the two corpses, even after just a day. Judging by the look on Ikeda's face, she was thinking exactly the same thing.

"And?" he said.

"They were Italians. Known to my colleagues in the abstract, but for nothing of great significance."

Ikeda's brow wrinkled, and as she opened her mouth to talk, Trapp's attention was caught by the sound of several high-powered motorcycles crossing the nearby Ponte Santa Trinita, a picturesque three-arched bridge across the river. It was a discordant sound against the scenic calm, but then again this was Italy, where the cities were old when cars were young, and as a result more people got around on two wheels than four.

"So you didn't find anything that connected them to us?" she asked. "No reason they wanted us dead?"

Alessandro shrugged. "They were not good men. Over the past three years, the AISE tracked the first man, Bernardo Rossi, traveling to Turkey twice and spending six months there each time. The second man, Alfredo Costa, we only have as visiting once."

Ikeda looked confused. "Turkey?"

Trapp put the pieces together first. "Syria," he grunted. "They were traveling to Syria to fight in the civil war. Which side for?"

Alessandro shrugged. "About as you would expect – whichever side paid best. Which was usually the regime. Or –"

"The Russians," Trapp finished, his jaw set and a dark flicker crossing his face. Everything that had happened over the past few days: Sokolov getting in contact after all these years, the Russian takedown of the British Airways flight, and now this – it all lead inevitably back to the Russians.

Inside the restaurant, a scuffle broke out. Trapp glanced up to see two white-jacketed waiters turning with surprise. The first headed inside, a look of outrage on his face.

Trapp squinted to make out what was happening. The large glass windows that looked out onto the terrace were well lit, and what he saw was enough to make his blood run cold.

He reacted instinctively, screaming a command as he rose, knocking the chair back against the wall behind him. "Get down!"

He reached automatically with his right hand for the pistol secreted inside his suit jacket. With his left, he yanked the rim of the circular dining table, yanked it up and threw it to the ground for cover. He grabbed Alessandro's arm, dragging the older man backward and shoving him to the ground without ceremony.

"What the hell are you doing?" he spluttered.

"Shut up," Trapp grunted, the cold metal of his pistol a comfort in his hand. He glanced to his right and saw that Ikeda had snapped into action without a second's hesitation. Her purse lay open on the ground, a silver pistol in her hands. Diners surveyed the chaos with open-mouthed stupefaction.

And then the gunfire split the air.

14

"Fuck," Trapp grunted as a wave of bullets chewed up the river wall, sending fragments of stone spitting and fizzing out in every direction, and terrified screams with them. "They're packing Uzis."

"What's the plan?" Ikeda asked, her voice calm, only a slight widening of the eyes giving away the fact that this was anything other than an ordinary day at the office.

Trapp allowed himself only half a second to consider his options. They were shit, and that was putting about as much lipstick on the pig as it would bear. Unlike in the movies, the table in front of them would do nothing more to protect them from the oncoming gunfire than disguise their precise locations. In any other situation, he would lay down a withering rate of fire and force the gunmen back, but there were too many innocents around.

One wrong move, one dead businessman or socialite would cause an international incident. All it would take was a single CCTV image of his face, or Ikeda's, and the Italian government would raise hell in the media until they got their man.

All that, though, was only a problem if they successfully

escaped with their lives... Trapp wasn't a betting man, but if he was, he would put worse than even odds on escaping this mess.

Still, he knew that if they all stayed in this precise position, their chances of survival would spiral very quickly down to zero. He needed to prevent them getting flanked, otherwise they were all dead.

"Fire for effect," he said, raising his voice over the relentless roar of gunfire. "Just distract them so I can take a look."

Ikeda nodded and raised her hand. As the third finger rose into the air, she sprang upwards and started firing at a stone pillar to the left of the glass doorway. The noise of this weapon, much closer than the onrushing hitmen, and without ear protection, was deafening. Trapp took the opportunity to dive right, behind a second pillar. He pressed his back against it, clutched his pistol to his chest, and turned to survey the situation.

There were four gunmen. Each was dressed the same, but slightly different, in a leather jacket and varying shades of denim jeans. Each wore a motorcycle helmet over their heads, the visor pulled down to protect their identity.

Amateur, Trapp thought, his lips curling with disgust. The helmets would obscure their peripheral vision just as much their identities.

There was, however, one point of similarity. Each of the four men was armed with an Uzi submachine gun.

The sight was almost too implausible to believe, but Trapp knew that it was absolutely, horrifyingly real. The gunmen were spraying indiscriminately, as though they didn't care who they hit, though as far as Trapp could tell, no innocents lay dead or injured.

Yet.

But if this went on much longer, there was no way that would last.

The first of the shooters emerged from the main body of the

restaurant onto the terrace, leading with his weapon. Trapp drew a bead, feeling the euphoric rush of adrenaline mixed with alcohol running through his veins. There was no way his aim would be steady enough this deep into the evening to have any confidence of making a headshot, so he aimed for the man's chest and fired twice.

The man's helmet splintered and painted the glass behind him red with splattered blood, just as his shoulder jerked, the force twisting him around as he fell. For half a second, Trapp frowned. He hadn't thought his aim was that bad, but then his brain processed Ikeda's pistol barking, and he yelled out, "Good shot."

One down, three to go.

Trapp quickly ran through his tactical position. The only way into and off the terrace was through the restaurant itself – or the river below. If it had been just him and Ikeda, Trapp would have dived, but he didn't know how deep the river ran, or whether Alessandro would be up to the swim.

So they would need to fight their way out. He had thirteen rounds left – twelve in the clip and one in the chamber. He would have to make them count.

"How's your ammo?" he shouted out, pressing his back against the pillar for a second time.

"Not great," came the immediate reply over a renewed wave of gunfire that was now coming disconcertingly close to their two positions. Several bullets impacted with Trapp's pillar, and sent shards of stone spinning in every direction.

"We can't let them pin us down," Trapp called out. "They've got the advantage in manpower, firepower, and ammunition. If we let them drag this out, we're dead."

"I concur," came Ikeda's calm reply. Her voice was slightly tight, but Trapp marveled that it didn't even sound like her heartrate was raised.

"How you doing over there, Alessandro?" Trapp yelled. From his current position, he couldn't see the old Italian spy.

By contrast with Ikeda, the older man's voice was strained. "I'm alive. But I'm unarmed."

"That's fine. Stay where you are. We're going to end this."

Trapp risked peeking around the pillar for a second time and saw a stream of restaurant guests flooding out behind the three living gunmen. The steady tick of a clock in his mind said that barely twenty seconds had passed since this whole mess had started. But this was the center of a major Italian city. They probably had no longer than ninety before the first police officers arrived on the scene.

With Alessandro in tow, they would be able to talk their way out of pretty much any mess, but Trapp had an intelligence veteran's instinctive dislike for attention. Talking their way out would mean interviews, pictures, police officers getting a good look at him. Once the initial terror of the crisis waned, passersby would take out camera phones, and Trapp's image would be plastered all over social media. His anonymity would be gone forever.

No – that outcome had to be avoided at all costs.

The only way out was through. Through the restaurant, and through the three remaining gunmen.

Trapp glanced behind him, and found several restaurant guests huddling behind their table, dishes forgotten, glasses knocked over and smashed, cutlery scattered in disarray. One of them, an older woman, had her hand clamped firmly over her mouth to avoid making a sound, but was weeping silently, her eyes bloodshot.

"It's okay," he murmured, crouching down and reaching forward. She flinched, and her husband pulled her backward, and away from this unknown terror.

Trapp winced, but didn't blame her. He grabbed a steak knife abandoned on top of the dinner table. It was smeared with meat juices, which he wiped against the white tablecloth out of habit.

"Cover me on three," he called out over a renewed wave of gunfire.

"Copy."

"One!"

"Two!"

He didn't remember saying three, but pushed himself away from the pillar, pistol clutched in a double-handed grip. The three gunmen were bunched around the door as they exited the restaurant onto the terrace, and the lead element's machine pistol was held outstretched in his hand.

Trapp reflexively and fired twice, not checking if he'd hit anything. The adrenaline was constricting his vision, and it didn't matter either way.

Eleven rounds left.

He didn't stop firing as he sprinted towards the doorway. The element of surprise was key. If he allowed the unknown shooters to regain control of the situation, then they would win. They had an advantage in firepower and ammunition, and for all Trapp knew they had backup hot on their heels.

No, this had to end now.

The first man fell backwards, collapsing against his two comrades and momentarily blocking the doorway. Trapp didn't know whether it was his shooting or Ikeda's that had done it, and didn't spare a second to find out.

His trigger finger squeezed again and again, the Beretta pistol now held only in his right hand barking out round after round as he fired indiscriminately toward the doorway. The restaurant behind the masked men was empty, at least in Trapp's direct line of fire, so he didn't have to worry about killing any innocents.

"One magazine left," Ikeda yelled out.

Unlike him, she was firing slowly and methodically. Picking

her targets only when an opportunity presented itself. For a brief moment, the staccato rate of fire from the Uzi machine pistols had faded as they struggled with the body falling against them. It was bad tactics, but good for Trapp.

First there was ten yards to the door, then five, and then he was upon the gunmen. Ikeda's support was useless now.

The pistol in Trapp's hand kicked one last time, putting a bullet in the now surely dead body of the first man in line. It clicked, and he tossed it aside, not looking as it skated along the terrace's paving stones. He switched the steak knife from his left arm to his right and charged the three men with his shoulder down.

It was an extraordinary sight.

His two remaining opponents were fumbling with the dead man's body, desperately attempting to push him out of the way. The motorcycle helmets they wore made them look like characters from a Halloween slasher movie. A bullet had impacted one of the men's helmets, smashing the visor, which hung askew, but seemingly not doing any further damage. Trapp caught a flash of dark brown eyes, and then he was upon them.

The impact pushed the four men back into the restaurant. But Trapp's targets were off-balance, and the extra weight of their dead friend carried them backward. The rearmost man tripped, sending all of them, Trapp included, tumbling to the floor in a sea of tangled, grasping limbs.

Trapp reacted quickest. He scrambled up, steak knife still clutched in the palm of his hand, leapt over the dead body of the first man, and plunged the knife into the stomach of the hitman to his right. It caught in the man's leather jacket, the blade shattering with the force of the impact, but puncturing his stomach nonetheless.

The trained CIA assassin discarded the weapon. It was useless now. He went for the dying man's Uzi, pulling it from hands that attempted numbly to resist, as the strength faded rapidly from his body, life blood pooling on the marble floor.

"You fucking," Trapp grunted, "Piece. Of. Shit!"

He reoriented the machine pistol and pulled the trigger. It cut the third man apart, punching a line of rounds from his crotch to the top of his head. He was dead in an instant.

Trapp didn't stop moving. He kicked away the pistol that had belonged to the first man to die.

"How we looking?" he called out, careful not to use Ikeda's name now that the fighting was over.

Alessandro's efforts to clean up the crime scene they had escaped the day before were one thing. That involved two dead hitmen, scum of the earth types that not even their own mothers would miss, and without any prying eyes to run to the media.

This was something else entirely. There was no way that the Italian police would look past an incident like this. It would be the first item on every news channel for at least a week.

"Oh, hell," Ikeda groaned from behind him, sending an ice-cold chill surging through Trapp's veins. In a louder voice, she said, "We've got a problem."

Trapp didn't turn back until he was certain that all the gunmen were dead. The one he'd stabbed in the stomach was the only one whose fate was in any doubt, but Trapp checked his pulse and found nothing. He spun around, hands stained with blood, and a terror in his heart that something had happened to a woman he had come to care about more deeply than he could ever have imagined.

His eyes searched out Ikeda's frame. Her pistol was held limply to one side, barrel pointing at the ground, finger off the trigger. She was looking down, shock drawn in tight lines on what he could see of her face.

"Talk to me!" he demanded, worry tightening his vocal cords. "Are you hurt?"

She shook her head silently, walked two paces forward, and collapsed onto her knees by a body. The weapon slipped from her fingers, and clattered against the stone terrace. An instant later, Trapp put it together in his head.

He walked numbly over to join her, barely aware of the crescendo of screams from the wave of restaurant goers now streaming from the restaurant's terrace, meals forgotten, lives forever shattered, or the sound of sirens wailing in the far-off distance.

Alessandro looked up from the ground, his mouth gaping wide, eyes glassy with shock. His suit jacket was askew, his white shirt speckled with dust and a spreading stain a little to the left of his heart that looked like spilled wine. Ikeda pressed her palms against it, desperately attempting to stop the flow of blood pumping from his veins.

Trapp knew just by looking at the old man that it was already too late.

"I –," Alessandro groaned, his voice weak. "I think I got in the way."

Trapp shook his head and attempted to calm the man. "Just relax. You'll be all right, I promise. Emergency services are on their way."

Alessandro choked out a laugh, then coughed, spluttering up blood that flecked Ikeda's dress and Trapp's new suit. Not that either could have cared less. Neither of them were immune to the shock of having a colleague or a friend snatched away from them in the prime of their life. It was, sadly, a hazard of the job when it came to their line of work.

But Alessandro Lombardi was different. For Trapp, he was a connection to a good deed in his past. He'd seen the wily old Italian spy as a friend, and looked back fondly on the memory of saving his daughter. And now he had cost him his life.

The Italian shook his head weakly, although the movement

was barely discernible as the strength began to fade from his body. "Don't lie to me," he whispered. "I know it's too late."

Trapp's jaw clenched with pain. He knew he would replay the scene in his mind a thousand times over, trying to figure out what he could have done differently, how he could have saved the old man's life. Lombardi deserved to retire, to spend time with his daughter and his grandkids, to eat at the finest restaurants and bask in the rewards of a lifetime spent in the service of his country.

Now he would do none of those things. And it was all Trapp's fault.

"Help's coming," Ikeda said in a soothing voice before glancing up at Trapp and flashing him a warning. He was aware of the sound of sirens, of course, which were echoing down the breadth of the river, beginning to drown out the sounds of panic in the streets.

Trapp knew they needed to move, to get ahead of the manhunt that would soon be closing on the city of Florence. But he couldn't bring himself to leave Alessandro's side.

"Get out of here," Alessandro croaked with dogged determination in his voice. "Take my case and run!"

Trapp squinted at the urgency in the old man's tone. But perhaps he was reading too much into it. "We won't leave you," he grunted. "We'll talk our way out of whatever trouble we find ourselves in."

"If I release the pressure," Ikeda mouthed in a voice that was little more than a whisper, "he'll die."

"I'm not deaf," Alessandro cough-laughed a second time. "I'm a dead man already. We all know it. So get the hell out of here!"

"Why?" Trapp said simply. He couldn't understand Alessandro's sudden insistence.

"In my case," the Italian coughed, his chest straining from the effort of speech, "you'll find everything you need. I didn't put it together until just now. But if you don't get out of here now, it'll be too late..."

His eyes flickered closed, and the strength seemed to sag from his body, as though he had given everything for one last second of speech. A wave of pain flooded through Trapp's frame. He thought he was done with this world, with death and struggle and grief. But it wasn't done with him. Not by a long shot.

"Is he..." Trapp croaked.

Ikeda nodded, sadness flashing in her own eyes. For Alessandro, but most of all, for Trapp himself.

It was as though the Italian's death released Trapp. There would be time to grieve later, time to process what had just happened, and eventually time to pay his respects to those Alessandro had left behind. He stood, mind snapping into autopilot, and made for the attaché case. He didn't bother opening it, merely grabbed the handle.

Ikeda looked up at him, still on her knees, dress and hands and forearms coated with sticky red blood, still glistening, a stark reminder that only moments ago it was pumping in the old man's veins. Now he was gone, his body little more than a husk where life had been.

"Come on," Trapp choked, a wave of grief welling up in his throat as he cast one last look at Alessandro's body – smaller in death than it ever was in life. "We have to go."

15

Florence was not Rome, and although the police arrived quickly, and in great and ever swelling numbers, their approach to securing the area was more enthusiastic than effective.

After wiping then tossing every weapon they had touched into the river, to at least slow down the collection of any forensic evidence – and hopefully hinder it entirely, Trapp cloaked Ikeda in his suit jacket to hide the bloodstains that soaked her dark dress, and they joined the terrified crowd fleeing the scene of the crime.

They were hurried on their way by panicked local police and *Caribinieri*, who still appeared to think they were dealing with a terrorist attack, like the ones that had recently rocked so many European cities. They returned to the Four Seasons, entering via a back entrance to avoid attracting attention, cleaned up and checked out, to avoid leaving the Italian police any more clues than were inevitable.

Three hours, a circuitous route and a stolen Fiat later, they arrived in the northern Italian city of Milan, from where they boarded the last train to Turin, a city of nine hundred thousand inhabitants nestled in the Italian Alps. It was close to the border with both France and Switzerland, which afforded them multiple avenues in which to run – if it came to that.

Aware that their cash wouldn't last forever, Trapp booked a middle-of-the-road business hotel near the airport. They burned the passports they had used checking in to the Four Seasons, and moved to the last identities in their possession – a Jason and Elizabeth Spiers from Cleary, Idaho. If they lost these, Trapp knew, things would swiftly go from bad to worse. The last thing they needed to attempt right now was running across Europe searching for someone to provide them with fresh papers. Clean documents were hard to come by, and the best forgers were often in the employ of one intelligence service or another, meaning it was possible that any new identity would be blown the moment they acquired it. After Alessandro's death, and facing an enemy of uncertain strength and seemingly limitless reach, it was a risk they simply could not take.

Trapp pushed the door to the hotel room open, out of habit collecting a copy of the *International Herald Tribune* that was in a small canvas bag around the door handle.

Ikeda instantly sank onto the double bed in the center of the small room, and he soon joined her. He set Alessandro's attaché case on the bedspread next to them and tossed the paper beside it. They hadn't opened the case yet. It had a brooding presence – a reminder of everything that had happened in the last two days, and everything that they had lost.

"I'm sorry," she murmured, rolling onto her side and stroking his hair. "About Alessandro."

Trapp winced. He wasn't used to processing his emotions out loud, less still with someone else listening. Even last year, when the best friend he'd ever had – Ryan Price – was murdered, he never truly grieved until he spent a few weeks working alongside Price's brother, Joshua. Hard work had broken down the barriers in his mind he'd erected against the grief, but the pair of them had dealt with their shared pain like men.

In other words, poorly. Drinking too much and telling stories about the man they had lost.

But Alessandro felt different. It wasn't just that he was taken in the autumn of his life. It was that he should never have been involved at all. Trapp knew that he had cost the old man his life. Stolen a father from his daughter, and a grandfather from children who would grow up never knowing the caliber of the man they had lost forever.

"It's fine," Trapp grunted.

Ikeda shook her head sadly. "It's really not, Jason."

But she knew better than to push the matter any further. At least, not yet. Trapp was still the same killer that he had always been. He would process the grief in his own way, in his own time. But he could already feel a seething rage beginning to build in his gut, flooding his system with heat and anger and light. He didn't just want to find whoever was responsible for Alessandro's murder; he wanted to put a bullet in their brain, and not stop till every last son of a bitch who had any hand in the man's death was lying dead at his feet.

He wasn't the kind of man who would make them beg for their lives. He would just end them, feeling no shame, no sadness, fueled only by a burning sense of justice that he was doing what was right – what needed to be done.

"I'm going to get them," Trapp replied instead.

"I'm right there with you."

Trapp shook his head. "No way. This isn't your fight. And besides, you're still hurting. I can't ask you to come with me, and I won't let you."

Ikeda snorted. "You didn't ask," she said tartly. "And I don't remember requesting permission. I'm coming with you whether you like it or not."

Trapp leapt to his feet and faced her with unaccustomed anger. "The hell you are!"

Ikeda could have chosen one of several options. She could have ground her jaw together, planted her feet like a bull and charged. She could have salved Trapp's ego, whispered sweet nothings into his ear until he was putty in her hands. The first of those would have caused sparks, though he would doubtless have seen sense in the end.

The second would have been a little less aggressive and a whole lot more manipulative. That too might have worked. In truth, there wasn't a lot Trapp could do to resist Ikeda's wiles, let alone her fierce determination.

But she chose neither of those angles. Instead she sat up, shrugged, and said, "It's not a choice, Jason. I'm coming with you, whether you like it or not."

Trapp merely blinked. Somehow, he knew that he was beaten. She didn't need to fight him, nor play with his emotions to get her way. She had made a decision, and there was very little he could do to stop her going through with it. Like him, that was just the way she was made.

"So." Ikeda smiled. "Shall we find out what's in the case?"

He grunted and turned away, knowing when he was beaten. He walked to the minibar, pulled out two bottles of a local beer, lifted off the caps and handed one to his newfound partner, taking a long drag of his own as he sat down on the bed next to her.

She shifted position, sitting with her knees collapsed underneath her, and dragged the black attaché case over. It was secured on either side of the handle by a combination lock. For a second, Ikeda's face clouded over with a frown before she turned back to Trapp. "Each tumbler is set to zero, zero, zero..."

Trapp grinned, despite the day they had, and the lingering

sensation that Ikeda had played him. "That's Alessandro." He shrugged. "*Was* Alessandro, anyway. Never was too concerned with operational security."

Silently, he wondered if that's what had gotten him killed.

Ikeda flicked open the catch on either side, and the locks sprang upward in unison with an audible click. Trapp knocked back another long swig of the beer and briefly attempted to work out whether he could be bothered to stand up and get another one. He decided against it, and instead watched as Ikeda lifted the black leather lid of the case.

"What have we got?" he asked.

"A file," Ikeda replied simply. She plucked a thin manila folder from inside Alessandro's briefcase and set it down on the bed before quickly rifling through the case's storage compartments and pockets. She glanced up at him. "That's it."

"I guess we should open it."

Both were unusually reticent, perhaps because opening the folder meant formally accepting what they truthfully already knew – that for the second time in as many months, their lives had been turned upside down. Reading what was written inside the manila jacket would be accepting a new fate, one which neither would necessarily be able to control. And yet, what choice did they have?

Finally, Ikeda let out a taut, strained sigh and flicked open the first page. She nestled against Trapp as her eyes flickered from left to right, then turned to him with mild confusion. "Who the hell is Igor Strelkin?"

The file contained images of the two men who had died at Castello Romagno, dressed as they had been when they graduated from basic training. Both had exemplary service records, according to the broken Italian translation the now deceased Italian spy had provided of their records. Trapp wondered what decisions taken had led them to this fate. It was an easy life for men with training but not a lot of prospects to fall into. And once in, it was hard to get out.

"Aegis Private Security," he murmured, seeing the company name in the files of both dead men, as well as the one that belonged to the third, the company's owner.

Although Trapp had never heard of it, it was clear that Aegis was a private military company –modern-day mercenaries. The two dead Italian hitmen were linked to the company by bank transactions that stretched back several years, and large transfers matched up exactly with the periods in which the two men were supposedly visiting Turkey.

But as Alessandro had made perfectly clear, and Trapp had guessed instantly, the visits to Turkey were no more than a paper-thin cover for their real activities: fighting alongside the regime in the Syrian Civil War.

"It's always the fucking Russians," Trapp muttered as he read the thin file from cover to cover.

"Huh?"

"Toss me that newspaper," he grunted. Ikeda did as she was asked, her gray eyes curious, but she remained silent and let him work.

Through all of the running and the fighting, Trapp had barely had a moment to catch his breath and think. Though he knew the outline of what had happened to the British Airways jet as it attempted to leave Russia, that was all he knew. He was sick of being off-balance, of being the dumbest guy in the room. That needed to change, and it needed to change fast.

The *International Herald Tribune* wasn't exactly the President's Daily Brief produced by the CIA, but it would have to do for now. Trapp was pretty confident now that the contractors from Aegis had nothing to do with the Agency, but until he was 100% sure, he wasn't planning on risking his life – and more importantly Ikeda's – on a hunch. He scanned the paper, his quick mind pulling out the most important details. He didn't stop to analyze them.

That would come later.

The paper had helpfully produced a small diagram of the plane's fateful final journey, as well as an icon that indicated the surface-to-air missile system that had destroyed it. As yet, the story's author reported, the Russians had not announced the reason why they had shot down the passenger jet.

Amateur aviation enthusiasts monitoring air traffic control frequencies had provided a transcript of Moscow Tower informing the pilots that there was an explosive on board, and that they were instructed to turn around immediately. However, Trapp read, sources inside the British intelligence services strongly contested that description of events.

He turned the page and saw faces staring back up at him. The faces of the dead. The icons were endless – smiling pictures taken from Facebook profiles, provided to the media by grieving families, or leaked by the investigation. Each image was labeled with a name.

"Anything?" Ikeda asked.

As Trapp looked back up at her, he wasn't sure. There was something here, he knew it, but what that something was he simply didn't know. He was no conspiracy theorist, but he had spent long enough in the murky world of intelligence and assassination to understand when something didn't smell right, and what had happened to BA 233 stank like a pail of fish heads forgotten in the summer sun.

"Don't you think it's just a little bit unusual," he said, "that I received a message from a source I haven't heard from in five years on the same day as the Russians shoot down a plane? That the next day, two guys try and kill us in cold blood, and that we discover they were paid by a former KGB operative running a private security company out of Turkey? And that just after we asked Alessandro to do a bit of digging, all hell breaks loose?"

Trapp dropped his gaze back down to the newspaper still spread out across his lap and idly began scanning the faces of the men, women and children who had been murdered by a Russian missile.

And then he froze.

"Sure I do," Ikeda replied, anxiously playing with a loose strand of her silky brown hair. "But what are we going to do about it?"

Trapp said nothing. His gaze was fixed unerringly on the newspaper in front of him. In an instant it fell into place.

"Hey," Ikeda said a little more insistently. "Did you hear me?"

Trapp heard her. But his brain was whirring in overdrive as it processed one of the images on the newspaper on his lap. A picture of a wiry gentleman in his late 40s, whose hair was beginning to thin. The photo looked to have been blown up from an identity document, but while the face was expressionless, there was nevertheless a wry humor in his eyes.

The photo was labeled Grigori Trubetskoy.

But Trapp knew the man's real name.

It was Alexy Sokolov.

16

President Nash's intended week of vacation at Camp David, the first time off he'd had in months, was for obvious reasons cut short after just three days. Marine One took him back to Washington, and he switched the golf cart and slacks for the Resolute desk and a crisply pressed dark suit.

He entered the Situation Room and pressed the assorted military officers, aides and members of his cabinet to sit. He took his place at the head of the long conference table and gratefully accepted a cup of coffee from the US Air Force steward.

"Okay," he grunted, but not before taking a long gulp of the hot black liquid. "Let's get started."

He wasn't exactly in a conversational mood, but better than anyone he knew his duty. In a straight tossup between endless – and mostly pointless – briefings on national security and playing golf, he would choose the three iron every time. Except, of course, he wouldn't. Nash might talk a big game, and grumble about having to attend the damn things, but he read his PDB from cover to cover each morning with a scrutiny few other presidents ever matched.

"Mr. President," his Chief of Staff, Emma Martinez, said, gesturing at a slight, tall woman with cropped blond hair. "This is Riley Simmons, the director of the National Cyber Security Division over at Homeland."

"Nice to meet you, Riley," Nash said with a half smile. "What brings you over here today?"

He had never met the director before, though he thought he remembered seeing her interviewed on CNN some months before, after a suspected cyber attack on California's electrical grid that had eventually turned out to be nothing of the sort – a coyote getting fried in a power substation, if he remembered correctly. She was in her late 30s, or perhaps early 40s, with a slim physique and a fierce intelligence in her light blue eyes. He made a note not to underestimate her.

"Thank you, Mr. President," Riley replied, bobbing her head. "I was asked to brief you this morning about a new virus my agency picked up late last week. We're calling it SANDSTONE."

She passed a series of printouts around the long conference table that detailed the virus's vital statistics. When one reached Nash, he couldn't help but notice that it looked kind of light on detail.

"And why is that, Ms. Simmons?" he inquired.

She shot him a smile, then flushed before the words stumbled out of her mouth. Nash barely noticed. He had long ago realized that there was something about the title of president that turned ordinarily intelligent, accomplished people into blithering halfwits. All told, Riley Simmons wasn't doing half bad. He'd definitely seen worse.

"It just kinda... sounded good, Mr. President," she said.

Nash shot her a reassuring, amused smile. "And if you don't mind, Director, perhaps you could tell me why it is that this

SANDSTONE virus has ended up on my desk on a Saturday morning?"

In truth, Nash was grateful for the break from outraged European leaders calling him about the shootdown of the British Airways jet over Belarus several days earlier. It was a little-known and – in Nash's view at least – significantly under-appreciated fact that most of the US president's time was spent dealing with diplomatic and foreign policy matters. Mostly endless, interminable phone calls with foreign leaders bitching about something or other, or more usually *each other*.

On this occasion, he agreed with all of them on the gravity of the crisis. He had motioned for a meeting of the UN Security Council to be held first thing next week, and had increased the readiness level of US forces on the European continent, as well as authorizing surveillance flights on a round-the-clock basis.

Riley nodded nervously. "Yes, sir. I'll do my best."

She leaned forward and tapped a button on a small, black rectangular remote control that had been placed on the conference table in front of her. A large LCD screen on the far wall of the room, facing the president, blinked into life. It was a map of the United States, depicted in a violet blue, with etched white lines indicating state borders and yellow dots marking out population centers.

Nash could just about remember a time when he could look at a map of his country and not immediately wonder which city, national park, airport or train line his officials were about to tell him was expected to be threatened next.

"What am I looking at, Director Simmons?" he asked.

"Sir, several days ago a honeypot computer system operated by my agency was infected with a string of malicious code. This happens several hundred times every day, so it is not altogether unusual. The next morning, which was last Friday, my researchers gave it a once-over."

Nash raised his eyebrow. "And?"

Simmons continued, her voice audibly gaining confidence now as she focused on her area of expertise. "A significant segment of this code was stolen from the National Security Agency two years ago."

Nash frowned. "Hold it right there. You're talking about the NSA? *Our* NSA?"

"That is correct, Mr. President." Simmons nodded. "A web server was left unprotected and penetrated by hackers, resulting in the loss of some of the NSA's most advanced penetration tools."

"I'm sorry," Martinez chimed in. "Penetration tools?"

Simmons winced as she explained, "In layman's terms, hacking tools."

"So you're saying someone's attacking us with our own code?" Martinez added.

"Not *exactly*," Simmons replied cautiously.

She tapped another button on the remote, and the image on the screen focused on the East Coast of the USA. Nash squinted at the screen, wishing he had his glasses, which he had come to need more and more over the past few months. A small smattering of tiny red dots were superimposed over the much larger yellow sections on the map.

"We created a hash of the viral code and uploaded it to monitoring systems across the country by the end of last weekend. Over the past three days, infections have been reported across the country, but so far mainly centered on the East Coast."

Simmons tapped another button, and this time the map focused only on New York City. A box blinked into existence on the right-hand corner of the screen, marking out the day and time. MONDAY 0800.

"This was our first infection snapshot. As you can see," she said, gesturing at the screen, where the existence of the red dots were few and far between, "at this point the infection was extremely light. At that time, it had not even been brought to my attention."

She tapped another button. The screen updated. TUESDAY 1600.

By now, the red dots were significantly more visible. They formed light clusters, a bit like chickenpox spots on an infected child.

Simmons tapped the button again. WEDNESDAY 2100.

By now, Nash began to experience a creeping sense of dread, though he could not put a finger on precisely why. The red dots were thicker now, like brake lights forming thick lines of color on the freeway at night. They followed paths that looked to Nash's untrained eye like roads, though they did not correspond with any of the thoroughfares that led in and out of New York City.

"Okay, I get it," Nash grumbled as Simmons changed the image twice more, to THURSDAY 1200 and then FRIDAY 1300 in quick succession. "It's getting worse. So what the hell is it? And more importantly, what are we *doing* about it?"

Nash was no Luddite. He had an iPhone just like anyone else, even if the geeks had locked it down to the point he couldn't even open his favorite crossword app. But when it came to talk of computer networks and hacking and vulnerabilities, he sometimes wondered if he had been born a little too early. Most of it went straight over his head.

Simmons grimaced and swept a curl of her cropped blond hair behind her left ear. "That's the million-dollar question, Mr. President. This virus is spreading faster than anything I have ever seen. It uses elements of the stolen NSA code, but most of the vulnerabilities our own tools were designed to penetrate have now been patched. Whoever built this virus iterated on our code, and they did a damn good job. My people estimate that within seven days, this virus will be on more than 90% of

Internet-connected computer systems in the continental United States."

"Ms. Simmons," Nash interjected, finally finding the words to voice a question that had bugged him from the start of the briefing. "Exactly what was the original NSA code designed to achieve?"

"Mr. President, have you been briefed on Stuxnet?"

Nash waved his hand irritably. "Refresh my memory."

"About a decade ago, the NSA, CIA and the Israelis were extremely worried about the Iranians reaching a breakout point at which they would be able to produce enough nuclear material to build a bomb. So they collaborated to build a virus that could, in theory, infect and destroy the Iranian centrifuges by modifying the rate at which they spun, causing power fluctuations and so on."

"Well," Nash grunted, "did it work?"

"Perfectly." Simmons nodded grimly. "But what worries me is that code of that nature could, in theory, be used to infect the power grid, the stock exchange, water treatment plants, the natural gas grid, any cloud computing system, the cellular network – you name it, if it's connected to the Internet, it's vulnerable. And..." She paused.

"Go on." Nash gestured. He wasn't liking where this was going.

"And, primary analysis of the virus collected in our honeypot systems suggests that a similar code base is present here."

"Well, if we designed this virus," Nash said, "surely we know how to defend against it?"

Simmons shook her head, her demeanor now shorn of all warmth, her expression pale. "No, sir. Partly that's because whoever's behind this has iterated on our code. But partly it's because most of the nation's infrastructure is run on thirty-year-old operating systems, when we're lucky. They are inherently insecure."

"Do you mean to tell me," Martinez said, her voice acid, "that we're currently a sitting duck? And if so, Director, what the hell have your people been doing over at Homeland? Sitting on your hands and waiting for the worst to happen?"

Simmons frowned, but not out of fear of the president's bulldog's cheap assault, or the woman's notoriously fiery temper. Nash was watching closely, and detected that the young director was made of significantly sterner stuff than that. She leaned to one side, clicked open a briefcase, and pulled out several bound sheets of paper. She began tossing them onto the conference table, one after another.

"This is the NCSD's annual report from 2018."

She looked up. Threw another one on to the table, her upper lip curled. Nash saw the eagle logo of the Department of Homeland Security emblazoned on the front of the report as it spun across the wooden surface.

"2017."

"2016."

Nash raised a single finger, his eyes flickering from his glowering chief of staff to the equally angry cyber security official. "That's enough, Ms. Simmons. Get to the point."

"The point, sir," Simmons hissed before taking a deep breath and visibly mastering her temper, "is that my agency flagged these risks year after year. I personally lobbied the White House, testified in front of Congress, did damn near everything in my ability to get someone to pay attention. But no one did. And now we are where we are."

Nash leaned back in his chair, his mind spinning at the prospect of a cyber weapon crippling the United States. Images of gridlocked roads, sparking power lines and empty grocery store shelves played across his mind.

"Well," he sighed, "we're all listening now."

17

Mike Mitchell, the director of the CIA's little-known Special Activities Division, rarely wore a suit. There was a time when he was among the Agency's most lethal assassins, more comfortable in the trenches of some little-known foreign battlefield than the equally contested – if less bloody – arenas of Washington's never-ending bureaucratic pissing contests.

He longed to return to those more carefree days. Back then, if one of the Agency's seventh floor suits had questioned his methods, he would've been as likely to introduce the man to his fist as offer his ear.

"Yes, Mr. President. Absolutely," Lawrence grunted. "I'll be in touch the second I have something actionable."

Mitchell watched as the new Director of Central Intelligence nodded several more times. His boss glanced up, looking at the new arrival, and gestured for him to take a seat in front of his desk.

"Yes, sir," Lawrence said. He put the phone down and closed his eyes briefly, dragging in a deep breath.

Mitchell wondered whether the phone call had been staged

for his benefit, though decided, as he assessed the man, that it was unlikely. They had followed markedly different tracks to rise through the ranks. For the first half of Mitchell's career, his file jacket had borne the initials 'NOC' for 'no official cover,' a designation given to CIA operatives who got the dirty jobs that the Agency needed done, but could never admit to. Years spent out in the field provided little opportunity to tangle in the Agency's politics.

Lawrence, by contrast, was an intelligence officer by trade. He'd spent time in the former Soviet Union, before the fall of the Berlin wall, but always from the comfort of the local US Embassy, from where he recruited and ran the Agency's local network of human intelligence sources. After that, he'd worked his way up the Europe desk in Langley, which he'd ended up heading for most of the last decade. It was, Mitchell knew, an entirely different vantage point to the intelligence game from his own. Lawrence's world was that of traditional spy craft, a business of attending cocktail parties, massaging egos and separating fact from fiction.

Mitchell's, by contrast, was of being the sharp end of the spear. Of acting on the intelligence provided by people like George Lawrence. Of getting his hands dirty so the suits didn't have to. And now, he reflected wryly, he was wearing one.

"Mike," he said, setting the secure phone into its handset before half-rising from his seat and sticking out his hand for Mitchell to shake. "I apologize for summoning you like this."

Mitchell released his hand and sat back down.

"No apology needed, sir," he replied, sensing that Lawrence was the kind of man who preferred to keep things formal.

"I'll be blunt," Lawrence said. "I need you to send over everything you have on the Hangman, and I need it done yesterday. Is that clear?"

"Do you mind if I ask, Director," Mitchell replied carefully, "why now? Your predecessors always preferred to keep a level of distance from my division and the precise details of how we achieve the goals we are tasked with."

Lawrence settled back in his leather chair and steepled his fingers together, glowering at his employee from behind his professorial beard.

"How this works, *Mike*," he said, emphasizing Mitchell's first name. "Is when I say 'jump,' you ask 'how high?' Got that?"

Mitchell winced at the use of the hackneyed cliché, though he displayed no outward reaction.

"Of course," he agreed without flinching. "My only concern is with protecting you, sir. If something goes wrong in the field, I'm the one who throws myself in front of the bullet. The second you know exactly what we do and how we do it, Congress can call you in front of them, and then – if you'll excuse the salty language, sir, you're fucked."

Lawrence softened his posture a little, apparently mollified by the suggestion that Mitchell was only looking out for him "I understand that, Mike," he said. "But this is bigger than you or me. The president's breathing down my neck about this whole Russia thing, and he wants to know if there's any connection to this SANDSTONE virus he just learned about."

"SANDSTONE?" Mitchell repeated, raising an eyebrow at the use of the unfamiliar term.

"Forget about it." Lawrence waved dismissively. "You'll be briefed on it soon enough."

Mitchell nodded, but made a note to ask Greaves to do some digging.

"Where's your boy right now?" Lawrence asked. "I want him in a conference room in this very building inside twenty-four hours. Grill him for everything he knows, and don't stop until you get my say so. Understood?"

Mitchell shook his head, knowing that his boss wouldn't like what he had to say, but deciding to tell him anyway. "He's a contractor, sir. I don't have him on a tight leash. That's the flipside of deniability – he doesn't work nine to five."

Lawrence slammed his palm down on the desk in front of him. Steam might have poured from his ears if it wasn't already billowing from his mouth. "Figure out where the fuck he is, and get him back to Langley. This is the CIA, you understand – not a summer camp. We have processes for a reason. Shove a black bag over his head if you have to, I don't care, just get it done."

For the briefest of seconds, a smile crept across Mitchell's face. He killed it instantly, transforming his expression into one of studied blankness, like a twenty-year veteran of the Chinese Politburo, but it was already too late. Lawrence glanced up, his fingers curling with irritation.

"Why the hell are you smirking?" he growled.

"If you think that's going to work, Director, you don't know Jason Trapp..."

18

T he Turk's name was Emin. He was sitting on a small table on the terrace of the Soho House hotel in Istanbul, sipping a bottle of beer that was glistening from condensation in the overpowering early evening heat and playing with his phone.

Trapp knew the man by reputation rather than experience. He was still stiff from the flight from Italy as he scanned the small terrace through the glass wall that led outside, picking out the two bodyguards that accompanied the gunrunner without needing to search particularly hard. They were posted at opposite ends of the terrace, one by each entrance to the main body of the hotel. He nudged Ikeda, who was holding his hand and leaning into his arm, and guided her attention to the two burly, suited men. The look he got back left him under no uncertain illusion that she had already scouted them out.

"How do you want to play this?" Ikeda murmured.

"He's an asshole, by all accounts," Trapp replied quietly, looping his arms around her waist and nuzzling her face, just like any other of the honeymooning couples currently inhabiting the hipster hotel. "But he's honest. All he cares about is the color of his clients' money. He won't sell us out. He knows he'd be out of business – or dead – in days if he started playing games like that."

She looked over his shoulder, studying the profile of Emin Aksoy. Her eyebrow kinked, and from the uncertain look on Ikeda's face, Trapp knew exactly what she was thinking. The Turkish gunrunner had chosen the location of their meeting, and judging by the central location, the quality of the hotel's furnishings and decoration, and the cost of the man's perfectly cut Italian suit, his tastes didn't run cheap.

"You think we have enough?" she said.

"Depends how upmarket we go." Trapp shrugged. "An AK-47 comes pretty cheap in this part of the world. Body armor and night vision, not so much."

"Come on then, honey." She smiled. "Let's go see a man about a thing..."

As they passed through the doorway onto the terrace, and before they made it to the rows of striped yellow sun loungers, Trapp's attention was fixed firmly on the nearest of the two bodyguards. In contrast to his boss, the man's suit was off the rack, and badly chosen at that. It hung low and loose and baggy, like a 1980s hip-hop artist, but even so Trapp could make out the bulge of an elephant gun in a holster attached to his shoulder. He made a mental note not to let the man get off a shot at him, if it came to that. Whatever caliber round was inside that thing would tear him to shreds given half a chance.

Trapp strode confidently toward the squat, shaven-headed man, and stopped a pace in front of him. "I believe I know a friend of yours," he said.

"American?" the bodyguard grunted.

"You got it."

The powerful Turk squinted in confusion before glancing over at his boss. Emin Aksoy nodded, and beckoned his guests over. Trapp started walking, but ran into a brick wall. He looked down to find the bodyguard's hand pressed against the center of his chest, the man's varicose forearm as impenetrable a barrier as any highway guardrail.

"Wait."

Trapp did as he was instructed, and the bodyguard patted him down. He watched with a little concern as the man squatted low, his suit pants straining against his enormous bulk, and then waited as the man repeated his task – with cursory disdain this time – on Ikeda. The dismissive way that women in this region were treated never failed to amuse Trapp.

More fool them.

His task complete, the bodyguard jerked his head at his waiting boss. "Go."

Trapp smiled thinly. "My pleasure."

He walked over to Emin's table, Ikeda's slight hand still clutched in his own. He wasn't nervous about the upcoming meeting, but neither was he foolhardy. Weapons traffickers weren't always the most congenial of individuals, and in his experience they could be surly, and prone to violence. Soho House wasn't exactly the gun bazaars of Waziristan, in the tribal areas of Pakistan, where Trapp had once had a pistol pressed to his temple while attempting to acquire a consignment of stolen Javelin antitank missiles, but it would only take one wrong move for one of the two big bastards near the doors to blow his head off.

He thrust out his hand. "Jason Spiers," he said. "And my wife, Elizabeth."

"Pleased to meet you." Ikeda smiled sweetly.

The Turkish gunrunner shook Trapp's hand, then kissed Ikeda's. He beckoned for the pair of them to sit down, and then waved for a nearby and attentive waiter, who made a beeline for the bar the second the drinks orders were taken.

"So glad you could make it," the Turk said in perfect English, laced only with the faintest of accents.

Trapp glanced around. "You picked a nice spot," he said.

Emin laughed. "I was in Syria last week," he said. "Doing business with the rebels. Believe me, after two weeks shitting in a hole and surviving on MREs, you would be grateful for a little taste of civilization as well."

"I imagine I would," Trapp said. He looked up as the waiter returned with a tray that contained another beer for Emin, one for himself, and a gin and tonic for Ikeda. He smiled at the memory of meeting her the first time, just a few weeks before. She was nothing if not a creature of habit.

"Thank you." She smiled, taking a sip. The waiter disappeared.

Emin jerked his head at the bar and gave Trapp a knowing look. "Perhaps your friend might like to wait over there while we talk?"

Trapp didn't reply for a second, wondering if Ikeda might say something. She wasn't exactly a shy, retiring wallflower. And, he considered, she could rip the Turk apart with little more than the beer bottle currently clutched in his palm. But she just smiled, somewhat blankly, and glanced at him instead.

"I don't think so," he said smoothly, his voice gruff. "She comes with me."

I wouldn't piss her off, buddy, he thought. *You don't know who you're messing with.*

"Have it your way," Emin replied, a slight look of disapproval on his tanned, boyish face. Trapp guessed that he was in his late 30s, but he looked a decade younger – and every bit the playboy that his reputation warned. "So how can I help you, my friend?"

Trapp cut to the chase. He was getting a smarmy vibe from this arrogant, new-money gunrunner, and didn't want to spend more time in the man's presence then he absolutely had to. "I need some hardware," he said. "And I need it fast."

"Do you mind if I ask why?" Emin inquired. He gestured at

the rooftops of Istanbul that stretched away in the distance of the setting evening sun, glowing a vibrant red. "We are a long way from Syria, my friend. There is no danger for you here."

"As a matter of fact, I do," Trapp replied, injecting a hint of danger into his voice – a bite that indicated he wasn't to be messed with. "Have you got what I want, or not?"

Emin leaned back, a smile playing on his lips, and took a swig from his fresh bottle of beer. When he opened his mouth, Trapp couldn't help but think that he sounded expensively educated, most likely in England – though he couldn't be certain whether that was truly the source of the man's cultured accent, or whether it was acquired, or affected, somewhat later in life.

"That rather depends on what exactly it is you are looking to acquire, does it not?" Emin said.

"Nothing heavy," Ikeda said, fixing the man with an incisive stare of her own. "But enough to get by."

Emin nodded. "I think I can manage that. Can you pay?"

Trapp shrugged. "You take credit card?"

"Everything but AMEX," the Turk quipped. "The fees are murder."

Trapp raised his eyebrow at the man's choice of words. "I can only imagine."

"In all seriousness, it's cash or wire transfer. I prefer cash, but I'm not fussy."

Ikeda smiled acidly. "Are we paying by the hour, or can we get moving?"

The Turk's mouth opened in a circle of surprise before he recovered his manners. "Of course," he said, with a smile that did not meet his eyes. "Meet me in the lobby in five minutes."

⌁

FIVE MINUTES LATER, as instructed, Trapp and Ikeda exited the elevator into the hotel lobby, arm in arm. They immediately noticed Emin's lean frame, head bowed as he typed furiously into a large cell phone held between his strangely slight, feminine hands.

"You think he's selling us out?" Ikeda murmured out of the side of her mouth.

"He doesn't know who we really are," Trapp said with a little more confidence than he truly felt. "At least, I don't think he does."

"You're just filling me with confidence," she replied dryly.

Trapp winked at her. "I try."

Things moved fast after they reached Emin. He turned around, winced, and said, "I apologize for what's about to happen. My men take the security of our operation very seriously."

"Oh good," Trapp said, rolling his eyes in Ikeda's direction. "I can't wait..."

They left the hotel in Emin's wake, stepping out into a heat that radiated from the city's blacktop, and which – without the breeze that graced the terrace atop the hotel – instantly soaked Trapp with sweat. Two brash Mercedes SUVs, painted black with tinted windows, idled on the street outside.

Emin turned to Trapp. "Don't worry," he said, a smile curling the corners of his mouth, "I'll take good care of her."

The man's eyes flickered hungrily in Ikeda's direction, but before Trapp had a chance to reply, he felt the ox-like hand of the Turk's bodyguard on his back, pushing him toward the rearmost of the two SUVs.

Just before he left earshot, he heard Ikeda whisper, "I'll be fine."

The bodyguard shoved Trapp into the SUV, clambering in behind him and slamming the door shut with a resounding thud. The seats were plush black leather and smelled new, and as Trapp's eyes were getting accustomed to the murky gloom behind the tinted windows, he heard the man grunt, "You wear this."

He looked up to see a black hood in the enormous Turkish bodyguard's outstretched hand.

"Yippee," he muttered dryly.

He didn't bother arguing with the man. Even setting aside the fact that the bodyguard could probably crush his skull between his gigantic butcher's hands, there was no point. His current conversation partner, if you could call him that, was a foot soldier with no decision-making authority. And besides, if they were going to have any chance of taking out Igor Strelkin, the Russian mercenary, then they needed firepower – and lots of it.

Trapp pulled the hood on, and his world went black. Then he pulled it off, only to see the bodyguard's pin-like, angry eyes fixed directly on his own. He shrugged apologetically and pointed at the seatbelt.

"Can't do it in the dark," he said.

Once he was properly secured, he pulled the hood back on and settled back to wait as the SUV pulled out into traffic, its powerful engine emitting a throaty growl. Though he couldn't see the chaos around him, the orchestra of horns and coughing scooters painted a vivid picture of Istanbul's traffic in Trapp's mind. It was probably for the best that he couldn't see the precise details of the unstructured, frenetic ballet of trucks and vans and cars all careering around him with reckless abandon. Never a man who liked to be out of control, his present situation was exactly that.

In truth, though, he had the better half of the bargain. He doubted that the smarmy Turkish arms trafficker in the vehicle with Ikeda would be shy about making a move on her. Not that he was worried. Hood or no hood, bodyguard or no bodyguard, if he put a foot out of place, let alone a hand, he knew that Ikeda would break it, no matter the consequences.

"How long's this going to take?" he asked, not expecting an answer. He didn't get one.

The SUV threaded through traffic for about forty minutes, though the first twenty of those were spent almost stationary. Once they got moving, Trapp gave up trying to follow the pattern of jerked, hurried left and right turns. He couldn't tell whether the erratic driving was done intentionally, to confuse him, or simply because that's the way the Turks learned.

Eventually, the SUV came to a halt. Unsure whether they were stopped at lights, he didn't say anything, but a second later he heard the thunk of a car door opening to his right.

"Wait here," the bodyguard muttered in thickly accented English. Then came the thud of boots impacting against the ground, then a crash as the door slammed shut again. The routine was duplicated as the driver stepped out. After his door, too, slammed shut, Trapp was left alone in silence.

"Fuck that," he muttered, pulling the hood from his face and sweeping his fingers through now sticky, flat hair. Night had fallen swiftly, and though a glow from the city's lights now colored a moonless sky, it was difficult to make out much detail about his surroundings through the SUV's tinted windows.

What little he could see indicated that they were now in an industrial area, hemmed in against one of the thickly wooded, steeply climbing hillsides that delineated Istanbul's various districts. Given enough time, a satellite photo and a hefty dose of luck, he could probably have narrowed down the exact location, but he neither needed nor wanted to go through that interminable process.

Trapp unclipped his seatbelt, then rolled his shoulders and neck from side to side. He felt like he hadn't got a good night's sleep in days, which was probably accurate, but didn't make him feel a whole lot more positive about his current predicament. He was about to go to war with a bunch of Russian mercenaries whose capabilities were unclear, for a reason that was equally shrouded in fog. And he was doing all this while thousands of miles away from home, with not just the disapproval of the Central Intelligence Agency, but the lingering possibility that they had sold him out hanging over his head.

It was the prospect of being hunted down by his own team that was on his mind when he heard Ikeda cry out.

19

Before Trapp was fully out of the Mercedes SUV, his partner already had the situation fully under control. Her black hood decorated the dusty road, and she was crouched over the prostrate form of Emin Aksoy, twisting the gunrunner's arm behind his back until he squealed in pain.

"You gonna do that again?" she growled into his ear, but loud enough that Trapp could hear.

"No!" the Turk squealed. "I promise."

Both the man's bodyguards had their pistols drawn and aimed directly at Ikeda's back, but they could not fire for fear of hitting their boss. Silently, Trapp closed the distance between him and the nearest of the two armed men. He stole a glance at the two drivers, who were standing together, cigarettes in hand, catching a smoke after the long drive, and now looking stunned at the speed with which events had proceeded, and didn't look like they wanted any part of a gunfight.

For a gunrunner, Trapp thought, Aksoy had terrible security. His men had thought nothing of the potential danger posed by the American woman, presumably thinking she was little more than arm candy. They couldn't have been more wrong.

His lip curled as he realized that wasn't even the worst part of it. In the commotion, they had forgotten about him entirely, which meant that he was able to sneak up behind the distracted bodyguard and deliver a kick to the back of the man's knee at precisely the same moment at which he grabbed the bodyguard's wrist, twisting it and applying pressure so that the pistol fell from his nerveless fingers and clattered against the ground. He danced forward, retrieving the weapon, and before the second bodyguard could react, he drew a bead on the man's skull.

"Now," Trapp said in a voice that carried over the background squawking of nocturnal birds and the low hum of machinery hidden in the darkened warehouses that lined the area. "Why doesn't everyone just relax."

He kept his eye on the guard he'd just disabled, who was rolling on the ground switching between clutching his knee and caressing his wrist. The man definitely appeared to be out of action, but Trapp had no intention of forgetting he was there – and repeating his opponent's mistake.

"I'm relaxed," Ikeda cooed. "What about you, Jason?"

"Cool as a cucumber," he replied, before groaning. "Crap, that was a terrible line..."

"I won't tell if you don't," Ikeda called back. She yanked Emin's arm. "Now," she said. "Are you going to keep those to yourself?"

"Get the hell off me," Emin grunted. "Or my men will shoot!"

"I don't think so," Trapp laughed. "Ask yourself whether this dumb sack of shit"—he jerked his chin at the one remaining armed bodyguard—"is likely to be a better shot than I am. If you think so, then by all means order him to take it.

"But if you don't"—he shrugged—"then maybe you should take a deep breath and apologize to the lady."

He watched as the Turk's head wobbled from left to right, as he took in the precise nature of his predicament for the first time. He could practically see the cogs turning in the man's skull.

"All right, all right," he moaned. "I'm sorry, okay?"

Immediately, Ikeda released the gunrunner's arm and jumped up, landing lightly on the balls of her feet. "See," she said sweetly, "that's all you had to say. Now – are we going to do business with each other, or not?"

Emin rolled onto his back, clutching his shoulder as a rictus of pain grasped his face, twisting it. He grimaced, rolled the offending joint, and then slowly clambered to his feet. "Fuck off," he grunted.

"Now"—Ikeda pouted—"that's not nice, is it?"

Trapp watched as an expression of relief washed over the bodyguard's face, and he subsequently lowered his weapon. When he was certain that the tension was fading away, he shoved the commandeered weapon underneath his belt, rather than returning it to its rightful owner.

Just in case.

"I'm sorry, okay?" Emin grumbled. "I was just being friendly."

"Yeah well, you can take your *friendship* somewhere else, buddy," Ikeda replied scornfully. "Why don't you just concentrate on showing us your merchandise?"

Trapp hiked up his eyebrow. *Remind me not to get on your bad side*, he thought.

Emin dusted himself down and cast a murderous look at his two bodyguards, along with the drivers, both of whom were doing their very best to stay out of sight, flushed embarrassment written on their faces. He growled an order in flowing Turkish, and his men snapped into action to escape their boss's ire, jogging toward the nearest of the drab warehouses and opening a series of impregnable-looking locks. One of them pulled at a thick length of chain, which clinked and clanked, and then tumbled into a rusty heap to the side of the door.

The same man grabbed a handle on the front of the metal shutters, grunted as he heaved upward, then ducked underneath. There were a few seconds of silence, and then an unhealthy electric groan rang out as an unseen motor whirred into action, rolling the rusted shutter door upward.

As it opened, and a set of strip lights blinked into life overhead, revealing rack after rack of deadly weaponry, and piles of green-tinted military crates, Eliza Ikeda was for once stunned into silence. Trapp's own mouth fell open with surprise he felt no need to conceal.

His gaze met Ikeda's, and a broad grin stretched out on both their faces.

Jackpot.

"Come on," Emin said in a taut, irritable voice, clearly still sore about kissing the deck a few moments before. "Pick what you want. I don't have all day."

"You're not worried about someone jacking this place?" Trapp asked, still somewhat stunned at the vast selection of weapons, explosives and endless crates of ammunition stacked against the warehouse's far wall. Though he knew Emin's reputation as a man who could get pretty much anything, given enough time and sufficient incentive, he hadn't expected a full-on damn military armory on the outskirts of one of Europe's largest cities.

If this was what he kept in the capital, Trapp could only wonder at how much hardware was stored nearer the front lines, across the border into Syria.

"People around here know not to mess with me," Emin sneered.

Trapp could tell that the prideful Turkish gunrunner was

still smarting from his humiliation at Ikeda's hands. Turkey wasn't Saudi Arabia, but neither was it Western Europe. In Emin's neck of the woods, men were supposed to be men, and women confined to the kitchen.

He glanced at Ikeda. *Not this one.*

Typically, her attention was presently absorbed by the nearest rack of rifles. She took a pace forward, glanced at a nearby bodyguard, and then half-shrugged, clearly coming to the conclusion that there was little the man could – or would, after what she had just done – do to stop her.

She removed an AK-74 assault rifle from the rack and checked it expertly. It wasn't loaded, but as far as Trapp could make out it was clean and in good working order. She glanced up at Emin, showing no hangover of animosity from his wandering hands a few minutes before.

"How much?" she asked.

Emin grimaced, and Trapp wondered whether he would refuse to answer the question. In the end, the lure of money won out. "Twelve hundred euros," he grunted. "If you take ten or more, I'll knock it down to a thousand apiece."

"We're not planning on invading Iran," Trapp said mildly. "Two should be fine."

Ikeda stuck out her tongue. "You're no fun..."

She set two of the rifles on the spotless stainless steel table that sat in the center of the warehouse of death, then her eyes alighted upon a case of grenades. Her neck spun around, and she looked at Trapp with laughter sparkling in her eyes.

Affecting a Valley girl accent, she pouted and said, "Hey, honey, can we get some of these? They'd look b-e-a-utiful on the nightstand..."

Trapp rolled his eyes. "Get whatever you want," he said, taking a pace toward her and whispering into her ear, "After all, the Company's paying..."

After the AK-74s, a selection of pistols clattered onto the

steel worktop, then a pair of Heckler and Koch MP-7 submachine guns, complete with suppressors, a pair of pump-action shotguns, a short case of flash bang grenades and – to satisfy Ikeda – a crate of the high explosive kind.

Trapp glanced at Emin, who was leaning against the warehouse's roller-shutter door, arms folded across his chest. He was watching the supermarket sweep play out with a barely concealed lack of interest. Trapp couldn't help but wonder how many times he'd seen this process play out before. Who had died because of the weapons he had sold. How many wives lost husbands, mothers lost children, brothers lost sisters and sisters brothers. But he put the thought out of his mind. This was a bloody business. And people like Emin were the lubricant that made it work, for both good and evil.

"You got anything accurate?" he said.

The arms dealer straightened up and walked languidly over to Trapp. "What kind of shot are you looking to make?"

Trapp shrugged. "No idea. I just like to be prepared."

Emin chewed the inside of his lip, then walked to the far end of the warehouse, to a section of crates that were lost in the murky gloom thrown by a busted overhead light. He bent down, opened the catch, flicked open the lid, and straightened, cradling a sniper rifle that Trapp didn't recognize. The weapon was over a meter in length.

"Zastava M91." The Turk smiled. "It's Serbian. 7.62 mm, ten rounds in the clip, should be good out to at least a thousand yards."

He handed the rifle to Trapp, who tested its weight, then pressed its stock against his shoulder and rested his chin against the action, staring straight down the barrel.

"If you want something heavier," Emin added, "I can get you a Barrett fifty cal. But it'll take a few days. I'll have to order it in. And it'll cost you."

"This'll do great," Trapp said, setting the rifle down next to the veritable arms cache that was quickly accumulating on the steel table. He wondered how the Turk's supply chain worked – did the man order in his hardware from a dark web version of Amazon, complete with two-day shipping? Then he decided he didn't really want to know.

He cast a practiced eye over the small stack of weaponry which Ikeda was still adding to, though at a slightly less furious pace now. "We'll need ammo for all of it. Don't be stingy. We're good for the money."

"You wouldn't be here if I thought that was in question," Emin replied.

He clicked his fingers at the nearest of his men and rattled off a stream of unintelligible words in Turkish that seemed angry, to Trapp's unpractised ear, and the light bodyguard proceeded to stand crate after crate of ammunition by the pile of guns, grenades, night vision goggles, body armor and other equipment that – like a kid in a candy shop – Ikeda had gathered.

"How much?" Trapp grunted, jerking his finger at their order.

"Thirty," Emin said after a second's hesitation. "But I'll knock it down to twenty-eight if you can do cash."

"No such luck," Trapp replied. "Give me your bank details and I'll arrange the transfer. Do you do delivery?"

Emin looked up with horror in his eyes that his professional reputation had been so impugned. "But of course…"

20

The hardware was delivered to Trapp and Ikeda's luxurious suite in the Peninsula Hotel the next day, several hours after Trapp made the transfer from a Cayman Island account to which he had access, to Emin's account in an equally shady offshore jurisdiction.

Trapp had no doubt that before long, an analyst in the bowels of Langley's New Headquarters Building would flag the unauthorized transfer, run it up the chain, and shortly after that a shit storm would break. But since he was on a separate continent, far from the long arm of the Agency's bean counters, he decided to worry about that another day.

Along with several thousand rounds of ammunition in various calibers, the Turkish weapons dealer had provided a crate of empty magazines. Trapp was lying on a thick leather sofa, a pile of empty to his left, a stack of loaded magazines to his right, when Ikeda jumped to her feet, a worried grimace on her face.

"Everything okay?" he asked, beginning to rise.

Ikeda danced across the suite barefoot, with the grace of a ballet dancer. She made it to the door, then turned back with a bashful smile on her face, and the 'do not disturb' leaf in her hand.

"Just peachy." She grinned, "But unless we're planning on giving some poor housekeeper a heart attack tomorrow morning, I figured it might be worthwhile hiding what we're up to."

Trapp glanced around the hotel room. A small box of fragmentation grenades packed in foam was sitting on top of the glass-fronted minibar, the couch beside him was showered with 9 mm brass jacketed rounds, and a pair of MP-7 submachine guns was broken down on the coffee table in front of him.

"You might have a point..." he said as he scratched his chin. "I guess that rules out room service, too."

Ikeda opened the door a fraction of an inch, to make sure that no passing vacationers could see the arsenal of death inside the hotel suite, reached out and secured the do not disturb sign around the door handle. As she closed the door behind her, turning to face him with a mischievous grin stretching across his face, she said, "With a mind that sharp, you should consider joining Mensa."

Trapp plucked a brass round from the couch beside him and threw it unerringly in the direction of her chest. The lithe CIA operative caught it easily, and pocketed it. "I'll keep that one for later," she said. "You never know when it might come in useful."

He glanced at the nondescript diver's watch on his wrist as she pattered over to him, and noted the time was a little after three in the afternoon. "How about I take you out to dinner, then," he said. "Somewhere nice?"

Ikeda kissed him gently on the lips, sending a frisson of excitement running down the nape of his neck. "I thought you'd never ask."

They spent the next few hours just like any other new couple, loading magazine after magazine, checking their body armor and night vision equipment, breaking down, cleaning and lubricating each piece of weaponry, and then stowing every last piece of equipment into black duffel bags that Emin had provided, which went into the walk-in closet, secured by luggage locks. It wasn't an impregnable security system, but Trapp figured it should be enough to hide the arsenal from a light-fingered maid, or any other prying eyes that had breached the flimsy first line of defense posed by the do-not-disturb sign on the door.

"So what do we know about Strelkin?" Ikeda asked.

She was sitting in front of a mirror-backed makeup table, perched upon a chair that looked like a piano bench, and wearing only a plain gray sports bra and a pair of equally functional underwear. Trapp cast his mind back to the first time she had stolen his breath away, in the lead up to the ill-fated operation in the Ritz-Carlton in Macau. Then, she'd worn a shimmering silk dress that left little to the imagination.

But while Eliza Ikeda was undeniably stunning, a woman who – if she chose to – could draw the attention of any man in any room, along with the jealousy of most of their wives, it wasn't shallow physical beauty that drew Trapp to her. It was something more indefinable: her poise, the way she carried herself, the physical strength of her athlete's body, and the equally impressive mind that lay behind her gorgeous looks.

Trapp glanced down at the open manila file that Alessandro had died to equip them with. The photocopied pages within were already frayed and creased from use.

"He likes the finer things in life," he said, reading from a summary that he had almost memorized. "Lives in a seven bedroom villa not right on the Bosporus. Set him back thirteen million euros."

Ikeda whistled. "Someone's doing well for himself..."

Trapp grimaced. He hated mercenaries. They could be valuable, and the United States was hardly a paragon of virtue when it came to making use of their services, especially in far-flung conflict zones where the public wouldn't stomach the death of American soldiers, but he knew too well that the only loyalty they showed was to the almighty dollar.

Or in this case, the almighty ruble.

And in this particular case, it was clear that Strelkin was making out like a bandit from the conflict across the Turkish border in Syria. He wasn't surprised that the man directed his operations from hundreds of miles away in Istanbul, rather than getting his hands dirty alongside his men. After all, why risk dying to get your paycheck, when someone else will do that for you?

Trapp knew that he was no saint himself. If there was a god up there, looking down on him, he would have to account one day for the people he had killed, the harm he had done. But at least he had done it for the right reasons – to keep his country safe from the demons around every corner. Strelkin was different. He didn't care who lived or died, as long as he got paid. And Trapp resolved that whatever it took, the man would get what was coming to him.

"According to this," Trapp said, tapping a printout of Strelkin's most recent bank transactions, "he eats at a restaurant called Mikla most nights."

His eyes bulged as he saw the size of the man's average check. "And he doesn't hold back."

Ikeda turned around, exposing her bare, toned stomach. "Then I guess I know where you're taking me for dinner."

THEY TOOK a cab from the hotel to the restaurant. Trapp was uncomfortably aware that the last time he'd gone out with Ikeda, a friend of his died. It was a known hazard in this line of work, but it didn't make it any easier.

Upon arrival, the maître d' led them to a pair of stools that looked out onto a backlit water feature, and then over the twinkling lights of the endless city below, and the glistening navigation lamps of the ships plying their trade up and down the Bosporus.

Trapp glanced around the restaurant. He saw an empty table by the opposite wall of the elegant establishment, which had a good line of sight to almost every other table in the place. He pointed it out, and said, "How about that one?"

The white-jacketed member of staff shook his head, an apologetic grimace on his face. "I'm sorry, sir," he said in accented English, "but it's reserved." He gestured out at the breathtaking views over the city. "And besides, these are the two best seats in the house."

Trapp reached into his pocket and pulled out several crisp green notes which he folded into his palm. "I'm sure they are. But my wife here"—he gestured at Ikeda—"has an absolutely terrible fear of heights. Is there anything you can do to help? It would be most appreciated..."

The maître d' accepted the offer without blinking, though his expression relaxed. He smiled and said, "On second thoughts, perhaps I can see what is possible."

Trapp smiled dryly. "I thought that might be the case."

He offered Ikeda his arm, and she accepted it as they walked over to the now magically free table. It didn't have the stunning views of their previous berth, but since they weren't only here for the experience, neither minded.

A basket of freshly baked sourdough bread and chicken salt butter was placed in front of them within seconds, followed shortly after by a glass of chilled white wine. He broke off a chunk of the bread, buttered it lavishly, and closed his eyes with delight as the rich, unctuous taste broke like a wave on his tastebuds.

He opened them again to see Ikeda staring at him with a lightly mocking smile. She raised her eyebrow. "That good?"

"How did you guess?"

"You look like you just had an orgasm..."

Trapp winked. "You know what they say about all work and no play..."

Though both pairs of eyes darted out and examined each of the restaurant's new arrivals, the first forty minutes of their meal passed much as any other date, although much to the consternation of a procession of waiters, they scarcely sipped at the wine glasses in front of them. Once bitten, twice shy.

"I guess he's a no-show," Ikeda said, glancing at the face of a wristwatch that sat on a thin silver band around her left wrist. "It's almost 9."

"Maybe he eats late?" Trapp grunted.

In truth, he was kind of hoping that Strelkin didn't show. He had every intention of finding the man, pinning him to a wall and shoving a pistol against his temple until he spilled every last piece of information they were looking for. But it could wait just one more night. He wanted to take Ikeda to a bar, to drink a cocktail, and then another, without worrying that the alcohol might throw off his aim if it came to a gunfight. And then he wanted to take her back to the hotel and see where the night went after that.

So of course, just seconds later, Ikeda's eyes narrowed. She consciously relaxed her expression, lifting her wine glass to her lips and mouthing, "I spoke too soon. He's at your six," from behind the glass.

Trapp knew better than to react. Strelkin had just arrived, and had no reason to believe he was being watched, let alone be aware of the identity of the two Americans who were doing the watching. There was no cause to hurry.

He lowered his voice. "What are we looking at?"

Ikeda didn't reply immediately. Her pupils flickered left and then right. "There are five of them. Slavic. Big, mean bastards. I guess they must be his men."

"Makes sense," Trapp replied. "It's just a local restaurant to him, judging by his bank statements."

Ikeda's nostrils flared with distaste. Trapp knew what she was thinking – that the Russian mercenary's luxurious lifestyle was only paid for through the death, mutilation and rape of thousands of innocent Syrian men, women and children. There was nothing gentle or honorable about the civil war taking place over Turkey's eastern border. It wasn't peacekeeping; it was ethnic cleansing. Assad, his Iranian backers and Russian enforcers didn't care who they had to kill, as long as they got the job done.

Or who they had to pay.

"Must be nice," she spat quietly.

Trapp watched out of the corner of his eye as the five mercenaries were led to a table ahead of him and to his right, now out of Ikeda's eyeshot. "Armed?"

She nodded imperceptibly. "Three of them are, at least, including our new friend Igor. And I'm guessing the other two aren't here out of the kindness of his heart."

Trapp grimaced. He hadn't expected Strelkin to come unprotected, but he'd figured one or two men at most. Istanbul wasn't the front lines, and the Turkish security services made sure that the violence didn't spill over into their flagship city. But clearly the Russian mercenary boss went to great lengths to ensure his own safety.

"You're right," he grunted, grinding his teeth together with irritation.

The weight of the pistol beneath his navy blazer was comforting, but he knew that he wouldn't be using it. Not tonight, at any rate. Five against two wasn't great odds in anyone's book. Trapp himself weighed a couple of hundred pounds on a good day, and was handily over six feet tall, but compared to the meaty Russian brutes in his line of sight, he was a child.

"We'll need to take him at home," he said. "On the move, maybe, but it's two of us against who knows how many of them. Better to do it when he's asleep."

Ikeda nodded thoughtfully. She took a sip of wine, strangely more relaxed now that they knew there was little prospect of coming to blows in the next few hours. And perhaps it had something to do with the fact that she couldn't actually see the several thousand muscular pounds of Russian prize fighters that Trapp was presently faced with.

He kept watching as Strelkin waved his hand above his head imperiously and bellowed, "Waiter!"

The entire restaurant hushed for a few seconds, all conversation falling away, leaving only cutlery chinking against china and the booming laughter emanating from the clearly already drunk Russian mercenaries. The maître d' who had sat Ikeda and Trapp quickly beckoned one of his colleagues over. Trapp paid attention as Strelkin made a circular gesture with his index finger and said something that looked suspiciously like, "Vodka!"

"What are you thinking?" he asked.

Though it would be almost imperceptible to someone who hadn't spent the last two months in her company, Trapp had – and it was as plain as day to him that she was mulling something over.

"The way I see it," she said, "we've got two choices."

"Go on..."

She jerked her head in the direction of the Russians' table, though the movement was so subtle it was clearly intended for Trapp's eyes only. "It sounds like those bozos are in for a heavy night, right?"

Trapp nodded. He followed the path of the white-jacketed waiter as the man made a beeline for the bar, spoke to the bartender, and returned with a frozen bottle of Grey Goose vodka and five shot glasses on a silver tray. As the man passed their table, he pointed them out. "Looks like it."

"Then we go in hard. Tonight. We wait till two or three in the morning, take out the perimeter security as quietly as we can, and then kill his bodyguards while they're sleeping off the alcohol."

Trapp had come to much the same conclusion in his own head. The Russians had the advantage of manpower, so a head-to-head contest would almost certainly end in their favor. The two freelancing CIA operatives, by contrast, had stealth, surprise, and the benefit of years of training on their side. They needed to play to those strengths.

"What's the other option?" he asked. "You said we had two choices."

Ikeda inclined her head, and a stray lock of dark hair tickled her chin before she huffed a puff of air out of the side of her mouth with frustration and tucked it away behind her ear. Trapp hid a smile.

"Yeah, I did. But you're not going to like it..."

21

Ikeda was right. Her second choice involved asking for help, and like men all over the world, Trapp preferred never to read an instruction manual, let alone phone a friend.

"Never going to happen," he said, shaking his head instantly. "We do this ourselves."

Ikeda didn't say anything. At least, not instantly. Trapp got the sense that she was sizing him up, trying to work out how best to pitch her proposal. And he got a creeping sense that however much he protested, she was going to get her way. The problem wasn't that she was as smart as she was persuasive; the problem was that she was almost inevitably *right*.

And that pissed him off. Trapp usually preferred the bull in a china shop approach – barreling forward and leaving every problem in shards behind him. Eliza Ikeda was a little more refined in her approach.

"We do this ourselves," she said, repeating his own words back at him, "and we most likely end up in body bags."

She gestured around the opulent, two-hundred euro a plate restaurant. "If he's bringing four of his guys along to eat with him in a place like this every night, then you can be sure he'll have a ring of steel around his villa."

Though he didn't say anything, Trapp had to concede that she was probably correct. He wasn't James Bond, and while he was handy enough with a lock pick, when it came to hacking through a building's security system, he was the wrong guy to call.

"And how do we know that we can trust Langley?" Trapp growled, slightly too loud. Thankfully it didn't seem like anyone overheard his indiscretion.

Ikeda glanced left and right and shot him a pointed look. "I don't know Mitchell. Never met the guy, though he's got a hell of a reputation."

"Uh huh," Trapp said noncommittally. "What's your point?"

She fixed him with a knowing stare. "He went to bat for me, Jason. When I was in that hellhole. You were the one who came and got me out, and I'll never forget that, but if he hadn't sent the Navy in after you, then we'd both have died there, and you know it."

Trapp did know it. He knew, in fact, that it would have been a whole lot worse. If the modified Marburg virus the North Koreans had been brewing in secret had made it into China, then tens, maybe hundreds of millions of innocents would have ended up dead – and it was just as likely that a nuclear war would have broken out, frying the American heartland in a single, horrific instant.

He closed his eyes and sighed. "So you're saying that you trust him?"

A gruff burst of laughter broke out, hushing the room for a second time, and when Trapp's eyes snapped open, he saw the crew of Russian mercenaries sinking yet another shot of vodka as their starters arrived.

"Sure," Ikeda said evenly. "I trust *him*."

Relationships, Trapp was swiftly learning, were all about

compromise. And so he proposed one, knowing that she was right, and that there was no way that Mitchell, at least, was responsible for Sokolov's death, or the two Russian agents turning up at his door. He could trust the man – his boss – even if he wasn't yet willing to allow the rest of Langley.

"Fine," he said gruffly. "I'll reach out. But only under two conditions..."

Ikeda pursed her lips together. "Shoot."

"First," Trapp said, jabbing out a finger and tapping it with another, "we scout the place out before we do anything else. Tonight."

She nodded. "Deal. And the second?"

Trapp grinned and pointed at a chocolate brownie on a rectangular black slate plate, accompanied with a single scoop of vanilla ice cream and lashings of dark chocolate sauce that had just been set down on the table next to them. "Let's get dessert."

22

Mike Mitchell's phone rang. He glanced at the screen and his head immediately tilted forward. He was expecting the call, but that didn't mean he wanted to answer it. Reluctantly, however, he did so, and pressed the secure cell phone to his ear.

"Mitchell, you there?"

"Director," Mitchell replied, his tone guarded. "How can I help?"

"Cut that shit out," Lawrence replied, his voice already frothing with rage. "What the fuck happened in Italy?"

The director of the Special Activities Division paused to collect his thoughts before replying, knowing better than to react to the flicker of irritation gnawing at him as a result of the DCI's tone. Mitchell was a proud man, with an ego just like everyone else, but he was also superbly self-controlled – a vital precondition for an effective operator in the field, and just as indispensable a quality in the treacherous political soup of Washington DC.

"I'm trying to get to the bottom of it, sir," he replied, not entirely happy that Trapp had thrown him under a bus.

"*Trying to get to the bottom of it,*" Lawrence repeated, his voice now dripping with derision. "Well, you know what, Mike? It seems pretty clear to me. This Hangman character of yours has gone rogue. He sold out Sokolov to the Russians, and now he's working contract jobs for them. First this Italian spy, and who the hell knows what he'll do next. It's a fucking disaster."

"No, sir," Mitchell replied firmly. "I guarantee that's not the case."

"And what evidence do you have for that guarantee?" Lawrence snapped. "Because I'm looking at images from Interpol with his face all over them. The director of the Italian security service just got off the phone with me, and he's furious, you understand? It took everything I had to convince him not to go to the press."

"Thank you, sir."

"I didn't do it for you, or your band of reckless cowboys down in SAD," came Lawrence's furious reply. "If word got out that one of our hitmen killed an Italian intelligence officer, it would be a diplomatic nightmare. Half of Europe would kick our station chiefs out, you understand? The French hate us already, the Germans are ambivalent, but something like this will rile the whole lot of them. It will set our HUMINT back years. You know what that'll cost this country?"

"He's not a hitman, sir," Mitchell insisted, adding some bite to his words, though remaining careful not to use Hangman's real name. The encryption was supposed to be unbreakable. But that didn't mean he trusted it completely. "He's an *operator*. All my people are. There's a difference."

"That's just semantics, Mike, and you know it," Lawrence said.

"No, sir," Mitchell replied firmly. "It's not. My people aren't cowboys. Hangman did *not* murder Alessandro Lombardi, and he sure as hell didn't sell out Sokolov. There's something else going on here, and I intend to prove it. The only rational explanation is that he thinks we might have had something to do with it. Hell, I'll stake my whole damn career on it."

There was a moment's cold silence before the director of Central Intelligence replied. "Mike," he said. "You already have."

⌇

AS MITCHELL ENTERED the sub-basement beneath Langley's New Headquarters Building that housed his two top analysts, Kyle Partey and Timothy Greaves, he was still smarting from the dressing down the DCI had handed out just a few moments before. So it took him a couple of seconds to notice that Kyle had a phone handset pressed to his ear, and at the sound of his boss entering the room, had stood up, and was now gesturing wildly over his head, beckoning for Mitchell to join him.

He did so, and a wave of relief flooded Kyle's face as he pressed the handset into Mitchell's hands, muttering, "It's Trapp" as he did so.

A mixture of relief and irritation battled in the director's mind as he relieved Kyle of the phone and placed it against his ear. Relief that Trapp had finally checked in, and irritation that it had taken so damn long.

Trapp's gruff, unmistakable voice barked out in an uncompromising tone that certainly didn't *sound* apologetic. "Is this line secure?"

Mitchell glanced at Kyle Partey, and mouthed the same question to the smartly dressed young analyst. The stress of his position was clearly beginning to show, and gray hairs had started sprouting among the forest of wiry black hair on his head.

Kyle waggled his hand in a "Kinda" gesture and muttered, "Keep it short."

"Jason, where the fuck are you?" Mitchell hissed.

The truth was, he was pissed off. A couple of days earlier, he had defended Trapp in DCI Lawrence's office. Said that he was a contractor, and couldn't be expected to stay on a tight leash. All that was the God's honest truth. And yet, Mitchell would have appreciated a freaking heads-up. Trapp had hung him out to dry, without so much as a hint as to what he was up to. And now he was calling in from halfway across the world without even a sliver of contrition in his voice.

"Turkey," Trapp said simply, his voice low and gruff.

"Turkey!" Mitchell exploded. "What the fuck are you doing in Turkey? The DCI wants your head, and he doesn't care how he gets it. He thinks you're knee deep in this Sokolov thing."

"The DCI can go to hell," Trapp replied.

Mitchell was surprised by how calm his operative's voice sounded over the phone, but he knew the man too well to believe that he was doing anything else right now other than boiling over with rage. Jason Trapp was not a man who responded well to overt displays of authority, and especially not to power plays. He hated the bureaucratic bullshit that emanated from every sinew of the Washington DC Beltway.

And the truth was, Mike Mitchell could hardly blame him. There was no point in bringing Trapp in to Langley for questioning. If anyone was going to get to the bottom of whatever the hell was going on right now, it was more likely to be Trapp than a whole army of analysts in Washington.

"Be that as it may," Mitchell said, stabbing his finger into the air as he rattled off each of the single-syllable words like well-aimed gunfire, "Lawrence is riding my ass about you, and I'm going to have to throw him a bone, or he won't stop digging. Now what the hell are you doing in Turkey?"

"Throw him whatever you want," Trapp said dismissively. "I don't give a shit. I need an SOG team at my location, and I need it yesterday. Can you get it done?"

Mitchell's mouth opened and shut several times blankly,

like a goldfish mindlessly bobbing along. SOG stood for Special Operations Group, the kinetic arm of the CIA's Special Activities Division – Mitchell's fiefdom. They were the Agency's special forces units. "Say that again?"

Trapp's voice carried more than a hint of irritation this time. "Four men. With their own equipment. Can you get them to me, or not?"

"You cannot be fucking serious," Mitchell said.

"I'm deadly serious, Mike," Trapp fired back. "I'm running down a lead over here, one that's tied into everything that's going on. And I need your help."

Mitchell ran his fingers through the close cropped – and now sadly thinning – hair on top of his head. He ground his teeth together with frustration. One part of him, a very big part, wanted to tell Trapp to go to hell. The operative only ever saw things his own way. He didn't see the big picture that he had to deal with, only the microcosm that surrounded him at any given time.

But as the silence dragged on, he considered the other side of that same equation. The thing was, Jason Trapp was the kind of individual who usually found himself at the very heart of the action for a reason.

"If you want me to run cover for you, Jason, I need something in return."

This time it was Trapp's turn to fall silent. Eventually, grudgingly, through no-doubt gritted teeth, the operative said, "No promises. But I'll listen."

"What the hell happened in Florence?" Mitchell asked, thinking back to the furious dressing down that Lawrence had given him only a few minutes before. "The Italians have images of you and Eliza, and believe me, they ain't freaking happy about it. One of their top guys is dead, and you blew through the net before they had a chance to ask you about it."

"That's why I'm here, Mike," Trapp said softly. "Alessandro

was a friend. If you think I would ever want him dead, then you don't know me."

Mitchell matched his operative's more emollient tone. "I believe you, Jason. But I can't help you if I don't know what you're up to. And I've got four dead Serbian mobsters lined up on a slab in a Florentine morgue with your name all over them. So why don't you start talking?"

There was a rustle on the line, as though one of Trapp's enormous hands had just covered the microphone, and he got the unmistakable sense that he was being discussed at that very moment. Not for the first time Mitchell reflected that his job rarely involved giving orders – or at least, giving orders that he expected to be followed.

To be successful as the director of the Special Activities Division meant leading men and women who were singularly focused, enormously dedicated, and more convinced of their own opinion than anyone else on the planet. The problem was, they were usually right. Mostly. His task wasn't to tell them what to do, it was to guide the world's deadliest, most effective killers into making the correct decision — and convincing them it was their choice all along.

There was another series of rustles and scratches, and Trapp's voice came back on the line. "Okay."

"Okay what?"

"Okay I'll tell you," Trapp said. "Believe me, Mike, I didn't want to be in the middle of this any more than you wanted it. But that's just the way it is. Four days ago, a pair of Italian mercenaries turned up unannounced and tried to kill me."

"Crap," Mitchell said, sucking air through his teeth. "Are you –"

"We're fine," Trapp said brusquely, "better than they are, anyway. I knew Alessandro from a job a few years ago. I didn't know who we could trust, so I went to him with the information. It cost him his life."

Mitchell could hear the grief in Trapp's tone. He'd never met Alessandro Lombardi before, but he knew the Italian by reputation. Everyone in the business did. He was a huge loss. "I'm sorry."

"Don't be. Before he died, Alessandro gave us a file. It contained the names of both the assassins and the man who employed them." Trapp paused, as though deciding whether or not he'd already said too much. "The guy's name was Igor Strelkin."

Mitchell frowned. "Never heard of him."

"Until a couple of days ago, me neither," Trapp said. "But he's a bad dude. Russian private military type. Highest bidder, no questions asked."

"So what's he got to do with anything?" Mitchell said, still not seeing how everything fit together.

"That's the million-dollar question," Trapp replied. "If I had the answer, I wouldn't need to bust down his front door and put my gun between his teeth, would I?"

Mitchell grimaced. "So basically, Jason," he said. "You've got nothing. Just a hunch. And you want me to back that up with four of my men, without the DCI getting a whiff of what the hell I'm doing. Is that about right?"

"I don't care if Santa Claus himself finds out what I'm up to," Trapp said, his temper rising. "Think it through, Mike. This BA flight goes down, killing an asset that I recruited five years ago. An asset who, if I'm not mistaken, gave us the best intelligence we've ever got on the motives, actions and players at the top of the Kremlin. Then the very next day, two pricks turn up at my front door and try and slot me. And it turns out that the two dudes are paid by the Russians. You don't think that's just a *little bit* suspicious, Mike?"

Trapp's sarcasm was as biting as it was justified, Mitchell thought. "All right, all right, I get it," he sighed. "So what's your plan?"

"I told you already. I'm going to knock on his front door, put a gun to his head and get him to tell me who the fuck paid him to have me killed. That's the key, Mike. Something big is going on here, and we need to find out what it is before it's too late. If you can help, great. But if you can't, then at least stay the hell out of my way."

The line went dead.

23

The four man SOG team each wore grim, competent expressions as they entered the hotel suite. They showed no sign of fatigue, though Trapp knew that it was at least an eleven hour drive from the border with Syria, and probably a couple of hours by helicopter from whatever dusty forward operating base they had been stationed at before that.

But after leaving Delta, Trapp had spent eighteen months with the Special Operations Group. He knew they were used to following unclear orders, on minimal sleep in the most desperate of circumstances. To them, this was just water off a duck's back.

"I'm Rich," a tall, wiry man with a thick salt and pepper beard said once the door to the suite had closed behind them. He was lean rather than muscular, but nevertheless radiated competence. Trapp assumed that he was the team leader. His face was tanned and wore the exhausted look of a man not long out of a combat zone.

"Nice to meet you," he replied, shaking the man's hand. He

pointed at Ikeda. "That's Eliza, I'm Jason. We're running point down here."

Surnames were neither asked for nor offered.

Rich nodded. "I know who you are," he said simply. He pointed at each of his three men in turn. "This is Andy, Rhett and Bruno."

In contrast to the team leader, his operators were each as powerfully built as the other. Two of them – Andy and Rhett – were around 5 foot 10, with inky black hair and Mediterranean complexions. They looked like brothers, although Trapp suspected that it was little more than a passing resemblance. The third, Bruno, was nearer to Trapp's own height, and had dark brown hair.

"Where's your gear?" Trapp grunted as first he, then Ikeda, shook hands with the remaining members of the team.

"The truck. Figured it would be better not to lug it up here if we didn't absolutely have to."

"Good call," he agreed.

"If you don't mind me asking," Bruno said, with a Bronx bite in his voice, "what the hell are we doing here? We had a bead on a real nasty Islamic State motherfucker. I was looking forward to putting a bullet in his skull. Now I find myself in this five-star hotel."

He glanced around as though he wasn't exactly impressed with the life of luxury Trapp and Ikeda were living while he and his boys were slumming it in Syria on behalf of their country. "And so I figure there must be a real good reason, you know? Because we already had a *real* good reason to stay where we were, if you get what I'm sayin'."

Trapp had been in the man's shoes more times than he could count. Hours, minutes, or even seconds from taking out a real nasty dude, only to get a call from some rear echelon motherfucker who wanted an update, or who got cold feet at the last moment over the geopolitical ramifications of knocking off some tinpot Middle Eastern dictator.

"I get it," he replied with equanimity. "And I won't forget you boys helping me out on this one. If there's anything I can do to help you whack your target when all this is done, just let me know."

Bruno crossed his arms in front of his chest, the action screaming his belief that he didn't need help from nobody. He had that ineffable special forces operator's arrogance about him. Trapp knew that the same acerbic confidence ran through his own veins, though he probably kept it in check a little better than the younger man.

And what about when you were his age?

Trapp's mouth wrinkled with the inkling of a wry smile. He didn't blame the man for his reaction. The team's previous target was most likely already long gone. He knew how it worked. When you identified a target's location, you got a window that might only be open for hours. That's why the United States had special operations teams forward deployed all over the globe. You had to hit hard and fast. By the time this job in Istanbul was over, the Islamic State leader would be in the wind.

Trapp didn't bother apologizing again. He knew the man opposite him wouldn't give a shit. So he turned away, walked to the assortment of couches that took pride of place in the center of the suite, and picked up the manila folder. He opened it, withdrew the picture of their target, and held it in the air.

"This is Igor Strelkin," he said.

"Yeah," Bruno said, a sneer crossing his face. "We know who that asshole is."

"You do?" Ikeda asked, a note of surprise in her voice. "How?"

Bruno's hands dropped to his sides. It wasn't an outright offer of a truce, but Trapp sensed that he at least had the man's attention. Beyond that, he wasn't surprised that the operator was taking the lead on behalf of his team, rather than its designated leader. Special forces teams, especially the Agency's, prized individuality, intelligence, and stating one's opinions.

"How much do you know about Syria?" he said.

Ikeda shrugged. "Not my ballpark."

Bruno's lip curled. "I didn't think so."

Trapp hid a smile rather than taking offense at the operator's dismissive tone. He knew exactly what the man must think of Ikeda. That she was an analyst, or some other breed of mouth breather from Langley who would only get in the way of getting the job done. But they hadn't seen how she operated.

She took a pace forward so that she was almost nose to nose with the SOG killer – or would have been, if he didn't have half a foot on her – and though her expression remained impassive, her voice took on a hard, biting tone. "You wanna cut that out?"

A mocking smile danced across Bruno's face. "You know, I don't think I do."

Ikeda nodded slowly, as though she was turning over the man's response in her mind. She chewed her lip, almost shivering with anxiety, and her shoulders slumped forward as though she was beaten. Bruno's face crowed with victory.

She started turning to her left, and at the precise second that Bruno's neck twisted to the right to share a triumphant grin with his teammates, she hooked her right leg around his, grabbed a firm hold of his right shoulder with her left hand, and then threw him to the ground in a well-practiced judo maneuver. Before he finished falling, she straddled him, and a flash of steel appeared between her fingers, then kissed the toppled operator's carotid artery.

"Now," Ikeda said, her voice perfectly calm, her eyes locked onto Bruno's shocked pupils. "Why don't we try that again?"

Neither Trapp nor any one of Bruno's three team members moved so much as a muscle to offer their support as a few seconds of silence filled the hotel suite. With four inches of razor-sharp steel at his neck and a hundred-ten pounds of crazy bitch straddling his chest, Bruno barely dared to breathe, let alone provoke Ikeda's wrath with a second ill-judged comment.

Trapp, for his part, knew that Ikeda was entirely in control. She was unflappable in the face of mortal danger, so he had no worries about her going head to head with a trigger-puller who was a little too high on his own supply of testosterone. She was just doing what had to be done for this crew to respect her.

The tense silence was split by a roaring peal of laughter. Trapp looked to his right to see one of the shorter operators, Rhett, practically doubled over, clutching his stomach as waves of hilarity rippled through him.

"Dang, she's a real firecracker," he grunted, shaking his head as he struggled to suck in a mouthful of oxygen. "You look like a real prick now, Bruno…"

Ikeda hopped lightly to her feet, landing without so much as a whisper. The blade – which Trapp hadn't even known she was carrying – quickly disappeared, and she reached down to offer the fallen special operator a hand up, not displaying so much as a hint of animosity.

He looked at it for a couple of seconds, as though weighing whether to accept the offer. Then, still lying flat on his back, he let his head tilt backward until it banged against the floor, then grabbed the proffered limb and pulled himself to his feet. He shook his head ruefully and said, "I take your point. My apologies."

"Accepted and forgotten," Ikeda replied warmly. "Now, if I remember correctly, you were saying something about Syria?"

Another wave of contagious laughter bubbled up out of Rhett's mouth, and Bruno shot him a black, embarrassed look. The teammate shrugged. "You better listen to the little lady," he chuckled. "I'm guessing you don't want to see her when she's angry..."

"Point taken," he muttered, closing his eyes briefly to reorient himself. "Okay, Syria. It's a fucking shit show out there. You got Islamic State, Al Qaeda, a few dozen local warlords, various rebel groups fighting against the government, the Kurds, a few of us, the Brits, the French, the Russian military, and then Lord only knows how many PMC groups running around. Mostly Russian."

Trapp nodded. "That's where Strelkin comes in, right?"

"Uh huh," Bruno agreed. "He's a real nasty dude, and I've met a few. The thing about Syria is it's a breeding ground for terrorists, right?"

"Right."

"Well, the Russians don't give a fuck about that. They say they do in the media, but it's just BS."

"So why are they there?"

"Propping up the Assad regime," Bruno replied, his face creasing with distaste as he unconsciously rubbed the back of his head to soothe the pain of his earlier fall. "It suits President Murov to have military bases in the Middle East, so he can't allow the government to fall. So he's got the Russian army, the Air Force, and a couple of special forces units in-country. But it's the PMCs like Aegis that do the real bad shit."

"Like what?" Ikeda inquired.

Bruno shrugged like it didn't bother him, but from the rigidity of his posture it was clear that it did. "Like wiping out rebel villages. Burning them to the ground, with women and children inside. His men steal, drink and rape with impunity. We sent it up the chain but"—he shrugged—"you know, *politics.*"

Trapp shared the man's disgust. War was a nasty business, and the American military wasn't exactly free of blame in that regard. But when US personnel went bad, they were court-martialed and sent to Leavenworth, not given medals to pin on their chests. He suspected the Russians thought a little differently.

"So how would you boys feel about paying Mr. Strelkin a visit?" Trapp asked, a grim smile on his face.

"How friendly we talking?" Bruno asked, looking up at him.

Trapp shrugged. "I've got some questions to ask him. But the prick sent a couple of hitmen after me, so I'm not exactly feeling too charitable right now. But," he said, holding up a warning finger, "there's one condition."

"Which is?"

"Whatever happens, it never happened, is that understood? This is about as deep black as it gets. If you guys don't want to get involved, I understand that. But I need you to walk out of here right now."

He held his breath and waited as Bruno looked around at the other members of his team. Suddenly the operator displayed no signs of frustration about losing his previous target. Trapp knew the look on his face. He'd worn it many times himself. It was the look of a hunter catching the scent of prey.

It was the team leader, Rich, who replied, after sharing a series of silent nods with his men. "I think you got yourself a deal."

24

Igor Strelkin's multimillion euro villa was situated in a quiet neighborhood, on a piece of land that both over-looked and ran down to the gently lapping waters of the Bosporus, which was good, because Istanbul was the kind of city that never slept. Mounting a ground assault on a compound in the center of one of the city's densely packed resi-dential blocks without the benefit of either support from local law enforcement or aerial cover would have been an invitation to disaster.

As it was, they all agreed that the tactical position was far from perfect. But, as Bruno growled, "Ain't that always the way..."

After several hours spent going over the available intel on Strelkin's residence, crew, and known security systems, the new arrivals bedded down for a few hours of needed shuteye.

As valuable as the addition of the CIA Special Operations Group team was for the successful accomplishment of Trapp's planned assault, another new recruit was equally vital. Dr. Timothy Greaves. But instead of carrying a rifle, Trapp judged that his specific suite of skills would be better employed in going head to head with the villa's security system. And besides, he was several thousand miles away.

"You reading me, Tim?" Trapp said softly, the throat mic that sat just above his collarbone sensitive enough to pick up the smallest of vibrations and convert them into usable audio.

"Loud and clear," Greaves said brightly, his voice typically taut with nervous energy. Trapp was never sure whether the NSA computer whiz – currently seconded to the Agency – was terrified of him, or whether the stress was simply as a result of the caffeine delivered directly into his system from the endless stream of Big Gulp cups of energy drink he guzzled through.

"What time is it there?" he asked, more to double-check that the comms system was truly working than for any great desire to make small talk.

The repercussions of the false flag attack on America's military satellites a couple of months before were still being felt in the Pacific, and the Air Force, along with several private space contractors, had spent the last few weeks blasting backup satellites into the skies. Luckily, though, most of the damage was confined to the skies over Asia. Trapp hadn't paid much attention while he was in Italy, but from what little news he'd read during his prolonged vacation, the analysts said that a runaway cascade of space debris had only narrowly been averted.

Thankfully, it was, which meant that Trapp and Ikeda were able to hook into the SOG team's digital communications net, which was capable both of short-range encrypted digital radio transmissions and long-range satellite link ups, meaning Trapp could coordinate both with the team on the ground, and the supporting elements back home. Tonight, that meant Tim Greaves.

"Coming up on 7 p.m.," Greaves replied.

Washington was seven hours behind Turkey, so it was almost two in the morning in Istanbul. The assault was scheduled for three in the morning, and the four-man CIA team had departed from the hotel suite several hours earlier to achieve their first objective.

Trapp's plan was unvarnished. It relied more on the element of surprise and overwhelming force than guile. But sometimes that was the way it had to be. Sometimes you weren't given the opportunity to build a mockup of the target compound and spend a month taking it down again and again under the watchful eye of instructors who had forgotten more than you would ever learn.

No, sometimes you just had to get the job done, relying on muscle memory greased a thousand times before, and skills acquired on nights just like tonight.

A rule of thumb in combat operations is that the attacker should outnumber the defender three to one. Less than that, and too much is left to chance. On this occasion, the ratio was questionable at best. But that was simply the hand they had been dealt. The plan was as old as time – a pincer assault, attacking both sides of Strelkin's compound at the same time and using the cover of night and the natural human inclination to exhaustion.

"Okay, Hangman," came the whispered voice of the CIA team leader through Trapp's headset. "We're holding tight just off the beach."

"What do you see?" Trapp asked.

"Lasers," came the soft-voiced reply. "A hell of a lot of 'em. Your boy better take them out, or we ain't going anywhere fast."

"Copy that," Trapp said, his voice registering no trace of emotion at the expected news. "Hold fast in your current position. How long do you need to hit the beach?"

"Sixty seconds from your mark," Rich replied. "Any faster and we might get spotted."

"Understood. Hangman out."

Trapp switched channels, reflecting that this was an officer's job. Back in Delta, some snot-nosed, newly-qualified but irritat-

ingly competent lieutenant fresh out of the Operator Training
Course would have handled comms and coordinated the
assault. It was a good shoot if the team leader never had to fire
his weapon. That was the job of trigger-pulling grunts like
Jason Trapp himself.

But the Hangman suspected he wouldn't have that luxury
tonight.

"You hear that, Greaves?" he asked, thumbing his mic.

"Loud and clear," came the man's excited reply. "It's what we
expected. Laser beams covering the rear approach. Hopefully
no pressure sensors, but even if they are there, as long as they're
on the same system, it doesn't matter. If you can plug me into
the alarm panel, I can give you two minutes. Long enough to
get into the house. After that, you're on your own."

Greaves, Trapp thought, had acclimatized incredibly well to
his new role supporting front-line operations. He had an
excitable personality, and questionable eating habits, but he
was damn good at his job, perhaps the best hacker, or computer
programmer, or whatever the hell he wanted to be called, that
Trapp had ever met. Certainly the best he'd ever worked with.
The top talent usually went to Silicon Valley, not the Central
Intelligence Agency.

"I need five, Tim," Trapp demanded. "Five minutes to hit
the house. Two is cutting it damn fine."

"No can do," Greaves replied, his voice carrying over a
rustle on the line. "That's –"

"Tim, stop shaking your damn head. It's blowing out my
eardrum."

"Sorry," came the muted reply.

"You were saying?"

"That's not how this works. Not from the exterior alarm
terminal, anyway. You get inside, get to the central control unit,
I'll give you all the time in the world. Strelkin is using a pretty
high-end system, with hard-coded access privileges, the whole

works. I can make the system reboot from an exterior terminal, which takes exactly 120 seconds, but if you don't get to that central panel in time, there isn't anything I can do to stop it lighting up. Not from here, anyway."

"Great." Trapp grimaced. He'd known that was what Greaves was going to say, but wanted to test him anyway, just in case he could pull a rabbit out of his hat. But that wasn't happening tonight.

"Okay kid," Trapp grunted. "Stay frosty. Hangman out."

Trapp swiveled in his seat and glanced at Ikeda, whose eyes were glued to a night vision scope, studying Strelkin's villa from a distance. "You listening to all that?"

"Uh huh."

"You ready?"

Ikeda tore her eyes away from the scope. In the gloom of the back of the van, Trapp could barely see her pupils, and like his, her face was darkened with camo paint, so she loomed from the darkness like a predator, her white teeth flashing ominously as she opened her mouth to speak. "I guess we'll find out..."

"Let's go," Trapp murmured.

Ikeda reacted without acknowledging him, checking that her Heckler and Koch MP-7 suppressed submachine gun was secured to the strap around her shoulder. The second she was satisfied it was, she smoothly opened the van's rear door and slipped out.

Trapp followed close behind. They both paused the second the van's doors were shut, ears cocked and listening for any sign that the slight movement had been detected.

"We're on the move," Trapp murmured into his throat mic. "Get ready."

"Copy that," Rich replied. "We'll be there."

You better be, Trapp thought, but did not say.

There was nothing more dangerous than an operation going off half-cocked, with half the assault force taken off the chessboard before things even really got going. There were a thousand things that could go wrong, eliminating the SOG team and leaving Trapp and Ikeda exposed to the full force of Strelkin's guards.

The lawn that led down to the water's edge could be mined, a high-explosive anti-personnel charge just waiting to blow off someone's leg, and wake the living dead, or else the paranoid Russian mercenary could have a guy set up with a machine gun overlooking the rear of the compound.

It wasn't *likely*, but it was possible. And that was the eternal dilemma of any ops planning officer – the crippling fear that they had overlooked something that would get a man killed.

In an ideal world, Trapp would have planned this differently. He would've used more men, to start with, and inserted them by air, rappelling down onto the roof, the lawn, and finally blowing a hole through the compound's outer walls to hit the villa from three directions before its inhabitants knew what the hell was going on.

Instead of interrogating Strelkin on-site, he would have extracted him by air, taken him to a black site, and gotten out of the danger zone.

"Let's move," Trapp whispered to Ikeda, shaking his head to clear it.

There was no sense in thinking about what could have been, especially now. That was a dangerous elixir, and one that would only scramble his mind, not help him get the job done.

The two CIA operators clutched their weapons and moved in a low crouch to the cover of a patch of scrub about thirty yards from the corner of the outer walls of the Strelkin compound. Again, they paused, sniffing the air to determine whether they had been detected, but found nothing. This time, Trapp tapped Ikeda's shoulder instead of talking. From here on out, they would communicate only through hand signals.

Slung over Ikeda's back was the suppressed shotgun. It would still be loud, but hopefully the weapon's bark would be reduced enough that it could be mistaken for the cough of an engine on the river. Trapp had an equally vital weapon, though one that was considerably less lethal. He cradled the canvas bag that held it like it contained a Faberge egg, not a rubberized, drop-resistant military-grade computer tablet.

Trapp tapped his throat mic twice, the pre-agreed signal that he was in position.

"I'm ready," Greaves replied immediately, his voice tight, professional.

One further tap signaled that Trapp understood. He quietly unzipped the bag and removed the tablet, cringing at the sound that the action produced, which was like a boulder tumbling through a shale rock field. Still, it was quickly over, and there was no sign of movement inside.

Trapp held the tablet up in front of him.

"Okay," Greaves murmured softly. "Remove the front of the panel. Do it slowly. I've got the circuit diagram in front of me, so as long as it hasn't been modified, then we should be fine. Still..."

Should be?

Trapp raged silently, unable to speak but desperate to chew Greaves out regardless. But he resisted, mastering the urge.

A single tap. He understood.

Trapp lodged the tablet into a strap on the front of his body armor, which kept it more or less in position, and removed a small screwdriver from inside the bag, which he used to loosen the front panel, one screw at a time, but leaving all of them in place. He could hear the hacker's breath in his headset, loud and heavy, and several times he thought he heard the crunch of food, or the crackle of a candy wrapper, which really pissed him off.

Next, he clicked a shielded flashlight on. It only cast a tiny beam, throwing barely enough light to see what he was doing, let alone be noticed. Still, he hid any excess light leakage with his hand as he shone the beam around the alarm panel, checking to see if there was any divergence with what Greaves had briefed him to expect. There wasn't.

But then again, he wasn't a damn alarm technician...

Gingerly, holding his breath, Trapp picked off the screws and removed the alarm system's metal panel.

"Give me some light, Trapp," Greaves said.

He grimaced, but did as he was told, shining the beam of the flashlight onto the exposed panel.

"Okay," came the reply, accompanied with a sigh of relief. "It's what we expected."

A single tap.

"You ready?" Greaves asked.

Again, a single tap.

"Okay, let's get started. You should see a bundle of electric cables, and then a thin, flat one, right? The light's not so good on the camera image."

Trapp flashed a thumbs up to the camera, indicating that he agreed.

"You're looking for the flat one. It's a fiber-optic cable. It runs to the central control unit. It should be attached to the keypad."

He squinted and then saw it before turning his head and flashing a signal to Ikeda to get ready. As he was turning back, he saw her communicate the message to the team waiting on the water, with a pre-agreed sequence of dashes over the radio.

"Yeah, you got it," Greaves said excitedly. "Don't pull it out until you're ready, okay?"

Thanks for the pep talk, buddy, Trapp thought, rolling his eyes. He realized that Greaves was treating him the same way he would handle a soldier fresh out of boot camp – like a live grenade, just waiting to blow up in his hands.

A single tap.

"Okay, when you pull the cable, you've got about two seconds to plug it into the tablet and initialize the routine. Any longer than that and the system will trip out. You got that?"

Greaves paused, but before Trapp replied he heard a sound like a palm slapping against a forehead. "Oh, that's right, you can't speak. My bad. Okay then, when you're ready..."

25

Rich swiveled his neck to look at his men, who had their bellies pressed against the deck of a low rubber dinghy, eyes trained on the target compound just fifty yards away across the placid water. The boat was just a civilian model, not designed for this purpose, but with a low profile and a quiet outboard motor, and would do the job as well as anything the DOD paid fifty times as much to acquire.

"That's the signal, boys," he murmured, acknowledging Ikeda's communication with two clicks on his radio. "Let's move."

Bruno started the motor, and it immediately chugged into life. Rich would have preferred to row or swim his way in, but it hadn't been possible to acquire either tanks, oars or flippers in the truncated time available to plan this op, so it had to be done the old-fashioned way.

The dinghy cut through the water slowly, barely leaving a wake as the motor drove it forward, but hewing exactly to the strict timeline ticking in the team leader's mind as he studied the landing point. Laser beams were still sweeping the villa's rear approach in unpredictable patterns, as visible as the trail left by a missile in the night sky through his night vision scope.

He knew that even if Hangman did his job, those beams would keep sweeping the night sky, searching for intruders, and sending back information to the alarm system's central unit. He would have no way of knowing whether the message was getting through until they hit the lawn, and probably not even then. The first sign they might get of discovery could be a stream of bullets chewing up someone's torso.

Thirty seconds.

Rich pushed away the premonitions of disaster and watched the lawn get closer and closer, his grip on his suppressed submachine gun firm. It was attached to his flak vest by an idiot cord, a lesson drilled into him by a sergeant long ago, a man who was as hard as a woodpecker's lips. Now it came second nature.

Fifteen seconds.

His men were silent, poised, ready for action, the only soundtrack the low groan of the boat's engine and the ragged breaths of men preparing to enter combat. They were some of the best men he had ever served alongside – not just the best of the best, but the best of the best of the *best*.

And that's a fucking mouthful.

It was, but as the last few seconds before the opening of their assault window ticked away, the truth of the statement was self-evident in Rich's mind. In the units they had been plucked from, mainly Delta and SEAL Team Six, they were known as men who paired controlled aggression and risk-taking with intelligence and decision-making that was second to none.

But almost alone in the great pantheon of American special forces units were the teams of the Agency's Special Operations Group. Unlike Delta, or the SEALs, his boys rarely got the luxury of an Air Force gunship hovering overhead, or a funeral with full military honors if something went wrong. No, if they screwed up, or even if they did everything right, but things still went to shit, no one would ever know their names. The Agency sure as hell wouldn't admit they had boots on the ground in a friendly country like Turkey. It was just how the game was played.

The clock hit zero at the precise moment the dinghy brushed the mud at the bottom of the black river and came to a halt.

"Go, go, go," he intoned, his voice low but clearly audible. A length of line was already attached to a metal stake, which he jammed into the hard-baked Turkish turf, securing the boat so their exit route didn't drift away.

His men surged onto the grass, not bothering to dodge the infrared laser beams that swept the villa's garden. What mattered now was speed. They had exactly 120 seconds to get up the lawn, enter the house, and wipe out everyone inside.

"Don't get tempted to waste the prick," he reiterated over the net. "Strelkin stays alive. Everyone else is fair game."

There was no response. None was needed.

They sprinted from the river toward a small outhouse at the bottom of the lawn. That was the first checkpoint. They ran in an uneven line, their weapon systems tight against their shoulders, ready to open fire with a second's notice. The house itself was dark, with only a few internal lights on and glowing through Rich's night vision goggles as bright as Vegas emerging from the dark of the Nevada desert.

How long had already elapsed? Five seconds? Two minutes was one hell of a tight schedule. They hit the outhouse. Andy and Bruno kept sprinting for the villa itself.

"Boss," Rhett groaned, his breath ragged from the strain. "Give me a boost."

The man's sniper rifle was slung over his shoulder, and Rich immediately dropped to a knee, offering up his interlinked palms for his operator's boot. "Ready?"

"You bet."

Rhett stepped on, and Rich boosted him up, letting out a low, involuntary grunt at the strain of the exertion. The second he was sure that the sniper was up, he followed behind his two other men.

"I'm in position," Rhett immediately stated over the radio net. "Nothing visible."

Rich was now ten seconds behind the other two members of his assault team. They were almost at the house.

And then one of the villa's outer doors opened.

"Shit," he breathed, the sound of his voice barely over a whisper. Had someone inside figured out what the hell was going on? If so, this could turn into a real shit show in no time at all.

"Take a knee," Rhett whispered. "I've got a shot."

Instantly, Rich did as he was instructed, watching as both Andy and Bruno followed suit ahead of him, silently holding their forward momentum, but keeping their weapons trained on this new development.

A man stepped out of the building, his head down. Was he armed? Through the glow of his night vision, it was impossible for Rich to say. If he was, it surely made no sense to leave the relative safety of the villa. Strelkin's men were trained, weren't they? That's what Hangman had said. It stood to reason that a man with even a basic grasp of tactics would know better than to expose himself to enemy fire.

Fuck, fuck, fuck.

Rich had to make a decision, and fast. Every second that drifted away was impossible to replace.

"Tell me what you see, Rhett," he murmured as quietly as he could.

"Hold," came the instant, calm reply.

Rich ground his teeth together. His sniper was acting in line with his training, but they didn't have time for that. Still, he knew better than to second-guess his man. Slow was smooth, and smooth – theoretically – was supposed to be fast.

"Okay, he's lighting up," Rhett finally whispered. "It's not Strelkin."

The decision was made in Rich's mind. He analyzed the situation, knowing both that Bruno was closer, and out of his sniper's field of fire. That meant that even if movement drew his attention, Rhett would be able to drop the Russian before the man had a chance to react. "Bruno, take him."

Instantly, a dark shape about ten yards away from the man, now smoking and leaning against the villa's exterior wall, rose like a wraith in the night.

Ninety seconds left, a quiet, insistent voice in Rich's mind reminded him.

He held his breath, waiting to see whether the smoker had noticed the change. Bruno took two measured paces forward, opened his stance, and fired two shots into the smoker's center mass. As the man began to fall, the operator sprinted forward once more, and fired a single safety round into the dead man's skull. It was an unpleasant business, but it had to be done. Dying men could be surprisingly noisy.

"Let's move," Rich growled. "They don't know we're here. Let's wake them the fuck up."

He got a muted, "Hell yeah," in response from someone, probably Bruno, who entered the villa first, through the open door the smoker had left behind. Real nice of him, Rich thought. Saved blowing through the glass with a shotgun.

"Tango down," Bruno said over the radio before Rich was even inside. He heard the telltale crack of a suppressed pistol, and then another. His headset crackled again, Bruno's voice, calm and businesslike. "Two."

Andy entered the building with his submachine gun up, sweeping from side to side as he was trained.

"I'm going upstairs," Bruno grunted over the net. "Cover me."

By the time Rich even made it into the villa, his aching bones protesting at the exercise after hours lying crouched at the bottom of the boat, he could only see the backs of his two men as they climbed the stairs, weapons drawn. He followed, but by the time he reached the top, it was already over.

26

Trapp entered Igor Strelkin's bedroom to find the man stark naked, with the barrel of a pistol jammed against his temple. The man's beady eyes were flicking frantically from side to side, as though he was searching for a way out of his current predicament. But given that his wrists were currently flex-cuffed behind his back and he was being held by a very pissed-off looking operator named Bruno, Trapp was certain he wasn't going to find one.

"How is he?" Trapp asked, jerking his chin at the prisoner. Ikeda entered after him and stood silently in the corner of the room, her dark eyes fixed intently on the man who had ordered her death.

Bruno shrugged. Trapp knew that the CIA special operator wanted nothing more than to put a bullet in the Russian's head. He didn't blame him.

"Alive," he said. "For now..."

Strelkin let out a strangled whimper, which Trapp took as a sign that the man comprehended English. "Who are you people?" he yelped, his command of the language strong, but nevertheless laced with a thick Russian accent. "You're fucking dead men, all of you."

Trapp ignored the man's frantic protests. "Did he cause you any trouble?" he said, directing his question at Bruno.

The operator let out a short, sharp, dismissive laugh. "This piece of shit? No chance." He sneered at his prisoner and jabbed Strelkin hard in his shoulder with the barrel of his pistol. "Closest he came was nearly pissing all over my boots."

Trapp hid a smile. "Sit him up on the bed."

Bruno nodded. "You want me to step out?"

He considered the question for a second. In an ideal world, the four-man CIA special forces team would never know who Igor Strelkin was, or why Trapp wanted to question him. But the events of the last few days had been anything but ideal, and there remained a very real possibility that he would need their help before this was over. Trapp glanced over his shoulder, meeting Ikeda's gaze, and they communicated silently.

Snapping his head back, he replied, "You can stay."

Trapp locked his eyes on to the Russian captive's. The man's pupils danced left and right, but slowly centered in his direction. Still speaking to Bruno, he said, "You okay disposing with this piece of shit?"

The reply came so swiftly Trapp wondered whether the Agency special operator knew he was playing bad cop, or whether he simply wanted to waste Strelkin that bad. He somehow suspected it was the latter. Not that he'd lose any sleep over it...

"You bet. You mind how it's done?"

Trapp shrugged. "Slowly. *Painfully.*"

Bruno nodded with satisfaction, a broad grin stretching across his face. "My kind of guy."

Strelkin watched the conversation develop with a mounting distress that was evidenced by the way his body began to shiver. Though the air-conditioning system was blasting out cold air,

Trapp guessed that it was fear, not the room's icy temperature that was causing the reaction.

"Who are you people?" the Russian moaned for a second time. "I can pay. If you leave now, I'll forget this ever happened."

Trapp looked over his shoulder to where Ikeda was standing impassively, her arms crossed. "You believe him?"

She sneered. "Not a damn word."

Right now, Trapp reflected, they were playing a three-way game of bad cop. It would probably be worth offering Strelkin a way out. But not yet. He'd let him sweat for a little longer.

"Do you know who I am, Igor?" he growled.

The Russian shook his head vigorously. His thin graying hair stuck to his forehead, limp with acrid, fearful sweat.

"Think harder."

"I swear, I've never met you before in my life. Please, I'll –"

"Pay?" Trapp laughed coldly. "I know. You suggested that already. Not why I'm here." He turned back to Ikeda. "What about you?"

An evil smile crossed her face. "Me neither."

Trapp shook his head. "I didn't think so. You see, Igor, I'm not here for your money. I'm here because you tried to kill me. Three days ago. You remember now?"

From the dawning light of comprehension now flaring in Strelkin's eyes, Trapp could tell that he did. But he detected another emotion now – outright terror. But was it of what they might do to him, or fear that someone else might find out?

"So you do remember." Trapp grinned.

"I've never met you in my life," Strelkin said, flecks of spittle flying from his mouth. "I'm a businessman. Why would I try and kill you?"

Trapp looked at Bruno. "If he lies to me again, shoot him in the knee."

"My pleasure," the powerful special operator crowed. He

lifted his pistol and aimed it menacingly in the direction of Strelkin's left kneecap. The Russian stared at him, his chest rising and falling rapidly, with snatched, terrified breaths.

The sight reminded Trapp of a nature documentary he'd seen as a child, set in the Serengeti in Africa. Even then, the documentary was old, and it depicted half a dozen native hunters, clad only in loin cloths that he suspected were donned more for the modesty of the viewers back home than because they were an accurate representation of local clothing preferences.

They chased a lame antelope for hours, until the poor beast's flanks were soaked with sweat and it could run no farther. The creature's mouth was coated with thick, white foam, and though it was clearly terrified as the hunters approached to put it out of its misery, it was spent, unable to move or think or run.

"It's the adrenaline, Igor," Trapp said in a clinical tone. "It's why you can't concentrate. It's why you can't breathe properly. Your body wants you to run, to get as far away from me as possible, but you can't – you know why?"

"Because if he does, he loses a kneecap?" Bruno interjected, his voice tight with mocking curiosity. "I ain't never seen a dude get far without one of those before."

Trapp turned shot the operator a black look. The man grimaced an apology.

"*Because*," Trapp emphasized, "you're a coward, Igor. You send people to do your dirty work, and you live here in luxury, drinking your nights away, hiding from the consequences of what you've done. Of the lives you condemned for your thirty pieces of silver. And"—he grinned—"because if you try and run, my friend here will shoot you in the knee."

He paced backward and forward in front of the bound captive, as if pondering his next question. Then he spun in place and fixed his gaze on Igor Strelkin once more. "So I'll ask you this once, Igor. And if I don't like the answer, I'll start carving bits off you, one by one. Do you understand?"

A hurricane of emotions crossed Strelkin's face. Trapp had seen the exact same process play out more times than he could remember. As a rule, he preferred not to torture people. For a start, it didn't work – at least, no better than simply building a rapport with a captive and convincing them that it was in their best interests to cooperate.

But when he was forced to interrogate someone, that someone was usually senior, experienced – so far removed from the consequences of their actions, for so long, that when they were confronted with the long arm of the law catching up with them, they didn't know how to react.

Strelkin nodded.

Trapp cupped his ear, leaned forward, and in a menacing, singing-song tone spat, "I can't hear you, Igor..."

"Yes, yes," the Russian panted, his head bobbing up and down as if to reinforce his point. "I understand. I hear you. But –"

"Oh, Igor," Trapp said, his nose curling from the odor of alcohol that emanated from his captive in waves, "it was all going so well. Here's how this is going to work. You tell me exactly what I want to know, no ifs, no buts, and I let you live. But if you lie to me, or I even *suspect* that you're holding out on the truth, you will die."

"You don't understand," Strelkin moaned. "I just did what I was told to do."

"The following orders defense didn't work at Nuremberg, and it sure as shit ain't gonna work now," Trapp grunted. "But just for a moment, let's pretend you're right. You were just following orders. Tell me who gave those orders, and you live."

Strelkin looked from him to Ikeda to Bruno and then repeated the process all over again, his dark eyes wet with terror and searching for sympathy.

He found none. He choked out a sob, shrugged, and said, "If I tell you, I die. If I don't tell you, I die. So what's in it for me?"

Trapp chewed his lip, as though he was truly considering the question. He wasn't. Not really. Ever since he'd seen the Russian mercenary boss drinking in the upscale restaurant the night before, he'd known that the man couldn't possibly be the person who'd given the order for him to die. He was just a glorified trigger-puller, a man who was paid – and paid well, judging by his opulent villa – to make problems go away.

Problems like him and Ikeda.

No, this was exactly what he wanted. For Strelkin to crack. To reveal himself for what he really was – a cowardly, transactional piece of crap. And one who would trade his life for information.

Trapp squatted down in front of his prisoner and molded his face into a reasonable, almost sympathetic expression. "You tell me who paid you to kill me," he said, "and I give you my word I'll let you live."

"Hey!" Bruno protested, unable to stop himself. Trapp glanced up to see him wince sheepishly before apparently determining that he'd already put his foot in his mouth, so he might as well blunder on.

He shrugged self-consciously. "I mean, I thought you said I could kill him."

Trapp wanted to chew the operator out. An interrogation was like a well-functioning restaurant kitchen – it wasn't just that too many cooks spoil the broth, but that someone needed to be in charge, to be the one calling the shots, or it all fell apart. That someone was him, not Bruno.

But then again, he considered, in the other man's shoes, he'd probably have said the same damn thing. He shrugged dismissively. "You can shoot him in the knee. How about that?"

Strelkin squealed in horror at the prospect of being maimed. He shook his head violently from side to side, body flopping on the bed like a fish out of water. Trapp delivered a swift, powerful, yet measured backhand that echoed around the room, and stunned the man into silence.

Bruno grimaced with distaste. "If we let him live, you know as well as I do that he'll only go back to slaughtering innocents. I know his type. He won't stop as long as someone's paying him."

"Both knees, then," Trapp said.

"He doesn't need knees to keep on doing what he's doing."

"Point taken," Trapp agreed. His eyes flicked up as he considered his options. And then they snapped back onto the silent, trembling frame of Igor Strelkin, who looked a shadow of the man they'd seen the previous evening, holding court in one of Istanbul's most expensive restaurants. "How about this, then – if you ever so much as blink the wrong way ever again, I'll come back, and I won't kill you. You know what I'll do?"

Strelkin stared back, unblinking, curiosity mixing with abject fear in his eyes. Saliva glistened at the corners of his mouth. Trapp's face puckered with distaste.

"I'll drag you across the border to fucking Syria, and I'll take you to Aleppo. And I'll strip you naked, tie you to a stake in the ground, douse you in gasoline, and then leave a sign around your neck telling the locals who you are and what you've done."

"You wouldn't..." the Russian whispered.

"Oh believe me," Trapp said, a grim smile stretching across his face. "Nothing would make me happier. I hear burning is a horrible way to die, but somehow I think it suits you, Igor."

He glanced at the watch on his left wrist, more for show than anything else. "You have five seconds to give me your answer."

"Four."

"Three."

"Two."

Trapp's mouth was opening to deliver a death sentence on the Russian killer when a high-pitched squeal escaped Strelkin's lips. "Okay, okay," he blubbered. "I'll tell you."

"I want a name, Igor. Now."

The mercenary looked panicked, as though he knew what he was about to say might cost him his life, just as easily as Trapp himself. But Trapp was in front of him, and whoever his puppetmaster was, he was a long way away.

"Kholodov," he whimpered. "His name is Roman Kholodov."

27

W hite House Social Secretary Philippa Kohli was waiting at the bottom of the thin stairwell that led from the rear of the Residence, anxiously massaging one hand with the other.

"Relax, Philli." President Nash laughed warmly as he reached her side. "It'll go fine. It always does."

She nodded, though she didn't seem convinced. "Yes, sir," she said.

"Now, why don't you run me through who I'm supposed to be button-holing tonight?" Nash said, passing a decorative silver soup cauldron, polished within an inch of its life, which had sat in that particular White House hallway for longer than anyone could remember. He paused in front of it, fixing his tie, which had come slightly askew, and double-checked that a piece of spinach hadn't stowed away between his front teeth, or a smudge of lipstick on his collar.

Fat chance of that, he thought wryly.

Though a few of his predecessors in the job had seen the trappings of the office as the world's most powerful aphro-

disiac, sweeping the women of Washington off their feet,
mostly that had taken place before the twenty-four hour news
cycle – and worse, social media.

No, Nash knew that if he so much as looked at a woman the
wrong way, it would be plastered all over the Beltway's gossip
columns in an instant. The ambulance-chasers in the worst
sections of the media would stop at nothing to dig up dirt on
him, or worse, the 'lucky' individual who caught his eye. It
would be quite the woman who would be able to face the
endless media scrutiny. No, President Nash had decided some
time ago that so long as he remained in office, he would have to
keep his fly buttoned up.

It didn't help, of course, that the very top echelons of the
political game in Washington weren't just populated by the best
and brightest, but by the best looking, with the brightest smiles.
Like one Philippa Kohli, who was wearing an evening gown in a
deep, rich maroon that hugged her body and reminded Nash of
his own wife, twenty years earlier, before politics, the death of
his son, the campaign, and then the divorce.

"Mr. President?"

Nash looked up and saw that Philippa was looking at him
with a quizzical, scrunched expression on her face. He smiled
apologetically. "I'm sorry, I was miles away."

"No need to apologize, sir. As I was saying, it's just a small
dinner tonight. About sixty guests from the automotive industry. You'll be sitting next to Kieran Walsh, the President of the
United Autoworkers union."

The president grunted, knowing that Kohli's office would
have been bombarded with letters from each and every last one
of tonight's guests, all looking to curry political influence with
the nation's most powerful politician.

"And what does he want from me this week?" he said.

"A bailout for the plant down in North Carolina," she said.

"And Ramon Sanchez from GM is here tonight as well. I arranged the seating plan so they won't be close together, but..."

Nash shook his head and chuckled softly to himself. Ramon Sanchez, the CEO of General Motors, had only this week announced his intention to close a manufacturing plant and ship all the equipment down to Mexico, leaving several thousand employees – and most importantly for tonight's festivities – almost two thousand *union* employees looking for jobs in a town that simply didn't have any to offer.

"But Walsh will be looking for trouble, and Sanchez will be more than happy to give it to him," he finished.

"Precisely, sir," Philippa replied with a tired sigh that indicated she knew Sanchez's acerbic manner – and penchant for causing trouble – as well as he did.

They rounded the corner and entered the hallway that led to the East Room, the magnificent reception room in the East Wing of the White House that had hosted hundreds, perhaps thousands of such events. Nash stopped in his tracks, turned to his social secretary, and asked, "How do I look?"

"Great, Mr. President," she replied, shooting him a smile. "Knock 'em dead."

Nash knew that his staff were protective of him, especially after the way that his political opponents had weaponized the disintegration of his marriage during the campaign. He saw them as family more than he did employees, and he felt they treated him the same way, though in his position it was hard to tell.

He also knew that tonight's dinner – although easily derided as just another stop on Washington's cocktail circuit – was of the utmost importance. The American economy had been rocked, not just in the preceding few months with the Bloody Monday terrorist attacks and the crisis in the Pacific, but through successive years of industrial malaise. Her people were hurting, and the companies that had once turned America's heartland into the engine of the world were now fleeing in search of cheaper labor and laxer regulation.

Tonight was about showing those same companies that America was open for business once again, and that her president planned to clear away every barrier they might face in the pursuit of that success.

Marine sentries in dress blues snapped crisp salutes as their president entered the East Room, and he reflexively returned the honor. He barely noticed as his Secret Service detail updated his position to their control room. The buzz of conversation died instantly as he entered the room, as though the proximity of power had somehow sucked the oxygen from the throats of the assorted throng, but a light, forgettable tune played from the ballroom piano that sat on the far side of the room, avoiding an awkward silence.

Nash accepted a glass of champagne from an attentive steward, raised it with a politician's broad smile, and said, "Don't stop on my account, ladies and gentlemen."

A titter of laughter broke out, and every face in the room turned in his direction. Nash winced internally. It was a constant challenge to remain grounded in this job. It wasn't just that an Air Force lieutenant colonel with a briefcase chained to his wrist was always within thirty feet of him, theoretically giving him the option of slow-roasting every square inch of Russia within hours, it was that when you were president, people laughed at every single one of your jokes.

Whether they were funny or not.

"The Navy has prepared a great spread for us tonight, and I'm sure I'll have a couple of moments to see each of you in person. Now, here's to getting to know all of you a little better."

Nash raised his glass and toasted no one in particular,

watching as the rest of the room aped him. He saw the squat, bullish UAW President, Walsh, already making a beeline for him. Typically, the man, a third-generation auto-worker from Detroit, had a beer in his beefy arms rather than a champagne flute.

The president beckoned a waiting steward over, pressed the glass of champagne into his hands, and said under his breath, "Get me a beer, will you? Quick as you can."

Philippa Kohli, ever-present at his side during these events, mainly to whisper people's names to him so that he didn't have to remember – or fail to remember and make a fool of himself – whispered, "Good move, sir. Walsh is real salt of the earth."

The white-jacketed Navy steward disappeared, and Nash turned back in the oncoming union man's direction. "Don't I know it," he muttered back.

As he was raising his arm to shake Walsh's hand, the lights went out.

You have got to be fucking kidding me, Nash thought, grinding his teeth together with frustration as, within seconds of darkness falling, several flashlights clicked on, presumably held by members of his Secret Service detail.

As protocol dictated, two agents hardened up on the president's position, suit jackets open at the waist, and hands lingering near their weapons.

"Sir, you'll have to come with us," one of the two men said, his voice clipped and professional, clearly former military.

President Nash leaned forward, placing his lips just a few inches from one of the man's cauliflower ears. "Son, unless a nuke is about to fall on the East Wing, I'm not going anywhere. And you can quote me on that. Understood?"

The agent looked up at him, though in the darkness, amidst the shadows thrown by battling flashlight beams, Nash couldn't make out his expression. He suspected that the man was wondering whether to simply bundle him out of the reception room and take him down to the bunker thirty feet beneath their feet.

"Sir, protocol –"

"Screw protocol," Nash grunted, a little more firmly than he'd intended. He shot the man an apologetic look, though doubted he could see it. More quietly, he said, "These people are here because I wanted to show them that America is working. If I run off and lock myself in a vault because of a freaking power cut, it will be the talk of the town by morning, and I may as well kiss the economy goodbye."

He could sense that the Secret Service agent in front of him didn't really give a damn about the economy, and that was fair enough. It wasn't his job to care – but it was Nash's. So unless they physically bundled him with them, he wasn't moving.

"Ladies and gentlemen," Nash said, raising his voice above the nervous chatter that had begun to fill the large room. "It seems that we're having minor technical difficulties, but it shouldn't be long now until –"

The generators in the White House basement kicked in, and a second later the glass chandeliers overhead were glowing with electric light. Nash's pupils shrank as night turned into day, but he hid the reaction as best he could.

Without missing a beat he said, "– we get the power back on. See?"

An anxious chuckle filled the room, though from fewer mouths then had laughed at his terrible joke a few minutes earlier. He clapped his hands together, knowing with a politician's innate instinct that he needed to take charge.

"Music!" Nash bellowed, searching for the pianist. "That's what we need."

The woman in question flinched as half the eyes in the room turned on her, cleared her throat anxiously, and began to play.

His chief of staff, Emma Martinez, entered the reception

room as the notes began to ring out, an anxious look on her face. She mastered the expression as she waded through the crowd of distracted guests, but Nash instantly knew that something was wrong. "Sir, don't react, but you're needed in the situation room."

28

"What are you going to do with him?" Trapp asked, referring to Igor Strelkin. The Russian mercenary leader was trussed up and currently the sole resident of the trunk of a rental car, a filthy rag stuffed in his mouth, and a length of duct tape across his lips.

Rich, the SOG team leader, spat a thin stream of tobacco juice against the concrete floor of the hotel's underground parking lot and shrugged. "I know a guy. He'll take care of him for a few days. Won't be pleasant, for Igor anyway, but he won't be talking."

Trapp raised an eyebrow. "But he'll live?"

"Why do you care?" Rich asked, seeming genuinely interested.

"I gave him my word," Trapp replied simply. "I won't go back on it. Not even for him."

Rich squinted, but apparently decided it wasn't worth his time to argue. "Your way it is," he said. "My guy will cut him free when you're done with"—he paused—"with whatever it is you're doing, anyway. Don't s'pose you fancy filling me in on exactly what that is?"

Trapp shook his head. "It's need to know, and right now –"

Rich laughed in spite of himself, and finished the joke. "– I don't need to know. I get it. I don't reckon you're gonna tell me if all this has something to do with the power going out back home, either?"

Trapp fixed him with an intense stare. "No, I don't think I am. But stay frosty. I've got a feeling that this is going to get worse before it gets better, and if it does, you and your team will be right in the middle of it."

"Sure," the team leader replied. "We'll be here if you call."

Trapp stuck out his hand, and Rich pumped it twice.

"I appreciate it," he said, tossing the CIA special operator the keys to the rental. "Take care of her."

Rich looked distinctly unimpressed at the size of the dinky little European town car as he snatched the jangling keys out of the air.

"Anything hits us in that thing," he replied, "I won't need to hold Bruno back from the piece of shit Russian in the trunk. We'll all be toast."

The remaining three members of the hit squad were already long gone, having departed on the very same boat on which they'd made their insertion. A cursory search of the place had been carried out, to identify any glaring pieces of forensic evidence they might have left behind, but the heavy lifting would be done by several incendiary devices that were now set all around the villa and programmed to go off a little before dawn. Trapp glanced down at his watch and saw that that was any moment now.

He wondered how the avaricious Russian would react when he learned that his home had been reduced to cinders. Then again, Trapp knew that would be the least of his concerns. He'd instructed Greaves to drain Strelkin's bank accounts, even the ones he thought the CIA didn't know about. By the time Rich's men let him go, every blood-stained dollar he had ever earned would be gone, donated anonymously via a shell company to a charity set up to take care of children orphaned by the war in Syria.

It was fitting enough. He wondered if Strelkin would agree, but decided he really didn't give a shit.

"Drive safe," Trapp replied.

Rich threw a mock-salute and pushed the button on the rental car's remote control. It chirruped twice, the headlights blinking on and off, and he turned to leave without another word.

"So," Ikeda murmured as they watched the last of the CIA team depart, gunning the small car's engine and squealing as he drove out of the parking lot with unnecessary haste. "What now?"

Trapp didn't reply all at once. He needed time to think, but as usual, events were moving too fast to allow sufficient processing time. Rich's question whether there was a connection between tonight's takedown and the power going out all across the continental United States was a perceptive one. He was certain that the man was right, and that everything that had happened from Sokolov's murder, right through the events in Italy and now the apparent involvement of this Roman Kholodov, was all connected.

He just didn't know how.

"We need to go to Russia," he said.

Ikeda barely flinched at his proposal. That was what he liked about her. He'd just suggested they venture into the belly of the beast, place their collective heads between a tiger's maw, or any of a dozen other trite clichés, and yet her decision was already made. Wherever he went, she would be right there at his side. She wasn't the following type.

"Are you going to book flights, or shall I?" she replied.

He winked. "Atta girl."

Ikeda leaned against his arm as they began the walk back up to the hotel suite. "So..." she ventured. "You got a plan?"

"Depends how you define 'plan.'"

She glared at him. "Spill it, Jason."

"All right, all right," he replied, a grin stretching across his face that was perhaps unwarranted, given the particular conundrum they currently faced.

"The way I see it, we have two options." He counted them out on his hand. "First, we go pay this Kholodov prick a visit. Run the Strelkin playbook again, bust in under the cover of darkness and do whatever it takes to make him talk."

Ikeda looked up at him doubtfully. "Sounds risky. Plus if he's smart, he'll know someone took Igor out, and he'll be on his guard."

He sighed. "Yeah, I don't like that one either. Kholodov is ex-KGB, and he's spent a decade as President Murov's personal bodyguard. His security will be top-notch. And I'd prefer not to infiltrate Rich and his guys into Russia if I can avoid it. Better to go in under the radar, poke around, see if we can't find some answers."

"So what's the second option?"

"Something we need to do anyway. Sokolov sent me a message. Whatever it was must have been important enough for him to risk his life to do so. Let's go find out what he wanted to say."

They stopped in front of the double set of elevator doors, and Ikeda pushed the button to call it. It lit up, and she stepped back. "Sounds good," she said, chewing her lip.

"You don't look convinced," he replied.

The elevator dinged, and the steel doors opened smoothly, to reveal an empty cabin, the floor-length mirror smudged from where a previous traveler had leaned against it. As they entered, Trapp's mind was filled with the endless details of what needed to happen next. The people they would need to see, the equipment they would need to acquire the things –

Ikeda's lips closed on his, and suddenly that train of thought evaporated, replaced instead with something altogether more inviting.

She broke away, and his vision was filled with the captivating sight of her slate gray eyes, the flush blossoming on her cheeks spelling out her desire as plain as day. "It's a good plan," she said, panting slightly as if overcome by what she had just done. "But we don't need to go tonight. The world can wait a few hours."

Trapp hadn't actually intended to hail a cab and head straight for the airport, so he was more than happy to let this unexpected – but auspicious – turn of events play out exactly as Ikeda wanted. He pouted. "Only a few?"

Ikeda pushed him up against the mirror, her lips hungrily meeting his own, her fingers running through his hair. The assault was as unexpected as it was enjoyable, and as the elevator doors closed behind them, Trapp forgot there was a world out there, and lost himself entirely in her touch.

She broke away, a wicked glint dancing in her slate eyes, leaving her prey panting in her wake. "We'll see about that."

29

The two men departed Leningradskiy Railway Station at 10:15 p.m., settling into a sleeper cabin booked several days earlier by a stranger that they had never, nor would ever meet. The two tickets were purchased with a pre-paid debit card, which was included in a thick manila envelope alongside two fresh passports and a second, smaller envelope.

Upon opening this, they found the address of the safe house to which they had been instructed to head to straight after completing their mission. Fifteen minutes after being unsealed – and thus exposed to oxygen—the small square of chemically-treated paper would be unreadable. Still, one of the two men, a thin, wiry individual of Georgian ancestry, took extra care to tear the instructions into dozens of pieces, each smaller than the last, then swallow them dry.

The name in his passport was Anatoly.

The other man, Yuri, was short, squat, with a boxer's nose and ears and a stocky, swaggering walk that always reminded his partner of a bulldog, or when he was feeling less kind, a silverback gorilla.

"How long will this take?" Yuri grunted, tearing open the plastic packaging around one of the fresh bundle of sheets that had been placed on top of each of the thin mattresses. "It's as hot as balls in here."

Anatoly sighed, closed his eyes and prayed that someone up there would give him the patience to last the journey. "You know how long," he said. "Fifteen hours, if we're lucky."

He couldn't see his partner's face, but he'd worked with the man long enough to know what was coming next. "I need a drink. Something strong."

"You can't," Anatoly chided. "We have our orders. When we're done, I'll drink with you for a week."

When they were done, he knew, he would *need* to drink for a week. Probably longer. He had done things in the service of his country that would sicken most ordinary men. There were those – many – who would simply never understand what the service of one's country sometimes required. Anatoly was not one of them. He was willing to get his hands dirty. But the things he had done still affected him. Drinking helped. For a while.

"Screw that," Yuri snorted. "You said it yourself. We don't arrive till past noon. I can have a drink. Hell, I could have a fucking bottle if I wanted. Who's going to know?"

Anatoly liked his partner, as much as he ever really liked anyone. It didn't bother the wiry Russian that Yuri was a rapist, or that he beat every woman he spent more than a night with, and even some of those. After all, Anatoly figured, who wasn't, and who didn't? That was par for the course, especially in the circles he ran in.

But if it came to it, he would put a bullet in the man's temple, and he wouldn't lose a night's sleep over it. He hoped, of course, that that eventuality wouldn't come to pass. Because, after all, he liked Yuri.

Then again, he liked money more. And the job they had

been given paid well, very well, and held out the prospect of far more lucrative work in the future.

And Yuri's problem was that he couldn't always keep his mouth shut. That wasn't an issue when the job was silencing some dumb bitch of a reporter who got too close to a story that wasn't any of her damn business. But when it came to something like this...

Anatoly opened his eyes, ran his tongue across the front of his teeth and grimaced. Yes, he would put a bullet in Yuri's temple if he needed to. But that would leave a body, and a body meant questions. Getting rid of a body was risky.

So it would be better all around to talk the man out of it.

"Beer," he grunted. "And only a couple. Get me one while you're at it."

"Beer!" Yuri snorted. "I told you, I want something hard. Something that will put me to sleep." Anatoly could hear his head rustling against the thin plastic casing of his mattress. "There's no point in that watery shit. It'll just have me pissing all night."

"It's beer or nothing," Anatoly said, lacing his voice with a harder edge.

He was the smaller of the two men, by a long way, at least by weight. But both knew that he could put Yuri down if he needed to. No weapon required. He was a killer. A child who had been born into a dying Soviet Union, a boy who had begged to survive, a teen who had scrapped and stolen and fought so he never had to beg again.

And a man who was feared throughout the Moscow underworld for feats of unmatched violence, a man with whom right-thinking individuals avoided making eye contact, for fear of provoking a mad, black rage. It was mostly, but not entirely, for show. Anatoly was usually in control. He just liked the fear his reputation elicited in others.

While Yuri was formulating a reply, Anatoly pulled a thin,

dog-eared paperback out of his rucksack. He had bought it at a second-hand book store in the Meshchansky District just a couple of hours earlier. It was a Russian translation of an American author, someone Anatoly had never heard of. It was a crime novel, about a serial killer preying on innocent women in Washington, and the FBI agent charged with tracking him down. Unlike most readers of the genre, Anatoly didn't picture himself in Agent Pope's shoes.

He saw himself as the killer.

The novel was simply research.

He hadn't acted on his desires, of course. Not yet, anyway. But one day, he would. Perhaps after this job.

"Beer it is, then," Yuri muttered ruefully, smacking his head against Anatoly's bunk as he clambered out of his own. "*Fuck.* I'll get you one."

"I thought you would."

~

THE TRAIN ARRIVED IN TALLINN, Estonia at 1:52 in the afternoon the next day. Anatoly had slept like a baby. Yuri grumbled that he was up all night, and judging by his bloodshot eyes and puffy complexion, Anatoly suspected that the man had not only drunk a couple more than the two beers promised, but something a little harder as well.

Tallinn train station was situated not far from the beautiful Baltic city's Old Town, but the two men were not there to sightsee. They found the car, a Skoda Octavia that was several years past its best, exactly where it was supposed to be, and retrieved the keys from where they were taped above one of the wheels.

The equipment they would need was in the trunk. Anatoly decided to drive. The last thing he needed was for the drunk in the passenger seat next to him to crash into something, and set them both on fire. Anyway, the final leg of their journey would only take a few hours. And with luck, Yuri would sleep through most of it.

"Does it bother you?"

"Does what bother me?" Anatoly asked, indicating left and guiding the batted Skoda down a cobbled street. He supposed that Riga, the capital of the small country of Latvia on the Baltic Sea, would be a beautiful city in the daytime. But it wasn't daytime, and he'd been driving five hours, listening to Yuri bitch about the women in his life not responding to discipline anymore, and being gassed by the man's second-hand cigarette smoke, so he wasn't too inclined to pay much attention to his surroundings, no matter what the guidebook said.

This comment, however, had come after several minutes of blessed silence. Anatoly had hoped that his beefy partner had tired himself out. Sadly, that didn't seem to be the case.

"What we're about to do."

Anatoly glanced at his partner, sitting in the passenger seat swallowed up inside a scuffed, dark brown leather jacket that had probably seen its best days even before the Berlin wall came down. He frowned. Yuri had never struck him as the kind of individual who was prone to attacks of conscience. He knew that because he'd seen the brute grab a bar girl by her pigtails and smash the poor woman's head into the bar half a dozen times, leaving her brain damaged, and then pour himself a drink by leaning over her unconscious body.

"If I did, I wouldn't be there," he replied. "Are you having second thoughts?"

Yuri shot a furtive look in his partner's direction. He knew better than to admit his true feelings, but they were written plainly enough on his squashed, scarred face. He was uncomfortable with their mission, and that was a problem. Anatoly could do it by himself, of course, but two bodies were better than one. Besides, Anatoly knew that sprinting wasn't his partner's strong suit, and as the old joke went, he didn't need to be able to run faster than the cops, he just needed to be able to run faster than Yuri.

He found a parking space by the side of the road, guided the Skoda into it, and killed the engine. The keys jangled, and then a silence filled the car's cabin, punctuated only by Yuri's shallow, panting breaths. Anatoly wrinkled his nose. He didn't know when he had come to the conclusion that Yuri needed to die. Perhaps it really was at the start of their journey together. But either way, he knew it now.

As long as his partner lived, the man would be a liability. Not just to their mission, or the man who had hired them – Anatoly's future patron, or so he hoped – but to Anatoly himself. And that was the realization that truly sealed the man's fate.

"Of course not," Yuri blustered. "I was just asking the question."

Anatoly nodded slowly, taking the measure of the man beside him. Did he need to act now? "Good," he said slowly, stretching out each syllable. "Because I need you by my side, Yuri. You can't freeze. Not tonight."

Yuri threw up his hands, as though he was offended by the suggestion. A spark of fire had finally ignited in the man's belly, Anatoly observed dispassionately. "Of course I won't freeze!" he protested. "You know me better than that."

"Then let's speak no more of it," Anatoly said, pulling the keys free of the ignition.

They waited there for two hours, studying their target, a grand twentieth century art nouveau building on the corner of a block, and waiting both for employees to depart at the end of a long business day, and the traffic in the area to diminish. And then finally, it was time.

Anatoly popped the trunk and removed a large black hiking rucksack from inside. The contents clinked as he pulled it onto his back. Beside him, Yuri did the same. The equipment inside wasn't sophisticated. But then again, not only did it not need to be, but the lack of refinement was intentional.

A rectangular black case was all that remained on the felt lining at the bottom of the trunk. Anatoly opened it and removed a weapon that was commonly available on the black market in this part of the world, an SR-2 'Veresk' submachine gun, along with several clips of ammunition. He handed the weapon and ammo to Yuri, and then removed a second for himself. He loaded it, selected full-auto on the switch on the left-hand side, and made it ready to fire.

"Let's go," he grunted.

Now that the task was at hand, Yuri's prior bout of nerves seemed to have subsided. Either that, or the Moscow gangland hitman had decided that it was in his best interests to swallow his conscience until the job was done. He pushed the trunk closed and followed Anatoly.

What they were about to do wasn't subtle. That was kind of the point. They walked toward the embassy, until they could see the red, white and blue Eagle-headed flag of the Russian Federation dancing in a light summer breeze, visible in the spotlights that shone up onto the face of the building. Perhaps as a boy the sight might have roused a swell of patriotism in Anatoly's breast, or given him second thoughts about what he was about to do. Then again, as a boy he'd stolen and stabbed his way to the top of a tiny heap of shit, and adulthood hadn't changed him much either.

Once they were within fifteen yards, Anatoly made out a plump, balding security guard in a guard booth on the corner of the building, staring down at a glowing screen.

"Keep an eye on him," he said in a low voice as he removed the rucksack from his shoulder.

Yuri muttered an acknowledgment, but he wasn't paying attention. Inside the rucksack were five or six glass bottles, the shape of milk bottles, and a can of spray paint. He turned to Yuri.

"I'll take the south side," he said. "Kill the guard first. Quietly."

His partner shrugged. "As you wish."

A surge of adrenaline exploded into Anatoly's veins, making him momentarily lightheaded. He pulled the open rucksack back onto his shoulder, but kept the can of spray paint in his hand. He walked toward the side of the embassy building, in full view of a security camera which he knew perfectly well would not be recording, shook the can in his hand and listened to it rattle.

Without pausing, he sprayed the words *Krievu fašisti* and *izdrāzt* on the building's light gray walls. 'Russian fascists.' 'Go home.'

Over the sound of the aerosol, he heard Yuri's knuckles rapping against the window to the guard booth, a squeal of hinges, muted conversation, then a grunt as a blade entered the guard's neck. Anatoly grimaced. He would miss his partner when he was gone. But it had to be done.

The can went back in the rucksack. He pulled the lighter from the pocket of his pants and a Molotov cocktail from the bag.

"You ready?" he called out.

"Sure," came the unenthusiastic reply that would have sealed Yuri's fate, had Anatoly not already made his decision.

Anatoly lit the strip of cloth that hung out of the home-made incendiary and watched as the reflection danced off the glass windows and the remaining cocktails below. And then he hefted his arm back and let fly.

The Molotov cocktail impacted with a whumph, and the flames began to greedily lick at the gasoline that now coated the outer walls. From the other side of the building, where Anatoly knew a series of wooden balconies lay, as opposed to the stone front on his side, he heard the same sound as Yuri let loose his own arsenal.

A few seconds later, all five of Anatoly's cocktails were gone, the glass shattered, the liquid inside running in burning rivulets down the side of the Russian Embassy to the Republic of Latvia. He stepped back and grabbed hold of the Veresk submachine gun.

It didn't take long.

Just a few seconds later, the embassy's fire alarm began to ring out, a nails-on-chalkboard squeal that pierced the otherwise placid night sky. Anatoly watched the building burn with a hungry glee that was only matched by an almost orgasmic anticipation of what was going to happen next. All thoughts of guilt were long forgotten. They might come later, or they might not.

There would only be half a dozen personnel outside, he knew. Anyone important had been given the night off. The Russians inside were cubicle drones. Duty officers monitoring secure traffic that would never come, not to a tiny embassy to an irrelevant diplomatic backwater like Latvia. But they had their orders, and so they would die.

The door on his side of the building slammed open, and a young man, perhaps in his late 20s, stumbled out, holding a jacket over his mouth and coughing through the smoke. A woman followed behind, and then another. They looked half-asleep, but the rearmost girl, a plump, short woman, was squealing with fear.

Anatoly pretended he was simply an onlooker, hiding his weapon behind the now empty rucksack, waiting until they were all in view.

"Shit, man. What the hell is going on?" the male refugee from the building yelled, his voice slack with horror.

Anatoly shrugged, but before he had a chance to reply, the staccato chatter of Yuri's submachine gun rang out. The embassy worker spun on his heel in search of this new disaster. He didn't see Anatoly's arm cutting through the air. He didn't see the hail of bullets that spewed out from the weapon as Anatoly depressed the trigger. He didn't hear the cries of terror from the girls, or the gurgling sound as that too was cut short.

And then Yuri's gunfire faded away, replaced by nothing but the crackling of flames and the spitting and popping of burning wood.

When the job was done, before the sound of the gunfire even stopped echoing along the narrow cobbled streets around the embassy, Yuri and Anatoly began walking back to the car. They did so with a measured step, neither hurrying nor walking with undue slowness. At this time of night, Anatoly knew, the police response time was more likely to be measured in fifteen minute increments than seconds.

It was better to walk, Anatoly knew. It looked more natural. Was less likely to draw unwanted attention than reckless flight. Sirens finally punctuated the night as they reached the Skoda.

"Open the trunk," Anatoly grunted, adrenaline pumping into his veins as his body prepared for what he was about to do.

Yuri squinted up at him in confusion, stopping at the foot of the car. "Why?"

"Just do it," he said, his voice harsh. "We need to move."

"Fine," Yuri grunted, throwing his hands up in confusion, but not arguing any further. The push-button mechanism that opened the trunk was stiff, and he swore as half his nail broke off in the process of pressing it.

"*Gavno*," he said, bringing his finger to his mouth and sucking on the injured nail. Shit.

Still leaning over, he began to turn back to face Anatoly, only to find the barrel of the wiry Russian's pistol in his face. A flare of recognition blazed in his dull, beady eyes. They widened, and his mouth began to open in horror, the hand falling away, or reaching for his own weapon, it wasn't clear. But before he had a chance to cry out, or to beg for his life, or try to fight, Anatoly pressed smoothly down on the trigger.

A bullet spat from the barrel, traveled just half a yard in the air, and broke Yuri's skull apart. The blood spatter coated the inside of the trunk. Before his legs fell away beneath him, Anatoly smoothly caught the two hundred pounds of now dead weight and used the momentum of the fall to push him forward into the trunk, hoisting his legs in after the dead man and then closing it over him.

"I'm sorry, my friend," he muttered as he made for the driver's side door with a face that showed not a hint of contrition. "But it had to be done."

30

The Agency safehouse was in the Barrikadnaya area northwest of central Moscow, not far from the American Embassy, and just out of the Garden Ring around the city. It was more of a safe *apartment*, Trapp thought as he climbed the steep flight of stairs that led up to it.

"I don't like it," he muttered.

Ikeda didn't say a word until they were inside, and the door bolted and triple-locked behind them. It was thicker than it looked, and Trapp suspected that it would stop most anything short of a breaching charge.

"We shouldn't be here long," she said. "And it's a city of apartments. It's all they have here."

"I still don't like it," he grumbled. "People will see us coming and going."

Ikeda squinted at him. "And?"

"You don't think it's a risk? This city has eyes."

She dumped her travel bag onto the floor and walked toward a small but well-appointed kitchen. She flung open a head-height cabinet, pulled out two tall glasses, and said over her shoulder, "No, *Jason*. I don't think it's a risk. When was the last time you took a vacation?"

The question threw him off balance, and it took his gray matter a few seconds to fire back up. "Um, last week?" he ventured.

Ikeda turned and shot him an acid look. "It was a rhetorical question, dumb ass." She grinned.

"How was I supposed to know?" he protested. "Anyway, what's your point?"

"My point," she said over the sound of the water tap turning on, and the drumbeat of liquid pounding against the metal sink, "was that if you'd actually taken a vacation at any point over the past ten years except the one we just cut short, you'd have known that this is how things work these days. People rent out their apartments on the Internet. In a neighborhood like this, the residents will be used to people coming and going."

Trapp supposed that he had vaguely heard of it. But Ikeda had unerringly homed in on a deeper truth, too – before her, he hadn't had a reason to take a proper vacation in years, and the Agency booking him a safe house certainly didn't count.

"You're sure?" he grunted, not sounding entirely convinced.

"About as sure as I can be," she replied, walking over to him, kissing him on the cheek, and pressing a glass of water into his hands. A few drops spilled over and splashed against his shirt.

"Whoops," she giggled, a vivacious delight spreading across her cheeks.

Trapp shook his head, and as he sipped, wondered whether her arrival into his life had been a blessing or a curse. It was *mostly* the former, he decided as the cooling liquid soothed his travel-parched tongue.

Mostly.

After all, before Ikeda shouldered her way into his life, there were few people who would have risked making fun of him the way she did so lightly. Those of his colleagues in the

Agency who knew his reputation knew enough not to mess with him, and those who didn't looked at his scarred neck, broad shoulders and squashed nose and invariably decided to pick on an easier target.

There was a clink as Ikeda set her own glass down on a see-through coffee table. "Come on," she said, jerking her head, "let's see what we've got."

The safehouse was laid out over a single floor, and tastefully – if sparsely – furnished with a couple of three-piece couches in an inoffensive pale gray fabric, with a few burnt orange sofa cushions scattered over them. Trapp raised an eyebrow at that, wondering which of the Agency's notoriously stingy bean counters had signed off on that particular expense.

A serving window separated the living room from the kitchen, and to its right was a doorway into a bedroom. At first glance, as he entered, Trapp saw nothing out of place. The bed was made, although a thin layer of dust covered a black television cabinet that sat at one end of the room, indicating that nobody had cleaned the place in several months. That made sense. It wasn't hard to work out that basic operational security meant that hiring a cleaning service for a safe house wasn't a good idea.

There was, however, one glaring difference between this apartment and an ordinary vacation rental. Ikeda and Trapp discovered immediately that the walk-in closet attached to the room wasn't that after all – or at least, it wasn't that anymore. It had been converted into a large walk-in safe. Ikeda punched a code from memory, and an electronic mechanism whirred into life, releasing several locking bolts.

Trapp did the honors, pulling the heavy steel door open and studying it with a critical eye. It was far from impregnable, he knew. The very best lockboxes were cast from a single piece of metal to minimize the number of seams and joins which could be a point of failure if attacked with tools. This safe, by contrast, had welding joints connecting each of its five faces. It had clearly been constructed in place, a conversion of the pre-existing room.

Then again, he thought, it would have been difficult to hide the addition of a ten-ton lockbox into the safehouse, since installing it whole would most likely have required the removal of one of the apartment's exterior walls.

"Jackpot," Eliza said, her eyes lighting up like those of a child on Christmas morning as she studied the treasures that lay within.

Trapp had to agree. Whoever had fitted this place out knew what they were doing. It wasn't just the sheer volume of fire-power that was so appealing to an ex-Delta operative like himself, though the racks of submachine guns, pistols, ammunition and other equipment could probably have satisfied the SEAL team that took out bin Laden.

The key piece of equipment that caught his eye, however, wasn't lethal at all. At least, not directly. He began setting it up.

"It's good to see you two," Mitchell said, his tired expression crystal-clear through the high-quality video system as soon as the connection stabilized.

"I wish I could say the same about you, Mike," Trapp replied. "But you're not looking too hot."

Mitchell chuckled, but it was clearly a forced laugh, one that was done for their benefit, and yet no more convincing for it. "I feel better than I look," he said.

"I'm glad," Trapp said, his voice betraying his true take. "How are things back home?"

Mitchell sighed, expelling a fast puff of air through his teeth. "Not so good," he admitted. "The power's going down all over the country." He glanced up, toward an unseen light source overhead. "We're fine here, of course. Enough generator fuel to keep us going for months. But I can't say the same for the rest of the country."

"We saw," Ikeda replied.

They had been following the news reports coming out of the US with obvious interest. The story in the media was that it was a computer virus, probably created by an Eastern European gang as a shakedown tool that got out of control.

"Could have been a whole lot worse than it is," Mitchell admitted. "Tim did a helluva job finding a vulnerability in the virus's control network, and penetrating it at precisely the right time to avoid a wholesale shutdown of the power network."

Trapp's ears pricked up at this. It was a piece of information that hadn't been released in the media, although he could understand why. It was bad enough that the power was going out at all, but if the public learned that every school, home, office building and hospital in the entire country could have been without power, then there was no telling what their reaction might be.

"You're getting a handle on things, though?" he asked, expecting a response in the affirmative.

Mitchell pushed his fingers through limp, flat hair in a vain and ultimately unsuccessful attempt to style it. "No."

"What do you mean, *no*?"

"It's a simple fucking word, Jason," Mitchell snapped, his irritation betraying both his exhaustion and the pressure he and the home team were working under.

Trapp paused and molded his expression into a mass of contradictions. His spectral eyes glinted with compassion, but his lips formed a hard, thin line. "We're the good guys, Mike," he said slowly. "Don't forget that."

It wasn't so much a rebuke as a reminder, and Mitchell took it in the spirit it was intended. He bowed his head.

"Sure," he said. And that, too, was about as much slack as Trapp ever expected to get.

"So what the fuck is going on over there?" Trapp asked, back to business. "The short version."

Mitchell ticked off a list of disasters on his fingers. "Like I said, electricity is on and off across the whole country. Dr. Greaves is fighting a running battle with the control network, but every time he penetrates a node, a new one pops up. It's like fighting a Hydra."

"Great," Trapp grunted.

His boss continued as though he hadn't noticed the interruption. "Every time the power goes down, that screws something else up. No electricity means no traffic lights means the roads are gridlocked, and that backs right up onto the highways. Another day like this and every urban grocery store in the nation will be empty. The president has ordered the release of strategic food supplies, and the military is ferrying food into major cities, but there are only so many helicopters to go around. Until we clear the streets, it's going to be touch and go."

"Damn," Ikeda whispered.

Trapp knew exactly what she was thinking. He was picturing it too. It was hard to imagine his country's peaceful streets could be afflicted by the same turmoil he'd seen in war zones across the globe. But he knew it was the truth. Panic was a natural human emotion. In times of stress, most people look out for themselves and their families first, and the thin blue line that stands between civilization and outright chaos can teeter, even crumble entirely far more easily than most could ever imagine.

"So what's the endgame, Mike. Who's doing this – the Russians?" Trapp asked.

Mitchell shrugged. "That's my working hypothesis. But it's circumstantial as hell. I need hard proof, something I can take to the President."

Ikeda glanced at Trapp, as though asking for permission to speak. He supposed he was technically her superior, though patently whatever dividing lines might once have existed between them were long ago blurred.

"We'll get it, Mr. Mitchell," she said. "If we can, we'll get it."

"Call me Mike." Mitchell grinned, a rare smile – at least under present circumstances – breaking across his face. "Mr. Mitchell was my dad."

"Mike it is, then," Ikeda agreed with a shy smile.

Trapp wondered what the hell they would do when this crisis was over. The month in Tuscany had been perfect, a much-needed sabbatical after years of unrelenting efforts that had ground him down more than he had first recognized. And Eliza Ikeda was a heck of a woman. Trapp knew that he wasn't the kind of man who could settle down in the suburbs, no matter how often he grumbled about the Agency, and about not getting enough time off.

He was built for this kind of work. It wasn't killing that he enjoyed, nor any of the other kinetic aspects of his job, as the CIA's training literature so dryly described them. No, when he was in the field, he was a hunter, a predator, searching for a prey as wily and slippery as anything nature could have devised. The hunt was like a drug, and Trapp never felt so alive as when he was shooting it directly into his veins. And what he did *mattered*. Maybe the rest of the world would never know that, but he did, and that had to count for something.

The truth was, Ikeda was fashioned from the same clay. It had taken him a while to stop thinking of her as a victim of the horrors she had endured behind the thirty-eighth parallel. But he realized that she never thought of herself that way. She was a survivor, just like him.

So what the hell does that mean for us?

He knew that they would never be a traditional couple, if that was even what they had become. To settle down and take desk jobs in Langley would be anathema to both of them. He couldn't imagine buying a four-bed in the Virginia hills and driving to work every day in a damn town car.

Perhaps you should just focus on one thing at a time, dumbass.

"Something funny, Jason?" Mitchell asked, raising an eyebrow.

Trapp wiped the smirk off his face. "In a dark kind of way, I guess."

"Care to share it with the class?"

"Not really, Mike."

"Then how about we stay focused on the task at hand?" Mitchell grunted.

"Works for me." He shrugged before leaning forward. "The way I see it, you're up shit creek without a paddle. How can we help?"

Mitchell rubbed his chin unconsciously, fingers scraping over several days of dark stubble. "Like I said, the Russians have their fingerprints all over this. I need you to bring me some proof, something solid that I can use to catch them red-handed."

"We'll do what we can," Trapp replied. "Anything else we need to know?"

Mitchell reached somewhere out of the webcam's field of view, and the sound of shuffling paper reverberated through the laptop's tinny speakers. They watched as Mitchell looked off-screen, his eyes scanning from left to right as he inhaled a document, then looked back.

"This guy Roman Kholodov. We don't know a great deal about him. Nothing concrete, anyway. I've got feelers out to NSA, FBI, the whole alphabet soup. Nothing yet. But he's close to Murov. Used to be the guy's bodyguard. Then nothing for a few years after that. It's like he sprang out of virgin clay, and just stumbled into possession of several billion dollars."

"Ain't that always the way?" Trapp muttered drily. "You at least got an address?"

Mitchell glanced back down. "Yeah. Not too far, a place called Soloslovo, just northwest of Moscow."

"Then I guess we should go check it out. That everything you got?"

"Pretty much," Mitchell replied grimly. "I appreciate it isn't much, Jason. The Russkies have got planes up in the air nibbling at NATO air defenses from Ramstein to Romford –"

Trapp squinted. "Where the hell is Romford?"

"Some rinky-dink English town," Mitchell replied, flicking his fingers dismissively. "But the Russians sent a Bear right down the English Channel, and the Air Force almost lost a Rivet over the Baltic Sea. They aren't playing around. We need to know why."

Trapp knew that the Bear was a Tupolev 95 strategic nuclear bomber, a common enough sight during the Cold War, but not often seen since. The thought sent a chill down his spine. "You got it, Mike. We'll do what we can."

"And then some," Mitchell replied flatly. "One last thing..."

Trapp looked up, warned by his boss's tone. "Yeah?"

"The DCI's breathing down my neck. Wants everything I have on you, and he wants it yesterday."

"What the hell for?"

Mitchell sighed. "He's a real by the book kinda guy. A top-tier analyst, but he doesn't understand Operations, and he just lost our top Russian asset in his first month on the job. My guess is he's looking for someone to take the fall, and your file, Jason..."

Trapp ground his teeth together hot enough to make a tendon near his temple pop. Judging by the reaction on Mitchell's face, he could hear it too. He knew exactly what his boss was suggesting, which was that he was no boy scout, and that his file would reflect as much. No one in the Special Activities Division was; that was just the way the game was played. The Agency had processes in place to avoid handing the dirt over to journalists, even ways of hiding it from congressional oversight.

But from the DCI?

"Bureaucrats," Trapp hissed, as though it were the dirtiest cuss word he knew. In a way, it was. "You don't think he might be able to pick a more convenient time to burn me?" he spat in a mocking, singsong tone. "I don't know, like when we're not in the middle of a major fucking geopolitical crisis?"

Mitchell raised his palms in a gesture both of agreement and supplication. "I know, I know. I get it. I'm running top cover, doing what I can. But I had to tell you. You're under the microscope on this one, Jason. One foot out of place, and..." He shrugged.

"The DCI can blow himself," Trapp said dismissively, his tone laced with scorn. "I'll do my job, Mike. Like I always do. Maybe it's time you did yours."

He killed the connection.

There was a brief pause before Ikeda said diplomatically, her expression deadpan, "Well, I thought that went well."

For a second, Trapp didn't know how to respond. And then it welled up inside him, a mixture of the humor of the situation, the stress and tension of the past few days, exhaustion and a kaleidoscope of other emotions beside, finally exploding in a volcanic fit of giggles. He laughed until his abdomen couldn't take it any longer, and then a little past that.

At first Ikeda just looked at him as though he had lost it, but after twenty seconds of that, she caught the bug, too. It was almost cathartic – a recognition of the near hopelessness of their situation, a calculation of their odds of success, and acceptance that no matter how bleak things looked, they would do their job anyway, because that's what they'd signed up for, and it had to be done.

Still, once the wave of laughter died away, a second's reservation filled Trapp's mind—the crash after a high. He reached out and grabbed Ikeda's hand and fixed her a look dead in the eyes.

"I need you to watch out on this one," he said. "Right now, I've got a target painted on my back. You heard Mike. If I screw up, some real big players will be looking to take me down, and they won't think twice about turning you into collateral damage. You could lose your career over this. Or worse."

Ikeda's face scrunched up. "You're the President's guy, Jason," she said. "He'll go to bat for you. He has to, after what you did."

Trapp sighed. "That would be nice, wouldn't it? But don't get your hopes up. That's not the way Washington works. We're expendable, it says it right there on the business cards. If we go down, no one's coming to get us."

She fell silent, and Trapp wondered whether she was reconsidering her earlier opposition. "If I lose my career over this, it's not the kind of career I wanted anyway. So what's the plan?"

Trapp studied her face for a long second, wondering if he should try and talk her out of it, and knowing there wasn't a chance he would succeed. She was as damn pigheaded as he was. Probably why he liked her so much.

"The way I see it," he said, "we've got two targets: the dead drop, and this prick Kholodov's place. We need to scope them both, and we need to do it fast." He shook his head, grimacing. "I don't know, it just kind of feels like we're running out of time."

And that was almost the worst of it, Trapp realized. It wasn't as simple a task as simply putting a bullet in the bad guy's forehead. He didn't know who he was supposed to be fighting. He was one of his country's most finely honed weapons, but without a target, he was almost useless.

"We need to split up," Ikeda said, her tone firm. "It's the only way."

For a second time that morning, Trapp realized, he didn't really have any other choice.

31

"Roman," President Murov said, a wide smile not reaching cold, dead eyes. "You are late."

Kholodov knew that he was not. However, he also knew that there was no sense in arguing with the most powerful man in Russia. He had worked for Murov long enough to know that the man was a master at pushing his sparring partners off-balance, even – perhaps *especially* – when those partners were his loyal servants.

It was a power game.

"My apologies, Mr. President," he replied, dropping his eyes to the floor in a gesture of mild subservience.

There were few men, he thought, who could inspire such a reaction in him. The past few years had been kind to Roman Kholodov. Very kind. He bought the houses he wanted, sailed on the yachts he craved, ate in the city's finest restaurants – and when he tired of those, he could fly half way across the world for lunch on his own jet and be back in Russia in time for dinner.

But Kholodov's power, such as it was, flowed from the enormous wealth he controlled. Wealth for which he was merely a custodian. A handsomely paid custodian, to be sure, but a caretaker nonetheless. Murov, by contrast, had the power of life and death. His signature moved armies, and the merest hint of a nod could condemn a man to execution.

That was true power.

Roman Kholodov shivered. He knew, had always known, that his current position was akin to dancing atop the blade of a razor. He was useful to his president. But the profits that flowed to him as a reward for that loyalty could not only be turned off at a whim, but stripped from him without recourse. No court in the land would dare attempt to reverse a decision that carried the signature of President Dmitry Murov.

Not that it would get to court, of course. A sensible man, put in such an invidious position, would understand that losing his wealth was at least preferable to losing his head. A less sensible individual would find that life in Russia is cheap, and the president very wealthy.

Murov waved his hand in a gesture of benefaction and said, "It is already forgotten. Please, sit."

Kholodov did as he was instructed, seating himself in one of the upholstered armchairs that sat in front of Murov's desk in his Kremlin office. As he did so, the president stood, turned away from his guest and walked to a small cabinet of polished hardwood that was built into the wall behind his workstation. He opened it, pulled out two crystal whisky glasses, and set them down in front of him.

"Scotch?" he asked, not turning.

Roman knew better than to turn his master down. "Please."

The amber liquid tinkled as it flowed from a bottle made from glass that was stained dark green, and decorated with a label that was yellowed with age. Kholodov shifted in his place, leaning forward with anticipation.

The Scotch glasses clinked together as President Murov carried them back to his desk in one hand. Roman almost reached out to grasp one as he placed them on the green leather surface, but restrained himself at the last moment, a twitch in his shoulder betraying the impulse. He felt Murov's eyes upon him, studying him, drinking in every last detail, and suspected that it hadn't been missed.

Murov sat. He leaned back in his chair, tipping the front legs backward, letting the silence in his office build – broken only by the metronomic ticking of a grandfather clock – then allowed the chair to topple back to the ground and pushed one of the two glasses toward his guest.

Kholodov accepted the drink, sliding it back with the base of the glass still against the leather, then lifted it clear and settled back into his armchair. He brought the crystal up to his nose, closed his eyes and took a long, deep sniff. The aroma was glorious. Cherries and smoke, aged for decades in casks of oak.

His eyes snapped open to find Murov's gaze locked on his own, as if demanding a response.

Yes, that is it, Kholodov thought. His president did not ask, he demanded. He did not wait, he took.

"Peaty," he said.

Murov lifted his own glass to his lips and took an unblinking sip. Kholodov copied his master dutifully. The whisky was amongst the best he had ever tasted, in theory. In practice, he could barely appreciate it as Murov's stare burned his skin.

"So," he said.

"So," Murov replied. A smile crept onto his face, dawdling at the corners of his lips. As before, it did not reach his eyes. There was something sinister about that, Kholodov thought. He wondered if his president found joy in anything, whether he took real pleasure from these power plays, or simply performed them as a matter of course.

Perhaps there was a sparkling wit behind that impassive

visage. But if there was, Kholodov was sure he would never know.

Kholodov cleared his throat. "You wanted to see me, Mr. President."

Apparently tiring of his little game, Murov glanced at his wristwatch – expensive, Swiss – and then back up at his former bodyguard. "Brief me on our operation," he said.

Kholodov nodded, happy to have returned to safer ground. The operation was something he knew like the lines on his own face, studied and practiced and updated and finessed over the years like the moving parts of a long-running Broadway show. And it was all falling into place.

Mostly.

"We activated the first phase of the virus last night, right on schedule," he said, wishing he had access to his notes on the operation to avoid making a mistake when recounting the details, but knowing that to commit something this sensitive to a medium such as paper would be folly of the highest order. A folly which a man like Murov would neither forgive not forget. "The early indications are –"

Murov cut him off with a dismissive sneer. Kholodov had worked for this man for decades, on and off, under various guises, and as a younger man had been willing to throw his own body in the path of an assassin's bullet to save his president. He had seen the man belittle visitors many times before, often raising a snigger behind his own impassive face, mirth inside unblinking eyes. And even with the benefit of all that experience, his boss's gesture still cut him deep.

"You have failed, Roman," the president said, his tone of voice measured, almost probing. "They still have power."

"Sixty percent of the country is dark, Mr. President," Kholodov rejoined.

"The FSB tell me they are bringing power stations back online as swiftly as we bring them down," Murov replied. "You told me that once the grid went down, it would take them months to repair it. But for that to happen, the *whole grid* needed to go dark at once, did it not?"

Kholodov paused for a second to compose himself, instead of immediately diving into the fray. He knew better than anyone that Murov prized control above all else – both his control over others, and their control of themselves. Rising to anger would only provoke that very same response.

And yet the truth was that anger crackled inside him. He had been over this with Murov dozens of times over the past few months, and had always maintained that he could not promise to knock out the US power grid, at least not completely, and certainly not with definitive confidence.

"That is true," he allowed, a muscle on his jaw twitching even as his tone remained composed. "But this was never supposed to be the destination, merely a stop along the way. As you know, the goal was merely to throw the Americanski off from our true aims."

Murov steepled his fingers, staying silent as he surveyed his subordinate. Kholodov's skin crawled underneath the onslaught of the man's intense, unbroken observation. Everything he had, he owed to the man on the other side of that desk. All the wealth, all the power, all the respect from his peers. And all of it could be undone at the stroke of a pen.

And it wasn't just his wealth, power and status that could be stripped from him. He was suddenly, uncomfortably cognizant of the fact that he was now a loose end. If it served Murov's purposes, the president would show him no loyalty, and he would be removed, taken off the chessboard for good.

"I will not fail you, sir," Kholodov said, his voice cracking slightly, rising an octave under the pressure of the examination and his sudden realization of the consequences of failure, and yet needing to say something for precisely that same reason. "I promise you that. The Americans will be humbled."

Murov raised his whisky glass to his lips and took a sip, though Kholodov could not be sure that the level of the liquid in the glass changed at all. Was he even drinking? Or was it all an act, a prop to put his guests at ease? With Murov, one could never know. Was everything a game – or was *that* in fact the true goal of the exercise, to make everyone who encountered him second-guess themselves, wasting their energy and attention parrying imagined stabs and thrusts?

"I trust you, Roman," Murov said, his tone indicating that his trust only extended so far. "And I trust that you will finish the job."

"I will, sir," Kholodov said, his voice scarcely stronger than a whimper. "I know what is at stake."

"Good," Murov said briskly, as if the previous tension was already forgotten. Perhaps for him it was, but not his guest. "This business in Latvia – terrible, isn't it?"

Kholodov saw no signs of grief on Murov's face, but then he hadn't been expecting any. After all, the attack on the embassy in Riga had been the president's own idea. Another move on the chessboard. A pawn sacrificed in order to engineer a more advantageous position for her queen.

Or in this case, her king.

"Terrible," Kholodov repeated dully, feeling as though his nerves were being stretched to their absolute limit. "But necessary."

"Of course," Murov agreed. "I can hear the protests from here. Our people are very angry indeed," he finished with satisfaction.

It was an age-old game, played by those in positions of power for whom human life was more of a currency to be spent in pursuit of a goal than an item of any intrinsic value. The Russian people were indeed angry, and their vehemence was growing hour by hour, fed by details strategically released in the state media, and spread like wildfire on the Internet.

"It is proceeding according to plan," Kholodov said, his satisfaction with his work tempered slightly by the understanding that he could not now be seen to boast, not after his failure – real or perceived – in America.

"The Young Guard?"

"Mobilizing as we speak, sir. There will be twenty thousand of them in the park by this evening."

The Young Guard were the youth action wing of the United Russia political party which Murov had long ago created to support his ambitions. They were a group who were as malleable as they were angry, and their anger could be shaped and directed, as was happening now. Russians were dead on foreign soil, and the youth, not remembering the pain and privation through which their forebears had suffered, were baying for blood.

There was a long silence, eventually broken only by a knock at the mahogany-paneled entrance to the presidential office. A young woman waited for half a beat before opening the door a crack.

"It's almost time, Mr. President," she said, pulling the door to behind her.

"Finish your drink, Roman," Murov said with a friendly smile, standing and removing his suit jacket from a hanger that hung off one of the flagpoles that bracketed either side of his desk. He shrugged it on and patted out a few stray wrinkles.

And he left, buttoning his jacket, murmuring something to the aide waiting outside. The wooden door made a clunking sound as it settled back into its frame, and Kholodov collapsed back into the thick armchair, his hands trembling.

He drank deeply from the whisky now that Murov was gone, trusting the fiery liquid to burn away his fear. He stayed there for a few long minutes, thinking of nothing in particular, finishing his drink because that was what the boss had instructed him to do. As he turned to leave, he saw a muted television screen, tuned to *Russia Today*. A chyron scrolled across the bottom of the feed, informing the viewers of the tragedy in Latvia. Four dead, and an embassy burned to ashes.

He paused in front of it, watching as President Murov stepped behind the plinth, his expression solemn. Kholodov touched a button underneath the screen, and Murov's voice blared out, cracking with emotion that he knew to be feigned.

"Russia will not simply stand by and watch as her citizens are humiliated, raped and killed. I swear to the people of this great nation that if these indignities do not stop immediately, the armed forces will see to it that they do."

32

I keda pulled out her cell phone and checked that she was at the right address. The phone was a burner, one of a number they'd found in the safe house, wrapped in fresh plastic, and accompanied with SIM cards from a variety of companies – all paid up for months. The address was the one she'd been given by the seller of a motorbike, using a local version of Craigslist, and she was here to pick it up.

"Looks like the right place," she muttered to herself.

It had taken about thirty minutes in the cab, but only because the traffic into the suburbs was bumper to bumper. The area was significantly more run-down than the Barrikad-naya district, but it felt lived in, rather than abandoned. There was, she mused, a distinct difference between those two states.

Ikeda found the right address, climbed the three wooden steps that led up to the house, and knocked on the front door. Nothing happened for a few long seconds, and she was drawing her knuckles back to try again when she heard footsteps, then the metallic scratching of a chain being unfastened and the thunk of the door being unlocked.

The seller opened it, and Ikeda found herself looking at a

man wearing a dark blue Adidas tracksuit, the white stripes that passed down the shoulders stained yellow with either sweat or nicotine, or perhaps a combination of both.

Gross.

She briefly considered turning tail and heading back to the safe house. If the motorcycle she was here to purchase was in the same condition as its owner, then she wasn't sure she wanted to trust her life to it. Hell, she wasn't sure she wanted to even *touch* it.

The man cleared his throat, opened his mouth, and a stream of Russian words poured out. Ikeda only recognized the last one. "Russky?"

She shook her head. She knew that one – he was asking if she spoke Russian.

"*Nyet*," she said. She did not.

"Is okay, I work as an electrician in London," the man smiled, revealing a gap in his lower set of incisors, though whether it was a result of poor dental hygiene or a fight, Ikeda did not know. She figured the odds were about equal. He held up the fingers of both hands.

"My name Ivan," Ivan said, poking himself in the chest. "Ten years," he said proudly, jerking his thumb at the small, two-story house behind him. "Then I buy this."

"It's lovely," Ikeda smiled, not really meaning it, but hoping it wouldn't show – and hoping even more that he didn't invite her in. "I'm here about the bike?"

The Russian squinted at her as though she was an idiot. There was a hint of truth to that, she allowed. After all, it didn't seem likely that a steady stream of American women turned up at his front door looking for anything else.

"Of course," the electrician said, his tone conveying his opinion of her more than his words. "I show you."

He reached inside the doorway, and Ikeda heard the jingle of keys being removed from what she assumed was a hook next

to the door. Keys in hand, he gestured for her to head back
down to the road. He joined her at the bottom, then led her
around the side of the small house. Tufts of grass rose through
cracks in the concrete, and a vine that she didn't recognize had
begun the slow, laborious process of enveloping this corner of
the house.

Ivan pointed at the vague outline of a bike that was
disguised by large sheet of blue canvas and secured by yellow
elastic ropes.

"Here is," he muttered, bending down to untie the
fastenings.

With a flourish, he pulled back the canvas and revealed the
same bike she'd seen in the pictures online. It was Japanese, a
Kawasaki, and had been a midnight black when it rolled off the
line a decade before, but had now acquired something of a
zebra effect through years of scrapes that had stripped away the
finish and left only scratched white plastic behind.

It wasn't exactly the Triumph she had left behind in Hong
Kong, a bike she'd saved for months to purchase, whose
leather she still dreamed of sometimes, but nevertheless Ikeda
liked what she saw. The bike, the model of which was named
Ninja, according to the small, scratched plate above the gauges,
looked nondescript, fast, and functional. And though it wore
plenty of cosmetic marks, it looked otherwise well-
maintained.

Ikeda's lips formed an upside down frown of approval, and
she glanced at Ivan. "Looks good. You mind if I take it for a
spin?"

The colloquialism stumped the old electrician. "Spin? I do
not understand."

She pointed at the bike, then the road, just about visible
down the side of the house. "Try it out, I mean. Make sure she
runs smooth." She patted her pockets down, for the thin sheaf
of ruble notes that she had liberated from a much larger stack

in the safe house, and held them out. It was about sixty thousand in local currency, just a bit over $900.

"You can keep hold of these. Just to keep me honest," she said, placing a ghost of a smile on her lips to assure the man that his bike would be safe in her hands.

The light of understanding dawned in Ivan's eyes, and he waved away the cash, tossing Ikeda the keys, which she caught in midair.

"I trust you," he growled, patting his belly and bursting out with a laugh that coated Ikeda's cheeks with flecks of spittle. Then he frowned. "But come back."

Ikeda put the key into the ignition, then wheeled the bike down the thin channel that hugged the side of the house, and onto the cracked asphalt of the road, balancing it on the kickstand for a few seconds as she bent down and gave the vitals a quick once over.

"I'll bear that in mind." She grinned, wondering if he would understand what that meant. She started up the bike, knocked back the kickstand, and balanced for a couple of seconds with a trailing leg, just listening to the throaty growl of the bike's engine. Shabby as her current owner appeared, he clearly knew how to maintain an engine. She threw Ivan a thumbs-up and fed the bike a trickle of gas.

It jumped forward, and Ikeda took it for a spin around the block, dodging several large potholes that looked at least two winters old, and significantly more threatening for it. When she was satisfied that the vehicle both sounded, smelled and felt fine, she returned to the house and paid Ivan.

"I'll take care of her," she said as the man was pocketing his windfall – exactly what he'd asked for, and twenty thousand rubles more than he expected.

He merely squinted in response, nonplussed at the notion that his former bike, now Ikeda's – at least for now, was anything more than merely an object. To her, it was. It meant freedom, and the warm summer air tugging at her hair as she tested her newfound purchase.

Anyway, that oversight was quickly remedied when she passed a military surplus shop, where she paid for an olive green helmet with a clear visor to protect against the wind and the bugs it carried, along with a spare, just in case.

For a short while, Ikeda simply drove around Moscow's Garden Ring, the multilane road built where the 17th-century city walls had once stood, drinking in the sights and sounds of an alien city and twice avoiding being clipped by truly desperate drivers, in each case by a mere hair's breadth. She crossed over a bend in the Moskva River, and then back again, gunning the engine until she pushed past a hundred miles an hour, the roar of the engine beneath her combining with the white noise of air whipping past her ears to produce an almost trancelike state, in which she forgot all of the killing and the fear of the past few days, and the weeks before that. Cars and trucks and sixteen wheelers zipped past, red and blue and white and then just a blur.

A horn blared, sharp and urgent, jolting Ikeda back to her senses. She tapped the brakes smoothly, bringing the bike back down below legal limits. A second later, she saw the cause of the unknown good Samaritan's warning – a four-door Ford with a blue stripe that ran just below the window line, and red and blue lights on top.

A cop car.

Part of Ikeda's mind absently celebrated the victory of capitalism over the Eastern Bloc's top-down model of communism. Even Henry Ford himself probably couldn't have pictured a time when the Moscow police force would have been buying American. And yet here was the living proof.

The other part of her mind, of course, held its breath and waited for the lights to spark into life, and a siren to blare its loud, discordant tune.

One, two, three, she counted in her head, and only when she reached ten and still the police vehicle had not responded did she finally relax, suddenly aware of a bead of sweat trickling down her left temple, and a clamminess on her palms. Her heart was jackhammering in her chest, and she forced it to slow.

"What the hell are you doing?" she cursed over the roar of the wind, knowing that the consequences of being caught speeding would most likely have been minor – just a ticket, and yet also horribly aware that she had broken the cardinal rule of tradecraft: never do anything that might attract attention, let alone suspicion.

Eliza Ikeda knew that her false identity was flawless. Yet there was no reason, none at all, to risk getting it flagged by a Russian police computer. Not when the stakes were so high.

She took the next exit, navigating toward the village of Solosovlo and ensured that she maintained a pace that was a couple of miles below the sedate speed mandated by the road signs. It was time to get to work.

33

Trapp walked to the Barrikadnaya Metro station, admiring the striking Soviet architecture of the station's main hall as he descended the escalator several hundred feet into one of the world's deepest subway lines, built amidst the fear and intrigue of the Cold War, when Soviet military planners assumed that American and British nuclear warheads would rain down on the heads of a terrified population.

His mind conjured a scene which could have been lifted from a Hollywood movie. Intercontinental ballistic missiles soaring through the stratosphere, each carrying dozens of deadly warheads many times more powerful than those that leveled Hiroshima and Nagasaki. He heard the ear-piercing sound of sirens screaming their warning, pictured the faces of weeping children, and pale-faced mothers dragging little hands and scurrying down below, to a safety that was nothing more than illusory.

He knew what would happen next. The American missiles would block out the city overhead, sealing the refugees into a stone tomb from which there would be no escape and no rescue. As fires blazed overhead, then faded as there was nothing left to burn, so would the survivors starve and wither away as there was no more air to breathe.

He shivered at the thought and banished it from his mind. After all, those days were long gone. The nukes were slowly being decommissioned, the bombers grounded, the launch tubes filled with concrete. The West had won the Cold War.

Hadn't it?

Trapp's striking, split eyes studied a decorative motif that was not as stark and brutalist as one might imagine. Huge chunks of dark, mottled marble, narrower at the base than the top, held up an arched ceiling, down which ran a zigzagging, artistic strip of lights that hung suspended from the ceiling. He somewhat suspected that those were not part of the original plans – evidence of the country's wealth returning after years in the wilderness – but everything else was.

He stepped onto a train carriage, painted white and accented with red, that would whisk him on line seven to the station at Kitay-gorod, near Park Zaryad'ye, situated adjacent to the Kremlin, which was his final destination.

Trapp held on to a steel bar overhead, swaying as the subway train rattled down the tracks. At first, beyond a brief attempt to endure he wasn't being followed, he didn't pay much attention to the bright-faced students, the teenagers holding signs, or the woman with the megaphone. He was lost in his own head until a group of them started chanting, beating against the carriage's toughened plastic windows and bellowing out a tune that he could not understand. Mostly, he tried to block out the sound, assuming they were sports fans on the way to a game.

Eventually, however, his eyes drifted to a small gaggle of the loudest chanters, those most insistent on being heard, and found they weren't dressed in ice hockey gear, but draped in

Russian flags and carrying placards and signs in the same, impenetrable language.

Was there a soccer game, Trapp wondered. The World Cup or something?

No – wrong time of year.

Then what?

His eyes focused on one of the signs, held by a teenager, his head shaved, who couldn't have been much older than sixteen. The placard had a white background, mounted on a wooden stick that was about four feet long. But it wasn't the design of the kid's sign itself that interested Trapp so much, but the design on it – the Statue of Liberty holding a knife to the throat of a Russian bear.

That's a new one, he thought.

Trapp had watched the burning of American flags at protests more times than he could count. Mostly through the scope of a rifle, though sometimes wearing a Middle Eastern keffiyeh, lotion that darkened his skin and long, flowing white robes to help him blend into an angry crowd that would turn on him in an instant if they knew his true identity.

This crowd was a little different, that was for sure.

"Oh, hell," Trapp muttered as he stepped out of the station's semidarkness and into a bright summer's day, both following and being followed by teenagers carrying signs and breaking into song.

Hell was about right, he thought. The area was alive, and not in a good way. Protesters streamed in every direction, holding signs above their heads, chanting, singing, wearing faces that were angry and bright, contented and sad. Many were young, college-age, even younger. But there were old heads as well, topped with gray, mounted on beer bellies, paired with biker jackets, or attached to sagging jowls.

But all, old or young, were heading directly for the park.

A little bit of activity Trapp could deal with – would even

welcome, to hide him from prying eyes. This was something else entirely. The entire park looked like it was playing host to a Russian version of Woodstock, except with angry political chants in the place of music.

This isn't good, he thought. *Not good at all.*

Trapp thought back to a cold December night, when he'd first met Alexy Sokolov, and showed him a dead drop location that lay between his workplace at the Kremlin and the Metro stop he took on his journey home. He remembered showing the man how to leave a signal that there was a parcel inside, remembered indicating the location where the message was to be left.

That night had been crisp and cold, with a light falling of fresh snow dusting paths that were cleared daily, but covering grass on either side that would not grow again for months. Their winter boots crunched against the snow, and Trapp had watched his source's eyes dart left and right with evident unease, searching for a hidden enemy, for the police to stream from the bushes and arrest them both.

"*Cut that out,*" he had hissed. "*You want to get us both killed?*"

Sokolov had shaken his head, fresh blood flooding to cheeks that were already dusted pink from the cold. At the time, and only in the safety of his own mind, Trapp hadn't thought the man would make it a month. But he'd taught Sokolov what he could, then passed him over to a real handler, and not thought of him again for years.

The park that night was empty and quiet, the backlit fortresses of the Kremlin looming overhead, the towers of Orthodox churches glowing like halos in the city's skyline, iron streetlights casting pools of light in an endless darkness, like stars in an inky black sky.

The contrast of that solitude with today could not have been more stark.

Trapp allowed himself to be carried toward the park among

the crowd, not resisting the flow of people, though not joining in with their songs. He could not have if he wanted to. He saw a discarded sign on the ground and grabbed it, assuming that it echoed the protesters' message, and hoping it would help him blend in. He decided to circle once around the park, scouting out the lay of the land, and not liking what he saw.

Some – not all, nor even many, but some of the protesters arriving were carrying large packs on their backs. Packs that contained tents and camp stoves and gazebos, and all the other little pieces of equipment that were required to form a camp. And one by one as they arrived, the campsite in the center of the park grew, decorated by flags and pennants on long wooden poles, fluttering overhead. Half the flags were recognizable – the eagle of the Russian Federation.

The others Trapp had not seen before, though the design stirred a memory in his brain. They depicted a bear, painted in blue, with the red blue and white of their country's flag overhead, and Cyrillic writing below. He wasn't a Russia expert, but he thought that it might be the flag of President Murov's political party, United Russia.

Trapp swore under his breath as he recognized that the protest camp – for that was surely what it was – was located exactly where he needed to go. Where the hollowed-out rock containing Sokolov's message would be, if the man had managed to leave it without being spotted.

Even that was not certain.

It was possible that even now, spotters from the FSB were watching the location with binoculars, waiting for Sokolov's contact to arrive, waiting to spring a trap. Trapp knew this dead drop was nothing more than a stand-in. Sokolov's handler, whoever the man was, would have given his charge new communications procedures, which meant that if anyone was waiting, then they were unlikely to be here.

What the hell was he going to do, he wondered. The assortment of tents, some streaky with dried mud, others fresh out of their plastic packaging, was growing by the minute, and quickly expanding into the area where the hollowed-out rock should be. He didn't like acting before he knew whether someone was watching him, and he certainly didn't like picking up a message this important with so many potentially unfriendly eyes around, but the truth was he didn't really have a choice.

He thrust his hands into his pockets, feeling the comforting weight of the pistol that he had earlier slid into the inside chest pocket of his jacket. It bounced against his pectoral muscles, but he knew that it couldn't help him. Not this time. If he needed to use it, then everything had already gone to shit.

Trapp decided that he didn't have time to wait. The rock garden was still mostly empty, though littered with discarded garbage – soda cans and, ironically, given the anti-American nature of the protest, empty cartons of McDonald's fries. But these kids were setting up to be here for a while, and though occasionally a police officer made his presence known, they were taking selfies with the protesters, instead of moving them on. The protesters were settling in for the long haul, and the cops didn't seem to mind.

So Trapp worked his way through the crowd, clutching his protest sign over his head, his eyes fixed on the spot where the rock should be. His eyes periodically glanced left and right, checking to see whether anyone was watching, and he didn't walk in a precisely straight line, but still he never deviated from his destination.

When he was only a few yards away, a small crowd of protesters – all men, most with shaven heads – began chanting and pounding their fists in the air as they walked in his direction. Trapp attempted to avoid them, but didn't notice a short, thin teen whose frame was completely obscured by his larger friend until it was too late. The kid collided with Trapp's shoulder and spun off him, momentarily falling to the ground.

"Sorry, buddy," he grunted out of habit.

As the words escaped his mouth, Trapp froze, realizing the mistake he had made by speaking in English. He glanced up at the man he had collided with, and found that he was little more than a boy, perhaps nineteen years old, wiry and with gray eyes that burned hot with rage.

"You're American."

It was a statement, not a question, and delivered as a harsh accusation. Trapp didn't need to lean on his years of experience in the field, or on his preternatural skill in reading a person to know that, from the sneer on the youth's face and the way his lips were drawn back in a snarl, revealing yellowed teeth, admitting his nationality would be a real bad idea.

"Canadian," he lied. "What's that got to do with anything?"

The kid blinked, knuckles white around his sign. Trapp watched as he processed this unexpected piece of information, wondering if it would change his opinion any.

"You're Western!" he snarled instead.

I guess not.

Trapp raised his palms in a nonthreatening gesture. "I ain't fighting with you there. But believe me, buddy, I'm no friend of the Americans."

"But you're Western," the kid said for a second time, as though his criticism was both inherent, implicit, and impossible to ignore.

Trapp decided to disengage, correctly surmising that no good could come of this encounter. He backed away, his boot kicking against a discarded soda can. The part of his mind that wasn't occupied with escaping the present situation without any trouble wrinkled his nose, and sniffed that protesters were the same wherever you found them.

Unfortunately, he only succeeded in backing into a brick wall. Only it wasn't a brick wall, it was a human, a male human whose blond hair was tied back in a ponytail, a man who had to be pushing three hundred pounds of mostly fat, and not muscle, and a male human whose arms were crossed over his chest.

The big guy had a straggly beard that was bare in patches, and on either side he had accomplices who wore expressions that were as grim as his own. There were five of them, plus the original kid, and while they were mostly young, that was more of a curse than it was a blessing. They were amped up on anger – jaws set, grimacing, looking for a fight and being egged on merely by the presence of other men.

This. Was. Not. Good.

The wiry kid snarled something in Russian, and Trapp wished he'd paid more attention in language school. In response, the fat one uncrossed his arms, took a step forward, showed Trapp both of his palms, and pushed him hard in the chest.

Although he was expecting it, the force of the blow surprised him. Jason Trapp was not a small man. He had a couple of inches on the brick wall, but even though his own frame consisted solely of lean muscle, the wall had a hundred pounds on him, the logic of which was remorseless. The force caused him to stumble backward, and then sprawl into the dirt.

"Fuck," he grunted, the wind momentarily squashed out of his lungs. The sign he had carried around for the last few minutes went flying, but by now Trapp had long ago forgotten it. He scrambled backward, knowing that in any combat situation – even a brawl like this one – to be static was to invite disaster.

Having put some distance between him and the small crowd of skinheads that was now growing by the second, as though somehow attracted by a pheromone that screamed drama, he rose to his feet.

Trapp watched as the brick wall's face scrunched up with confusion, as though attempting to process something with a motherboard that simply wasn't up to the task. That seemed about right, he thought. The big dumb fuck looked like merely learning the alphabet would be a challenge, let alone anything else.

Trapp showed the crowd his palms in the universal sign of peace. But, for the moment at least, they seemed to be occupied in conversation, all carried out in a language he did not understand, at a blistering pace that meant that even if he did, he would probably struggle to keep up.

He attempted to make use of the momentary distraction and edged away from the group, knowing that all he needed to do was get around them, and then he would be at his target. The rock he was looking for would be about the size of a man's fist – only big enough to contain a small flash drive. Much easier than the old days, when the choice was paper or microfilm, each presenting their own challenges.

"Have you got a gun?" the wiry protester asked, stabbing his finger at Trapp.

Oh, shit.

He played for time. "Huh?"

"My friend"—the wiry kid jerked his thumb at the wall— "said he felt a gun."

Trapp shook his head, trying to play it cool. "No way. It's a cell phone. Tell your buddy he doesn't know what a gun feels like."

"His father owns a gun shop," came the sneering reply. "You think we are fools?"

The response stopped Trapp cold. Of all the big ugly bastards in all the world, he had to get pushed by the one who worked in a freaking *gun shop*. A more lucid part of his brain hoped that Ikeda was having a better time right now than he was. Because there was every chance that the next few seconds were going to hell in a hand basket.

The kid's face took on a sly, questioning expression. "What are you doing here?" he demanded. "Are you a spy?"

Trapp cast a surreptitious glance around himself, searching for a way out. None was apparent. The crowd of skinheads was growing fast, and coming from all directions. They were just kids, clearly from some youth protest group, but that didn't make a bit of difference. Thirty of them at least were converging on him in a loose, multi-layer circle that would be impossible to dodge through.

"What the hell are you talking about?" he replied, curling his lip in a contemptuous sneer. He glanced at a beer can held by one of the kids, and said, "You've been drinking. Your friend is mistaken. Let's leave it there."

"Open your jacket," the wiry kid spat, apoplectic with rage, yet also slyly calculating. "Prove you don't have a gun, and you can go."

Fuck.

Trapp's options were narrowing fast. He considered unleashing a display of fearsome, controlled violence on one of the protesters. Probably the big guy – who for all his size was unlikely to be a trained fighter. He could get close enough to strike a blow at the man's throat, and put him out of action before he had a chance to respond.

If there were only a few of them, even perhaps ten, that was the choice that Trapp would have made. But there were fifty of them now, jeering and screaming and waving their signs with malevolent rage. There was no way that he could fight his way out of this. He could take one of them down, two, maybe three, but after that the sheer weight of bodies would subdue him.

He couldn't allow that outcome to happen. He had a job to do today, one that was vital to the security of his country. Whatever the message Sokolov had left, it had cost the man his life.

"Okay, okay," Trapp murmured softly, showing the crowd around him his palms in the universal gesture of peace. "I'll show you I'm not armed, okay? If that's what it takes to get you guys off my back, I'll do it."

His mind was made up. There was only one way out of this.

"Slowly," the wiry kid snarled. "In fact –"

Trapp suspected that the kid had clocked that asking a man who was possibly armed to get out his weapon was a really dumb idea. He moved too fast for him to respond, unzipping his jacket and removing the pistol in one swift movement.

The safety was already off.

He heard a gasp, and grinned when he noticed the collective flinch from the crowd as they realized what he was holding. "I guess you were right, motherfucker."

And then he fired the weapon five times.

34

Trapp swore at himself for letting it get this far. For just a fraction of a second he paused in stasis, the barrel of his pistol pointing directly at the wet turf. He could see the divots where the spent rounds had torn at the grass, and out of his peripheral vision he could see a glittering brass shell casing lodged among green blades.

"Fuck."

The protest erupted in chaos, with terrified screams splitting the air, and after one long moment in which everyone remained perfectly still, people began to run in every direction, which Trapp saw as though he was a camera placed at the epicenter of an explosion.

The wiry kid and the brick wall were the first to run, the former faster than the latter, skinny arms pumping at his sides as he sprinted away from the madman with the gun.

Trapp was already moving as he began to catalog his options. He quickly scanned the chaotic landscape, and saw that the hundreds who had heard the gunshots had begun to run, triggering further thousands into panicked flight, though from what, this latter category could not know. The farthest edge of the crowd still held their signs and placards aloft, though he could see heads turning to listen to the screams, then those same placards falling as their owners pitched them to the ground as the shockwave from the explosion of panic continued to gain pace.

He figured he had about thirty seconds before he had to bug out. The cops were mostly arrayed around the edges of the park, a hundred yards from his current location in any given direction. It was possible that one of them had witnessed the entire event, though unlikely. He couldn't dismiss the possibility out of hand, but ranked it low in his mental threat grid.

That meant two things: that the first responders wouldn't know exactly where to head, and that they would be fighting against the flight of the panicked crowd when they started running into danger.

Twenty-nine seconds.

Trapp knew he couldn't rest for a moment longer. If he was caught here, then the best case scenario was that he would spend the rest of his life behind bars, tried either as a spy or a terrorist. But he figured that it was unlikely he would be given the respect of a journey through the notoriously corrupt Russian justice system. No, he would be taken into the custody of the FSB, and disappeared.

But his captors would not forget him. Not by a long shot.

He broke into a run toward the rock garden he had pointed out to Sokolov all those years before. The farthest edge of the tent city the protesters had started to construct was about twenty yards north, and he saw a shaven-headed kid, no older than twenty and dressed in a camouflage jacket crawl from the nearest tent, pulling his khaki pants up around his waist as he staggered to his feet. A fraction behind him followed a girl, buttoning up her blouse, her whimpering cries of fear carried on a light breeze.

Despite himself, the corners of Trapp's mouth kinked up in a smile. *Keep it in your pants, kid.*

But apart from them, he was alone for thirty yards in every direction. Seen from above, the scene would have looked like the eye of a swirling storm, an island of calm serenity surrounded by walls of terrified, fleeing humanity.

He was on the rock garden then, the pistol now shoved into his belt loop. He would need to dispose of it, but now was not the time. It might still come in useful.

Twenty-six seconds.

Trapp's wraithlike eyes scanned the garden, searching for anything that looked out of place. He split the area into a grid, as he had been trained at the Farm, and moved his eyes along predictable, parallel lines, both vertical and horizontal. They swept across the grid, looking for a tiny, telltale scratch of colored chalk. Adrenaline surged inside his veins as his brain screamed a warning that time was ticking away, that men with guns were coming for him, and that if he did not get out of here soon, it would be too late.

The chemical made him jumpy, and twice he caught himself skipping a grid square, and forced himself to slow down, to turn back his gaze and search again. He clenched his hands into fists, his muscles vibrating with tension.

A fountain sat at the center of the garden, and the center of his search grid. A protester's backpack lay against it, the drawstring at the top open, and the clips undone. Junk food spilled out from the toppled pack, wrappers that Trapp did not recognize, but flashes of color that only clouded his vision, causing his brain to report false positives.

Focus.

There was litter everywhere, both blown by the wind and intentionally discarded. A flash of silver caught his eye, the inside of a torn-open chocolate bar, and then it wheeled through the air, carried by a gust of air.

"Come on," Trapp grunted to himself. He allowed himself a glance up to assess his tactical position. The park was by no means empty, but the eye of the storm had grown exponentially in only the time it had taken to breathe in a few deep gulps of air. Now he could see little knots of congestion at the far edges of the park, where police officers clad in neon vests fought against the panicked flight of the crowd.

Fifteen seconds.

And that was an optimistic estimate, Trapp knew, because now he could see an officer in the distance, making a beeline straight for him. The man was wearing an orange vest over his uniform, like the others, his arms a mere blur at his sides.

He snapped his gaze back to the rock garden and crouched down, both to narrow the distance to his target, and in the vain hope that it would hide him from the prying eyes of the cops. His focus passed over the mottled stone weathered by acid rain and erosion, chipped in places, mossy in others, and his heart began to beat faster and faster as his brain processed the reality that things had gone very, very wrong indeed.

And then he saw it.

Something out of place, like the rocks all around him, yet also not – as though it was trying too hard to fit in. As though it was...

Manufactured.

His hand reached out to grasp it, but he was too far away, and he stood to give himself the ability to take a step forward.

And then he heard the beating of boots against damp grass, a muffled cry in a language he didn't understand, and a chill ran down his spine as he realized.

Six seconds.

Only he didn't have that long, not really. The cop was too close, and as Trapp turned to face this new threat, the officer's hand moved to the pistol held in a navy blue holster at his waist. The man was young, not much older than the protesters he was here to watch over and keep in line, and he didn't have the experience to know that he should have armed himself already, or that the rush of adrenaline can make a man's fingers numb.

The cop's momentum carried him close to his target, too close, and as the weapon finally came free of its holster, the arm beginning to rise in order to take aim at the suspect, Trapp grimaced an apology. The onrushing officer didn't have time to process the unexpected image of a man with glittering eyes and a total absence of fear before Trapp's arm chopped down on his wrist, anesthetizing it and sent the Makarov pistol flying.

The cop yelped something in Russian which Trapp did not understand, and his foot caught against a rock on the ground, sending him stumbling forward, off balance – and also out of Trapp's reach.

"Crap," he muttered, reaching for his own pistol and hoping the young cop wouldn't make him fire it. He drew it in a smooth motion, the thick fabric of his overhanging jacket tugging at the hammer, but not enough to impede the weapon's progress.

He didn't like killing the boys in blue, no matter which country's flag was on the patch on their shoulder. This man – a boy, really – was no different. He wasn't a soldier, and this wasn't a war. But the world of espionage was so often a gray zone that faded to black, and if Trapp was forced to waste the kid, he would. He might lose a few nights sleep over it, the guilt might chase him into old age, if he ever made it that far, but he would do it, and deal with the consequences later.

Trapp's mind considered all this as the cop staggered forward, almost toppling onto his hands and knees before he arrested his forward motion. The man spun around, and Trapp saw a flash of dark eyes, scared now, searching for his fallen weapon.

"Don't fucking move," Trapp yelled, not knowing whether the man in front of him understood a word of English. His brain screamed at him that he needed to get moving, and fast. But first, he needed to put this cop down.

The missing pistol was closer to him than it was to its rightful owner. Trapp saw a telltale tension building in the kid's legs as he tried to psych himself into diving for it. But he moved first, rushing forward and kicking the weapon out of action, sending it spinning into the grass twenty feet away. Hope died in the officer's eyes, then, and knowing that his brain would not yet have formulated a secondary course of action, Trapp picked his moment to strike.

"Down!" Trapp yelled, jabbing the muzzle of his pistol forward in a motion that would have a weapons instructor cringing, but which he knew would add to the kid's mounting fear. He translated his original command by pointing angrily at the ground, and yelling again, "I said get down!"

The captured cop's resistance crumbled, and he collapsed to his knees. Trapp closed the last couple of steps that separated the two men, reversed the pistol in his hand and smashed it down on the cop's head. It wasn't a killing blow.

He hoped.

He grabbed the Russian cop's slumped body, stripping the man of both his orange vest, upon which Trapp could now see the Cyrillic word for 'POLICE' was inscribed, and the blue uniform jacket underneath, which was accented with a thin red stripe beneath each shoulder, and the red and gold emblem of the Moscow Police Department on the breast pocket. He dumped the kid's radio, careful not to leave a print, since he knew that he would be unable to understand a single word spoken over the police net, and shrugged the jacket over his own shoulders.

It would have been a tight fit even without his own layers of clothing. On top of those, the zipper of the jacket barely fastened, leaving him looking like the Michelin man. It wasn't much of a disguise, but Trapp only hoped to sow a second's doubt in the minds of the man's comrades.

He stuffed the neon vest inside the jacket so that it was out of view, and then spared no further thought for the unconscious officer. The struggle had taken him a dozen feet away from the dead drop location, and he hurried back over to it, picking up an object that both looked like a rock, and felt like a rock, but was machined out of carbon fiber and painted, rather than having been formed during the formation of the earth herself.

He heard shouts closing on his position, but guessed that for a few more seconds, at least, the police would be caught on their heels, not knowing who to look for, or in which direction to direct their search. He kept himself low, heading for the collection of thirty or forty tents, and circled the small, newly-erected encampment to put some distance in between him and the cop's body.

Trapp didn't attempt to open the dead drop device, not yet. Once he emerged on the far side of the tent city, his boots met firmer ground – paving stones arranged around a large statue that looked like a jagged steel wedding ring, standing vertically upon a stone plinth. The statue was adorned both with Russian flags and hand-painted bedsheets daubed in Cyrillic slogans. It was a strange sight, now that the protesters were gone, leaving only their garbage and placards on the ground in their wake, a post-apocalyptic hellscape.

Keep moving, he reminded himself.

To stop right now was to submit to certain capture. Capture meant that whatever intelligence was contained inside the dead drop – *if* anything truly lay inside – would fall into enemy hands. Capture meant torture, and a slow, inevitable, horrifically painful death.

It meant never seeing Ikeda again. And that was unacceptable.

Trapp darted between tall, spindly tree trunks with thin, silver bark that marked them out as birch. Their thick green canopy danced lazily in the wind, and then he was back on the grass, running toward the edge of the park. He saw a cop heading in his direction, and then another, and he slowed his pace, so as not to draw unwanted attention.

"*куда ты идешь*," the nearest of the uniformed officers yelled, confusion carving wrinkled lines into the man's face. But Trapp had no idea what he was saying, and he kept going, not stopping, nor answering, knowing that if he so much as opened his mouth then the game was up.

Though he kept walking forward, his pace fast, Trapp kept the corners of his eyes trained on the man who had opened his mouth, knowing that common sense was tangling with duty, and wondering which would win out. Would he see through Trapp's paper-thin disguise, realize that he'd never seen this man before, or clock that he was wearing denim jeans instead of blue uniform pants?

Or would he keep going forward, toward the sound of gunfire that had rocked the protest fewer than sixty seconds before?

Trapp's fingers inched closer to the weapon that was once again stowed in his belt, now beneath two layers of jacket. The cop's decision would determine the course of the rest of his life – specifically, whether he lived to see it, or died right here and now.

In truth, the man's decision would also guide Trapp's own fate, for if he was forced to open fire then there would be no escaping the wrath of his comrades. Not for a second time.

Don't do it, he urged.

As he kept moving, rejoining a path again, only twenty yards away from a small group of protesters who hadn't vacated the park entirely, the cop seemed to come to a decision. He shook off his confusion and returned to the pursuit of a man he didn't yet know he had already lost.

Trapp joined the crowd, not yet allowing himself to wallow in the wave of relief coursing through his body, and pushed through it, ignoring questions barked at him in a foreign language. He galloped down a set of steps, past another pair of cops rushing in the opposite direction, barely meriting a second glance on this occasion.

As he left the park, crossing a road that was cordoned off to traffic at either end, he breathed out a long, deep, endless sigh of relief that flooded out of him with the relentless power of the Nile emptying into the Mediterranean Sea. It was only now that he recognized how fast his heart was beating, or felt the beads of sweat dripping off his forehead – both more a result of tension than exertion.

"That was close," he groaned, cursing himself for breaking the cardinal rule of espionage and thrusting himself into the center of attention. "Too damn close."

And it was far from over. He might have escaped the first cordon of cops, but before long the whole of central Moscow would be on lockdown. He needed to get out before it was too late.

Trapp fought against his instincts and slowed his pace, walking casually down a side street, past a government building with a small brass plaque outside which read, 'Federal Agency for State Property Management' in English letters under the Cyrillic. He kept his head low, pointed at the ground, hoping that it would obscure him from the surveillance cameras that dotted the area, but knowing that it probably wouldn't.

That's a problem for another day.

He cast a quick look around to make sure no one was paying him any attention, and when he was certain that they were not, he ducked into a space between two parked cars, crouched down, and pulled on the neon vest he had previously stowed by his breast. Again, the disguise was skin deep, but if one of the cops he'd just passed managed to radio in a description, then perhaps this costume change might add a layer of distance. It was better than nothing.

He started walking again, slowly enough not to draw the eye, fast enough to put as much distance between himself and what was about to turn into a very hot crime scene as possible. As he walked, his fingers played with the rock he had carried all this time, searching for a seam or a catch. He knew that it would not be locked, or contain the kind of self-destruct device so beloved of Hollywood movies. There wasn't the space, and besides, any competent intelligence agency would be able to defeat such protections quickly enough.

Trapp found it, worked the bottom of the rock open, and saw a memory stick sitting in a foam indentation. He pulled it free, put it into the coin pocket of his denim jeans, and dumped the two halves of the rock into an overflowing trash can.

It was only then that the question came to him. *What the hell do I do now?*

35

The village of Soloslovo was 20 miles from Central Moscow, about thirty minutes by car in light traffic, or twenty on a high-powered motorcycle the likes of which Eliza Ikeda rode as she zipped past, around and through the bumper-to-bumper vehicles which lined the streets between the third and sixth of Moscow's concentric ring roads, their exhausts pumping thick clouds of smoke into the air.

There was little to distinguish most of her journey from any of a dozen run-down former Eastern Bloc cities. It was Moscow, but she could have been anywhere. Hulking concrete apartment blocks rose like jagged teeth to either side of the highway, a dull gray that matched the clouds scuttling across the sky.

It was a relief to leave Moscow proper and enter the country, passing through sections of thick pine forest, and past communities that were at turns glistening examples of the country's surging oil wealth or spotted with decaying remnants of long-abandoned Soviet heavy industry.

Little distinguished Soloslovo from any of half a dozen similar villages that Ikeda growled past, except the quality of the blacktop. It took her a little while to pick up on the fact, and it wasn't until she was guiding the bike to a stop in what passed for the town's main strip that her brain put the pieces together. The first fifteen miles of the journey had been a masterclass in dodging potholes, and Ikeda had been forced to draw on skills drilled into her at the CIA's tactical mobility school at Camp Peary to avoid aping Superman and going straight over her handlebars.

The last five, however, were more akin to cutting through the calm, still water of a mountain lake, as Ikeda – a competitive long distance swimmer – had done many times before. It was the first sign that Soloslovo was more than the McMansion town filled to the brim with McMansion people that it first appeared.

The second was the cars.

"Dang," she muttered as she pulled off her helmet and ran her fingers through her hair, her eyes tracking a matte black Bentley Continental – at least three hundred thousand dollars' worth of vehicle – as it passed her by.

Ikeda hadn't paid much attention to the billboard signs that lined the last few miles of asphalt into town, but now she remembered that at least a third of them had been advertising high-end foreign vehicles. Bentleys, of course, but also Rolls-Royce, Aston Martin, Ferrari and Porsche. No American brands, she noted with a half-smile.

I guess they save those for the cops.

She pulled an elastic hair band from her jeans pocket, stretched it out over her fingers, and quickly tied her hair into a neat ponytail. With that job done, she quickly checked that her pistol, a compact 9 mm Sig Sauer, was secure in her waistband after the journey, hidden behind the leather jacket she had donned just in case she came tumbling off the bike – an eventuality that thankfully hadn't come to pass.

She scanned her eyes around the neighborhood before dropping them down to the screen of the phone, checking for a message from Trapp. There was nothing, which wasn't surprising. He had his own shit to do, and she knew him well enough by now to understand that he wasn't the kind of guy who either needed or wanted to be attached to her with an umbilical cord. That was just fine with Ikeda. She valued her own space too highly to be with a man who wanted to crowd it.

She frowned, her slate gray eyes suddenly sightless. Was that what they were? Together?

Cut that out, girl, she grumbled to herself. Assuming they survived this present difficulty, there would be plenty of time to figure out exactly what they were, and where they were going.

She grazed the backs of her fingers against the butt of the pistol one more time to reassure herself that it was still there, and then got to work. She had devised a cover story for her presence in the village. If she was asked, then she was a high-end international realty consultant scouting out a home for an American banker who was being assigned to the Moscow office of his firm. No, she couldn't identify the firm – client confidentiality. *I'm sure you understand.*

That would be enough to pass more than a cursory inspection. Even so, she didn't expect to need it. From her limited experience with Russians, she found them to be a reserved and private people. Not rude, nor unfriendly, just...

Cold.

There was truly no other word for it. Although Russia was perhaps her own country's foremost competitor, and sometime enemy, Ikeda did not believe that any people were truly evil, and certainly not the Russians. They simply took a little time to warm up, which was hardly surprising, given the turmoil that had wracked the country over the preceding century. For much of it, sharing too much with the wrong person could lead to a knock on the door in the middle of the night, a one-way ticket to Siberia, or an even worse fate.

America was not exactly perfect itself, she knew, and when

it came down to it, was there truly any difference between a people who would smile at you when they stabbed you in the back, and one who simply remained impassive from the start?

Not so much.

Ikeda snorted, and for a second time reminded herself to concentrate on the task at hand. All they knew was that Roman Kholodov, the man whose name had come up during the operation in Istanbul, had a house here in Soloslovo. Her job was to reconnoiter the place, work out what kind of security was being employed, and see if she could determine a route into the building – ideally one that didn't require the kind of kinetic method they had employed in Turkey. Istanbul was a long way away from Russia, and the mercenary was a low level player in the grand scheme of things. His disappearance probably wouldn't even bring a tear to his own mother's eye.

She didn't think that anyone would weep too deeply over Roman Kholodov's disappearance either, but that wasn't the point. If they took him out before they had an actual plan, somebody would notice, and that might have unpredictable – possibly devastating – consequences.

Ikeda drummed her fingers against her denim pants as she walked down the main thoroughfare, her eyes flicking left and right and drinking in every detail of the place. In truth, there wasn't much to slake her thirst for information. Soloslovo was a quiet place, heavy on real estate, but light on everything else. There were three small grocery stores, an expensive bar set in a building constructed entirely of white marble that looked tacky as hell, and not a whole lot beyond that.

"What the hell do people do here?" she muttered.

Ikeda checked the map on her phone, noted that the battery was already half-drained, and resolved to avoid using it as much as possible. She had a good head for directions, and her spin around Moscow had given her enough of a sense of the city's layout to get by. She would be able to make her own way back to the safe house, with or without assistance from the long arm of one of Silicon Valley's premier mapping products.

Just this once, though, it came in useful.

With the location of Kholodov's mansion now fixed in her mind, she replaced the phone in her pocket and set off on foot. There was a light breeze, and although when the sun's rays reached her, it was burning hot, they were nevertheless intermittent. As she had discovered with the roads, the village was impeccably well-maintained. The grass medians were neatly tended, the sidewalks free of litter and debris.

It's nice for some.

The area still bore signs that in the distant past it had been an agricultural community, though those days were clearly long gone. A grain silo, rusted and askew, looked like the leaning Tower of Pisa, and wore a bright yellow sign marked with black Cyrillic characters that Ikeda could not read, but nevertheless understood. It was marked for demolition.

In its place, no doubt, a soulless glass and brick mansion would rise, like all the others that lined the streets at fifty yard intervals. Ikeda wrinkled her nose. She didn't have any of her own, but nevertheless shared a healthy distaste for that most gauche of things: *new money*. And new money was something that Soloslovo had coming out of its ears.

As she reached the edge of the village, still a few hundred yards away from Kholodov's property, she noticed that the area had subtly changed. The mansions were spaced further apart now, and set into plots of land that she guessed measured up at about an acre. Some of the plots were surrounded by neatly placed fir trees. She didn't know a whole hell of a lot about gardening, but what little knowledge she had was enough to tell that they hadn't been there long. The trunks were light, bark thin, and the spaces between the dark green branches indicated that they hadn't yet grown into their full size. They were older than the McMansions they guarded, but not by much.

Kholodov's compound, when she reached it, was both obviously his, and obviously a compound – a designation ordinarily reserved by the media for properties owned by warlords in far-flung, war-torn countries. But the owner of this particular property cared little for aesthetics. That was no slight on the architect of the mansion, which while not to Ikeda's personal taste, was nice enough – in an ostentatious display of wealth kind of way.

No, she mused. *It's the whole razor wire and metal spikes thing you've got going on, buddy. It's not exactly friendly.*

The wall itself was stark gray concrete, and almost perfectly square, with each section measuring around fifty yards. Easy enough to climb, Ikeda thought, until you reached the razor-sharp obstacles mounted on top. They would be a problem. Not an insurmountable one, but a problem nonetheless. Almost any security system could be breached, her training had taught her. The mark of their success lay in how long they slowed a would-be assailant down.

It was the cameras that worried her more. There was a veritable thicket of them – three at each of the corners, covering every angle, and a dome spaced every fifteen yards down the wall. There wasn't an inch they wouldn't cover. The question was – who was watching on the other side? An army, or just a spotty night watchman working his first job out of high school. It was impossible to be sure.

She looped around the fence, careful to stay out of sight, noting the camera positions, committing blind spots to memory, and searching for an easy way in.

None presented itself.

When she had all the entrances and exits mapped, along with surreptitious shots of anything that merited further study, she turned back toward the village, deciding that the risk of being spotted outweighed the value of whatever intelligence she might be able to glean. She grimaced unconsciously as she walked. Kholodov's compound wasn't a fortress, but it wasn't far off. A head-on assault would be almost impossible.

She took a different road back, where she stumbled on a collection of concrete apartment buildings that were almost tumbling down. Electricity cables hung like rats' tails from nearby pylons, low and tangled.

An old woman sat at the side of the road, tending a sad, rickety cart stacked with apples that were equally so. A rumble of hunger in Ikeda's stomach told her how long it was since she last ate, and she reached out for one. "How much?"

The woman, whose hair had long ago faded to white, and which was mostly tucked behind a hand-patterned scarf regardless, leaned forward and replied in a low, scratchy voice.

"I'm sorry," Ikeda said apologetically. "I didn't catch that."

The babushka cleared her throat, and Ikeda noticed how small the old woman looked, how bowed by the strains and stresses of life. She had to be close to eighty years old, though she supposed that perhaps she'd simply lived a harder life than most. The evidence was right in front of her, after all, for instead of enjoying a comfortable retirement, the old lady was plying a thankless trade.

"You are American?" the babushka croaked, speaking slow, half-forgotten, yet perfectly passable English. Her cheeks, carved into valleys and canyons by age, warmed into a smile.

"How did you guess?" Ikeda grinned, surprised to find an English speaker out here.

"I love America," she replied, her face entirely without guile. "So for you, girl, nothing."

Ikeda reached into her leather jacket, shaking her head even before the woman finished speaking. After the disappearance of her mother just months after she was born, and her father's death thereafter, she'd been raised by her grandparents

– a halcyon period of calm in an otherwise fractious childhood. She could not in good conscience take from this woman without paying.

"I insist," she said, passing over a note that was equivalent to a week of the woman's pension, though that wasn't saying a whole lot. The babushka's gnarled fingers didn't rise up to meet it, so she tucked it beneath an apple, taking the one next to it and polishing it against her blouse.

She leaned against a concrete fence post next to the old lady, and took a bite of the apple. Its skin was leathered and waxy, like the woman who sold it, but it was sweet, and still possessed enough crunch to satisfy Ikeda's immediate pangs of hunger.

"How long have you lived here?" she asked. "Your English is great."

It surprised her. Russians, particularly those of the babushka's generation, were not known for their foreign language skills – and certainly not for their proficiency with English. After all, for most of her long life, America and the West were the imperialist enemy – to be feared, not studied.

The babushka beamed once again at the compliment. "I was, how you say...secretary. For Party boss. Many years. My husband was manager on state farm."

Ikeda chewed on the apple, enjoying the brief interlude of normality after the craziness of the past few days. It was nice to enjoy the country as a tourist might, instead of applying the suspicious demeanor the Agency had instilled into her. It was an attitude that might save her life, and yet at the same time it was an acid that, left unchecked, could eat away at her soul and make that very same life not worth living.

"Sixty years," the babushka added, book-ending a few seconds of silence.

"What's that?"

"You ask how long I live here," she nodded, the movement jerky yet purposeful. "Sixty years."

Ikeda let out a low whistle. In a little over thirty, her own life had spanned Japan, Hawaii, California, Hong Kong, China, even North Korea, and many other countries besides. It was almost incomprehensible to her that someone could have lived in a place like this for quite so long.

"You must like it," she said, coming to the end of the apple, her mind wandering as she tried to determine what to do next.

The babushka's response surprised her. The old woman spat forcefully against the ground and cursed in Russian. "You are nice girl, yes?"

The question caught Ikeda off guard. She wasn't immediately certain how to respond. "Um, I guess so..."

"I am old. You think I want to sell apples by side of road? Bah!" She shook her head violently. "We had a life, and they took from us. Took *everything*."

"Who did?" Ikeda asked, her curiosity piqued.

"We were budgetniki. We worked hard for the state all our lives. They came to my husband's farm, told the workers they would get apartment for papers. What did we know? They were liars. My husband said no, so they beat him. Then he said yes."

What Ikeda came to understand was that the 'papers' were shares in Soloslovo's largest – and for several generations, only – employer, a Soviet state farm. After the fall of communism, the workers were issued shares in their former workplaces, and those shares were often stolen by unscrupulous bosses. Some workers traded what they thought to be worthless scraps of paper for a bottle of vodka, but the babushka and her husband had known better. She was educated, and he had street smarts of his own. But that didn't matter when gangsters came to town equipped with pistols and crowbars. They got what they wanted – the land on which the area's many gleaming mansions now stood.

And poor, hard-working retirees, all of whom had known nothing but the hardships of the communist state, were left with nothing, just a pension that wasn't enough to cover the heating bill. And the land, the babushka asserted, went straight to President Murov's closest cronies as a reward for their service.

"What do you mean?" Ikeda asked, her interest long past idle curiosity.

"Bodyguards," the babushka hissed with derision. "FSB, KGB, I don't know. All the same. Gangsters. *Pigs!*"

That fit, Ikeda thought. It was a page straight out of 'Dictatorship for Dummies'– reward the people who kept you safe. Keep them close to keep them loyal. And it also explained how Roman Kholodov had come into his fortune. Little was known about the man until he suddenly, mysteriously became a billionaire. Now the pieces fit together in her mind. Kholodov was just a front man, a convenient body behind whom the Russian president could park a portion of his ill-acquired fortune.

The information also suggested that Soloslovo would be crawling with security. It wasn't just the roads that were in good condition; it would be the police response times also. And that, she considered, was somewhat less than optimal, at least where an assault was concerned.

"Why pigs?" Ikeda ventured, curious at the level of disgust in the old woman's voice. It pointed to a specific outrage, surely too.

"You saw the big house?" the babushka asked, pointing in the direction of Kholodov's compound.

"Uh huh."

"That man, he is animal. Every night, same time."

Ikeda frowned. "What happens?"

"Girls. Young girls!" The old woman squawked, practically quivering with anger. "A man drives them to the house. On this road. They stay an hour, maybe two. I see them return, always crying."

She spat at the ground for emphasis. But Ikeda didn't feel her anger. A hunger gripped her, a realisation that maybe, just maybe, they had a way in.

The phone in her pocket buzzed – two long pulses, with a short break in between that signaled a message had arrived on the encrypted platform she was using to communicate with Trapp. The message would delete itself if it remained unread for longer than an hour, but she had no intention of leaving it that long.

Ikeda pulled the slim black device out, allowed it to interrogate her fingerprint, and checked the screen. What she read chilled the blood in her veins.

"I'm sorry," she choked, unable to tear her eyes away from the screen. "I have to go."

The message was simple. It read: '911.'

36

T rapp walked almost a mile on foot before ditching the police vest in a trashcan, along with the jacket underneath it. He glanced around to ensure no one was watching, then rummaged among the garbage, pulling out a greasy fast food wrapper and what looked suspiciously like a bag containing a soiled diaper, and dumping them on top.

He wrinkled his nose, looking down at his fingers with more than a little distaste. It wasn't exactly crawling half a mile through a sewage line, as he'd once done near the presidential palace in Kiev, but still, every man had his foibles, and one of Trapp's was his fondness for personal hygiene. It was a desire he could forgo for the sake of his country, but that didn't mean he had to like it.

Then again, he was pretty sure he wouldn't enjoy spending the next fifty years in a Siberian jail, either.

He snorted. *Like they'd let you last that long.*

Next to the garbage can was a docking station for the Moscow push bike rental system. Trapp pulled a prepaid Visa debit card from the inside of his jacket pocket, suffering a momentary but heart-stopping panic as he briefly thought he'd lost the memory stick, and unlocked one of the bikes, taking care to wipe the screen clean after he was done, to avoid leaving his prints behind.

He checked his phone and found a message from Ikeda. It was terse. "Coming."

"Real hard-core, secret agent guy," Trapp muttered, mounting the bike and beginning to pedal. In his denim, he looked a little like an oversized hipster. *Very* oversized, and not a little ridiculous. But it was the best option he had, and his desire to get away was constantly reinforced by the echoes of sirens bouncing down Moscow's wide boulevards.

It had taken fifteen minutes to get to the bike station, and Trapp knew that he had to move fast. The cops would most likely be setting up checkpoints any second now, if they hadn't already, and he needed to get away from the center. Moscow was a city of almost twelve million souls, and outside of its glitzy core was a warren of concrete apartment blocks, narrow streets and downtrodden neighborhoods where the locals had no particular love of the deeply corrupt city police.

Several times, he passed Metro stations, which offered the false prospect of whisking him out of danger and back to the safe house in just minutes, but he knew better than to venture below ground when the cops were after him. In the subway, the authorities had the upper hand. They could regulate access, stop a train on the tracks, and hundreds of feet below the surface, he would be trapped, with no way out, and no realistic prospect of finding one.

Two miles later he stopped at a Paul Smith on Neglinnaya Street, a British fashion brand which produced clothes that really didn't suit him, dumped his jacket in the trash, and purchased a dark red sports coat with a white zipper, and a ridiculous black fedora to complete the look.

He kept his jeans, partly because he couldn't find any with holes big enough to fit his thighs amid the sea of skinny jeans,

and partly because he had an irrational fear of losing the
memory stick which contained the only will and testament that
Alexy Sokolov had left behind.

He checked his phone again. There was a message from
Ikeda.

'Where are you?'

Trapp exited the boutique, typing a reply into his phone,
and didn't hear the siren, because it wasn't blaring. An instant
later, he cursed himself, seeing the silent blue and red lights
flashing on top of a cop car that was driving slowly down the
quiet street. Moving naturally, but as quickly as possible, he
dropped to the ground, pretending to lace his shoe, and hiding
the bulk of his frame behind a row of parked cars.

Idiot, he cursed, furious with himself. His pulse was racing,
and he struggled to master it. Had they noticed him? Should
he run?

If he did, they would doubtless come after him, whether
they knew who the hell he was or not. That was what the boys
in blue did back home, and he had no reason to believe it
would be different here.

So don't fucking run. Act natural.

It wasn't the mere presence of cops that worried Trapp. He
had a pistol, and if they came after him, he would be forced to
take them out. He had no doubts that he would be able to react
faster than a couple of half-trained officers, and he had enough
rounds left to turn the windshield into a spider web of cracks,
and any soft flesh behind it into jelly.

No, it was the memory stick in his jeans that now felt like it
weighed half a ton. If there was even a slight chance that it
might contain information vital to national security, then he
couldn't afford to lose it. No matter the cost.

The police lights reflected off the shining glass fronts of
numerous high-end shops, mostly bearing names written in
Cyrillic characters that he did not recognize, and containing

items that he would not want to own even if he could afford to.

Which he could not.

There were two officers, Trapp saw, a driver and his passenger, both scanning the street. One was female. Could he kill a woman?

If I have to.

It was the truth, and Trapp knew it, but it was an unpalatable one. But the stakes were simply too high to allow a little thing like a conscience to stand in the way. Nations were like tectonic plates, especially those the size of the United States and Russia. Their actions decided the fate of billions, reshaped futures too numerous to count, powered by forces that were simply impossible to restrain.

And where does that leave you?

All this flashed through Trapp's mind in the space of a scant few seconds. He was still collapsed in a false crouch, pretending to tie an imaginary shoelace, but he couldn't hold the pose for long without drawing suspicion. His phone, still clutched in his hand, buzzed.

'What's your location?'

Okay, good. The idea that he had a partner somewhere out there comforted Trapp. It was still two against twelve million, which made for positively inclement odds, no matter how you cut it. Still, it was a whole lot better than *one* in twelve million.

Trapp stood slowly, so as not to draw the eye of the passing officers, and hunched his frame, knowing that if his description had been passed to the city's beat cops, then his unusual height would be the first thing they were looking for.

He tapped out a message, sending Ikeda the area and the street. Her reply arrived quickly, as though she too was hovering over her phone.

'Okay. I'm ten minutes out.'

Ten minutes was a whole lot better than an hour, Trapp

mused as he kept his head turned in the direction of the phone and slightly away from the police car, but in a situation like this it was as good as a lifetime. He scanned the street with his peripheral vision, attempting to see what the two officers were doing by checking the reflection in the glass window of the furniture shop.

No joy. The car's flashing lights made it impossible to tell. Had it slowed even further? His heart began to race again, adrenaline pumping into his system and making his hands sweat. The phone felt slippery between his fingers.

"Fuck," Trapp whispered, forcing his mind into overdrive. He needed options, and he needed them now.

He had a couple of choices, neither of which were optimal. But whichever he chose, he knew, he had to act fast. To continue hovering like this would simply invite trouble.

He could enter a shop, either the Paul Smith he'd just left, or one of the many identikit boutiques that lined the shopping boulevard. That option had the advantage of taking him out of the direct line of sight of the officers inside the car, but it also limited his routes of egress. Each shop would probably have a rear entrance, to allow stock to arrive, but he didn't know where those might lead. If the cops had already called in a suspect, then he might only be boxing himself in.

Option two was to walk south down the street, in the opposite direction of travel to the police, maintaining a casual pace. There were plenty of tall men in Russia, his hair color was disguised by this pretentious hat, and he was wearing a different outfit entirely. They probably wouldn't notice him, and by the time he was around the corner, he would be a ghost.

On the other hand, if they had already seen him, then a foot chase down the streets of Moscow was unlikely to end well. He didn't know the lay of the land, he didn't speak the language, and they could almost certainly call in reinforcements faster than he could think up an exfiltration route.

"Think, Jason, think," he whispered.

An idea occurred to him, hokey, but effective enough. Trapp brought the cell phone to his ear, faking a call. As he did so, he turned his head a fraction of an inch, but enough that his peripheral vision now swept across the street. The police car was slowing. No, stopping.

Shit.

Inside, now.

It was a shitty option, but they were all shitty options. He walked, didn't run, into the furniture store next to the clothes shop he had just left. It had glass doors out front, but they were narrow – not nearly wide enough to move bulky furniture in and out of, confirming that there must be a service entrance out back, and more importantly, a service entrance that led to a *road*.

Unless they build the stuff inside?

"It's not fucking IKEA," he muttered aloud, as much to reassure himself and stave off the growing stress that was swiftly beginning to strangle his decision-making functions. He couldn't allow that. He needed to think clearly.

"Hey, buddy, there a bathroom in this joint?" he said.

The reply came in Russian. Trapp waved the guy away, muttering, "Yeah, yeah, I get it. You no speak English."

The store was set out over one floor, as far as he could tell, and if he'd had the time to pay attention to the merchandise, Trapp might have wondered who the hell would buy any of this shit. Ostentatious chandeliers dangled overhead, attached to price tags that might bankrupt small African nations, and the floor was dotted with sofas and couches that were probably made from exotic animal skins sourced from those same countries, but which were the definition of form over function.

How long had it been since Ikeda gave him her ETA, a minute? Less? It was hard to tell. Blood was rushing in Trapp's ears in time with his heartbeat, and that was way too fast, and getting faster, the noise strangling his threat perception and inviting him to make a mistake.

He scanned the store, searching for something he could use, still moving ever farther inside. It was big, almost thirty yards wide, and about twice as deep. A glint of light attracted his eye.

Okay, a mirror, finally some good news. I can work with that.

Trapp walked toward it, quickening his step now he was out of direct view of the street. He figured that if the officers entered this establishment, it meant they knew who he was, or at least suspected. Dollars to doughnuts it also meant they had called it in, which meant he'd need to move fast, or he was screwed.

He reached the mirror, stopping in front of it, shifting left slightly, then stretching his arm out as if to check the price tag. Instead, he repositioned it, so that the angle covered the entrance to the store, as well as giving and narrow view of the street.

Crap.

Not good. Really not good. The cop car was most definitely stopped. It was hard to make out for sure, but it looked like one officer was climbing out the passenger side door, the woman inside speaking into her radio.

In truth, it was almost a relief. The tension of not knowing his fate had been worse than knowing he was made. At least now he knew that he had only one option left – to get the hell out of here, no matter how he accomplished it.

Trapp barely looked at the phone in his hands as he side-stepped the mirror, returned to the tiled path through the store, and began typing a hurried message.

'I've got trouble. Cops, two of them. Leave me if it looks bad.'

He didn't wait for a response, understanding that the business end of the motorcycle wasn't exactly a great spot for texting and riding. He had at least eight minutes on his own, and only a wing, a prayer, and a 9 mm pistol on his side.

No – wait, there was one more thing he could use. He glanced back at the screen of his phone, swiped through a couple of apps, and found it. A location beacon that would update Ikeda with his precise coordinates. Easier than being glued to a cell phone in the middle of a firefight, and it was all commercially available. A couple of bucks in the app store. That was the real triumph of capitalism.

Concentrate, Jason.

Now he chanced a glance over his shoulder. If they were entering the store, then they could only have one target, unless the police in Moscow were paid a damn sight more than their brethren back in the US of A.

In truth, he had expected to see precisely what he did. Two officers, one with her pistol drawn, but held at her side, the other with his fingers resting lightly on the holster. Still, as if any further confirmation was needed, this settled it.

It's time to go.

Though Trapp had mocked the idea earlier, the furniture store was in fact laid out like an extremely high end IKEA – sample rooms were constructed out of furniture: beds, chests of drawers, children's nightlights, and other items he couldn't even begin to describe. The layout was that of a maze, winding and obstructed, meaning that if he needed to run, his quickest route to the other side – and hopefully to the service exit he was looking for – would be over the merchandise, not around it.

Trapp sidestepped a browsing customer, all faux fur, six-inch heels and glittering Swarovski crystals. His mind conjured up an image of Ikeda in that kind of outfit, and he almost snorted.

Almost.

His shoulder clipped the woman as he passed her, spinning her around, and almost sending her tumbling. He didn't bother turning back, but heard the sound of her stilettos scraping the tiles like a newborn giraffe on an ice rink. She chased his departing back with a stream of unintelligible Russian curses.

The sound was chased by another cry, commanding and strident, a man's voice that drowned out that of the offended woman. *"Politsiya, ostanovis!"*

He understood that one, Trapp thought grimly, equipping himself with the pistol and hoping he had enough ammunition left to slow them down. The metal grip felt strangely comforting, but he didn't truly want to open fire on a couple of innocent police officers, or in a public space, not least for a second time that day.

He spared a look over his shoulder, but found his view was obscured by a large oak cabinet. Would it stop a bullet?

A mental stopwatch started ticking in his subconscious. How long was left? Seven minutes?

And then what?

37

The bike mounted the sidewalk twice as Ikeda gunned the engine, dodging red lights at every opportunity, using active pedestrian crossings to get a jumpstart into freshly empty sections of roads. She left a trail of chaos and waving fists in her way, and she really didn't give a shit.

"I'm coming, Jason," she muttered to herself over and over again, almost as a mantra.

She would never forget what he had done for her when she was in that North Korean camp. Never forget that he'd crawled down a mountainside, not slept in days, knifed a camp guard in the neck, frog marched another through his own base, and rescued her with little more on his side than sheer force of will.

So copping a traffic violation? Yeah, she could probably handle that. She let go of the left handlebar, keeping hold of the right, and the throttle jammed down, feeding gas into the piston which exploded beneath her, sending a metronomic vibration through her body, chattering her teeth and turning her entire vision into a blur.

With it, she reached inside her jacket and removed the phone.

Slow is smooth, and smooth is fast, remember.

The last thing she could afford to do was drop the device and have it smash into a thousand pieces. It was her only way of contacting Trapp. She powered up the screen, splitting her attention between the road ahead and its display.

Ikeda clenched her right fist in satisfaction when she saw what he'd done, inadvertently dumping what felt like at least an ounce of gasoline into the engine, and letting loose a burst of power that sent the front wheel skipping up off the asphalt. "Smarter than you look, Jason!" she yelled with glee.

She tapped the message – a set of live coordinates – and a map screen flashed into existence on her phone. It contained two icons, a red arrow, shaped like a guitar pick, which denoted her target, and a small blue circle, moving rapidly down a street.

Too rapidly.

A flash of yellow darted into the street, attached to a pair of kids' shoes. Ikeda saw a pair of blond pigtails, a white face, lips parted in a smile, turning back to her mother. She saw the panic inscribed on that same mother's face, no doubt picturing every parent's greatest fear.

The world slowed down.

Ikeda was alone on the asphalt. The nearest car behind her was at least thirty yards back, since she was pushing ninety miles an hour in the center of the city. It wasn't safe. Actions like this had consequences. The kind of consequences that left you scarred for life.

A fly swatted the visor of her helmet, exploding on impact, causing her fingers to jerk spasmodically at the controls of the bike. Still holding the phone, her left hand hit the brakes as hard as she could without flying over the handlebars. The fly's body, now little more than mush and the remnants of an exoskeleton, scraped up the clear visor, leaving a trail in its wake.

The girl stopped dead, right in the middle of the road. Only twenty feet separated her tiny frame from almost certain death.

Holy fuck.

The mother came rushing out into the road, entering into a vicious three-way dance with potentially lethal consequences. Adrenaline pumped into Ikeda's system, causing her vision to narrow into the point of a telescope, focused on the girl's pale face, which still bore an expression that was more confused than terrified.

The girl's mother was wearing a dark orange coat, a flash of color against the surface of the road. The movement attracted Ikeda's attention, and it made her mind up.

"Left!"

Shit. Shit. Shit.

Ikeda did not know whether she was screaming, whether she was shouting, whether the girl was crying, or her mother was calling her back. She didn't know whether the kid would dart into her path, or even get pushed. All she knew was that she needed to hug the curb as close as humanly possible. She could not, would not allow any harm to come to this child.

Around the street, dozens of horrified faces turned to the bike's throaty growl, all watching a tragedy play out in slow motion. Ikeda did not see any of it. She jerked the controls hard to the left, and missed the girl by a couple of feet, although if she was asked later in life, she would swear blind that it was by no more than inches.

"Oh my God, oh my God," Ikeda muttered, adrenaline still coursing through her veins, making her jumpy, making it difficult even to see the speed gauge above the handlebars. The bike was still bleeding momentum, slowing almost to a crawl. The engine quieted, but even so the street for a second, then two, maybe three remained deathly quiet.

And then the girl started sobbing. Not sobbing, really, so much as bawling, sending great shrieking cries of terror echoing down the wide city street. They drowned out the raging of a torrent of blood in Ikeda's ears, the rapid, ragged, uneven tenor of the breaths she was dragging into her own lungs.

But to Eliza Ikeda, the girl's cries sounded like a choir of angels. Because she was still alive.

She swiveled her head, looking over her shoulder, just to check that her mind wasn't lying to her, just to check she had not actually killed the little girl.

Uh oh.

The girl was most certainly alive, swaddled in her mother's arms, heaving great, jerking sobs, coating the woman's shoulder in a river of salty tears. The kid's mom couldn't have cared less about the reckless, out-of-control motorcyclist who had almost killed her daughter.

But the dad did. At least, Ikeda assumed that the large, balding Russian charging toward her with an expression of pure, unadulterated anger on his face was related to the little girl. It had taken the bike almost thirty yards to come to a complete halt after she had passed the kid. He looked like a slow starter, but he'd already eaten up ten of them, and was building momentum fast.

It went against every grain of moral fiber that Eliza Ikeda possessed, but she knew she had to get out of here. Getting off the bike, apologizing, hell – slicing her driving license into two – that would be the right thing to do. She'd fucked up, and she would probably see that little girl's face in her dreams for the rest of her life.

But sometimes life split into forking paths, both of which were correct, but only one of which could be taken. And a man's life rested in her hands.

Still, Ikeda's muscles seemed locked into place, as though a combination of an overdose of adrenaline, and a healthy dose of shock were both reverberating around her body. She could see the powerful Russian charging toward her, the analytical part of her mind cataloguing him as a threat.

Fifteen yards.

And yet she could not move. Again, a flash of yellow as her mind replayed the incident over again, this time painting the surface of the road red as her subconscious extrapolated what could so easily have happened.

Ten yards.

That voice again, calling out a threat warning like the navigator in the back of a fighter jet. The Russian was getting closer and closer, and part of her wanted to feel his wrath, allow him to take out his rightful rage upon her. She deserved it.

And yet it could not be.

Ikeda glanced back down at the screen of the phone. It was still shining bright. She knew where she had to go. And she gunned the engine, not looking back, not needing to.

And it felt like crap.

38

"Come out," a Russian voice called, thickly accented, but perfectly understandable. "You have no trouble. We just want to ask questions."

"I bet you do," Trapp said underneath his breath, careful not to give away his position. He was crouching behind the frame of a bed near the back of the store. On top of the sheets was a wispy bedspread that looked like the skin of some ethereal creature, all shimmering fibers and glitter. It was making his nose twitch.

He bit his tongue hard, bringing a ghost of a tear to his eyes. The last thing he needed right now was a sneezing fit. It seemed to do the trick.

He could see the service exit from his current position, or at least a set of double doors with a brushed metal plaque on the front which he was pretty sure said 'Employees Only,' except in Russian.

The problem was, there was a twenty foot distance between him and the way out, and it was in full view of two crouching Russian cops, both of whom were armed. So the question was simple – could he get to, and more importantly *through*, those doors before the Russians pumped him full of lead?

It was dicey.

Would they even shoot at him? Back home, Trapp reflected, they probably would. He had a gun, after all, and he sure as hell wasn't sprinting for the exit without it, which meant they would be perfectly within their rights to open fire.

"So how much range time do you guys get?" he whispered.

That was the real question, after all. Trapp knew that he could close the distance to the doors at full sprint in under three seconds. Call it another second to break through the lock, if one existed, and he'd be out of sight inside five.

But five seconds was an eternity for a trained shooter, and he would be entirely without cover the entire time. He glanced at his phone again, hoping for a message from Ikeda to flash up. He would settle for a fucking love note at this point, though a ride out of this joint would definitely be preferable.

"You are no trouble," the male officer called out, meaning something else but getting his point across nevertheless. "Come out, hands up."

"Fat fucking chance," Trapp muttered, his mind made up.

He exploded up from his haunches, settling into a double-handed shooting stance, figuring that the cops would most likely be no better trained than their counterparts back home. While their brains were still processing the sight of him, he fired.

Once, twice, a third time, and in the confined environment of the furniture store, it sounded like a whole battalion opening up. The cops ducked, and he saw the flash of a blue jacket as one of them dived for cover.

Trapp waited, counting out a full two seconds in his head, just to let the Russians get comfortable. Then he fired again, three shots this time, aiming for the spots the Russians had just vacated. He didn't want to kill them, just put the fear of God into them.

And then he ran.

He headed straight for the doors, not bothering to look back, knowing that the two officers would hear the sound of his boots thundering against the store's tile floor, and hoping that they wouldn't be able to react fast enough. It wasn't like he had a choice. He'd heard them calling the sighting in, heard the dispatcher acknowledging, and heard a veritable armada worth of units reporting that they were en route.

He had to get out of here, and he had to get out of here now. There was no other option.

Trapp ran with his legs at full stretch, and half a second before he reached the double doors, he sighted the lock, which was just above waist height. It was a small vertical oblong, with eight metal buttons on the front. In short, it was a piece of junk.

He bounced off his leading foot, hurling himself into the air, and putting the full force of his two hundred some pounds into his heel, which collided with the rightmost of the two doors three inches above the lock. The instructors at the Farm would have given him hell for his technique on that one, but it did the job. The lock splintered, and the two doors swung open in front of him.

Crack!

As he passed through, a chunk of wood exploded about two feet from his left ear, and he heard the roar of loud yet wayward gunfire as the two cops opened up, yanking furiously at their triggers in a way that sent rounds flying in almost every direction except the one Trapp was sprinting in.

The doors swung closed behind him, but by this point he was twenty yards down a narrow concrete tunnel that led to a storeroom, lit by a bright white artificial light that hurt his eyes.

He reached the end of the tunnel, entered a large room that

was full of parallel metal racks, all piled high with cardboard boxes, and stopped. His footsteps echoed around the tunnel for a couple of seconds after he arrested his forward momentum, and his breath sounded overly loud in his ears.

How long since he sent that message to Ikeda? Six minutes?

There was no way to be certain, and that was almost worse than knowing that the worst-case scenario was already upon him. At least then he could be prepared for it.

Trapp turned, mastered his breathing, and tried to work out how many rounds he had remaining. Fourteen in the clip and one in the chamber when he started. How many had he fired at the park, five?

Plus another five just then, hotshot.

So five left if he was lucky, plus another fifteen in the clip, and then he was out. And Trapp knew better than most that the human brain was notoriously poor at accurately measuring ammunition expenditure in combat. He might as easily have just a single round left. He tried to measure the weight of the weapon by feel, but there was too much adrenaline flowing in his system, his blood pumping too fast, his hand too shaky to be anywhere close to sure.

"Come on, assholes," he grunted, amped up on the tension of combat. He had nothing against the two cops who were chasing him. They were only doing their jobs.

But so was he.

Okay, what now?

If the local cops were anywhere close to competent, then they would already have radioed in the events of the last few seconds. Additional units would be routed to the rear of the store, they would know he was armed, and the odds were good that they would open fire without asking any questions.

It was the way he would do it.

That left him with only one option. The same one as before:

he needed to move, to do so fast, and if possible to stop anyone from chasing him. He waited for half a second more, eyes trained on the double doors that lead from the main body of the store.

Had one just twitched?

"Screw it."

He fired twice, paused, then emptied the clip. Three more rounds impacted the doors, two on the left and one on the right, punching large holes in the flimsy plywood. Tiny splinters showered against the ground, falling more like snow than rain.

"That should keep 'em guessing..."

Trapp ejected the spent clip and pocketed it, rather than leaving it for a forensic team to go over. The rounds that he'd already expended were clean and untraceable. Every last round would have been loaded by someone wearing cotton gloves, purchased commercially. The ammunition itself would be unremarkable – high quality, but mass-produced. It wasn't the movies. He didn't have a signature round which a genius cop could use to hunt him down.

He smacked his last remaining magazine into the pistol, chambered a round, then spun on his heel, jogging rather than sprinting, in order not to make too much sound. Unless they had a death wish, the cops behind him would probably choose to hold their position, rather than running blindly into a hail of gunfire.

That should buy him the time he needed to get away.

How long now? Three minutes?

"*Hell.*"

Trapp saw movement to his left as he ran and raised the pistol in a single smooth movement, slowing his momentum as he did so. It was almost impossible to fire accurately while moving, and he knew better than to try. His finger was grazing the trigger, body acting on muscle memory, when he jerked it aside.

It was only a warehouse worker, his face pale with fright, and a cigarette burned almost to extinction hanging out of his mouth.

"Don't fucking say a word," Trapp hissed, pressing his left index finger against his lips, not knowing if the man spoke English or not, and not particularly caring. The message was clear. And judging by the look of terror on the wiry man's face, he wasn't planning to move a muscle.

"Where's the exit?" Trapp said, his eyes scanning left and right, not seeing it.

The man pivoted slowly in one place, his arm rising in an almost zombielike fashion, its leading finger limp, the limb itself trembling.

"Atta boy." He grinned. "Now, remember what I said…"

Trapp ran for the door, casting a single look over his shoulder to make sure the worker had not moved. He hadn't. In fact, the cigarette was still burning, less than a quarter inch away from his lips. Trapp winced. Either the guy was exploring a second career as a fire eater, or that was about to hurt.

The exit to the street looked pretty similar to the double doors he'd kicked his way through before, except these were painted black, and had parallel bars across them. Fire exits, no kicking required. His hip would thank him for that later, Trapp knew.

He slowed just in front of the doors, leading with his left hand, keeping the pistol tight against his right shoulder. He could hear sirens, but not too loud. Still far enough away to give him hope. There was something else, too, a low rumble.

An HVAC unit, maybe?

There was only one way to find out. He crouched, keeping his large frame low to minimize his profile, and pressed against the bar on the right-hand door, clicking the lock open. He pushed with his left hand, and stepped through.

A second later he discovered the source of the sound.

It was a goddess astride a grumbling black steed, holding an olive green helmet out to him, with her own pistol in her right hand.

She jerked her head at the bike. "Get on."

39

The bike's engine pulsed beneath Trapp, and its worn tires bit against the potholed surface of the narrow service road which ran down the center of the block, lit only by a narrow rectangle of sunlight far overhead.

He clung on to Ikeda's firm torso for all he was worth, his pistol once again stowed, at the front of his waistband this time, not the back. Safety on, just in case he accidentally shot off parts that were more precious to him than most. You could recover from a through-and-through gunshot wound to the thigh. The same injury to his groin didn't bear thinking about.

Ikeda pushed down hard on the throttle, and the bike responded, jarring over the uneven surface. She dodged a piled-up molehill of recycling bags, though the rear tire split open one of them, scattering scraps of paper wildly, a flash of white against the darkness of the asphalt.

She braked hard, bringing the bike almost to a halt as she pivoted on a central axis, then gunned the engine again, bursting through a passageway that led out onto a wide city street. They drew only a couple of half-interested glances as she accelerated out into traffic.

"Damn, girl," Trapp yelled over the roar of the pistons, and the air whipping past his helmet. "Who taught you to drive?"

No response.

Then again, he hadn't really expected one. She had more important things on her mind, like getting them the hell out of here without being arrested on charges of espionage. And now they were out in the open a peal of sirens, echoing in every direction, reminded Trapp that those consequences were very real indeed.

At the end of the street, a cop car, lights flashing, whistled past, weaving through traffic. A heartbeat later, a second followed. Ikeda slowed, and even though Trapp's natural instincts screamed that they should go faster, his training sang a different story.

The cops would expect him to have escaped on foot. For a few more seconds, perhaps a few more minutes, they would be looking for a lone shooter. That would change, of course, the second they looked at the store's security footage, interrogated the warehouse worker he'd almost shot, or heard from any of the other witnesses they had ridden past.

But all that would take time. And even when they put the pieces together, *if* they put the pieces together, it would take even longer to communicate their description to the chasing pack.

"Okay," Trapp heard Ikeda say just in front of them. "That's not so good."

Not so good, Trapp thought, was putting it mildly. Two police cars had closed off the street, turning diagonally into each other and forming the point of a diamond. It was a hastily arranged roadblock, but no less effective for it.

The front doors of both vehicles were open, and the officers were sheltering behind them, weapons drawn.

"You think they know who we are yet?" Ikeda called out.

Trapp instantly understood what she was thinking. It was a

gamble, that was certain. But he didn't see they had any other options, and they definitely couldn't wait. Every second that ticked past dragged them inexorably closer to the cliff edge of disaster.

"I guess there's only one way to find out..."

Ikeda laughed, an incongruous sound amidst the tension of the moment, and yet one that somehow salved Trapp's nerves. Because there was no doubt about it, he was nervous as hell.

The bike's engine was barely whispering beneath them now as Ikeda crept through traffic at no more than a couple of miles per hour, not wanting to draw the attention of the four police officers. It was difficult to make out at this distance, and through the narrow focus caused by the adrenaline coursing through his body, but at least two of the cops looked young, fresh out of the womb, let alone the police academy.

That was both a good and a bad thing, he reflected. Good, because they would be inexperienced. It was always harder to go toe to toe with someone whose rough edges had been sharpened through years of practice.

Bad, because inexperienced men made rash decisions. Decisions like shooting first and asking questions later.

Two bumpers ahead, the passenger door clunked open on the vehicle at the head of the quickly growing procession of traffic. It was an old, battered Soviet-era town car, half the size of most of the gleaming German machines that typically plied the streets of contemporary Moscow, as out of place as a plague boil on a supermodel.

A man stepped out, his shaven head practically gleaming. He threw his arms wide, like a quarreling Italian, and bellowed something in irate Russian, instantly drawing the attention of all four officers.

Trapp opened his mouth to make Ikeda aware of the opening, then slammed it shut as he realized she was way ahead of him. She increased power to the engine, feeding it a morsel extra gas, doubling their pace, but only taking it to a sedate four miles per hour. At the same time, she weaved the bike to the other side of the exasperated Russian's car, ducking down low to avoid being seen. Trapp copied her.

Smart cookie, he thought.

It was difficult to make out what was happening with the confrontation now, but Ikeda kept the bike crawling slowly forward, until only half a bumper separated the bike from the front of the rusting vehicle.

"Here we go," Trapp muttered.

For the first time, the cops seemed to recognize what they were doing. Their reaction was slow, Trapp noted, which suggested they hadn't yet worked out how he had made his getaway. One, a plump man, held up the palm of his hand and gestured at them to stop, though his attention flickered back and forth between this new threat and the earlier confrontation. Like the rest of them, his weapon was drawn, but held loosely at his side. It was as good an opportunity as they were likely to get.

Trapp tapped Ikeda on the shoulder. "Now!"

As usual, she was way ahead of him. The bike jumped forward with the acceleration of a rifle bullet, splitting to the right of the roadblock and mounting the curb onto the sidewalk. It was low, but still enough to send a jolt of pain through Trapp's coccyx and right up his spine.

He turned his head to the left as they passed the cars, watching with disapproval as open-mouth expressions of surprise appeared on four faces in turn, necks snapping left as they watched the bike go past.

And then it was over, the cops in the rearview mirror, the bike rocketing down the empty street, and through a four-way junction just before the lights flicked red.

40

"I'm getting an upload from Hangman, boss," Dr. Timothy Greaves said over the sound of crunching Cheetos. He wasn't a complete animal, he thought, reflecting the irony inherent in playing out to the stereotype everywhere – he wasn't spitting chunks of cheese puff all over his keyboard.

After all, he had *standards*...

"Boss –?"

There was no reply. Greaves lifted the two big cans of his headphones away from his ears, rested them around his neck, and swiveled his head. The small basement office was empty.

Huh.

He wondered if Partey and Mitchell had told him they were going anywhere or not. He couldn't remember anyone tapping him on the shoulder, but then again, judging by the collection of crushed energy drink cans and foil junk food wrappers that surrounded his workstation like the opening credits of the film WALL-E, he probably wouldn't have noticed. When he sunk his teeth into a problem, it was like a hunting lion clutching on to a sprinting antelope – he was in for the ride, wherever it took him.

Greaves glanced downwards, rolling his eyes as he noticed the thin layer of orange dust that coated his shirt.

Hunting lion is putting it kindly, he thought wryly.

Compared to the sleek, powerful frames of the golden-maned predators that prowled the Serengeti, his own was decidedly less impressive. There was a time, about six months earlier, when he had thought he might try getting into shape. It was shortly after a psychopathic domestic terrorist wearing the staid, unlikely uniform of a Mormon elder had attempted to send him on a one-way journey across the River Stix.

For a couple of weeks after that, he'd actually tried jogging. But Virginia in February wasn't exactly balmy, and after making it a mile and a half from his new house one Saturday evening, he got a stitch, and almost froze to death on the journey back.

That put an end to that.

Still, he mused, surveying the detritus on his desk with some embarrassment, he really needed to at least cut the junk food out. Okay, maybe not *out*, but at least *back*. He could do that, couldn't he?

Yeah, but diet soda tastes like crap... he thought sourly.

"So does diabetes."

You're talking to yourself...

"Go to hell," Greaves grunted.

His computer pinged, indicating that the download was complete. He cracked his knuckles, glanced around the empty office one more time and shrugged. He was used to being ignored. It did not bother him. You didn't join the Central Intelligence Agency for the public acclaim, and certainly not the NSA, his previous employer. If anything, the black hole at Fort Meade was even more secretive than the CIA.

And although he might not look it, Dr. Timothy Greaves was an extremely self-confident individual. Prowling lion he might not be, but in his field, he was among the very best. Perhaps even *the* best. He truly was a hunter, and although his hunting grounds were composed of bits and bytes and lines of code, the actions he took had very real consequences.

People had died because of information he'd uncovered; Greaves knew that without a doubt. Men and women both. Sometimes, in the depths of night as he stared up to the ceiling, caffeine and taurine and Lord only knows what else coursing around his system after a day spent behind his computer monitor, he imagined their faces. Created stories and narratives and lives in his head to replace those which had been lost.

Those were sleepless nights indeed.

But at the very same time, Greaves knew that he had saved more lives than he had ever cost. And those that had been lost, snuffed out through his deeds, if not by his own hand, they were the bad guys, weren't they?

Sure, keep telling yourself that...

Perhaps his doubts were no different from those of any operator in the field. For while Jason Trapp could pull a trigger and kill a president, the lines of code that he wrote could bring down nations.

Or save them.

The encrypted file finished extracting, the success announced by a second melodic chime from his computer. That was definitely one of the things he liked about working for the government – money was no object, and that was especially true for the Special Activities Division. Mitchell's operators needed the best of the best, and they invariably received it.

Greaves just got to tag along for the ride, and in his case, that meant access to the most powerful supercomputers money could buy. He tapped a command into the keyboard, pressed the return key, and as the file opened, his eyes widened with surprise.

"Holy carp," he muttered, making the lame joke even though – or perhaps because – he was alone.

He removed the cans from his ears for a second time, glancing around the room. Someone needed to be here to see this, didn't they? Should he call someone – Mitchell, perhaps? The boss would know what to do, wouldn't he?

The thing was, other than the sound of his own ragged breathing and the hum of hibernating computers, no one else was in the office. His eyes flickered to the bottom corner of his screen, noting the time. It was 2:15 in the morning.

"I guess that explains it."

Greaves cocked his head to one side. What to do? He could call Mitchell at home. He didn't know the man's number, but the operator would put him through.

Yeah, buddy, maybe you wanna take a rain check on that one?

The truth was, Mike Mitchell gave Greaves the willies. The director of SAD wasn't a big man, barely cresting 5 foot seven on a good day, and the hacker comfortably had a hundred pounds on his boss.

And then some...

But size was not everything, Greaves knew. Nor age. Mitchell was in his late 40s, hair graying at the temples, knee creaking when he got up, in a way it probably never used to. But there was a look in his eyes that chilled him to the bone. He didn't know precisely how Mitchell had made it to his current rank within the Agency, but he was pretty sure it didn't involve sitting behind a desk.

No, Mike Mitchell was a killer. Maybe not anymore, but once. And Timothy Greaves preferred to keep himself a degree or two removed from the trigger pullers. His work, he assured himself, was intellectual. It was a battle of wits, pitting his own against the world's very best hackers and computer programmers, and usually coming out on top.

Always, he corrected himself.

So maybe this could wait until he knew exactly what he was dealing with. It looked good, but he didn't want to risk waking Mitchell up and then being forced to explain it was nothing.

It wasn't nothing, of course. Greaves could tell that just from glancing at the code. But at the same time, what he had received wasn't even in the same ZIP code as actionable, not yet. It was a chink in the armor of the virus that was devastating computer networks, the power grid, water treatment facilities and pretty much everything else that ran on silicon in the United States. Which was pretty much everything these days.

But it was nothing more than that. It was an opening that he would need to winnow away at until it became a weapon. Greaves had been fighting a losing battle against the virus for several days, knocking up scattered victories here and there, doing more than any other single individual on the US government's payroll, but all the while knowing that even though he might win a few battles along the way, he was losing the war.

This code, though, was the key. It was like the a-bombs dropped on Hiroshima and Nagasaki at the end of the Second World War, Greaves thought. Back then, the whole country was talking about the possibility of a million dead soldiers and Marines, and then *BOOM*, no more Japan.

He clapped his hands together, though the strident crack was barely audible over the European techno pumping through his headphones. The impact stung his palms, and he winced as he rubbed them against his thighs, glad that no one could see.

Some hunter.

But there was a caveat. A really big caveat. If the politicians learned about this, they would want to use it. That had to be done, of course. There was no point building a weapon that never got used, especially when someone was attacking you.

But it had to be deployed at the right moment. And the right moment would also be the moment of greatest danger.

Like a battlefield commander exposing his flank to the enemy in order to lure them into an ambush, so it would be here. To truly halt the virus, they would have to wait until it had almost defeated them, infected every system, penetrated every computer. Any sooner, and the counterstrike would be effective, but not fatal. The virus would survive to fight another day, and the vulnerability would be patched...

Greaves had met President Nash. He *liked* President Nash. In his opinion, President Nash was a real standup guy.

But would he be able to resist the lure of fighting back against the computer virus that was devastating the American economy? Would he, knowing they had a weapon, want to deploy it before the time was right?

"It's 50-50," he muttered over the sound of a pumping techno beat, barely aware of how loud his voice sounded in the silent office.

He didn't like those odds.

41

The intercom on the top of the Resolute desk buzzed, startling the president from doing nothing more important than staring blearily into space. How long had it been since he'd last gotten a full night's sleep? A week?

Feels like longer.

His entire adult life, Charles Nash had watched as bright-eyed, eager first-term presidents were inaugurated, and then swiftly aged from the relentless pressures of the job. And yet just like every ambitious politician before him, and no doubt those after, Nash had never believed that he too would be subject to those same inexorable laws of nature. But little more than eight months into the job, he was learning that a month spent in the Oval Office was equivalent to three on the outside, and his graying temples and growing paunch were evidence enough of that.

And, he thought with a trace of bitterness, *even Wilson and Roosevelt didn't have to contend with an existential threat to the homeland.*

Those men had led the nation through the two largest conflicts the modern world had yet seen, but had done so at a time when America was truly an island. Her sons might bleed and die on far-flung battlefields, but through it all, their country sailed serene, protected by an ocean-sized moat on either coast.

But that luxury had dissipated long ago.

"Director Lawrence is here to see you, Mr. President," came the voice of Nancy Logan, his no-nonsense personal secretary, a woman of diminutive stature, in her mid-50s, who was the scourge of the West Wing, resolutely guarding the most valuable commodity in Washington: access to the president. She was his last line of defense against the wolves that circled every minute of every hour of every day, and who would drain him dry if they were given the opportunity.

Nash blinked once, attempting to shake the weariness from his head, but knowing he was fighting a losing battle. What he needed was a solid twelve hours between the sheets, though he would settle for six. He hadn't felt this tired since his first weeks on Parris Island, three decades earlier.

He leaned forward and held down a button on the intercom. "Thanks, Nancy. Send him in."

"Yes, Mr. President."

He tapped the button again. "And Nancy?"

"Yes, sir?"

"Go home already, will you? It's late. Send someone up from the pool."

"I'll go ahead and send Mr. Lawrence in, sir," came the cool reply of a woman who had been here long before him, and would be long after. Nancy Logan was not the kind of woman who paid heed to anything so illusory as an executive order.

And he was damn grateful for it.

The door clicked open, and a short, stout, bearded man entered, clutching a battered black briefcase. Nash rose from behind his desk, pushing the Kevlar-lined executive chair back.

"George," he said, pasting a smile on his face, "thanks for coming in."

"My pleasure, sir," came a slightly wan response from the new DCI as he crossed the dark blue carpet of the Oval Office. Nash knew that beneath the upholstery lay pressure plates that were constantly monitored by the Secret Service, so that they knew the position of all occupants of the office at all times.

A meeting with the DCI wasn't exactly a high priority for his detail – if Lawrence had made it through four decades of security screenings, he was probably good – but the agents would be watching anyway.

"I know it's late," Nash said apologetically, gesturing toward the parallel sofas in the center of the room. "Take a seat. Can I get you a drink?

"Whatever you're having would be great, Mr. President," Lawrence replied. His voice – his whole demeanor, really – was more professorial than Nash might have expected for someone in his role. He wasn't exactly 007, that was for sure. Still, Nash had watched his confirmation hearings up on the Hill, and had approved of the forensic manner in which Lawrence had torn apart specious lines of questioning. The man was startlingly intelligent, of that there was no doubt, and he had an encyclopedic knowledge of both the Agency within which he served and the external threats to the nation that he had pledged his life to defend.

"Scotch." Nash grinned, rolling up his shirtsleeves as he walked toward a cabinet to the right of a muted television set that was constantly scrolling news headlines. The offending piece of technology caught Nash's attention – and his ire. He turned it off. "The more expensive the better."

"I guess I'm a peasant, then, Mr. President. I'm a bourbon man, myself. But I am more than willing to be led astray."

Nash clinked two classes together, setting them next to the

bust of Churchill's head, and reached for a bottle of Oban, eighteen years old. He twisted his neck to survey the director. "Ice?"

"No, sir. Neat is fine."

"Good," the president chuckled. "You passed."

He doled out two home pours, then walked over to Lawrence, setting one of the glasses on the coffee table in front of his guest, who occupied himself with setting his briefcase on the table and opening it, retrieving a slim manila file before taking a sip.

"How are you, George?" he asked, taking a seat on the opposite couch. He lifted the whiskey tumbler to his nose and savored the rich, spicy aroma of the fine scotch. "You look tired."

It wasn't exactly polite to say so, but it was true. Had those gray streaks in the man's thick brown beard been so prominent a couple of months prior, when he'd nominated Lawrence for the CIA directorship? He couldn't remember, but he didn't think so.

"You know what they say, Mr. President. Play stupid games, win stupid prizes. I'll get some shuteye when this is all over."

He reached for the tumbler on the table in front of him and took another sip, the furrowed wrinkles on his brow dancing either with delight or disgust, it was difficult to say. "I understand you've been briefed on Crimson Sunset?"

Nash set his scotch on his thigh. "The Russian wargame down in the Baltics? I sure have. Looks like a big one."

"That it is, sir. At least two divisions of mechanized forces are arrayed along the borders of Lithuania, Latvia and Estonia. Plus three divisions of infantry and a significant amount of air support. Enough to wipe those countries off the map. I'm told that there are some very nervous generals sitting in the E Ring right now."

Nash nodded. "I can imagine. I feel the same way. And you're sure that all this is a wargame? It wouldn't be the first time the Russians have kneecapped someone in this neck of the woods. Probably won't be the last, either."

Lawrence took another sip of whiskey, though Nash noted that he looked uneasy. He was seated on the very edge of the couch, his posture as ramrod straight as his rounded belly would allow, his fingers steepled over the tumbler he held against his lap. He looked stressed, though the president couldn't blame him for it. The director had only been in the job for a month when this crisis hit, barely enough to get his feet wet.

"That's correct, sir. Georgia back in 2008, the Crimea in 2014. They've got form, that's for sure. But all three countries are NATO members, which wasn't the case before. It would be a real ballsy move to make, no doubt about it." He coughed awkwardly. "I hope you don't mind my language, sir."

"Not at all, George," Nash chuckled. "I'm a Marine, remember? Ignore the fancy suits. I still eat worms given the chance."

The director winced, though he hid the reaction well. Nash noticed, and cursed himself for insensitivity. He softened his voice. "I'm sorry, George. Your son?"

"Yes, Mr. President. He was First company, Third Marines. A real good kid," Lawrence croaked, clearing his throat in an attempt to maintain control.

"I bet," Nash said, searching for the director's eyes and holding his gaze. They were glistening, but Nash regarded him with pity and understanding, not scorn.

"I know what it's like to lose a boy," he said. "You never forget. You never get over it. There's no shame in admitting it, George."

"No sir," Lawrence agreed, reaching for his whiskey and knocking back a liberal dose. "It's been seven years. You never do. I'm sorry about yours, sir. I heard."

The whole country had heard, Nash mused. His opponent, or at least an unscrupulous PAC connected to the campaign, had weaponized his late son's drug problem. They pulled the ads after one of them made the national news, but by then the damage was done. The memory still boiled Nash's blood.

"Thank you, George. What was your boy's name?"

"Grover, sir. Grover Lawrence. You want to know the truth?"

Nash smiled. "Of course."

"I never liked the damn name," Lawrence half-laughed. "Sounded like a damn retiree. How can you look at a newborn and call him *Grover*? But my wife chose it. My ex-wife, I mean. And you don't argue with a woman who's just been through thirty hours of labor."

It was the president's turn to wince, though with a politician's skill, he was better at hiding it. He brought the tumbler to his lips and took a long sip, this time enough to burn his throat. The conversation was dredging up painful memories, not just of the son he'd lost, but the wife who'd left soon after.

"Sounds like a president," Nash agreed. He raised his glass. "To Grover."

"To Grover," Lawrence agreed, raising his own. "He was awarded the Navy Cross, you know?"

"I didn't," Nash replied, genuinely interested. "What for?"

"Posthumously," Lawrence said, his eyes glistening once again. "Crossed two hundred meters under heavy fire to reach an injured brother, according to the citation. Dragged him the whole way back to a corpsman without sustaining so much as a scratch. And then he died when his MRAP hit an IED on the way back to base a month later. Life's not fair, you know?"

Nash stayed silent, allowing the man to grieve in his own way. He had prompted it, after all, asking the questions, probing. The question lingering in his mind was whether Lawrence was up to the job. Had he made the right decision when he nominated the man to head up CIA? He was clearly under a tremendous amount of pressure. It wasn't exactly a surprise, given the almost unprecedented nature of the dual crises assailing the country both at home and abroad, but neither could it be ignored.

"No," he agreed. "Life's not fair."

What he left unsaid was what he could do about it. George Lawrence was patently a good man. A patriot who had given everything for his country. Not just his son, but his marriage. Nash had lived through a similar pain, and thrown himself into his work to hide from it, just as Lawrence had clearly done.

And yet Nash was considering asking him to resign. It would be a politically catastrophic decision in the middle of a crisis and would open him up to deserved criticisms from both sides of the aisle. How could the country have faith in his decisions when they had already been proved so wrong? But it wasn't the political consequences that concerned Nash. Asking Lawrence to step aside would break the man. His job was all he had left.

Still, it might need to be done. Nash could not allow the director of such a critically important intelligence agency to remain in post if that person wasn't up to the task, no matter who it was, or for what reason.

"How are your people holding up, George?" Nash asked.

Lawrence looked up, cleared his throat several times, and said, "They're doing their jobs, sir."

Nash studied the director for several long seconds, examining every nook and cranny, and every tremor on the man's face. "But..."

Lawrence flushed, understanding that he was being read, and not liking it – but knowing that it also meant that he was in no position to dissemble. "But I'm not sure everyone's on board, sir."

The president's left eyebrow hiked up. "Explain."

"Do you know the name Mike Mitchell, Mr. President?"

Interesting, Nash thought. If he had asked Lawrence to name a thousand people he thought were not team players, Mitchell would have been dead last.

On reflection, second last.

"I'm aware of him," he replied in a neutral voice.

"Sir, this is all internal stuff. Just bureaucracy, really," Lawrence said, making a belated attempt to row back on the direction he had taken. "It's way below your pay grade."

"Keep going," Nash said firmly.

"Mr. President, I believe he knows something he's not telling me about our Russian asset, the one who died last week. Mitchell runs the Special Activities Division," Lawrence said, and Nash noted the way the man's lip curled as he said those three words, "and he's slow-walking getting that information to me – particularly with respect to one of our NOCs, the man who recruited Sokolov."

"NOCs?" Nash asked.

"It stands for 'no official cover.' sir," Lawrence said. "Deniable operatives. The Russians call them 'illegals.'"

"I get it," Nash grunted. "This operative, who is he?"

"That's classified, Mr. President," Lawrence prevaricated. "And besides, I only know his codename."

"I want to know, George," Nash said, his tone uncompromising. "Now."

Lawrence blinked several times rapidly, as if processing the unexpected direction this conversation had taken. "Yes, sir," he said. He looked down at the folder next to his briefcase and opened it, as if to buy himself time to figure a way out of his predicament.

Nash waited patiently. He had a very good idea which operative had recruited Alexy Sokolov – one that was based on nothing more than a hunch, but which he was sure was correct.

Lawrence rustled a sheet of paper, then looked up, wearing a pained expression. "His codename is Hangman, Mr. President," he said in a tone that suggested that he was neither sure why the president needed to know, nor impressed that he had asked. "That's all I know."

Nash paused for a long beat, reflecting on the paths that were open to him. The last thing he needed was infighting within CIA, especially at a time like this. He needed the agency lean, focused, and pulling in one direction. Ordinarily, the way to achieve such an end would be to ensure that the organization was marching to the beat of the director's drum. But these were far from ordinary times.

"My understanding is that the Special Activities Division exists to provide the Agency with unconventional solutions to complex problems," Nash said. "And it's a complex world out there, that's for sure."

"That's correct, sir," Lawrence agreed, with all the enthusiasm of a condemned man arguing for his own execution. "But in my view, the CIA has moved too far away from its original mission of providing the nation with well-sourced intelligence. We should not be in the business of murder."

"I'm not going to tell you how to run your agency, George," Nash said in his best presidential voice, the one he used to deliver home truths to people who didn't want to hear them.

It carried a tone that told the recipient of said advice not just to shut the hell up and listen, but to act upon it if they hoped to keep their job. It pained Nash to use it on such a good man, but he figured it was better than throwing Lawrence out on his ass without giving him a fighting chance.

"No, Mr. President?"

"All I will say is that not too long ago, the Hangman saved my life. He saved the lives of a whole lot of people in this town, perhaps including your own. And he did so without ever once asking for recognition. Hell, he's the reason you're in the job you're in. When I nominated you, I wanted someone who would return CIA to its former glory, to be the Agency this country deserves. Not burn it to the ground.

"You might not like it, George, but sitting behind that desk," Nash said, indicating his mighty oak workstation, "carries with it a responsibility like you cannot imagine. You know, I never wanted to be a foreign policy president."

"No sir?"

"I've been to war, George. It's hell. And I have sent men into combat, knowing that at least a few of them are going to die. I've been at Andrews at four in the morning as those bodies come back in flag-wrapped coffins. But you want to know something?"

"Of course, Mr. President."

"I've learned it's a whole hell of a lot cheaper to spend a single life today than ten thousand tomorrow. Because never forget, those are the stakes we're playing for. Just knowing what the bad guy is up to isn't always enough. Sometimes you need to bloody his nose and let him know who's boss. And maybe someone has to die to get it done. One of our guys. That's a cross I will bear for as long as I may live. But it's one I will carry with pride."

Nash slugged the last of his whiskey and morosely considered pouring another. The conversation had taken a turn he hadn't expected and had dredged up painful, long-buried memories. The bottle, still half-full, called out to him, but he resisted its song. It might be a long night, and he would need a clear head. He set the tumbler down on the coffee table with a clink and looked back up at his guest.

"That will be all, George," he said, in a tone of finality.

Lawrence nodded, eyes clouded, seemingly lost in thought as he closed his briefcase. His voice, when it came, was subdued. "Good night, Mr. President."

"One last thing, George," Nash said, looking up at his departing guest. The DCI turned, but did not speak, perhaps tangling with his own demons.

"There's nothing either of us can do to bring your boy back.

Believe me, I feel your pain. But there are thousands of kids just like Grover. Kids who we are sworn to protect. Don't stick your head in the sand and pretend you're just doing your job."

Nash closed his eyes and allowed himself to dream of a better, kinder world. Lawrence's footsteps faded away as the door to the Oval Office clicked shut.

42

"**F**uck, that stings," Trapp grunted, grinding his molars together as waves of pain lashed at his shoulder. The most immediate source of that pain was the antiseptic lotion that Ikeda was pouring onto a deep graze that ran from the middle of his back to the top of his shoulder, though the original cause was clipping the offending body part against the side of a colossal, concrete Cold War-era architectural monstrosity as they darted through a narrow passageway on their way out of Moscow.

"You got lucky."

"Sure doesn't feel that way," he remarked acidly.

Ikeda was astride his back, the rough fabric of her denim jeans scraping against the bare skin of his torso. He winced as she roughly daubed the edges of the cut with antiseptic, exhaling through his teeth, then bashed his head against the mattress of the double bed in the safe house's only bedroom as the stinging sensation returned in full force with the application of an extra-large Band-Aid.

"You big baby," she chuckled. "I'm all done."

Trapp attempted to peer over his own shoulder, but saw

only the tanned woman on top of him and not the cut itself. "That's going to be a bitch to get off," he grumbled.

"Better than letting it get infected," she pointed out. "I thought you were supposed to be a tough guy, anyway?" she said, running her fingers sympathetically across the lash welts on his back, long-healed, but an ever-present reminder of the life he had so long ago escaped. Her hands traced a multitude of injuries on his body, uncovering wounds from different phases in his life like an archaeologist sifting through the dirt over a lost city.

"I'm usually drunk or unconscious when they start patching me up."

The movement of Ikeda's fingers stopped, and Trapp almost pouted.

"Hold up," she said. "I missed a spot."

The bottle of antiseptic popped open, and cool liquid flowed onto his mid back, followed by a wave of hot pain that elicited a muted hiss from his mouth.

"Quit squirming," Ikeda muttered, "or I'll have to tie you down."

"You'd like that, wouldn't you?" Trapp mumbled, sensing that she was taking altogether too much pleasure in torturing him like this.

"Oh," she whispered, leaning forward and kissing him on the back of his neck, "you have *no* idea..."

Hell, he thought as the unexpected touch redirected his blood flow. *I'm only human...*

43

The plan was rushed, which was never good, but it wasn't like they had any other choice. It relied on the flawless functioning of any number of moving parts, the failure of any of which would throw the whole operation into chaos.

Trapp was sitting in the driver's seat of a stolen white Lada Granta, a thoroughly unremarkable model of a Russian car brand he thought had gone bankrupt well before the end of the Cold War.

Apparently not.

The odometer had markings that went all the way up to 150 kilometers per hour, but he would be surprised if the car was capable of making it much past seventy. Then again, if everything went right, it wouldn't need to.

He was sitting at the side of the road about thirty yards ahead of an area of road construction that had turned two lanes into one, marked out by red and white barriers, and flashing orange lamps. The clock on the dash read eight-thirty in the evening, but this far north, the sky was already dark. It would be pitch black inside the hour, and though the days were still hot as summer meandered into fall, the nights cooled fast.

He would have turned the engine on to run the heater, if not for the fact that the interior of the Lada lit up like a slot machine every time he put the key in the ignition, and there seemed to be no way of altering that fact. So instead, he slowly froze.

Trapp reached across and opened the glove compartment. He'd stolen the Russian car from outside a Stalin-esque apartment block on the edges of a less than salubrious part of Moscow. The Russian capital was a city of excess, with probably a higher concentration of luxurious German automobiles than Berlin itself, but this was a worker's car.

His gloved fingers retrieved the car's insurance documents, and he used his cell phone's camera to snap a picture of the address in the top right corner. If he got the chance, he vowed, he would reimburse the owner for the inconvenience, and the fees that the cops would no doubt levy to retrieve the vehicle from the impound lot.

The phone buzzed in his hands, startling him amid the silence of the empty car, even though he was waiting for it. He unlocked it and opened the messaging app, knowing that he would read one of only two possible options. Either the operation was burned, and he needed to bug out, or it was a go. Adrenaline started pumping in his veins in preparation for either scenario.

The message was simple: *Black Mercedes E class, Moscow plates, registration Y2017BT. Sixty seconds.*

The last part of the message was superfluous. They had done several dry runs that very afternoon, testing the distance from the highway turn-off to this exact spot, until the exact timetable was indelibly printed onto his mind. There was little traffic then, and there was less now.

"Here we go," Trapp muttered, turning the key in the ignition and ruining his night vision all in one go. He didn't expect to need it, but years of training to avoid this precise eventuality made him resent the designers of the crappy Russian automobile regardless.

The Lada lit up, and Trapp didn't bother indicating as he pulled out onto the road. The engine did not so much growl as cough as the car's tires kicked out a spray of rocks before biting against the asphalt. He only drove forty yards before parking. He popped the hood, opened the door, and walked to the front of the vehicle before lifting the thin sheet of metal and propping it up.

Like an athlete going through his pre-game ritual, Trapp tapped the 9 mm pistol behind his back. He'd discounted the option of going with a shoulder holster, which would have made for easier access, but also posed an increased risk of being noticed. He was hoping to avoid bloodshed. At least, to start with.

Trapp leaned against the side of the vehicle, arms crossed, head turned slightly to the right to watch the unlit road. His eyes dropped briefly to the faded green glow of his diver's watch, which indicated that about thirty seconds had passed since he first got the message, then back. Right on cue, a set of high-beam headlights lit up the road, an oasis of light amid the darkness.

His heart was beating fast, now. The target shouldn't suspect a thing, but even the best laid plan could go wrong, and this was far from that. He was in an unfriendly foreign country, with no diplomatic cover, and no backup, save for a second, singular headlight following the approaching car, about fifteen seconds back.

The thrum of the Mercedes's engine was audible a couple of seconds later, then the hissing of its rubber tires against the recently laid asphalt as it came to a halt a little before the start of the construction zone.

For a few seconds, the vehicle just sat there, powerful headlights fixed on Trapp as though he was the star of a one-man show, practically blinding him. Nerves began to rise in his throat the longer the standoff continued, though all told it might only have lasted twenty seconds.

"Come on, asshole," he muttered under his breath. "Bite."

The individual in question did as requested, in a particularly Russian fashion, opening the door of the car and spitting a stream of unintelligible Russian words which Trapp assumed were especially vituperative curses.

"Hey buddy," he called out, raising his voice to be heard over the backing vocals. "You gonna help, or what? You ain't going anywhere if you don't."

The reply came in Russian, and sounded as angry as it did unhelpful. Trapp threw his arms to the side, feigning irritation, then jerked his thumb at the Lada. He mimed a pushing motion and waited, gambling that his unwilling conversation partner had places to be, and a customer to please, and thus couldn't afford to take the five-mile detour that avoiding this road would entail.

He guessed right.

The engine died, though the Mercedes's headlights remained on, and Trapp heard footsteps walking toward him before he saw their owner emerging from the light as though reenacting the resurrection.

"Damn," Trapp muttered underneath his breath. "But you're a big fucker."

It was an understatement. The Russian was about his height, but had at least fifty pounds on him, split evenly between fat and muscle. He was wearing a dark suit, slightly too tight, and the outline of a shoulder holster was visible beneath it even at this distance. Given the size of the guy, the weapon he was packing was probably an elephant cannon. Trapp made a note not to test his aim.

The voice grumbled to itself the entire way, and Trapp was left with the very distinct impression that its owner was used to getting his own way.

"How about we try and change that," he whispered.

He held out his hand as the man came up to him, but wasn't rewarded with a handshake. The man simply stood there, hands on his hips, his face looking like it had been smacked repeatedly with a heavy cast-iron pan.

"You speak English?" he asked, dropping his arm to his side.

The Russian – the *pimp*, Trapp corrected himself – shook his head. "No English," he replied, his accent so thick it suggested he was telling the truth. The man's gaze remained locked on to Trapp's face, boring a hole right into the center of his skull with the intensity of his smoldering rage.

Who pissed in your cornflakes? Trapp didn't say.

"You gonna give me a hand, or what?" he grumbled instead, slowly turning back to face the perfectly healthy Lada, but keeping his eyes on the big guy the entire time. He jerked his finger at the open hood. "I think it's the carburetor."

The second the Russian's eyes broke away from his own, following the gesture, Trapp spun into action, rotating his body clockwise and driving his left leg into the man's ankle. The impact wrenched his hip flexors, almost tearing them from their sockets, and he was worried that the big guy wouldn't go down. But when he began to fall, it was like an avalanche forming – just a tremor at first, then a tremble, and then a wholesale collapse.

Trapp sensed the arrival of Ikeda's bike, but kept the entirety of his attention focused on the man at his feet. The unexpected impact with the hard asphalt had stolen the air from the Russian's lungs, but he could still pose a threat.

Smoothly, he reached back with his right hand, grabbed the pistol, and fired three shots in the shape of a triangle around the pimp's sprawling body to make his point.

"Don't fucking move," he said, his voice rough, flecks of spittle flying from his mouth, glowing like sparks in the light thrown by the Mercedes's headlamps. "The next one goes in your skull."

He had the good sense not to move.

"You there?" Trapp called out, the adrenaline of combat fading now and widening the scope of his senses. His heart was still racing, palms slick with sweat, as his body reminded him that the Russian was still a hazard.

"Yeah," came the reply. "Car's clear. Just a girl." Then a curse, leaden with horror. "She's young."

"Take the keys," Trapp said. "Then come here."

A couple of seconds later, Ikeda was by his side. She was armed, her pistol drawn. "I told the girl to stay where she was," she said.

"Good." Trapp jerked his chin at the fallen Russian. "Take his weapon and then frisk him."

This was no time for niceties, and Ikeda was professional enough not to need any. She moved gracefully, as she was trained, staying out of Trapp's field of fire and plucking the Russian's pistol from its holster with two fingers before tossing it out of reach.

"Just give me a reason, scumbag," she hissed, ramming the barrel of her pistol against his skull, and sounding like any New York cop as she did so.

But Trapp did not blame her. He could not. He had no particular love for pimps, found the whole concept of sexual exploitation repellent, especially when the girls in question were underage. He knew that his mission was not to deliver justice for all the wrongs in the world. But fixing some of them couldn't hurt.

The pimp grunted with pain, but he seemed cowed, at least for now, and didn't move as Ikeda expertly frisked him. He was probably shocked from the sudden reversal in his fortunes, Trapp judged. How long that would last, he didn't know.

"I've got a knife," Ikeda called out, her gloved fingers removing a small blade from a sheath strapped to the man's ankle. She threw it aside, and the metal clinked against the hard surface of the road.

"Okay," she said, stepping back. "He's clear. Oh, *fuck*…"

Ikeda's neck snapped right, and it took all of Trapp's willpower not to copy her. He had a pretty good idea of the problem.

"Go," he grunted.

Ikeda didn't wait. She broke into a sprint, heading straight back for the Mercedes.

"Like the lady said," Trapp repeated, his voice cold as he fixed his gaze on the Russian's gleaming eyes. "I'm just looking for a reason…"

To his right, Trapp heard a clip-clop sound, like a shoed horse, only lighter, and then a whimper of fear. The girl was running.

This was the problem with running an operation like this, he knew. They were way past short-handed. This was bordering on reckless. They should have had a backup team ready to close on the stop the second he'd taken down the Russian.

Shoulda, woulda, coulda…

A cry of pain caught Trapp's attention, and despite himself, he turned his head. The Russian moved fast, and he was already half-up by the time Trapp's neck began whipping back. Something dark and thin whistled upward out of the darkness, striking the pistol from his fingers and sending it skittering across the surface of the road.

Not good.

He didn't have time to focus on what was happening with

the girl. The Russian was bigger than him, and now he'd lost the element of surprise, the man's additional weight would quickly begin to show.

Trapp automatically took several paces backward, his mind automatically cataloging the situation. The Russian had somehow acquired a short length of rusted, reddish rebar. He didn't even want to imagine the consequences of being struck with a weapon like that. It would shatter bones if he was lucky, and lead to severe internal bleeding if he wasn't.

The Russian lurched toward him, driving forward with the rebar as he powered off the ground and fully upright. It was a mistake, though Trapp wasn't close enough to fully capitalize on it. He did what he could, driving his clenched fist down onto his opponent's outstretched wrist, then rotating his body to the left in the same movement.

The pimp tumbled forward, still moving as the rebar dropped out of his suddenly unresponsive fingers and clanged against the road.

Fast, but not trained, Trapp noted. His opponent had probably relied on brute strength his entire life. That was a great strategy. Until it wasn't.

This was one of those times.

The Russian arrested his forward momentum and spun around, eyes searching for Trapp. His shirt was untucked, jacket popping at the seams, and his expression wild, yet strangely indecisive. His gaze dropped to the deck, hunting for the weapon, and as he bent down to grab it with his functional remaining hand, the left one, Trapp surged forward, twisted his torso, and hit him as hard as he could in the temple.

For a second time, the pimp went down like a sack of bricks, thankfully just stunned, not dead. This time, Trapp didn't stop moving. He flipped the man over, ground his face into the dirt, and grabbed both his wrists, then drove his unoccupied elbow into the Russian's unprotected back, not hard enough to do any damage, but enough to hurt. "You guys never learn, do you?"

Ikeda called out over the sound of the Russian's moans and Trapp's own ragged, heaving breaths. "You all good?"

"Getting there," Trapp replied grimly. "I guess he only needs one hand to drive."

44

"You speak English, honey?" Ikeda asked, though the question provoked no immediate response.

The game she was playing was a delicate one. The girl was sitting in the back seat of the Mercedes, wrapped in Trapp's jacket. Sensibly, he had left the two of them alone to talk as he disposed of the stolen Lada, surmising – probably correctly – that she would feel more comfortable in female company.

Even draped in the large item of men's clothing, it was impossible to hide from the reality of the situation. The girl was young, certainly younger than eighteen, and dressed in a sparkly cocktail dress that barely passed her upper thighs. Her eyes were dull, perhaps from the effects of opioids, though she seemed otherwise healthy. Ikeda suspected that simply meant the pimps had not controlled her for very long, rather than being a marker of their kindness.

She tried her best to keep her emotions from displaying in her eyes, but feared she was fighting a losing battle.

It's not disgust, she wanted to say, hell – scream. *It's pity*.

But she knew that pity could be just as devastating for a

victim to see, so she chose a question instead, a simple one. "What's your name?"

The girl's reply was slow, almost halting, as though it had been an awfully long time since anyone showed her a scrap of kindness.

"My real name," she said, her voice at once girlish and hoarse, "my real name is Sasha."

Real name? Ikeda wondered silently. And then the realization that these men had given her a stage name, like an animal, before they sold her like meat.

"Nice to meet you, Sasha." Ikeda smiled, holding out her hand to give the girl a semblance of normalcy. "I'm Eliza."

Sasha studied her hand nervously, but did not take it. "Who are you?"

"We're –"

Ikeda was about to say that she was here to help, but stopped herself just in time. It would be a lie, and Sasha would have been lied to too often for one so young. The truth was that she was not here to help. Sasha, the pimp, they were both just a means to an end. And while they would do what they could for the girl, saving her had not been their original goal.

"The man he was taking you to tonight," she said, jerking her thumb at the trussed, gagged Russian who was breathing heavily in the front seat. "Have you met him before?"

"Yes." The reply came immediately, and with none of the disguised, carefully moderated language with which Ikeda had swaddled her question. "His name is Roman. He has fucked me before. Three times," she said, holding up as many fingers.

"I'm so sorry, Sasha," Ikeda whispered.

"Why?" the girl replied, frowning with genuine confusion. "What did you do?"

"Nothing," she said quietly.

And that's the problem.

"Are you going to kill him?" Sasha asked bluntly.

"Who, the driver?"

"No. Roman."

Ikeda licked her lips uncertainly. "We need to ask him a few questions," she finally replied.

A coy smile crossed Sasha's lips. "I think that is yes," she said, her accent faltering for the first time. "He likes to hurt girls, you know."

Ikeda didn't, but she could believe it. There wasn't a hint of guile in the young girl. She just hoped that no matter how much pain Sasha had lived through in her short life, she would one day be able to outrun those demons.

"He will pay," Ikeda said, reaching out and squeezing Sasha's fingers in her own. "I promise you that."

"Good," Sasha replied simply, but with conviction.

"I need to ask you a few questions. Is that okay?"

"Yes."

Ikeda gestured at the bound pimp. "Does he speak English?"

Sasha laughed, the sound laced with unadulterated contempt. "Him?" She shook her head. "He is uneducated pig. No English. No nothing, just Russian."

"And you?"

"I am from Latvia," Sasha replied, flicking her hair with pride, a girlish expression that made Ikeda hope that all was not lost for her. "But I speak Russian, English also, not so much French."

"You're a very smart girl, you know that?" Ikeda said, squeezing Sasha's fingers once more.

"I think no," the girl said, her face dropping. "I think it is not smart to meet people like him."

Ikeda looked at the Russian and then back again, wishing that she did not have to ask this question. It would have been easier if Sasha were older, if she wasn't an innocent victim in all this. But it was unavoidable. "Can you translate for me?"

Sasha's eyes narrowed with a hint of shock at the ask, a reaction that Ikeda took like a punch to the gut. And yet, after a moment spent processing, she acceded to the question with a curt nod.

"Thank you," Ikeda said softly.

As she began to speak, the thin expression on the young girl's lips began to change, widening into a broad smile, and from there into outright glee.

"Tell him that we are going to pay his friend Roman a visit. He is going to get us through the front gate and past the guard. If I suspect for even a second that he's playing me," Ikeda said, reaching for a black Israeli combat knife and stroking the pimp's cheek with its 9-inch blade, "then I will gut him like a catfish. Tell him to nod once if he understands."

Sasha waited until Ikeda was done talking before she began to translate, rattling off Ikeda's demands in crisp, clear Russian. Ikeda could tell how much pleasure the girl was deriving from driving in the metaphorical knife. She couldn't blame her.

Finally, the pimp nodded.

"Good." Ikeda smiled. "I guess we should get going."

She saw Trapp hovering a few yards away, out of Sasha's sight and beckoned him over. "This is Jason," she said softly. "He's a friend, okay?"

"Nice to meet you, Jason," Sasha replied shyly.

They shook hands. It was strangely formal, and yet Ikeda felt the girl grew in stature from the ordinary human interaction. She cursed the cruel world that had thrown Sasha into this horrific situation.

I'll find a way to help you, she thought. *I promise you that.*

"Cut him loose," she said to Trapp, sneering derisively at the injured pimp. Turning back to Sasha, she said, "Can you take that jacket off, okay? I'm going to sit behind him, and he's going to drive us in. You'll tell me if he puts a foot out of line?"

"What is 'foot out of line?'" Sasha asked, frowning.

"It's an American phrase." Ikeda grinned, wondering how the hell she was going to explain it. "It just means, 'if he does something wrong.'"

The girl flashed her a conspiratorial smile. "Okay."

She sidled out of the jacket, which Ikeda took from her before sliding onto the back seat behind the driver.

"What about your friend?" Sasha asked, her eyes following Trapp with measured concern as he untied the pimp's hands and made sure there was no immediately obvious evidence of the struggle.

"Who, Jason?" Ikeda grinned. "He's going in the trunk..."

As Trapp got himself set in the back, Ikeda grabbed the knife and worked it through a seam in the rear of the driver's seat. She pushed the blade through the foam padding until it stopped at the leather on the other side, but did not pass through.

"Tell him to start the car," she murmured as the trunk thunked closed. "But not to drive, not yet."

After Sasha did as she was asked, the silent Russian turned the key in the ignition, and the Mercedes sedan's engine grumbled into life.

"Hands at ten and two," Ikeda snapped. "And get your foot off the gas."

Sasha relayed the instruction, adding a hard edge to her own voice. Ikeda shot her the A-OK sign. Maybe there could be a place for a girl like her at the Agency.

Ikeda leaned forward, placing her palm around the grip of the combat knife, and matched eyes with the Russian pimp through the rear mirror. "Before we get moving," she said, her voice even, yet cold. "I want to make one thing absolutely clear."

As Sasha translated, she worked the knife through the leather shell of the Mercedes's driver's seat, until the faintest whisper of a crack signaled that it had punched through, and was now only a fraction of an inch from puncturing the Russian's back.

"You feel that?" Ikeda spat. "Here, why don't you get a taste of your own medicine?" She rammed the knife forward, stopping it before it had jumped more than a quarter of an inch – enough to break the skin, enough to hurt, but a long way from doing any real damage.

That's a shame, she thought coldly, feeling no sympathy for the man in front of her.

The Russian squealed in pain, and Sasha laughed, clapping her hands together. Ikeda's eyes flickered left, away from the mirror, and in the direction of the young Latvian girl. Was this the best way to help the kid process the horrors she'd lived through?

Probably not. But it was *a* way, even if it would probably end up as just another tangled web for the shrinks to unpick.

Ikeda returned her focus to the rear mirror, and the tear glistening in the Russian's right eye. She held the gaze, counting out ten full seconds before she spoke again, then withdrew the point of the knife from the pimp's back. "If you do something I don't like, I'll sever your spine, do you understand?"

Sasha translated, but the Russian did not reply.

"Do you understand?" Ikeda spat, quivering with rage. She wanted to do it here and now and dump the pimp's body on the asphalt, as he had no doubt done so many times before, disposing of the used-up bodies of poor young girls who never stood a chance.

This time, after Sasha spoke, the pimp's head jerked up and down like a bobblehead as he whimpered in acquiescence. She flashed him the compact 9 mm Sig Sauer pistol she was keeping between her legs, just in case he got the wrong idea, or tried to play the hero.

"Better." Ikeda smiled. "Now, let's go."

The remainder of the journey was short, and they arrived at

the outskirts of Soloslovo just a few minutes later. The Mercedes jolted over a pothole, making the Russian's eyes narrow with worry, as he presumably wondered whether the impact would be enough to send the blade through his spinal cord.

It neither would, nor could, but Ikeda took inordinate pleasure in letting him twist in the wind.

The engine of the Mercedes purred as it slowed in front of the gate to Kholodov's compound. Ikeda felt a tremor of anxiety wash through her, and she consciously focused on her breath, calming it, mastering it and her rapid heartrate in turn. She needed to focus. Trapp was in the trunk, which meant he was out of commission for the present. Anything that happened in the next few seconds was her responsibility.

A man stepped out of the guard hut. Beside her, Sasha's breathing was tight and uneven, but not panicked by the sight of him. Through the Mercedes's tinted windows, Ikeda scanned him for any sign of a weapon, but saw nothing.

Doesn't mean it's not there, she reminded herself.

Next, her eyes darted up to the white housings that contained the surveillance cameras that were monitoring the front entrance to the compound. Nothing looked different from the day before, but it was impossible to be certain.

The Russian rolled down the window, and Ikeda jammed him in the back with the point of the knife – again showing him just enough of the blade to convey her point, without actually harming him. He flinched, but wisely didn't complain out loud.

The guard spoke in a gruff voice, directed at the pimp in the front.

Sasha leaned over, and surreptitiously whispered a translation into Ikeda's ear. "He says we're late, and that the boss"—her voice faltered—"will be angry."

Ikeda squeezed the girl's hand, conveying silent reassurance, and then let go, allowing the hand to drift toward the butt of her pistol. It was ready to fire, and she knew that even in the confines of the car, she would be able to put three rounds through his chest before he could blink.

Should have told Sasha to cover her ears.

It was too late now. The guard grunted something else, and Sasha leaned over to translate again, but Ikeda motioned her head fractionally, warning her off. The pimp, sitting in the driver's seat, rolled down the rear window, and the gate guard peered in to the rear of the vehicle.

Ikeda held her breath. What the hell was going on? Did the guy suspect something? What if he asked to search the vehicle?

If that happens, you take him out.

There was no other way. Not with Trapp out of action and a wildcard in the driver's seat. The pimp would need to go, too, Ikeda realized. It wasn't something she would lose any sleep over.

The guard's lips formed an upside-down frown, and Ikeda realized with distaste that he was checking her out. Her right leg began to tremble, and she bit down on her lip, concentrating on the pain and forcing it to stop.

Just act normal.

The man just stood there, peering in, studying her face, then her tits, then the rest of her body for an uncomfortably long period of time. Just as Ikeda was preparing to draw her weapon and open fire, figuring that he must suspect something was wrong, his neck turned to the left, and he started laughing, and reached in to the driver's window, slapping the pimp on his shoulder.

The guard said something in Russian, eliciting a noncommittal grunt in reply, and then flicked the driver a thumbs-up before turning back to his shack.

Ikeda let out a deep sigh of relief as the gates began to open, revealing a short, tree-lined driveway up to the main house. From satellite photos – just Google Earth, nothing classified –

she knew that there was a second structure to the east of the main building, most likely a parking garage.

"Tell him to park the car," she said, still watching the pimp for any sign he was about to make a move.

There was none. He did exactly as he was ordered, guiding the vehicle into a covered structure that was open on both sides – just a roof on stilts. But it was dark outside, and Ikeda could see no sign that anyone was watching.

"Kill the headlights," she ordered. "Then pop the trunk."

He did as he was commanded. Trapp moved like a wraith the second it was open, springing from the rear of the car, opening the driver's side door, and punching the brutish Russian square in the face.

He grinned at the two women in the passenger seat. "You don't know how long I've been waiting to do that..."

45

Trapp secured the half-conscious Russian pimp by both his wrists and his ankles, then bound the two together so that he was hunched over and incapable of movement. Next, he dragged the man out of the driver's seat and hoisted him over his right shoulder, thankful he only needed to shift the guy a few short yards. He wasn't certain he would have made it any further.

He dumped the body in the trunk that he had only just vacated himself, then rested one hand on its open door, breathing heavily and pretending to survey his handiwork, but mainly just recovering from the exertion.

"You're one big bastard," he grunted, taking a little pride in the fact that he'd come out on top, gagged the unlucky soul, then slammed the trunk compartment shut.

He watched as Ikeda crouched on her haunches by the open car door, still holding the combat knife, and said, "I need you to stay here, okay, Sasha? Keep the doors locked, sit in the driver's seat, and if anything goes wrong, honk the horn as long as you can. We'll be right out."

"I want to come with you," she protested.

Ikeda shook her head, and Trapp noted the haunting sadness contained within the action. Like his partner, he wanted nothing more than to help this girl work through her demons. But they had a job to do. He consoled himself with the fact that the sooner they got it done, the sooner they could get out of here. But, as so often with intelligence work, it was scant consolation.

She chewed her lip, as if coming to a decision. She thrust the vicious Israeli knife toward Sasha, handle first. "Here," she murmured. "If anyone tries to hurt you, you have my permission to cut them, okay?"

Sasha nodded, though even from his distant position, Trapp sensed the reservation in her posture. "Okay," she said softly. "I will do as you say."

"We'll be right out, okay, kid?" Trapp said, walking toward Ikeda and closing the door, knowing that she might not have the strength.

"You sure that was a good idea?" he asked once it was shut. "With the knife, I mean."

Ikeda's eyes flashed with fiery irritation. "Yeah, Jason," she said. "I'm sure."

He held his hands up. "Just checking," he said as the Mercedes's lights flashed, and the locks clunked into place. "I need your head in the game, okay?"

"Believe me," she said flatly. "It is."

Looking at her, he did. How could he think anything else? She wore the expression of a woman on a mission, a woman who would not be stopped, no matter what obstacles fell in her path. Who was he to question that?

Trapp checked his pistol, ejecting the part-spent magazine and pocketing it before inserting a fresh one and chambering a round. He didn't anticipate getting into a gunfight, but he was prepared for one. Over his shoulder, he threw a small rucksack which contained a few vital ingredients for the recipe he planned to cook up that evening. He practiced drawing the pistol once to ensure that his movement wasn't restricted by the bag on his shoulder, and when he was certain, he clicked his tongue with satisfaction.

"Okay, let's go," he said.

He walked a couple of paces behind Ikeda, thinking not for the first time that night how incongruous her outfit was – high-waisted silk pants and a midnight-blue blouse that glittered like pinpricks of starlight.

It wasn't quite as revealing as the short cocktail dress which barely covered Sasha's body, but it accentuated Ikeda's frame in all the right places – though it also precluded the option of her carrying even a compact pistol, now she wasn't shielded by the car. She was armed only with a stiletto-bladed knife, not stored in a nest of hair, like in the movies, but in a plunging pocket of her pants.

They walked around the side of Kholodov's gaudy mansion and finally came to the front door. As before, Trapp stood a pace behind her, with his hands clasped across his front, his face molded into an impassive expression that gave nothing away, not least the rage simmering behind them. He glanced up and noted that a security camera enclosed in a subtle dome was focused directly on their faces.

Ikeda reached out and pressed the doorbell. The chime, cheerful and discordant, echoed throughout the large house.

"Once we're in, check that the footage doesn't upload to the cloud," she murmured from the side of her mouth before it faded away.

Trapp nodded almost imperceptibly, knowing that she could see him in the reflection of the frosted glass to the right of the front door.

There was a short pause, then they heard the sound of foot-steps, barely audible at first, then louder. It sounded like a succession of stones dropping into a deep well. This was the moment of truth. They did not know who they might encounter on the other side of that door.

A guard?

There was the metallic scrape of a lock opening, and then it opened. Trapp tensed, standing on the balls of his feet, and noticed Ikeda doing the same, preparing to pounce.

No, not a bodyguard. Roman Kholodov.

He was wearing a black silk robe, tied loosely around his waist, and fluffy slippers. A succession of emotions worked their way across his face: at first blackness, then surprise, followed quickly by confusion.

He opened his mouth, and said, *"Kto ty, chert voz'mi?"*

Trapp wasn't exactly sure what that meant, but judging by his tone, he figured it was the Russian equivalent of "Who the hell are you?"

He couldn't be certain, but he sensed that Ikeda's face had widened in a sickly-sweet smile that mirrored the tone of her voice. "The agency sent me," she said, giving voice to a dual truth. "Sasha couldn't make it tonight."

Again, waves of surprise radiated across Kholodov's face, mixed with irritation. He was clearly a man who was used to getting his own way. That was about to change.

"I am not interested," he said in English, moving to close the door.

Ikeda took her cue. She sprung forward, driving off the balls of her feet and spiriting the stiletto blade from her pocket in the same instant, pouncing on the odious Russian billionaire and holding the knife to his throat before he had even a chance to blink.

"I bet you're not, Roman," she hissed. "You like them young, don't you?"

She didn't allow the Russian to respond before hooking her left leg around his ankles and toppling him, anticipating the sudden and immediate collapse and holding the blade to his neck the entire way down.

Trapp followed behind, closing the door silently and drawing his weapon as he watched Ikeda place her hand over Kholodov's mouth. She leaned in close and whispered, "Don't make a fucking sound, or I will slit you from ear to ear."

She made an incision, not much more than a paper cut, in truth, just below his right ear. It was enough to draw a bead of blood which sparkled in the light thrown by an ostentatious crystal chandelier that hung overhead, but not enough to do any real damage. Still, the Russian flinched, and Trapp wondered if he might piss himself on his own marble floor.

Adrenaline injected itself into Trapp's circulatory system, sharpening his senses. He snapped his attention away from Ikeda, knowing she had the Russian under control. He rotated a hundred and eighty degrees in place in a fraction of a second, bringing the muzzle of the pistol to bear first on two doorways, and then up a bifurcated staircase that led to the second floor of the mansion. His eyes flickered, searching for targets.

"Clear," he muttered under his breath.

Still holding the pistol raised and ready to fire, he swiftly divested himself of the rucksack and handed it to Ikeda without looking. He didn't say another word. They both had roles to play. She would not struggle to control the old Russian alone.

He heard Ikeda unzip the bag, which made the sound of a chainsaw being fired up in the silence of the mansion's entrance lobby. He winced, but then it was done, and he heard the clicking of flex ties as they secured Kholodov's wrists, then a grunt as she rolled him over, then duct tape securing his mouth. All the while, Trapp held his pistol steady, eyes flickering up and down, side to side, covering all potential angles from which an assailant might emerge.

"Make a sound, it'll be the last thing you do," Ikeda spat at the prisoner, voice low and cold.

Finally, she tapped Trapp on the shoulder and held up her own pistol. "Let's go," she muttered.

They cleared the first floor as a pair, Trapp covering doorways as Ikeda darted through, then reversing as they bunny-hopped through the enormous residence. Trapp's heart pounded in his chest, thudding so loudly he was sure it must be audible throughout the building.

Ninety seconds later, they were done. Kholodov was still where they had left him, lying on his front on the marble floor of his own mansion. He had moved a bit, squirming across the floor toward the front door like a snake on its belly, but not far. Trapp wasn't sure what the hell he was planning to do when he got there, but dragged him back to the center of the lobby anyway and gave him a vicious but measured kick to the ribs to subdue him. Not powerful enough to do any real damage, but enough to make his point abundantly clear.

Ikeda pointed upstairs, and he nodded.

They repeated the same process again, clearing bedroom after bedroom, all empty. Throughout the process, neither operative spoke a word, moving in perfect synchronicity, as though they had done this a thousand times before. They had, in training, but never together, and never with so little support. House clearing operations even at the best of times were risky affairs, and this was far from one of those. Neither of them was wearing body armor, they couldn't use flash bangs to distract their quarry, since stealth was paramount, and they were armed only with pistols.

Trapp froze, his subconscious alerting his body to an unknown danger well before the conscious mind became aware of it. His closed left fist darted up, stilling his partner, and he rotated his neck, owl-like, searching for the source of the sound. He stopped halfway, and jerked his head at a door at the end of the hallway, perhaps to a storage closet, from behind which he could hear the faint sound of –

Cheering?

He squinted, wondering whether he was hearing things, but cleared his mind. He braced the pistol in his grip, then jerked it at the door handle. Ikeda nodded once, immediately understanding what he wanted her to do.

The door opened outward into the hallway, or at least it would when Ikeda pumped the handle. That meant when she pulled it back, it would take her out of the game for at least a second, maybe two, leaving Trapp to negotiate whatever danger lay inside on his own.

That's why they pay you the big bucks.

He held up his left hand and started a silent countdown from three.

Two.

One.

Eliza yanked back the door, and he charged forward, pistol at the ready, finger grazing the trigger. A man was sitting behind a desk on the other side of the door, large headphone cans over his ears, watching a soccer match on a large television display. Sound leaked out of the headphones, tinny and loud, enough to be audible through a thick wooden door.

You dumb motherfucker.

Trapp stopped dead behind the man, the muzzle of his pistol steady, trained on the back of his head. He was wiry, short, and totally entranced in the game, his hand forming a fist and punching the air with satisfaction as his team scored, and the camera panned on a player wheeling away in celebration before sliding on his knees in front of a delirious crowd.

Around the security guard was a bank of monitors, trained on every conceivable angle both inside and outside the mansion. A wire was hanging out of the central display, the one currently displaying the soccer game, and instead another fed toward the security guard's laptop.

Trapp shook his head, disgusted by the lack of professionalism. Finally, the man reacted, though whether it was to the sound of Ikeda entering the security booth, the door clattering against the wall behind her, or he was simply going to take a leak, Trapp didn't know.

The guard spun around on his chair, hands rising to take off his headphones, and then freezing in midair.

"Rise and shine, asshole," Trapp said in a low, menacing voice. Which, it turned out, was unnecessary, since before his headphones were off, the man simply fainted, slumping against his chair and sliding half off, his knees sagging limply to one side.

Trapp just stood there, feeling slightly foolish, his muscles beginning to tremble as the adrenaline faded. He'd entered the room prepared for combat, and found only this sorry excuse for a warrior.

He glanced at Ikeda. She shrugged and said, "What the hell do we do now?"

46

The dingy basement beneath Kholodov's mansion told Trapp everything he needed to know about the man as he trudged down a flight of dimly lit stairs to the bottom, the billionaire's bound form slung over his shoulder.

The space was poorly lit, smelled of damp, and he sighted rat traps in dark corners, but it was neatly organized, as though whatever poor cleaner was hired to clean the enormous property – easily a full-time job – took pride in what Trapp was certain was a thankless task.

"How long till someone comes looking for you, Roman?" he muttered into a quiet that was punctuated only by a *tink-tink-tink* sound of water dripping against a metal basin. It was an irritating noise, but Trapp knew better than to silence it. If it annoyed him, then it would be equally unsettling for Kholodov.

The gagged Russian moaned, though whether it was an attempt at a reply, or simply an expression of fear, Trapp didn't know. Nor did he care. The man on his shoulder disgusted him. Every time he pictured the young Latvian girl's face in his mind, flinching with fear as she looked at him, he knew she saw in his own lined face every man who had ever abused her. It was a look of fear and repulsion, and it was one that Jason Trapp never wanted aimed at him again.

It did not matter that he had never hurt Sasha. Someone had. They found a vulnerable young girl and lured her into a life of subjugation when she was still supposed to be a child. Trapp didn't know if she had family, someone to look out for her. Perhaps no family could have stood in the way of the violence of the men who controlled her.

But he could. Ikeda could.

Trapp threw Kholodov onto the ground, imbuing the action with the contempt the man deserved. The fall winded the Russian, stealing the air from his lungs, forcing him to hyperventilate in search of oxygen. He lay face down on the filthy ground, struggling to breathe as Trapp searched for something to put him on.

He found a folding chair and manhandled Kholodov's prone form onto it, grunting as he struggled to lift the Russian's bulk. He slit the bonds that secured his legs before he was aware of what was happening and waved the blade in front of Kholodov's face to remind him of the consequences of stepping out of line.

Just give me a reason.

But Kholodov was meek as a lamb. The man's crocodilian eyes studied his captor, searching for an opportunity to escape, but Trapp suspected that he knew he was beaten. Whatever shape he'd been in as Murov's bodyguard, the prime of his life had long deserted him, replaced by a doughy midsection and a shrunken musculature that posed no threat of resistance, let alone escape.

Trapp secured the Russian's legs to those of the chair with duct tape found among the basement's cleaning supplies and then tied his arms behind his back before roughly ripping the tape from his lips.

Kholodov's eyes glistened from the pain, and Trapp grinned wolfishly at the sight. "Comfortable?"

His captive said nothing, though the man's gaze flashed a mixture of rage and fear. Trapp understood the reaction. He had seen it often when humbling powerful men. Their brains struggled to process their new station in life, atrophied by years of unquestioned authority. As Murov's bodyguard, Kholodov had wielded a certain kind of power. More when the Russian president made him a very wealthy man.

"If you let me go," Kholodov murmured, his voice low and hoarse, "I will pay you whatever you want. I am not stupid enough to attempt to scare you. You are clearly a very capable man."

"I try," Trapp said, inclining his head.

"There is cash in this house. A few hundred thousand, maybe a million. Euros, dollars, a few rubles, but I think you don't want those?"

"I don't," Trapp agreed amiably, answering the question, but with a different meaning than Kholodov might expect. He reached for Ikeda's stiletto blade and began to pick his nails clean, enjoying the way the Russian's gaze tracked every flash of steel.

"You are a sensible man," Kholodov said, his voice growing in confidence as he began to sense a way out. "A million is a lot of money. It will buy you women, cars, drugs..."

"All very appealing," Trapp agreed noncommittally.

Kholodov didn't seem to sense his flippant tone. "But a million won't get you very far. What you want is real money, yes?"

"I guess," Trapp said, enjoying Kholodov's attempt to buy him. It wasn't going to work, of course, but it was important to give the man hope, to allow him to believe once again in his own infallibility, to think he had secured a way out.

"A hundred million," Kholodov proposed triumphantly. "It's

all I can pull together at short notice. I will send it to any bank account you choose. Right now. My banker will release the funds the second I am free."

"Interesting," Trapp murmured, pretending to consider Kholodov's proposal. He waited until he saw the anticipation begin to crest in the Russian's eyes, and then crushed it. "But I'm afraid I'll have to pass."

"A hundred and ten million!" Kholodov yelped as Trapp tossed the stiletto blade from one palm to the other. "It's all I have. Dollars. I'll do it right now."

"It's not your money I'm here for," Trapp said, exploding forward and placing the tip of the blade underneath the man's chin, a spot at which he could drive it through his palette and into his brain.

"Then what?" Kholodov squealed.

"Information." Trapp took a step back and was pleased to see a dark circle had formed in the center of Kholodov's crotch, an ammonia stink quickly filling the air.

"What information?" he moaned.

Trapp decided to take a different tack. He suspected that Kholodov would talk; he seemed like the kind of guy who would sell out his own grandmother to keep breathing just a day longer. The real trick was to separate the lies from the truth.

"You know," he said in a conversational tone that belied the rage simmering inside him, "my friend up there, she really hates rapists."

Kholodov's chin jerked upward instantly, defiance glittering in his dark eyes. "I –"

Trapp waved away the Russian's protest. "I don't like old men who hurt little girls either, but she has this bug up her ass about it, you know?"

"I don't hurt girls," Kholodov moaned. "I swear to you."

"What about Sasha, Roman?"

"What about her?"

"You think her pimp treats her well? You think she enjoys climbing onto a wrinkly old bastard like you? You think she fucks you because she *wants to?*"

Kholodov's chin dropped against his chest. "I pay them. I pay them well. It's not my fault –"

Trapp cut him off with a short, hard laugh that cracked around the room like a gunshot. "It never is with pricks like you," he spat, watching as Kholodov flinched in terror with every harsh word. "I guess it's easy, with all your money, to not have to think about all the people you squashed underneath you as you climbed to the top."

He grinned. "And if it does, I bet a billion dollars pays for a hell of a good therapist..."

"I don't –"

"Hurt women," Trapp groaned. "I didn't believe you the first time, Roman, and I sure won't the next. But I digress – where was I?" He slapped the knife against his palm. "Oh yeah. Like I said, my friend doesn't like men like you. You know what she does to them?"

Kholodov shook his head reluctantly, though he was now hanging on to every word as though his life depended on it.

"She cuts off their balls," Trapp growled.

He glanced up to where Ikeda was waiting at the top of the basement stairs, framed by a rectangle of warm electric light that barely penetrated the dark below, and tossed the blade dismissively to the floor. "He's all yours."

TRAPP WENT UPSTAIRS and left Ikeda interrogating Kholodov below. He closed the door, cutting off the man's high-pitched squeals. They were beginning to give him a headache.

Next, he grabbed the satellite smartphone from the rucksack he'd brought along, selected a contact, and started speaking the second the connection initialized. "Mike, you there?"

"Jason – tell me you've got good news," Mitchell replied, stress battling with relief in his tone. He looked exhausted

"Working on it," he replied. "We just jumped Roman Kholodov. Ikeda's working him over now." He sneered. "I don't think he'll hold out long."

"She is?" Mitchell asked in surprise. "I thought you–"

"Trust me, Mike, she's got this one," Trapp said, cutting his superior off at the pass. "She's real fucking motivated, if you catch my drift."

"You're the boss," Mitchell replied, not sounding entirely convinced, but knowing better than to question the judgment of an operative in the field. Particularly *this* operative.

"You got a sitrep for me?" Trapp asked.

"Sure do. It's a quick one. Short answer is, we're still up shit creek without a paddle, and the water's only getting murkier. Might have a hole in the boat too, for all I know."

"Um, boss—?" a familiar voice piped up in the background. It belonged to Tim Greaves. "That's not...*entirely* accurate."

"You got something to add, Doctor?" Mitchell asked irritably, turning away from the camera so the screen filled with an image of the back of his head.

"Yeaaaah," Greaves agreed nervously. "I've been working on something Jason sent over."

"Enlighten me," was all Mitchell replied. His tone did the rest of the work.

Half of Greaves's face joined his boss's on screen. He was almost physically cringing, but built up the courage to talk. Almost. "Thing is, I guess, that dead spy—"

"Alexy," Trapp interjected firmly.

"Yeah," Greaves stammered, "Mr. Alexey. He stole the source code for this SANDSTONE virus from Kholodov. And, uh... I think I've figured out how to boomerang it back onto them."

"You're saying you control this thing now?" Trapp demanded.

"Well, kinda..." Greaves prevaricated. "I don't have *operational* control. Not at a granular level, not yet. But I've altered the code so that it's infecting Russian systems at a 10:1 ratio over ours. Plus I can probably isolate most of the systems over here from any execution orders. If they activate the virus, they'll take down their whole internet. We'll get a glancing blow, but they'll put themselves out for the count."

"So do you control it, or don't you?" Trapp asked, frustrated.

"No. But if the Russians deploy it, it'll only blow up in their own face."

Trapp closed his eyes. A kernel of an idea was beginning to brew in his mind.

"So do we tell them?" Mitchell mused on the other end of the line. "It's kind of like mutually assured destruction. They can't risk using it. But if they don't know, it's useless."

"No!" Trapp practically yelled, as behind him a door opened and closed. "Whatever you do, let's keep this in-house. I've got an idea. The start of one, anyway. I need some time to work it through."

Ikeda appeared at Trapp's side, drawing the attention of three men on two continents.

"The Russians want the Baltics," she said simply. "They've got troops on the borders of Estonia, Lithuania and Latvia. Planning to go in under the cover of night and the chaos caused by this virus and sew them up before we have a chance to respond."

Trapp's mind went into overdrive as a week's chaos clicked into place. He knew that nothing would stop Murov from executing on his desire to re-unite the former Soviet Union, piece by bloody piece. The truth was with a day or two's notice, there wasn't much President Nash could do to stop an invasion, and once the Russians were dug in, no American president would spend tens of thousands of young American lives to prise them out.

If they were going to stop things from unfolding very unpleasantly for the population of the Baltic countries, it would have to be done quietly. And with Kholodov working with them, however unwillingly, they had a way of making it happen.

"Mike," he said urgently, over a hubbub of raised voices. "We can stop this. We won't wait for the Russians to blow themselves up. We'll set the timetable, and then we'll keep the receipts. Kholodov is our ace in the hole. Let's use him."

"Jason," Mitchell asked pointedly. "Forgive the mixed metaphors, but do you think he can be trusted to play ball?"

Trapp curled his lip contemptuously. "I don't plan on leaving him a choice."

"I'll need to get approval for this," Mitchell cautioned. "It's above my paygrade."

"Then get it done, Mike. Quickly."

Trapp outlined the rest of his plan and set the wheels in motion. There was a lot to do, and not a whole hell of a lot of time to accomplish it in.

The second the call ended, Ikeda dragged him into the basement by his arm, fingernails digging into his flesh hard enough to leave deep ridges in his skin. He didn't have a choice in the matter — she was seething. "We can't let him go," she spat, each word punctuated with a stab of her finger at Kholodov's body. The man's chest was rising and falling rapidly, causing Trapp to fear that he might be having a heart attack.

On second reflection, he didn't really care.

"We won't," he said, keeping his voice low, so that the subject of their discussion could not overhear them. "I promise you. He'll get what's coming to him. Just not yet."

"Then when?" Ikeda hissed, her voice loud enough that it attracted Kholodov's attention. He looked up, the whites of his eyes flashing like a terrified deer at the end of a long hunt, driven to the depths of exhaustion, unable to move, but waiting to die.

Trapp gripped his partner by her shoulders and moved her a few feet farther away. "Soon," he whispered. "He can still be useful."

"Useful," Ikeda spat, the words sliding off her tongue with evident distaste. "How useful? Enough to buy his life? His *freedom?*"

Trapp gripped her shoulders tight, hard enough to hurt, as he pulled her out of Kholodov's earshot. He needed to get through to her, fast, and he needed to do so without the Russian becoming aware of it.

"Fuck no," he muttered the second they were clear. "That prick's gonna get what's coming to him. I promise you. But we can't waste him yet. Like I said, he's still of use to us." He paused, fixing her with a meaningful stare. "But there are lots of ways he can be useful to us. They don't all need him to be alive, you dig?"

Ikeda attempted to pull away, bitter frustration evident in her voice. "Jason—"

"No, Eliza," Trapp said harshly. "This one's not up for debate, okay?"

She simply glowered at him, her icy eyes hot and black with rage.

Trapp grimaced and measured his tone as he attempted to break through her anger. "Go get Sasha squared away, okay? Take her into town, give her some money and tell her to keep her mouth shut. We're going to be here a while, and we can't have her hanging around."

"And what about the prisoners?"

Trapp thought about the pimp in the trunk and the two

security guards and decided he had no sympathy for any of them. He shrugged dismissively. "They can rot. We'll deal with them at the end. But Sasha can't wait, okay? This is no place for a little girl."

Ikeda sagged at that, almost toppling toward Trapp, who caught her easily. "Okay. You're right," she whispered, her voice almost girlish as she sought reassurance. "But you promise he'll pay?"

"Oh," Trapp spat, unconsciously squaring his chest. "Believe me, he will..."

47

Mitchell grimaced as he caught sight of himself in a glass reflection as he crossed from the New Headquarters Building on the Langley CIA campus to the old one, which still housed the Agency's famed seventh floor. Technically he had access to a small private office of his own up there, but he never used it. For all he knew, it might have been reassigned long ago to someone who valued the real estate a little more highly than he did.

The reason for his ire as he surveyed his appearance was the undeniable fact that he looked like he'd slept in his suit. It was rumpled and creased beyond any chance of recovery, and would need to be dry cleaned and pressed before he would next be able to wear it in polite company. Add to that, he was almost certain he was carrying with him the unmistakable funk of body odor, a sign that he hadn't showered in almost two days. There hadn't been time.

The lunchtime rush was fading by the time his leather soles clicked across the marble floor of the lobby of the OHB, and he drew no glances of recognition as he signed himself into the building. His pass got him access to the elevator that ran to the seventh floor without further questions, and he rode the groaning machine up, doing his best to straighten his shirt and tie, though knowing the efforts would no doubt prove fruitless.

The elevator doors pinged and opened on the wood-paneled seventh floor. This time, the sound of Mitchell's footsteps was swallowed up by the thick cream carpet as he walked unerringly to the director's office, stopping for no one. The tapping of fingers on a keyboard echoed in the small anteroom that guarded access to the DCI.

Mitchell came to a halt in front of the dragon and spoke without standing on ceremony. "Is the director in?"

Lawrence's executive assistant, a prim woman in her 40s, stopped typing and looked up. A flash of recognition in her eyes was the only sign of warmth he got.

"Do you have an appointment, Michael?" she asked sweetly.

Mitchell knew, however, that behind her pleasant exterior lay a backbone fortified with steel. Whatever the spies and operators thought, it was the executive assistants who truly ran the CIA's enormous bureaucracy. The truly skillful players spent time buttering them up. A bottle of wine at Christmas, that sort of thing. Mitchell had never played that game.

"I do not," he said, silently ruing that omission now. "Karen, it's urgent."

Karen spoke in a tone that conveyed the distinct impression that if she could, she would be rolling her eyes. "It always is, in this place," she said, conveying the message regardless.

"Just check for me, will you?" Mitchell urged, his tone practically begging.

She held up a finger instead of replying, picked up a handset, and punched a button on her phone. She pressed it to her ear and waited an inordinate length of time as Mitchell shifted his weight from foot to foot. Surely she was just messing with him? How did he even know who she was ringing? It could easily be the catering department.

"Director, Mike Mitchell is here to see you," Karen finally said, her voice completely free of emotion.

The man in question ground his teeth together. Would it kill her to just send them in? Still, he knew better than to get on her bad side.

"Yes, Director," she said softly. "I will."

Karen replaced the handset in its cradle before looking up at Mitchell, who spoke impatiently. "Well?"

She paused before replying, as though taking a little pleasure in drawing out his torment. "The director will see you now," she finally said.

Mitchell impetuously reached out and squeezed her hand in thanks. "I appreciate it, Karen," he muttered, already turning away, his mind consumed with the gravity of what he was here to convey. "Remind me to get you something nice for Christmas."

"Mm-hmmmm."

He entered Director Lawrence's office suite and closed the heavy door behind him, aware that his previous visit hadn't proceeded as smoothly as he might have hoped.

Who are you kidding, Mike? He thinks you're an asshole.

The question of whether or not the feeling was mutual rested in large part on how the present meeting proceeded.

"Mike," Lawrence said, gesturing at a seat opposite his desk. "To what do I owe the pleasure?"

"It's not a courtesy call, sir," Mitchell said, sitting down and tugging the material of his jacket free from underneath him. "In fact, I don't think you're gonna like what I have to say."

Lawrence shot him a weak smile, and Mitchell noted how tired the man looked. His gray-flecked beard, ordinarily neatly trimmed, was decidedly on the wild side, and was dusted with crumbs from a half-eaten sandwich that lay on a white porcelain plate on top of his desk.

"I'm sadly coming to the realization, Mike," the director

said, "that unpleasant conversations make up about 90 percent of my job."

"Do you have a pen, sir?" Mitchell asked, his throat suddenly dry.

Lawrence's eyebrow kinked upward with genuine surprise. "A pen?" he repeated absently, patting his pockets down. His head danced left and right as he searched the surface of his desk for a writing implement, and then he leaned to one side, opened a drawer, and removed a black fountain pen, which he handed to his subordinate with a quizzical expression in his eyes. "Can you tell me why?"

Mitchell didn't reply. He retrieved an envelope from inside his jacket pocket and a single sheet of typed paper from within that. He unfolded the letter and scrolled his signature at the bottom of it before handing it to his boss in silence.

"A resignation letter?" Lawrence asked when he was done reading. "Mind if I ask why? It's kind of thin on detail..."

He nodded. "Intentionally, sir."

"How very theatrical," Lawrence remarked dryly. He leaned back in his chair, and a flicker of interest marked his expression, a hint of light amidst the gloom.

Mitchell let out a mild snort of laughter that seemed to quell some of the tension that was building in the office. "I guess you could say that. The truth is, Director, I haven't been entirely honest with you."

"I gathered as much."

"I've been running a side operation without your knowledge over the past few days, attempting to work out who's really responsible for the BA shoot down."

"Uh huh," the director replied noncommittally.

"You don't seem so surprised, sir."

Lawrence ran his fingers through his hair and let out a tired sigh. "This operation doesn't have anything to do with the mysterious Hangman, does it?"

Mitchell was too experienced to betray any hint of the mild shock of surprise that coursed through him. He'd expected to incur the director's wrath, his outrage – but not this. Whatever *this* was. Instead of rage, Lawrence merely seemed...

What? Amused?

"You know, Mike," Lawrence began slowly, fixing his subordinate with a surprisingly intense stare. "I never really liked your department."

"No, sir," Mitchell replied without emotion.

"In my book, by the time someone pulls a trigger, we've already screwed up," Lawrence continued. "We missed something. And someone had to die to atone for that error."

Mitchell fought the urge to argue back. Ordinarily he would fight SAD's corner with every fiber of his being, but there was something in Lawrence's voice that told him to hold off. The director's tone wasn't accusatory, but instead somehow introspective. As though he had come to a realization.

The DCI looked down at the resignation letter that was now sitting on the desk in front of him, slightly creased from its journey. He chewed his lip, as if coming to a difficult conclusion, and then returned his gaze to Mitchell once more. "Am I to understand that the reason this letter has made it to my desk is because you've found a solution for our present crisis?"

"That is correct, Director," Mitchell agreed, the words escaping through lips tight with the realization that his career now lay in Lawrence's hands. His solution, such as it was, only existed because he'd disobeyed his superior's direct orders in the first place. The DCI would be well within his rights to jettison him from Langley without a second thought.

Lawrence closed his eyes. "Mike, I trust that what I say will stay between us."

"Of course, sir," Mitchell nodded, though his boss couldn't see. "My lips are sealed."

"I had a difficult conversation with our mutual commander-in-chief recently," Lawrence admitted. "I only agreed to take this job in the first place because I wanted to change the Agency. We kill too many people. Drones, paramilitaries, all that sexy shit."

Mitchell remained silent, unsure where the conversation was heading.

"My view has always been that if we have a hundred Alexy Sokolovs, we don't need a thousand Hangmans." He paused, frowned, waved his hand with irritation. "Or Hangmen, I guess."

"Sure, Director, but –"

"I was reminded"—Lawrence grinned to soothe the sting of the interruption—"in no uncertain terms that sometimes one Hangman is all it takes. Just as one good intelligence source can prevent a war, so can a man with a gun. As long as it's the right man, with the right gun. Do you understand?"

Mitchell thought he did, and he was equally sure that he didn't. He desperately wanted to know what had flipped Lawrence's opinion on its axis, but he knew better than to ask. "I think I do, Director," he said.

Lawrence chuckled dryly. "At least that makes one of us. So tell me, Mike, what have you got for me?"

Mitchell took a deep breath and started. "The Russians are planning on running their Crimea play, but this time on the Baltics. They are going to roll up Estonia, Latvia and Lithuania all at once, using the cover of this SANDSTONE virus to prevent us from responding. Their next play is to take down Wall Street, alongside our military command and control networks. By the time we're in a position to respond, they'll be dug in. Game over."

Lawrence grimaced. "What's your level of confidence on this?"

"Rock solid," Mitchell replied instantly. "You could say I have it from the horse's mouth."

"I'm sure you do," the director replied in a voice that was neither pleased, nor – critically – displeased. "The question is, what do you propose we do about it? The way I see it, the Russians have us in a bind. Sword of Damocles at our neck, the whole nine yards. We're fucked."

Mitchell shook his head. What he was about to propose would test the mettle of even the most gung ho intelligence professional, and for all the man's personal charm, Director George Lawrence was better known for his quiet, measured focus on discreet intelligence gathering than his record for authorizing audacious operations.

There was a reason for that. At Langley, 'audacious' was another word for 'risky,' and any sensible bureaucrat knew better than to court risk.

"I don't think so, Director. The Russians are planning to send in their little green men ahead of the main invasion, just like they did in the Crimea and Ukraine. They'll take out key military, political and communications installations and generally spread chaos before the main force sees combat."

"What's your point?"

"We know who they are, where they are planning to cross the border in each country, and when. I'm already getting my men into place. I suggest we roll them up."

"And you need my authorization?" Lawrence murmured. "Makes a change, I suppose…"

Mitchell winced at the reproach. "For something this big, absolutely, sir. My unit is relatively small. We are not equipped for an operation of this magnitude."

"What about the virus? The Russians have us over a barrel; you said it yourself."

A wicked smile stretched across Mitchell's face. "What if I told you we have a solution to that problem as well?"

"I'd ask you what you're smoking," Lawrence grunted. "Why's this the first I'm hearing of it?"

"There's a catch," Mitchell admitted. "My team has gained a measure of control over SANDSTONE. We are limiting its spread in the US, and we've quietly flipped it back on its creators."

"You mean –?"

"Precisely, sir. If the Russians initiate it, they'll only blow themselves up." Mitchell grinned. "And believe me, I can't wait to watch."

Lawrence fixed him with a piercing stare. "And what about collateral damage? You're telling me you've found a silver bullet? Color me skeptical, Mike."

"I'm not saying there won't be blowback," Mitchell agreed. "But it'll be limited. A few local power grids briefly knocked offline. Maybe the president has to shut down the NASDAQ for a few hours. But it's worth it, Director."

"Why?"

Mitchell grinned slyly. "Plausible deniability. We're gonna get the Russians to activate this ticking time bomb all by themselves. It's going to blow up in their faces. You think they'll ever admit how badly they screwed up? No. They'll bury the whole thing. Greaves is penetrating every military network they have. We'll take them all down at the same time. Stop the Baltic invasion in its tracks."

"This is dicey, Mike," Lawrence breathed. "Damn dicey."

At least he didn't say 'risky'. Mitchell winced.

"It always is in this line of work, sir," he said simply, holding his breath as he waited for the director's final decision.

He didn't think he was about to get sacked, and he was willing to take this all the way to the top either way. But whatever happened, they needed to move fast. In under twenty-four hours, the first Russian units would begin infiltrating the Baltic states. It was the only chance they would get to bloody the bear's nose. After that, the risk of all-out war would be too great.

"Fuck," Lawrence grunted, rubbing his eyes and forehead almost obsessively. Long seconds ticked by as Mitchell waited on bated breath.

"Okay," the director muttered, and then a second time, his voice a little stronger, "okay. I'm in. We're going to do this. I still have some friends down in that part of the world."

He reached forward and pressed a button on the phone on his desk, but didn't lift the handset. "Karen – get me the head of the Latvian STU. Quietly, you understand?"

"Yes, Director."

Lawrence killed the line and shook his head, his eyes unfocused, lost deep in thought. "I guess we're actually doing this."

48

"What's his name?" Rich asked. The leader of the CIA's special action team was itching to shoot someone, and the adrenaline surging in his body was a sign he might not have to wait too long.

The immediate catalyst for the chemical's release was the appearance on a bank of small surveillance cameras of a small sedan car, traveling with its lights off, closing on the Vainagi border crossing on the Latvian border with Russia. The border post was unmanned at night, monitored remotely, but not closely. At least, that was usually the case. Tonight, although Rich hoped that the targets of their surveillance were blissfully unaware of the fact, the scrutiny on the remote area was intense.

"Anatoly Molotov," the Latvian muttered, his voice low, but his scornful tone no less obvious for it. He glowered at the surveillance monitor, as though visualizing what he wanted to do to the man. Rich suspected that whatever it was, it wouldn't be covered by the Geneva conventions. He didn't really care.

"Like the cocktail," Rich observed. "Fitting."

His partner in the command tent that night was Zaks Lodins, a captain in the Latvian Special Tasks Unit – the diminutive country's small but highly effective special forces task force. Lodins's men were far from lavishly outfitted, but what equipment they did possess was neatly and impeccably maintained. Rich liked what he saw.

The Latvian captain nodded. "It is as you say. Like the cocktail."

The command tent was set up inside one of the warehouses that made up the isolated border post. There was little chance of light from the small screens leaking out of the warehouse itself, but Lodins had decided to erect the canvas covering just in case. Rich approved of the man's attention to detail. It boded well.

The computer operator changed the view on the main screen, focusing on the sedan, which was beginning to slow as it neared the border complex. The driver parked the vehicle about 50 yards away and exited it.

Capt. Lodins muttered something in Latvian into his radio and held his fingers to his ear as he awaited the response. He turned to his CIA counterpart. "This pig is wearing a border guard uniform."

"As we expected. You're sure it's him?" Rich asked. He wasn't precisely sure how Trapp had come across the information that had led to the current operation, but it was impeccable. He had the names and unit designations of the Russian special forces operators who were crossing the border that night, as well as photos of the man they were to meet there.

"It is him," Lodins confirmed disdainfully. "Same face as the man who attacked the Embassy in Riga. My men memorized the photograph."

"Good enough for me," Rich grunted quietly, eyes glued to the screen. He knew that his own operators were seeded in the darkness alongside Lodins's men, waiting for the order to strike. For once, that decision was out of his hands. The Latvians were running the show. It was their country, after all.

The plan was simple: to wait until the Russian little green men were across the border, and then to hit them hard and without mercy. They would not be expecting trouble, not out here in the middle of the forest. If it was possible to take them prisoner, then those were Lodins's orders. But if that did not prove possible, then neither Rich nor Lodins would shed a tear. The Russians would never admit to losing so many operators on the Latvian side of the border, because admitting that would mean admitting they'd planned to invade.

Rich knew that scenes just like this were being played out at two more border crossings into Latvia, and several more across Estonia and Lithuania. It was likely, even probable, that men would die tonight. Probably some of the good guys, too.

But that was the luck of the draw. And this was the kind of operation that every operator dreamed of. Killing terrorists was fun, but it was also easy, like knocking out a toddler with one hand tied behind your back. Taking on the Russians, by contrast, that was real geopolitical shit. The kind of operation that affected the fate of nations.

The radio crackled quietly again, and Lodins listened. He looked up at Rich. "Activity on the other side of the border, my friend. Twelve SUVs."

Rich whistled under his breath. "Damn. Just like we thought."

Lodins nodded. He seemed jumpy, but Rich knew the feeling. Waiting for action was always the hardest part. He decided to steady the man's nerves. "You seen combat before, Captain?"

"A little," Lodins allowed. "Afghanistan, three years ago." His chest puffed up proudly. "My country is small, but we played our part in the coalition."

Rich slapped him on the back, grinning broadly. "If you've tangled with the Taliban, the Russians will be a cakewalk, trust me."

Lodins fixed the CIA man with an intense stare from beneath his dark helmet. "They controlled my country for three generations. I will die before I let that happen again."

I bet you would, Rich thought silently. He respected his counterpart too much to put his sentiment into words.

The Russian operative, Anatoly, walked toward the border fence.

Rich leaned forward, studying the small screen intently. "What's he holding?"

"I think you call them bolt cutters," Lodins replied.

"Shit's about to get real, real fast," Rich muttered.

The convoy of Russian special forces troops was just about visible on one of the surveillance cameras now. It was made up of a mishmash of Japanese and Russian automotive brands, and no two vehicles were the same. It was difficult to be sure, but few of the SUVs looked new – most instead were about five years old. It was a sensible decision; they would blend in better that way.

"Sixty seconds out," Lodins murmured. He repeated the same statement to his men, or at least Rich assumed he did. He activated his own mic and relayed the same message to his CIA operators. They were working hand in hand with the Latvians, but it was always better to make sure everyone was singing off the same hymn sheet.

He grabbed his personal weapon. "I'm going out there."

The sensible decision would probably have been to remain in the command tent, but this was Lodins's operation, and he was calling the shots. Rich decided he would feel more comfortable with a finger grazing the trigger instead of sitting inside a canvas tent and a metal box.

"Stay out of sight," the Latvian warned.

"You got it," Rich agreed amiably, feeling no rancor at the suggestion. He would've said the same thing.

He exited the warehouse from an door on the opposite side to where the action was about to go down. The hinges were thickly oiled and made no sound as he opened, slipped out, then closed the door behind him. The air outside was brisk compared to the thick funk inside the command tent, and from outside he could hear the growl of engines making their way to the border crossing.

"I got eyes on, boss," Rhett whispered over the team net. "This Russian prick's just waiting for them."

Rich clicked his mic twice to convey that he understood. He sidled down the side of the warehouse, trusting his eyes rather than the night vision set on top of his helmet. A nearly full moon was beating down overhead, bathing the border complex in a faded facsimile of daylight. He stopped just before the end of the warehouse, paused, and poked his head around. Just like Rhett had warned, Anatoly was waiting at the border, the gates now dragged wide open, his arms crossed across his thin chest. He was nervously bouncing from foot to foot.

Though his grim, camouflage-painted face betrayed no sign of it, inside, the CIA operator's heart felt like it was beating faster than a hummingbird's wings. The next sixty seconds might determine not only his own fate, but that of an entire region.

"They're a hundred yards out, boss," Rhett reported. "Starting to slow."

Rich did his best to slow his own breathing, resting his chin against his weapon, placing his eye against the scope. His finger rested gently against the trigger. Sixty Latvian commandos and three CIA special operators were lying in wait in the forest either side of the road at that very second.

"Fifty yards," his subordinate murmured.

After that, the Russian vehicles passed through a turn in the road and became visible through the thick tree line. They were running without lights, but the moon hanging bright overhead reflected against a dozen windscreens, painting their location for all to see.

"Don't fuck it up, guys," Rich whispered in a voice that was audible only to himself. Capt. Lodins had combat experience, but Rich doubted that all the men under him had. It would only take one over-enthusiastic, adrenaline-soaked soldier to fire a single round, and the whole damn rodeo would be blown to hell.

He flicked over to the Latvian command net, knowing he wouldn't understand a word, and not caring, figuring he'd pick up the basics pretty fast. After all, how many different ways could there be of saying, *"Kill the bastards"*?

The SUVs crossed the border at no more than five miles an hour, drove another 20 yards, and came to a halt in front of the waiting Anatoly. The operative's arms dropped to his sides, but he made no other move.

Playing it cool, Rich thought, a mirthless grin crossing his face. *It won't save you.*

The last vehicle in the Russian convoy slowed to a stop, and one by one their engines died, until all Rich could hear was a gentle popping hiss of cooling machinery, and the muted sound of his own breath.

The interlude was brief.

Captain Lodins' measured voice gave the command, and all hell broke loose. A tongue of flame belched out of the forest on the left-hand side of the halted convoy, and a stream of fifty caliber machine gun fire cut the last vehicle to shreds. Hundreds of rounds impacted the chassis, punching through and eviscerating everyone inside. Though it was impossible to make out against the darkness, a spurt of thick, dark blood coated the inside of the windshield, before that too crumbled against the weight of incoming fire.

Rich instantly turned back to his team's radio net, and muttered, "Engine blocks, kids. Don't miss."

The order was superfluous. His team knew their jobs. They would execute their part of the mission without needing to be told twice. But that was the eternal curse of the mission commander.

A rumble from behind Rich caught his attention, but he ignored it. It was the next phase of the plan clicking into place.

Another wave of gunfire followed immediately as the heavy caliber machine gun roar began to fade away. It crackled like fireworks on the Fourth of July, but Rich implicitly knew the difference. This was well aimed gunfire; his men and the Latvians aiming for the engine blocks of the eleven remaining Russian vehicles.

Sparks glinted on the hoods as round after round impacted with the front of the SUVs, bullets ricocheting and splintering in machinery, until the powerful engines were shredded into confetti.

For a long, long time, the Russians simply didn't react. In truth, their inaction probably spanned fewer than half a dozen seconds, but amidst the combat it might as well have been a lifetime. Perhaps a swift, violent, relentless counterattack might have saved them, though it was unlikely, or even a headlong retreat.

But neither occurred.

Anatoly was the first to break and run, sprinting forward through the hail of gunfire, rather than back toward his vehicle. He was heading for safety in Russia, rather than hoping to disappear in Latvia.

"Fuck," Rich mumbled, at the precise moment as an enormous surplus U.S. Army mine resistant armored personnel carrier screeched past his position, thundering toward the conflagration unfolding down below.

They needed Anatoly. Ideally alive, not dead, but they couldn't afford to lose him either way. Rich dropped his eyes back to his scope. It was a difficult shot to make, especially with adrenaline pumping in his veins.

"I've got him in my sights," he said into his throat mic, warning off the rest of his team. "It's my shot."

He didn't hear whether they acknowledged him or not as he tracked the Russian operative's sprinting, crouching form as it weaved low beneath gunfire. Rich saw the intermittent flashes of luminescence that marked out gunfire, but not the shots themselves as his world diminished to only what was visible through his gunsight.

"Come on, you bastard," he urged, though whether he was referring to himself or the Russian, he did not know. Anatoly ducked behind the shredded final vehicle in the convoy, hiding out of Rich's sight. Only twenty yards separated the Russian spy from the border of his motherland.

The Russian special forces teams were beginning to spill out of their vehicles now, hurriedly snatching at their weapons, firing messy, poorly-aimed shots into the darkness, desperately trying to fight the wraiths who were cutting them down, to do anything to even the odds.

Rich paid attention to none of it. His breathing was calm, now, almost meditative as he waited for Anatoly to make his break.

Breathe in, breathe out.

In, out.

Now.

The Russian sprinted, hands held tight against his ears as though afraid of the noise exploding all around him, running frantically for safety. Rich tracked him, lining up a shot. More flashes, more light, the screams of dying men ringing out all around. An engine roared into life, and then died as a hail of gunfire squelched it out.

Rich listened to none of it.

He breathed out.

He fired.

A single shot rocketed from his barrel into the darkness, and half a second later impacted Anatoly's thigh, sending him stumbling to the ground, unbalanced, so he impacted hard with one shoulder.

Rich winced. "That's gotta hurt."

For a few seconds, Anatoly didn't move. The experienced CIA operator began to wonder whether he'd accidentally killed him. It was easy enough to do. Like shooting out tires in the movies, disabling someone with a bullet was an almost impossible feat. Not because it was particularly difficult to aim a shot and take out someone's kneecap or ankle, because that was just a physical action which could be trained, but because large blood vessels run to almost every point in the human body. If you sever an artery, it's lights out.

Fortunately – or perhaps unfortunately, depending on your point of view – for Anatoly, he quivered into life as Rich watched through his scope. The CIA man winced, although he could not hear the inevitable screams of pain over the roar of gunfire. Inch by inch, Anatoly began dragging himself toward the border.

"Sorry, buddy, no can do," Rich muttered. "You ain't getting away with it that easy..."

He zeroed in on a spot a couple of yards away from Anatoly's head and fired once, twice, and then a third time. Sparks glinted and died against the asphalt as the rounds impacted, chewing up the road in the darkness.

Anatoly froze, his head searching everywhere for the source of his faraway tormentor. Rich grimaced as he watched. He took no pleasure in torturing the man. But he had a job to do. They needed Anatoly to confess for his sins.

And pay for them. Both death and escape were fates far too kind for a man of his unpleasant nature.

Perhaps convincing himself that the gunfire was random, the Russian spy began to drag himself forward once more, hands against the torn-up road. Rich almost thought he could hear the man moaning.

He fired again. And again. And again, until his magazine was empty and his ears rang with the repeated sound of gunfire.

Finally, Anatoly seemed to get the message. He collapsed against the hard ground, and this time Rich was certain he could hear the man's cries.

He pulled his eye away from the confines of his rifle's scope just in time to see the Latvian armored personnel carrier swerve around Anatoly's prone form, sealing off the border, and with it the Russians' only chance at escape.

All around, the gunfire began to fade. Half a dozen Russians lay collapsed on the ground around their eviscerated convoy, unmoving, bleeding out with limbs at impossible, unnatural angles. The Latvian commandos began to move in on foot, at first just dark, indistinct shadows in the darkness that materialized into men of flesh and blood, and carrying weapons of death. They surrounded the destroyed, steaming convoy, and began yanking terrified men from their vehicles and professionally binding them.

Just once, one of the little green men tried sprinting for the border. A Latvian commando pulled out a pistol, casually took aim, and a second later the Russian was dead.

It was as good as over.

At least, his team's part in it was. Whatever else it might take to halt the Russian menace, he did not know, but Rich took pride in a job well done.

He keyed his mic. "Report."

One by one, his men checked in. They were alive. So was he. It was a good day's work.

"Captain Lodins," he said, turning back to the command channel. "Give my congratulations to your men. They are as good as any I've ever fought with."

"Thank you, my friend."

49

"You ready?" Trapp asked quietly, gently holding each of Ikeda's cheeks in his large palms.

She nodded resolutely, her soft skin caressing Trapp's callused fingers. "You bet."

"Good," he said simply.

Turning away, he raised his voice and said, "Are you ready, Roman?"

The door to the billionaire's dressing room squeaked as the humbled man exited, now properly dressed for the first time in twenty-four hours. He was wearing a neat, navy blue Italian suit. The tailoring disguised his excess bulk as well as could be reasonably expected, which was to say, not very well. He was hunched over, as though the fight had been beaten out of him.

Kholodov rested his head against the door and mumbled, "You can't make me do this."

"Oh, that's where you're wrong," Trapp assured him. He had no need to brandish a weapon. Roman Kholodov was under no illusion about the power his captor possessed. "Either you do as I say, or I will kill you. It's that simple. Do you understand?"

"No, I –"

Trapp's voice acquired the texture of coarse sandpaper and dropped to a deadly quiet. "It's a simple fucking question, Roman. Do you want to live, or not?"

Kholodov's lined face showed traces of the man's exhaustion as it trembled with barely-suppressed emotion. He sagged. "I understand."

"Exceptional," Trapp said, losing patience and grabbing Kholodov by the shoulder, though he was careful not to decrease the billionaire's perfectly pressed suit. "Let's go."

He led him downstairs, Ikeda following suit, to Kholodov's office. It was, as their prisoner had explained, essentially a nerve center for the plan he had put together. Every single element of the plan, from controlling the SANDSTONE virus to contacting individual unit commanders in the field, could be stage-managed from that very room, though the operation itself both could and would run like clockwork without him.

Trapp glanced at Ikeda as he pushed Kholodov into a leather-backed executive chair and initialized a bank of cameras aimed directly at his face. "It's all set up?" he asked.

She nodded.

"Okay," he muttered, turning back to Kholodov and removing a pistol from the small of his back in the same move. He aided unwaveringly at the Russian's skull. "You so much as blink wrong, asshole, and I'll put a hole in your forehead. Understood?"

"How many times do I have to tell you," Kholodov moaned, his face pale, "I will do exactly as you say. I want to live."

"That's a pity," Trapp snarled. Wisely, Kholodov didn't reply.

"Dial it up," Trapp said, glancing back at Ikeda, who was leaning over a computer terminal. She nodded silently, and Trapp removed himself from the conference system's field of view, inserting an earbud at the same time to allow for a real-time translation from Langley. An anger was burning inside him now, but he kept himself entirely still, the pistol remaining

firmly in Kholodov's line of sight. Just a reminder of the fate
that awaited him if he failed to do exactly as he was told.

The computer chimed as the conference system activated.
Trapp half expected to hear an old-school modem sound as the
scrambler initialized a secure line, but there was nothing of the
sort. It was all digital these days. The world was starting to pass
him by.

"Roman." The Russian president, Dmitry Murov, smiled
thinly, though the translator relayed his words with a distinctly
Texan twang. "How nice of you to call."

Kholodov tugged at his shirt collar anxiously, and Trapp
held his breath, wondering if the man was about to blow the
operation to hell and back. Murov had the power to send in the
FSB, and if that happened, he didn't rate either his or Ikeda's
chances of escaping the country alive very highly. "Of course,
sir. I wanted to confirm that you are happy to proceed with"–he
paused, coughing slightly before continuing—"the operation."

Murov's face wrinkled with disdain. "You have your orders,
Roman."

Kholodov bobbed his head nervously. "What we have
planned, sir, it is momentous. I just wanted –"

Murov cut him off. "Our men are getting into position?"

"Yes, Mr. President," Kholodov said, his voice weak, but
audible. "As you know, they are operating under a communications blackout. They will check in once they are safely across
the border."

"Good." Murov smiled. "Roman, you have done well, my
friend. Tomorrow will be a new dawn for the Russian Federation. We should never have allowed our Baltic cousins to leave
our embrace. But that was another generation's mistake. It is
our duty to right that wrong."

"Yes, Mr. President," Kholodov said, nodding his head a
little too fast. Sweat glistened on his forehead, and Trapp

worried that it would be visible through the conference system's high definition video cameras. "A glorious day indeed."

Murov squinted. "Are you okay, my friend? You sound unwell."

For a second, Kholodov glanced off-screen, at Trapp. He ran his finger across his throat and gestured at the captive billionaire to play his part. The man did so, returning his gaze to the eye of the camera in front of him and shaking his head anxiously.

"No, Mr. President," he squeaked. "Just a little nervous."

"You have no reason to be." The Russian president smiled broadly. "The plan is flawless. The Americans won't know what we're doing until it's too late. And it's all your doing, Roman. You should be proud."

"I am," Kholodov murmured, his face ashen. "Believe me, Mr. President, I am."

"You don't sound it," Murov grunted, his expression black. He shook it off. "But once this is over, my friend, I will reward you greatly. Anything you ask."

"Thank you, Dmitry," Kholodov said. "Do I have your permission to initiate the virus?"

Trapp held his breath. This was the moment of truth, the final piece of information they needed to catch the vicious bastard red-handed. As Murov dragged out the silence before he replied, Trapp's tension only grew. Did he suspect something?

Finally, Murov spoke. His voice was cold, twisted, but it came through the speaker's crystal clear. "Do it, Roman. Humble those arrogant Americans." He leaned forward, finger massive in his camera's field of view. "And don't contact me until it's done."

The screen went black, and the speakers emitted a quiet hiss. Trapp didn't dare speak until Ikeda threw him a thumbs-up to indicate the call was over. He sighed quietly. "You get all that?"

"Uh-huh." She grinned, ejecting a memory stick from the computer and slipping it into her jacket. "Every last word. We got him."

Trapp clenched his fist with satisfaction. They had what they came for, evidence that the Russian president himself had conspired not just to invade three of his nearest – if not closest – neighbors, but also to attack the United States herself.

"What now?" Kholodov whimpered.

"Now, Roman," Trapp chuckled coldly, "you do as the president ordered."

"What do you mean?"

Trapp shrugged as though the answer was obvious. "Activate the virus."

"But..." Kholodov stammered. "But why? It will destroy your country."

"We'll see about that," Trapp replied, grabbing Kholodov once again and maneuvering him in front of the nearest computer terminal. He jabbed his finger at the screen. "You know what to do?"

"Of course," the Russian replied, throwing Trapp an anxious look, as though he thought he was playing a game that he didn't understand. In truth, he was. But Trapp had no intention of enlightening him.

Kholodov's fingers hovered over the keyboard for a few seconds as he grappled with indecision Trapp dug his fingers into his shoulder and delivered a firm, painful reminder of who exactly was in charge. Kholodov squeaked, but finally set to work. He called up a computer program that wasn't nearly as complex-looking as the Matrix-esque cascade of green text that Trapp had pictured.

A minute later, he looked up from the screen with a

pleading expression in his eyes. He spoke in a cracked, uncertain tone. "It is done."

Trapp glanced at Ikeda, who reached into her jacket and removed a flashlight.

"How long do you reckon?" she asked.

"Guess we'll have to wait and see..."

It didn't take long. Less than a minute later, every light in Kholodov's office died, along with all the computer equipment and every electrical system for almost five hundred miles. Except, of course, Ikeda's flashlight, which instantly clicked on, illuminating her face.

In the darkness, Kholodov whispered, "But how..."

Trapp smiled, though the expression held not even a hint of warmth, and probably wasn't visible in the darkness regardless. "Trade secret," he said, clapping the man on the back.

Ikeda raised her voice, a ghostly presence in the near-darkness. "I suggest, Roman, that for your own safety you don't mention to your boss that you had any part in what happened today, okay?"

The broken billionaire nodded blankly. He knew too well what the consequences would be of admitting betrayal to a man like President Dmitry Murov.

"And don't run, either," Trapp added. "Because if you do, I'll find you. You understand?"

"Yes," Kholodov whispered.

"Excellent." Trapp grinned, turning to leave as Ikeda's flashlight flickered against the office's cream walls. "Roman, you've been a blast. We'll be in touch."

50

T*hree weeks later.*

SUMMER WAS TURNING to fall as the bow of the MV Icarus cut through the thick, mineral-laden waters of the Black Sea, her powerful engines barely more than idling now as she reached the culmination of a journey that had spanned two continents, sixteen days and six thousand miles. It was the last voyage that the gleaming blue-hulled super yacht would ever make.

The keel of the two hundred foot long Icarus had been laid down in a South Korean shipyard only five years earlier. She was commissioned by a shell company, a cutout, and her builders were told that she was to be owned by a Middle Eastern oil and gas magnate, though as long as the construction payments arrived on time, the Koreans didn't care.

In truth, the Icarus was built to the tastes and specifications of a senior member of the Sinaloa Cartel, one Jesus Gonzalez, and completed her maiden journey only two weeks before the estimable Señor Gonzalez was captured by a company of the Infantería de Marina – the Mexican Marine Corps—acting on information supplied by one of his own *companeros*, and extradited to the United States. The vessel was seized by the US Coast Guard and had been kept in a dry dock near Miami for much of the previous sixteen months.

After the reprehensible Señor Gonzalez's conviction in federal court four months earlier, the Icarus became the legal property of the US government, and was scheduled to be disposed of at auction, until the boffins in Langley identified a more dramatic purpose for her.

On her present voyage, she was crewed by nineteen sailors from one of the Naval Special Warfare Command's Combat Service Teams, the unsung heroes who provide logistical support to the Navy's special operators across the globe. They were fourteen men and three women who could be relied upon to keep their lips sealed, a vital precondition for a mission that had been designed to be whispered about for years to come, but never formally acknowledged. Upon successful completion of the operation, it would go down in special forces lore, and the eighteen sailors under the command of Lieutenant Harry Charnaud wouldn't pay for a beer in a Coronado bar until at least Christmas.

Hopefully Christmas 2025, he mused.

The voyage had been pleasantly uneventful. Halfway across the Atlantic, the Icarus had met up with the USNS Yukon, an underway replenishment oiler, under a heavy cloud cover, two thousand miles from the nearest set of prying eyes. His sailors had carried out the subsequent refueling with commendable ease on the unfamiliar vessel.

Lieutenant Charnaud entered the Icarus's wraparound bridge clutching a steaming hot mug of black coffee. Everything was better on a super yacht, he thought ruefully, especially as whoever had fitted the thing out had gone to great lengths to ensure that, should she face inspection, there would not be as much as a hair's difference with any other such yacht at sea. The steaks were expensive and imported, the wine collection vast, the bedding thick and luxurious.

"Police that salute, sailor," he snapped, catching a glimpse out of the corner of his eye as he scanned the horizon for any sign that they were under observation.

"Sorry, sir," Chief Petty Officer Miguel Reyes muttered, hands dropping to his sides at the same rate at which his cheeks welled crimson. "It won't happen again."

"See that it doesn't, Reyes," Charnaud said. "And it's Harry, remember. I'm no lieutenant, not right now."

The lieutenant watched as Reyes processed the second part of his reprimand.

"Sorry, Harry," Reyes mumbled, almost choking at the unusual informality. "I'll keep that under advisement."

Charnaud hid a grin. The chief petty officer was a damn fine sailor, having spent over a decade aboard U.S. Navy frigates before he transferred over to Coronado. Old habits died very hard, and he couldn't entirely blame the man for automatically referring to him by his rank.

"But Captain will do just fine," Charnaud added, a smile tickling his lips, and letting Reyes know that he was mostly just playing with him.

"Yes, Captain," Reyes agreed with evident relief.

He, like the rest of the crew, was dressed in dark blue slacks and a sparkling white polo shirt with the yacht's name embroidered in gold thread over the left breast. Contrary to naval regulations, half of the male sailors were growing facial hair, which would of course be shaved off the moment they returned stateside.

Lieutenant Charnaud had borne the age profile of his crew in mind when drawing up a list of sailors to assign to this operation, and so while the entire crew was in excellent physical condition, a fact that might draw the surprised attention of a particularly diligent Coast Guard inspector, they did not otherwise deviate much from the appearance of the crews of the other super yachts that plied the warm waters of the Black Sea.

"How's everything looking?" Charnaud asked amiably, taking his seat in the captain's chair on the bridge. Unlike most of the Navy's own vessels, he could call up any relevant piece of information on a terminal in front of him, but he was an officer who valued the input of the sailors under his command. He knew that many of them had been at sea when he was still in college – and he knew better than to ignore their experience.

"Tanks are little low, Captain," Reyes replied. "Just a shade under three thousand gallons left."

"More than enough," Charnaud said amiably. "We'll be on station by nightfall. After that"—he patted the workstation in front of him—"this old girl won't be going anywhere in a hurry anyway."

Reyes glanced around, a wistful expression on his tanned face. "You sure it's the only way, Captain? Just – it's a real shame. This boat's a beauty…"

Charnaud winced as he took an overenthusiastic gulp of his coffee. When the burning lava java had finished coursing its way down its throat, he said, "You know the drill, Reyes. Ours is not to reason why…"

"Yes, sir," the sailor agreed. "But I ain't gotta like it."

"I'm with you there," the lieutenant agreed, suspecting that no matter how long he served in the blue water navy, he would never command a boat quite like this again. Or, for that matter, take part in a mission like this one.

"Chow's good," he said, listening out for the barely audible grumble of the yacht's high-powered but whisper-quiet engines. They were better than anything the Navy had, and would be perfect for a covert insertion off an unfriendly coast.

Yeah, and ten times the price…

"I ain't arguing with you there, Captain," Reyes agreed. He glanced at an LCD screen in front of them. "Recommend course change to heading 275. Got a sandbar marked on the charts."

"The con is yours," Charnaud said immediately, knowing that Reyes was a better boat driver than he would ever be. And he would never live it down if he beached a two hundred million dollar yacht off the coast of Turkey, that was for sure – even if the Icarus was to be scuttled the next night either way.

"Aye, Captain. Making heading 275." Reyes reached for a computer joystick that wouldn't have looked out of place in a teenage boy's bedroom and gently guided the Icarus to her new course. He looked up, shaking his head in wonder. "Course is 275."

"Course is 275," Charnaud acknowledged out of habit.

"Real damn shame," Reyes muttered underneath his breath, shaking his head. "And ain't that the truth."

THE HELICOPTER'S rotors were first audible shortly after nightfall, though over the water it was difficult to make out which direction they were coming from. It wasn't the first time that the crew of the Icarus had heard the sound of rotor aircraft – most of the super yachts that roved the waters of the Black Sea had space for at least a small one – but it was the first time since their voyage had begun that one had landed on their own helicopter deck.

The relative comfort of the Icarus, at least compared with a typical U.S. Navy vessel, had dulled the monotony of life on a ship at sea, but only a little. So any sailor who was not actively occupied at their duty station was out on the foredeck, watching the arrival of their guests. Anything to break with routine.

"Kill the deck lights," Charnaud ordered the second the helicopter touched down.

"Killing deck lights," Reyes acknowledged.

"Lieutenant Charnaud," a tall, powerfully-built man said not long after, dropping a long canvas case at his side and stretching out his hand in greeting. "Name's Jason. Nice to meet you."

"Welcome aboard, sir," Charnaud said, keeping his expression and tone professional, and stopping himself from succumbing to the desire to ask his visitor exactly what the hell it was that they were doing so close to the Russian coast. His eyes flicked down to the case at the man's feet.

Looks like a rifle, he thought. *A big one.*

"The pilot says we're not far off?" Jason said, his own eyes conspicuously following the lieutenant's down to the deck, and then back again.

Charnaud nodded, feeling suitably chastised. He didn't know who on God's green earth this mysterious individual was, but it wasn't hard to make at least a somewhat accurate guess. He had to be a special operator. Maybe a SEAL, though the lieutenant doubted it. More likely Agency.

Behind him, a woman stepped out of the helicopter.

For a second time, Jason's eyes traced the path of the lieutenant's and back again. Charnaud cleared his throat, and wondered what it was about the man in front of him that was throwing him off his game. He looked much like any of the special operators who cycled in and out of Coronado, the same powerful, muscular physique, constantly darting eyes, and a mild tension in his posture that suggested he was ready to snap into action at a moment's notice. But there was something different about this one, Charnaud thought. It wasn't just that he was older, but also more self-assured. Less testosterone-filled, and yet seemingly no less deadly for it.

"We're about three hours out," Charnaud said, happy to

steer the conversation back to safer ground. "But I can cut that in half if you want me to. This baby's got some real powerful engines. Would be nice to see what they are capable of."

"Maybe next time," Jason said, the wry smile on his face indicating that he too knew there would be no next time. "Better not to raise any eyebrows."

"No, sir," Charnaud agreed, kicking himself for suggesting it.

Real smart, big guy, he thought.

"We brought you some presents," Jason said, nodding at the helicopter which was now tied firm against the deck. "Let's get them unloaded and set up. I want you and your crew on the chopper by oh three hundred. Can you get it done?"

Like Reyes before him, it was Lieutenant Charnaud's opportunity to wish he could snap off a salute. There was something to be said for military protocol, after all. "Yes, sir," he said. "We'll be ready."

"Good man." Jason grinned. "See that you are."

TRAPP WENT BELOW DECKS, Ikeda at his side, in search perhaps of the most important person aboard – at least, if they hoped to escape this particular misadventure in one piece. They found him on the yacht's diving deck, a dedicated area near the rear of the vessel which contained a Triton miniature submarine, enough scuba sets to outfit a platoon of SEALs, and a work area the equal of any Navy destroyer.

He let out a low, impressed whistle. "So this is it."

A powerfully built man with sandy blond hair emerged from the rear end of the sub, wearing an oil-stained boiler suit and carrying a wrench. "It's a real nice piece of kit, sir, and I'll tell you that for nothing. I take it you're the guys who're taking her for a spin?"

The real nice piece of kit in question was dangling from a hoist, to allow for ease of access during maintenance, and secured at each of its four sleek corners by a length of line, in case the Icarus encountered inclement weather – unlikely at this time of year in the Black Sea, but not impossible.

"That's right." Trapp jerked his thumb at Ikeda. "That there is Eliza, and I'm Jason. You mind walking us through what this baby can do?"

"Tim O'Reilly," the mechanic said. "Machinist's mate, chief petty officer." He winked lasciviously. "Though I guess I'm not supposed to tell you that until we reach port."

Trapp chuckled. "I reckon I can keep the secret."

O'Reilly nodded thoughtfully and whacked the large wrench against his open palm, just once. "You know, I'm betting you can. I'll run you through the modifications I've made if that's okay with you, sir?"

"Just Jason is fine," Trapp said. "And that sounds pretty damn good to me."

The machinist's mate glanced at Ikeda. "Anything you wanna ask, don't hesitate. I could talk about this puppy all day."

"Got it," she said.

"So," he started, leading them round to the rear of the sub, "the base model – and I mean base, not basic," he grunted. "'Cause I don't think anything on the Icarus is basic, if you follow me."

Trapp glanced at the pristine row of scuba kits. They didn't look to have ever been used. Then again, the boat's original owner was sitting in a federal maximum-security jail right now, with no prospect of parole, so that made sense. "Uh huh."

"Like I was saying, base model, she's got a range of about thirty miles depending on current. I took a look at the charts, and it looks to be pushing your way, so you'll have a tailwind of a couple of knots an hour."

"How do you know where we're going?" Ikeda asked sharply.

"Begging your pardon, ma'am?"

Trapp glanced at his partner's suddenly alert posture. "I think what my"–he coughed, suddenly self-conscious—"my colleague here is asking is how do you know what our target is? That's compartmented information."

O'Reilly rolled his eyes. "I've been around the block a few times, sir. This ain't the first time I've sat a few miles off an unfriendly coast working on a mini sub so you special ops types can go for a dip. You pick up a few things, and the friendly inhabitants of Georgia weren't the bastards who just tried to nuke our economy, and they sure as shit didn't just try and invade half of Eastern Europe. That narrowed it down some."

He paused, and Trapp cast a critical eye over the Navy mechanic, watching out for any sign that he was lying. But O'Reilly was relaxed, his posture languid and unconcerned – and besides, he was talking sense. The tiny nation of Georgia, for so long an unwilling member of the Soviet Union, was located no more than fifty miles from Murov's villa in Sochi. It didn't take a rocket scientist to work out where they were headed.

"Copy that, Petty Officer," Trapp said, shaking his head. "I guess we should've known better than to bet against an old seadog like you."

"Damn straight." O'Reilly grinned, running greasy fingers through his light hair, but leaving no identifiable oil trail. "Now – where was I?"

"Before you were so rudely interrupted?" Ikeda said, throwing her hands up in mock apology. "Tailwinds."

"Exactly!" O'Reilly replied, slapping the mini sub's side for emphasis. "With the current flowing your way, unmodified, she'd probably push forty miles in range, but it's dicey. Water's warm, so there shouldn't be much of a drain on the battery on that front, but you never know."

He dragged a step ladder and climbed up three stairs, pointing to an unwieldy modification on the rear of the sub. "I've added on about sixty kilowatt hours of juice. Enough for another twenty, twenty-five miles."

"What about air?" Ikeda interjected.

"There's just the two of you, right?"

"Correct."

"You should be fine. With how much these things cost, the designers over-engineer. Hell, this thing's probably never been taken out for more than an hour, but the tanks on the back will do three people for twelve hours, or the two of you for eighteen. The batteries will be long dead by then."

"Good work," Trapp said approvingly. "You've tested it?"

O'Reilly shrugged. "Best I could without actually getting her wet, sir. But she'll do the job. You have my word."

"She better." Ikeda grinned. "Because I promise you, Petty Officer, if I drown in this thing, I'm coming back to haunt you."

The look on O'Reilly's face suggested he could think of any number of more chilling threats, but he was too polite to say it. Or perhaps sufficiently respectful of Ikeda's implied skill set. "If you die –"

He immediately clammed up. Trapp's eyebrow rose. "Go on, Chief..."

"My apologies, sir. I was gonna say that if you die, it won't be in this thing. Coulda picked a better way of making my point, I guess."

"Don't sweat it," Trapp replied, waving his hand. "You've done good, Tim. And if you haven't, it won't just be this pretty lady's ghost who's coming to haunt you..."

"No, sir," O'Reilly replied.

"What about when we're done?" Ikeda asked.

"You're ditching it at sea, right?"

Trapp nodded. "Correct."

"It's not designed for an underwater exit, so you're going to have to do things the old-fashioned way," O'Reilly said, patently relieved to be back on firmer ground. "I've modified the safety lock so that the hatch will open underwater, but you'll still need to equalize the pressure."

"How?"

O'Reilly chuckled and pointed at a large electric drill that was sitting on the yacht's steel deck. "Like I said, old school. Just bite through the Plexiglas shell, wait for it to fill up, and she'll open easy enough. You won't want to be too deep when you do it, though. She'll start sinking quick once she loses that extra buoyancy."

Trapp grimaced at the thought of being trapped in the sub as it sank toward a cold, dark grave at the bottom of the ocean, desperately scrabbling to get out before it was too late.

O'Reilly noticed the expression on his face and hastened to interject, "Don't worry, sir. She's got directional thrusters. If you angle those up before you leave, she'll hold steady enough. I've set it up so those will short out about five minutes after the hatch opens. You think that's long enough for you to get clear? I can work on it some more. Won't take long."

"Sounds good to me," Trapp replied, impressed at the sailor's foresight. "That everything?"

"Just about." O'Reilly nodded, offering out his hand and shaking both of theirs in turn. "And if you don't mind me saying, sir, give 'em hell."

51

I t was a near-perfect morning on Russia's Black Sea coast, and the MV Icarus bobbed at anchor a kilometer from shore, among a collection of yachts that varied from plentiful twenty-footers to boats that dwarfed even the Icarus itself.

Trapp and Ikeda had spent most of the morning working aboard the boat, wearing the same white and blue crew uniforms that the departed team of Navy sailors had worn before them and performing essential at-sea maintenance tasks, just in case anyone was paying attention, though probably not very well. Trapp suspected that someone on Murov's security detail had probably swept the yacht with high-power binoculars, perhaps even several times. But he doubted that they had received anything more than a cursory inspection. Sochi was the natural home of the Russian elite, and the super yachts floating off the coast were as common a sight as the supermodels that flocked to the seaside resort's many luxurious beach clubs. They were the last place any reasonable individual would expect a threat to emanate from.

Which of course, Trapp mused, meant that the Icarus was the perfect place from which to attempt such a feat.

And make no mistake: if we pull it off, it will be a hell of a feat.

He was standing on the wraparound bridge of the Icarus, a pair of binoculars held loosely in his hands. He scanned the horizon, starting his search far away from his intended target, and rotated slowly to his right, scoping out the deck of a yacht only a few hundred yards away, from which a helicopter was beginning to rise, its rotors beating a wash against the sea and causing it to foam and surge against the Hermione's golden hull.

"How are we looking?" Ikeda purred, dragging her nails across his back, and causing a shiver of pleasure to run the full length of his spine.

If he hadn't grown accustomed to the way she moved with a silent, predator's grace, Trapp might have jumped out of his skin. But he was, and so he did not. Instead, he kept the binoculars pressed tight against his eyes, barely holding as the field of view passed over the ostentatious yacht to their port side.

"Our boy's away," he murmured, tracking the helicopter for only a fraction of a second, just in case someone was watching, and continuing to rotate across the horizon.

"Right on schedule," Ikeda commented.

"Yep."

"You ready?"

Trapp said nothing as the binoculars alighted upon the terrace of the villa approximately a kilometer and a half distant from the yacht. The binoculars were powerful, but not powerful enough to make out the faces of the people moving about upon it, who at this distance seemed like stick figures.

"As I'll ever be..." he finally murmured.

"Then I'll see you topside," Ikeda said, correctly ascertaining that he was preparing himself for the task they were about to attempt, and understanding that some things were best accomplished in private.

He took a moment to compose himself, slowly mastering

his breathing until he knew that he was truly ready for what was to come, then clambered up a maintenance ladder that ran to the top of the yacht.

The Barrett fifty cal sniper rifle was a monster. This particular unit was *officially* never manufactured. There was no record of its serial number in any database, whether at a retailer or in the computers of the Barrett Firearms Manufacturing company. For that matter, the rifle itself bore no identifying markers, no serial number, and before it was acquired by the Central Intelligence Agency, it had never been fired, to ensure there could be no record of the rifling pattern.

Like the man who was about to caress its trigger, it was a ghost. Fittingly, Ikeda had spray-painted it white, in an Arctic camouflage pattern, to make the weapon indistinguishable from the color of the radar deck which crested the Icarus.

That morning, they had erected a small canvas shanty to cover an area of the yacht that contained several radar domes, communications antennas and several satellite dishes that were designed to ensure that the previous owner of the yacht was able to remain in constant contact with his business activities, and spent several hours disassembling one of the domes and pretending to repair it. It lay in pieces, amidst a sea of tools and screws and electronic components, most of which Trapp had no inkling as to their purpose.

Thankfully, for the task he had in mind, that was not required.

"You have the detonator?" he asked.

Ikeda nodded, pulling back a white sheet and revealing an innocuous rectangle of black plastic, which she quickly covered once he signaled that he saw it, though unless Murov's people had a drone hovering 20 feet overhead, it would be invisible. A little farther underneath the sheet, he knew, was the rifle, already loaded with a ten-round box magazine, filled with hand-filled, steel -tipped anti-personnel rounds. Pretty much any round fired from the Barrett would tear the human body to shreds, he knew. But he didn't intend to take any chances.

Not on this mission. There was too much riding on it.

"Got it," she confirmed.

As usual, before entering into combat, Trapp began to experience a familiar dryness of the mouth. Perspiration started forming on his palms, and he wiped them against his dark uniform slacks. He swallowed, hard.

"Let's run through the plan one last time," he said in a transparent attempt to take his mind off the tension.

"The helicopter should land in about three minutes," Ikeda said. "It's a five minute walk from the helipad to the terrace where Murov is waiting. We search for a counter-sniper team. If we see one, we take them out first."

"Good," Trapp said, pleased. That had been her idea. At this distance, with the sound of crashing waves in the background, the noise of even this beast of a rifle being fired would be barely audible. "What next?"

"We wait until Kholodov's sitting next to President Murov. Then we take the shot. The second it's fired, we toss the rifle into the sea, punch the detonator, and start the timer. Detonator goes into the drink next. Then we run for the sub."

Trapp closed his eyes, picturing it like a rally driver visualizing a particularly troublesome course. The explosives would detonate seven minutes after they were initiated, first aerosolizing a small amount of jet fuel, then igniting the main charge. The Icarus would be destroyed, and what was left of its hull would sink directly to the bottom of the Black Sea.

"You think seven minutes is enough?" he asked.

A vision of a shockwave pulsating out from the Icarus filled his mind, surging through the water around the hull, reaching out and snapping the miniature Triton submarine in half. It wasn't his death he was worried about, he knew; it was Ikeda's.

"Eggheads at Langley said so, didn't they?" Ikeda replied,

referring to the Special Activities Division's in-house brain trust, a tight-knit collection of scientists and engineers who provided support for the Agency's most difficult to achieve, most secretive operations.

She shrugged, though Trapp privately thought it looked a little affected, and said, "Seven minutes will be fine."

"You're right," he said, glancing at the diver's watch on his wrist, though his mind had kept almost perfect time since the helicopter lifted off from Kholodov's gaudy yacht "We better get into position. Kholodov's thirty seconds out. That means Murov will be heading to the terrace any moment now."

"Got it," Ikeda replied. She looked at him expectantly. "So?"

"So what?" he asked, although he already knew the question.

"Who's gonna take the shot?"

Trapp didn't reply immediately. He wanted to be the one to pull the trigger. Five years had passed since he had first recruited Alexy Sokolov, and he'd barely known the man then, let alone now. But an anger burned within him, fierce and unquenchable at Alexy's untimely death, a death that occurred in service of a country he never got the chance to truly know.

That anger rose in his throat like lava spurting from a volcano, urging him to take the reins. But the anger belonged to a man named Jason Trapp, and Jason Trapp was not on the Icarus; Hangman was. And where Jason Trapp wanted to wreak a vicious revenge on the men who had wronged him, the men who had stolen Sokolov's life before time, Hangman was cool, calculating.

More to the point, before setting out on this journey, he had traveled with Ikeda to a firing range at Camp Peary, the CIA's secretive training center, and both had taken hundreds of shots at this distance, with a repurposed mechanical bull beneath them simulating the swaying of a yacht's deck.

"You're better," he admitted without rancor. It was the truth.

There was only a fraction in it, but Ikeda was the better shot at this distance. He was good, but she was a natural. "Take it, if you want it."

"He was your friend, Jason," Ikeda whispered, referring not now to Alexy Sokolov, but to a man named Alessandro Lombardi, who had died in the Italian city of Florence just a few days earlier. "But I liked him too. And I think he would have come to like me."

Trapp said nothing. He nodded once and walked to the far side of the yacht, idly playing with the canvas shanty. He caught Ikeda's eye and nodded. "Now," he grunted, releasing a line, and allowing the sheet to fall, providing a few seconds of cover.

Immediately, Ikeda dropped to the deck and lay flat, rolling beneath the sheet until her frame was completely hidden. She rearranged it so that a small section sliced in the fabric was perfectly aligned over the scope of the fifty cal, with enough space for a small hand to alter the elevation knob.

"You're clear," he said quietly, scanning the scene to make sure there was nothing that could be seen from a distance. Nothing to give away their intentions.

But there wasn't.

He yanked the line back, reassembling the shanty to its original position, then took a cross-legged position next to the radar dome and retrieved several items from the deck, including a wind meter and a smartphone, on which was loaded a ballistic calculator. He held the wind meter aloft.

"Wind, three miles an hour," he said softly. "Direction six o'clock."

That was good. The wind was low, and coming from a direction that would not inflict a lateral force onto the bullet. Wind, as every sniper knew, was unpredictable, but he didn't think it would change much in the next few minutes.

The range they already knew, dialed in via GPS, but he double-checked it, just to be sure, and communicated it to the shooter. That was what Ikeda was now. Not a human being, not a woman he was coming to love, but merely an extension of the rifle in her hands.

A weapon.

It was a waiting game now. And they didn't have long.

52

President Dmitry Aleksandrovich Murov was not a man who tolerated failure, nor those who came bearing news of it. He was, however, an individual with a quite unhealthy fascination with meting out the consequences of such failures.

It was the only way, he knew, to keep people in line. They needed to fear him, and fear what he was capable of, or why else would his subordinates continue to follow his commands? He shivered at the prospect. It could not be allowed to come to pass, since the consequences of losing control would no doubt cost him not just his fortune, but also his life.

"He is here, Mr. President," a member of his security detail announced in a low voice after placing his fingers against his ear.

"Send him down, Boris," Murov said with a dismissive gesture of his fingers. "And then we are not to be disturbed. Is that understood?"

"Yes, Mr. President."

"And Boris?" Murov said.

"Sir?"

"Mr. Kholodov has failed me, and betrayed his country," Murov said, the first part the truth, the second a lie, though no change in his expression indicated either fact. "He will need to be removed."

Echoing his boss, Boris betrayed no emotion. He was the head of the president's security detail, a rising star in Murov's inner circle, and this was not the first time he had eliminated an individual who had raised his president's ire. Before Kholodov, his targets were mostly journalists, whistleblowers, and other such undesirables, but he had no moral objection to murder. Murov knew this without needing to ask, for the man would not be in his employ if he did.

"Of course, Mr. President. It will be as you command. How should it be carried out?"

Murov knew the question his man was asking – not instructions on the precise method with which he should dispatch the wayward Roman Kholodov, but whether the execution should be quiet, or...

"Make it a statement, Boris," he murmured.

"Yes, Mr. President."

Murov settled back in his seat and sipped on a steaming china cup of Colombian coffee. Not bad, he decided. It was as important to appreciate the little comforts in life as the extravagant ones. He still remembered the hard-fought, starving days of his youth, and he had no desire to reprise them. He hadn't known what Colombian coffee was, back then, but he always knew he wanted to find out. And he had. He had achieved everything he'd ever desired.

And so much more.

The beating of helicopter rotors passed overhead, though he barely paid attention to them, content with his thoughts and his coffee, and the views of an endless horizon, with enormous, glistening yachts sparkling on top of it like precious gems.

He spied Roman Kholodov's vessel, an ostentatious golden

monstrosity that fouled his view. It was his yacht, really, Murov thought, paid for with his money. The fact that the money truly belonged to the citizens of Russia, though those benighted people would never see it, never entered the Russian president's mind. As far as he was concerned, his assets and the state's were one and the same. Interchangeable.

As long as the money flowed in the correct direction.

A few minutes later, he heard two sets of footsteps approaching. "Mr. President, your guest."

Murov turned in time to see his bodyguard give him a nod before the man turned to leave. He took up a position fifty yards from his boss, covering the only path down the steep cliff that led to the marble terrace, and thus ensuring his master's safety.

By Boris's side stood a cringing Roman Kholodov, the pallor of his face a sickly yellow, his shoulders hunched over with exhaustion.

No, not exhaustion – acceptance.

The thought brought a cold smile to President Murov's lips. He beckoned the broken man over, reveling in the fact that, like a beaten dog, Kholodov knew what was about to happen, and yet would do nothing to stop it. The man had billions of dollars of Murov's money in his bank accounts. Enough money to run, to pay for the finest plastic surgery, to purchase perfect false documents.

People had tried before, Murov knew. None had succeeded. His people had hunted them to the ends of the earth, and then beyond, if needed. Those who ran suffered only weeks, months, even years of the certain knowledge that one day their country would find them, and that on that day, they would suffer an even slower, more painful demise than they could possibly have anticipated.

"Roman," Murov said with a tone of pleasant surprise in his voice that belied the reality of the situation. "You came."

Kholodov bowed his head and murmured, "Of course, Mr. President."

Murov beckoned him over. The man's death would be public, of course, but it would be quick, for he had come to meet his fate when others before him had not. And wasn't that a mercy?

His mercy.

Roman Kholodov, the man who was Boris before Boris was Boris, took a seat opposite his president, the man he had served faithfully most of his life. He was practically trembling, mute with fear. He pulled at his fingers, hands moving endlessly, fruitlessly. This time, there was no offer of coffee, no hospitality, no butler on hand to take a drinks order or to provide breakfast.

There was no sense in wasting money on the damned.

"Roman," Murov said, as though he was addressing a small child. "What is the matter?"

The dishevelled billionaire did not, could not look up to meet the gaze of his former master. "I failed you, Dmitry," he moaned. "I thought I could –"

"And you have come to ask forgiveness, yes?" Murov asked, his expression warm and kindly, his tone echoing the same emotion.

He had no intention of granting the man clemency. It would set a bad example. But he liked to watch his victims twist, displaying the same detached, sociopathic curiosity as an ordinary housecat playing with a doomed rodent.

The game was simple. Give them a taste of freedom, then snatch it away.

For the first time, Kholodov looked up, his eyes betraying a dull, disbelieving hope. He knew, of course, that no such forgiveness would be granted. He had watched this scene play out too many times before, though always with others playing the part of the victim. And yet he was a man, and so he allowed himself to believe that there was a chance.

"Please, Mr. President, I beg you –"

There was a clatter high above the terrace, then a sound like the beating of a tin drum as a small shower of rocks and shale came flying off the cliff. Murov was curious, but he did not snap his neck upward, as his bodyguard Boris did, nor even with the alacrity of the condemned man in front of him. It was not presidential.

The second event, however, was harder to miss. The body of a man, clad in black, wearing the dark fatigues of the Presidential Security Service, and a matching red and white patch on his left shoulder, plummeted from the top of the cliff and fell face first against the marble tiles of the terrace. He landed with a sickening crunch, and Murov distinctly heard the sounds of bones cracking as his own mouth fell open with muted shock.

But it was not the fall that killed the man. The rear half of his head was missing, simply gone, as though torn away by some rabid animal.

"Mr. President!" Boris yelled, beginning to sprint toward his charge. "Get down!"

Murov glanced to Kholodov, then the dead man in turn, his limbs numb with a cocktail of horror and shock. This could not be happening, not here. He was the president of the Russian Federation. This was his backyard. Russian warships patrolled the coast. His men had surface-to-air missiles covering the skies, and a full company of heavily-armed soldiers from the National Guard occupied a barracks that was just ten minutes away.

Then he caught Kholodov's horrified stare. It was as though the man had realized something, or perhaps just accepted his fate. And then Kholodov's head was gone, too. The bullet imparted such a terrible force to his former bodyguard's torso that it toppled the chair over behind him.

Murov could not move.

He was trapped in position, on the terrace he loved, over-looking the sparkling Black Sea, and waiting to die. He heard the gunshot, the one that had killed Kholodov, rolling over the water a second later. It was barely audible over the ragged panting of his breath.

"Dmitry," Boris yelled, using his president's first name. Murov looked up with dull, terrified, uncomprehending eyes. His bodyguard was close now, just a few yards away. Boris would know what to do.

And then Boris fell, a spray of red and white showering the air behind him. The white was bone fragments, Murov under-stood, as a moment of horrified clarity swept over him. Someone was out there, and they could kill him at any moment. None of his men would be able to rescue him in time, if they even could at all. No matter how many they sent, they would all die in vain. And then they would stop coming, for no man would put himself into hopeless harm.

He was a dead man.

His coffee cup lay on the ground, shattered, a pool of black liquid steaming against the cream-colored marble. A stream of yellow joined it, trickling down his pants leg, then flowing with reckless abandon as he relinquished all control over his bowels and his body. An acrid stink of ammonia and iron filled the air, blood and urine mixing into a potent, foul combination.

Murov was weeping now. Gripping the table in front of him, trembling, and pissing himself, waiting to die.

"Do it already," he whimpered, then bellowed an inchoate scream into the skies. "Just kill me!"

But the bullet did not come. Not in that moment, nor the next, nor the ten minutes which followed. Dmitry Murov, the president of the Russian Federation, sat in a puddle of his own waste, tears coursing down his cheeks, surrounded by the bodies of men who had died serving him, showing him a loyalty they would never have received in return.

And yet he lived.

He understood why. The Americans were sending a message. They could reach out and pluck his life at any time, in any place. They had not done it this time.

But they could have.

53

EPILOGUE

Trapp and Ikeda launched the miniature submarine into the water long before President Murov stopped wondering whether he was about to die. They activated the detonator just before closing the hatch, initiating a five-minute ignition sequence that would send the Icarus to the bottom of the Black Sea, the corrosive saltwater quickly eliminating any forensic evidence that survived the fire, long before any realistic hope of recovery. Not that they expected any. The Russians would want to hush the whole event up, not draw attention to it.

Ikeda pushed the Triton minisub's throttle as far forward as it would go, but they were only a few hundred yards away when the Icarus met its end – the sub's design focused more on endurance than straight-line speed. They didn't see the explosion, but they both heard and felt it as a shockwave surged through the water, causing a resonant *twang* as the sub's observation dome vibrated as the energy passed through it.

"Any closer, and we'd be kissing the bottom any moment now..." Trapp muttered.

Ikeda shivered, though whether it was from what he said or

the sight of the sunshine overhead dwindling like the view of the sky from the bottom of a well, Trapp did not know. "I hate it down here," she said, knuckles white around the joystick.

"Tell me about it," he replied, reaching over and giving her shoulder a reassuring squeeze.

She's trembling, he realized.

He knew why. In a way, killing a man from a thousand yards away and through a scope could be more intense than doing it up close and personal. When you track your kill through a high-powered lens, wait for the perfect moment to press the trigger, then watch as your quarry continues talking, smiling, laughing, and *living* for one, two and then a third heartbeat, it's just different.

No matter how much training an individual goes through, Trapp knew, when you fight a man face to face, instinct takes over. Adrenaline floods the nervous system, heightening aggression and hiding the prospect of death. Your opponent isn't just an enemy, he's a threat to your very survival.

And that's easy to rationalize.

But killing a living, breathing human being at a distance is different. He poses no threat to you. And you see the expressions on his face up until the moment his head splits open like a burst watermelon, as the blood paints a red mist into the air and his lifeless body topples backward in slow motion.

"He raped those girls," Ikeda whispered.

The sub's engines were just idling now, its forward momentum slowing, then fading entirely, and her eyes had adopted a glassy look. Now that the immediate flight from danger was over, she was slipping into shock.

"Not just Sasha. There were others. Who knows how many poor girls he abused over the years?"

"He's gone now," Trapp said firmly, reaching forward and shifting her fingers from the controls of the sub. "You did that. He can't hurt anyone else. Not anymore."

He kept talking, his voice quiet and deep, saying nothing in particular as he pulled Ikeda's trembling frame toward him and enveloped her in a warm embrace. He kept talking so that she knew he was there, so that in some deep part of her mind, there was a connection to reality, a way back to the land of the living.

What she was going through right now was natural. It was part of the process, and there was no shame in it. Trapp had seen men like this before, on more battlefields than he could remember. It had happened to him, still did, on occasion.

"Just breathe," he murmured, glancing behind him to where O'Reilly had stowed the diving equipment. And, he saw, snacks.

He tore the wrapper off something sweet, a bar of chocolate, and thrust it toward her, waving it under her nose until the smell of the sugar made its presence known. She nibbled at a corner obediently, but chewed numbly. It didn't matter. Trapp just needed to get some calories into her.

"You'll be fine," he whispered. "Just keep eating."

For a while, they just sat there, on plush leather executive seats, in the most unusual of settings. It was almost like being back in the womb, Trapp mused as they drifted, barely moving in a sea of darkness, just swaying in the gloom. The sub's floodlights were at the lowest setting, not to reduce their chances of detection, which was almost nil, but to conserve battery power.

His shoulder felt cool, and he glanced down to see that Ikeda was crying silent tears that felt thick and heavy against his shoulder. And he crooned a half-remembered song from his childhood, just a little kid's nursery rhyme. And as he sang, he remembered nights spent in darkness like this, hiding from the wrath of a father who hated him, and a mother who had lost the will to care.

And for a time Trapp, too, wept. His eyes were dry, but in that place, clutching against a woman who had so swiftly made herself into a rock, he released a sadness he had carried with him for years.

And then it was over.

"I'm okay," Ikeda croaked, pulling herself away. "Really, I'm okay."

Trapp didn't ask if she was sure. "About time." He grinned, gesturing out of the sub's observation window and into the darkness. "You even sure we're heading the right way?"

She acknowledged his weak attempt at humor and seemed grateful for it, firing a half-smile right back at him. She cleared her throat and said, with a little hint of attitude, "I don't know, *Jason*. I never went to the Naval Academy..."

"Clearly." He smirked, relieved that she truly did seem okay. "But we really should get going. I've got a feeling that our friends up there"—he jerked upward with his thumb—"aren't going to be too happy."

The thought was sobering. They were still forty miles from Georgia's territorial waters, although the experts at Langley had assured them that, even if their exfiltration method was somehow detected, a vessel of their size and speed would be almost impossible to track in the noisy littoral waters off the Russian coast. Since Ikeda had taken out the counter-sniper team, and they had launched their tub from the backside of the Icarus where no prying eyes were watching, it was almost a certainty that they had not been noticed.

But there was always a chance. And the prospect of the Russians mobilizing the police, Army, Navy, Coast Guard, and whatever else they had on hand was a sobering one, especially down here, all alone, with no rescue coming. For all his previous confidence that Murov would prefer to keep a lid on what had just so nearly happened to him, Trapp's mouth was suddenly dry.

"Aye aye, Captain," Ikeda said, throwing him a mocking

salute. "I don't suppose you wanna work the charts and tell me where we're supposed to be going?"

"Shouldn't the captain –" Trapp started before waving his hand amiably. "Never mind." He pulled a chart from the storage compartment and studied it, even though he'd already memorized the details.

"Set heading 153," he said, tracing a path that led from an approximation of their current position to their eventual destination – and the final resting place of the luxurious miniature submarine. Hopefully without them inside...

They could head to the surface if they needed to take a GPS fix, and would probably be able to detect the satellites while remaining a couple of feet underwater, but if he could avoid taking that risk, he wanted to.

Ikeda stuck her tongue out of the side of her mouth as she consulted a compass on the dash in front of her. "Heading 153 is..." she said, playing with the joystick, "set." She glanced up. "What the hell are we supposed to do now?" She looked at him hopefully. "Did you bring a pack of cards?"

He had not.

It took almost eleven hours of mind-numbing boredom before they made it to the final waypoint, a little behind schedule, but still within mission parameters. The sun was beginning to set overhead, which meant they needed to move fast for the cover story to work.

The submarine's current position was about fifty feet below the surface, according to the depth gauge, and over a deep ravine in the seafloor. It might as well have been a mile. The dark was beginning to play tricks on his mind. He didn't even want to think about what was underneath him. Just thousands of feet of nothingness, so much nothingness that once the sub was scuttled, it would never be found.

"Heading topside," Trapp muttered, playing with the controls.

They began to rise, and he felt a deep sense of relief overcome him every foot closer to the surface they got. Behind him, Ikeda groaned as she pulled on a wetsuit and struggled to hoist tanks of oxygen onto her back in the cramped conditions. Trapp was already fully kitted out – there was only space for one person to do it at a time.

"You look like an idiot." Ikeda grinned when she was done.

"Speak for yourself..."

Trapp began drilling, just as O'Reilly had instructed. The little sub began to fill with water, and began to sink, before the thrum of the thrusters stabilized it. Just when he'd decided they were about to die, with the cabin completely full, he heaved open the dome, and they broke free of the vessel, their faces breaching the surface a few seconds later.

"Can you see it?" Ikeda asked, removing her mouthpiece.

The 'it' in question was a recreational diving boat that was waiting for them closer to shore, about a thousand yards away. The plan was to make the swim underwater, to avoid any chance of detection. They were already in Georgian coastal waters, but Trapp was certain that if the Russians knew where they were, then there was at least a chance they would act first, and deal with the consequences later.

After all, what the hell were the Georgians going to do about it? They already got invaded once...

"They'll be there," Trapp said, with a little more confidence than he felt.

Not because he suspected that they might have been forgotten, even abandoned, but because no operative in the field is ever truly certain of surviving until they are back home, and sometimes not even then.

They each pulled on their flippers and sat, bobbing on the surface of the ocean for a few seconds, far enough away from land that in the fading light, they were almost invisible. Still, lingering was a risk, and they both knew it. "Let's go."

Ikeda pulled on her diving mask, then glanced down at the sub, almost out of sight beneath them. "You don't want to say a few words?"

Trapp remembered the darkness down there, and even though the machine had carried them out safely, holding up its end of the bargain, he never wanted to go back. "Good riddance," he grunted. And dived into the warm, salty waters of the Black Sea as the sub began its long, final journey to the bottom.

FIFTEEN MINUTES and one course check later, they made contact with the boat, which had a skull and cross bones flags fluttering in the breeze, just like it was supposed to. It was a nice touch. Mitchell's idea.

Strong arms hoisted them out of the water, and a second later, before his mask was even off, a beer was pressed into Trapp's more than willing fingers. He tore the mask from his face, wiped the salt from his eyes with the back of his salty arm, which didn't help much, and saw a smiling, familiar face staring back at him.

"Thanks for making it, Rich," he said. "Believe me, you're a sight for sore eyes."

"You got 'em real worked up, guys." Rich grinned. "Russian Navy's out in force, shaking down any boat bigger than a damn canoe. I spent the afternoon listening in. The squids know something big happened, just not what." He shrugged. "Shame you couldn't go for the big kahuna while you were at it."

Trapp saluted Ikeda with his beer, then downed half the bottle, sighing as the cool liquid soothed jangled nerves. "Now, ain't that the truth."

It was a five-hour drive to the largest Georgian air force installation, the Vaziani Military Base, situated about fifteen miles from the country's capital, Tbilisi. They stopped once, for fuel, though Ikeda and Trapp stayed inside a large German SUV with heavily tinted windows. There would be no record that they had ever entered, spent time in, or departed the small country.

The SUV passed through the base's gates, and Trapp noticed that the guard booths were empty and the barriers raised. He suspected that in about sixty seconds, neither of those two facts would hold true.

Rich leaned over and shook each of their hands in turn. "Nice working with you guys." He grinned. "We should do it again sometime. I kinda like your style."

"Likewise," Ikeda said. "Thanks for the ride."

Trapp just nodded. He was exhausted, not from the swim, not from the drive, or the somewhat less than breakneck underwater ride to escape Russian waters, but from the weeks of planning that had led to this point, the loss of a friend in Italy, and the shattering of a briefly idyllic Tuscan vacation.

He knew that Rich wouldn't mind. Like him, the man was a warrior. Sometimes it was better not to speak.

The SUV drove right onto the runway, and though it was late, Trapp guessed that this particular section of the base was empty out of choice, not circumstance. He heard the aircraft's engines before he saw it.

"I called ahead, while you were sleeping," Rich said, by way of explanation. "Told 'em to warm the old girl up. Figured you wouldn't mind."

"Not a bit," Trapp replied simply. It was the Lord's honest truth. He knew that, at best, a week of intensive debriefings lay ahead of him. But still, he couldn't wait to get home.

The C-130's ramp was open, glowing a ghostly green in the darkness. As the jet wash passed across lights glistening in the darkness, they blurred, though Trapp was not entirely sure it wasn't simply out of exhaustion.

They exited the vehicle and said their goodbyes to Rich before the SUV disappeared into the darkness. Ikeda kissed Trapp on the lips and whispered, "Let's go home."

Was that what America was? he wondered as they entered the US Air Force Hercules transport aircraft, feet tramping against the metal ramp and clanking. Home?

The truth was, he didn't know. Trapp supposed it was, in a way. The only home that he had ever known. The US Army had adopted him like a son, and was a better father than his own, twice as harsh, but infinitely times more fair – because at least it fucked everyone equally hard.

He wasn't the only screwup in boot camp, nor the only recruit running away from a life that had rejected him. But he was perhaps the one who adapted to his new life best, finding that he had a natural aptitude for hard work. He wasn't the biggest, tallest, strongest or even the bravest of the men and women he had served alongside since before his facial hair even grew in ratty clumps, though he held his own in each department. What set him apart was the discovery of an ability to push himself beyond the limits at which most men buckle, and inner resilience, as much mental as physical, which got him noticed and set him on a career path he would never have picked for himself.

Trapp had been at this for nearly twenty years. A few of them stationed at Fort Bragg were the closest he'd come to stability. Then it was a couple of months here, a week there. Never long enough in any one spot to put down roots. There were women, too, but never seriously. It was hard to find someone who truly understood what his job entailed. Especially since it was classified.

So no, he realized. America was not home. At least, not in a way that anyone else might understand. But it was as close to home as he could reasonably expect. Not the place, but the people. The men and women he'd sweated, fought and killed alongside, they were blood. They'd saved his life, and he'd saved theirs.

Mostly.

There were some who would never come back. Some he had loved as friends and brothers. One in particular who he would never see again.

But perhaps there was hope for him yet.

Mike Mitchell was waiting halfway up the Hercules's ramp, standing silhouetted on a green background, his hand outstretched.

Trapp shook it wearily, longing to slump down in one of the noisy plane's jump seats, lean against the red webbing that stood in for a seat back, and pass out. He glanced around the plane's interior, empty except for a few ice coolers, stacked upon each other. "You couldn't plump for something a little more comfortable?"

"She was on a scheduled flight from Germany," Mitchell explained, grinning. "Don't worry, the director's Gulfstream is waiting for you there. We thought it might be a little suspicious if we sent it to pick you up. Don't want to make it easy for the Russians, you know?"

"They'll know we did it." Trapp shrugged. "What's the difference?"

Mitchell nodded. "Oh, they know, all right. But they won't be able to prove it. And that matters."

"I guess," Trapp said, making a beeline for the nearest section of seating, as Mitchell first greeted, then embraced Ikeda, saying something to her that wasn't audible over the background hum of the powerful Rolls Royce turboprop engines.

The cargo bay of an Air Force Hercules was a far cry even from flying in the back on one of the big commercial airlines.

Not a whole lot in the way of creature comforts, and noisy as hell, to boot. But to Trapp, it was like returning to the womb. He'd spent a career on these puddle jumpers, skipping from hotspot to hotspot. They were usually the last slice of peace he would see before going looking for trouble, or the first sign of salvation on the way out.

Ikeda came and sat next to him, carrying a can of some Georgian beer which bore a label that Trapp could not read. He popped it and took a sip. He couldn't care less what blend of herbs and hops had gone into making it. Trapp was no craft beer snob. As long as it was ice cold, which this one was, he was happy.

Trapp wished he'd packed a book. Little could beat a cold beer and a good read on a night flight. Something to while away the hours till they reached Germany. Hell, even a Jack Slater book would scratch that particular itch.

Mitchell wisely took a seat at the opposite end of the Hercules's cavernous interior, knowing better than to disturb his two operatives right now. There would be a time for debriefings and endless after-action reports so sensitive that only a single copy would ever be committed to paper before being locked away in the CIA's archives. But this was not that time.

"How you doing?" Ikeda asked softly – or at least as softly as was practical over the roar of the engines as they began to power up for takeoff.

Trapp opened his mouth to reply and shot her a sheepish grin as the engines roared, first prodding then kicking the lumbering aircraft down the runway and into the sky. Instead of replying immediately, he reached out and simply squeezed her hand. When the mechanical grumble finally quieted enough to talk, as the Hercules levelled out above the first layer of cloud, he bobbed it open and closed like a goldfish as he struggled to corral fractious, competing thoughts into a semblance of sense. Through the weeks in between the ending of the initial crisis and the mission they'd just completed, they had studiously avoided any discussion of what came next.

It was easier to focus on sniping drills and SCUBA practice than tangle with the much more complex issue of what the future posed.

"I guess that's the question, isn't it?" he finally mused, letting his head drop tiredly back against the webbing.

"Uh huh," she replied. "That's why I asked it, dumbass..."

"Buzz off," Trapp grumbled good-naturedly. "It's been a long day."

"Stop avoiding the question, Jason," Ikeda said sternly. "I know you well enough by now. Cut it out."

Trapp threw his hands up in mock-surrender, swaying as the cargo jet hit a patch of unannounced turbulence. "Okay, okay," he mumbled. "You want the truth?"

She arched an eyebrow. "You planning to lie?"

"I guess not. Okay, here goes. I don't think I can give this up. You don't want the white picket fence life, and neither do I. But I don't know where that leaves us."

"I figured as much," Ikeda replied, her face registering no discernible expression.

Trapp grimaced. What was going on inside that head of hers? Couldn't she just say something? Anything...

"Something you ate?" she asked, raising her eyebrows a second time.

"Nuh uh," Trapp muttered, shaking his head. "I ain't playing that game. What do you think?"

"I think, dumbass," Ikeda said slowly, enunciating the words with elegant precision, "that's exactly what I expected. You're like me, Jason. We're not *normal*. We'll never *be* normal. And that's fine."

"It is?" Trapp replied, a little confused.

"Sure." She smiled warmly back, leaning in and pecking him on the lips. "If I wanted normal, I probably wouldn't have joined the Agency, okay? And neither would you. I don't know what the future holds, Jason, but I'm pretty sure we don't need a matchbox in the suburbs to make things work between us."

"We...don't?" Trapp replied dumbly. Why was it that his higher functions seemed to shut down in this woman's presence, he wondered.

"No, Jason," Ikeda said, kissing him again. "We don't."

"And what happens when you go back to Hong Kong, and they send me to, hell, I don't know, *Iran*. What then?"

"I don't know, Jason. But we'll make it work."

THE HERCULES BOUNCED over a small patch of turbulence, jerking Ikeda back into the world of wakefulness. She scrunched up her eyes, freeing them of sleep, and glanced to her left, where Trapp was passed out, his body hunched over, head resting on her shoulder. She didn't move. It felt nice. Something human amid the rattling of the enormous military machine currently attempting to grind her teeth to dust.

"He's an old pro," Mitchell said, speaking loudly over the engine whine and indicating Trapp. "Take a nuke to wake him up right now."

Ikeda smiled thinly, not out of dislike for the man, but simply because he inhabited a different world. She was a relatively junior field agent, and he was a creature of the Agency's seventh floor, the suits, though his khaki combat pants and field vest begged to differ. Still, she was aware that he wasn't just at the top of the totem pole, but on an entirely different one to her.

She picked her words carefully and said something banal. "I bet."

Geez, girl, that was the best you could come up with?

Still, Ikeda kept her face impassive and hoped that Mitchell would turn away.

He didn't.

Instead, he undid his canvas harness, squirmed out of it, and walked over to her, indicating the empty jumpseat to her right. "You mind?"

She would have preferred to avoid the conversation, especially with Trapp fast asleep, but didn't say so, mainly because Mitchell headed up the Special Activities Division, which made him the wrong kind of guy to cross. She knew little about the man himself, except what Trapp had told her, and he wasn't exactly a loquacious conversationalist.

Ikeda gestured at the empty seat and spoke guardedly. "Sure."

"You handled yourself well this past week," Mitchell said, his tone light, as though he was commenting on the weather.

"I guess."

"You did," he replied, as if to settle the matter. "I was impressed."

She inclined her head. "Thank you, sir."

"You can cut that out." He grinned. "It's not the way we do things in SAD."

"I'm not *in* Special Activities, sir," Ikeda shot back, quickfire.

"What if you could be?" Mitchell asked with an easy, yet probing smile. "Would you come on board? I wasn't joking when I said you've caught my eye. Trust me, that's not an easy thing to do. I want you to join us, Eliza."

Ikeda froze. Of all the conversation topics she'd expected, a job offer certainly wasn't one of them. Her eyes flickered to Jason's exhausted, slumbering form. "Sir —"

"Mike," Mitchell corrected gently.

Ikeda frowned. "Yes, sir. Mike, there's a complication."

"Okay, there usually is. What is it?"

She glanced at Jason, then back again. "Um—"

Mitchell laughed softly. "I see. You mean he's the complication."

"Yes, sir," Ikeda answered, her cheeks blushing red as she slipped back into formality to deal with the awkwardness. "We're... I guess you could say we're an item."

"An *item*," Mitchell repeated gaily. "How very mid-century of you."

"Yes, sir," she said, unbalanced by the tone of his reply and tripping over her tongue as she attempted to explain. "So I understand that, you know, it won't be possible. But I want you to know I really appreciate the offer. In any other circumstance, I'd love the job."

"Why wouldn't it be possible?" Mitchell asked, wearing a sly frown.

"Because, well..."

"You think I care if you guys are screwing?" He laughed coarsely. "Hell no. It's about time he found someone."

"But aren't there policies about that kind of thing? I don't know, fraternization?"

"With the enemy?" Mitchell jibed. "This is the CIA, not the FBI. We don't have a problem with our people hooking up, so long as we know about it. Heck, half the spies we sent behind the Iron Curtain during the Cold War were husband/wife double acts. It's a good cover."

Ikeda grimaced. She'd known about that corner of the Agency's history, of course. But that was different, wasn't it? Intelligence gathering was a far cry from the wet work handled by Special Activities.

"I— I guess..."

Mitchell extended his hand. "So you're on board?"

She shook it without thinking, and Mitchell stood. "Glad to have you with us, Eliza," he said, starting to walk away. "I think you're going to enjoy yourself."

Ikeda leaned against the webbing, her head spinning from the hairpin change of direction her life had just taken.

"Well," Trapp mumbled, half-snorting as he roused himself. "I guess that solves that problem..."

She elbowed him in the ribs. "You were awake the whole time?"

"Yep. Figured he'd try something like that. Mike always did have an eye for talent."

Ikeda melted into him as she nestled into his side, a smile on her face even as she murmured, "Jackass."

ALSO BY JACK SLATER

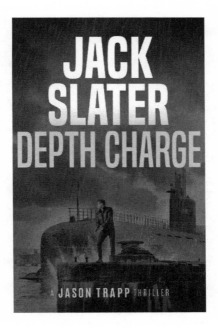

The clock is ticking.

In the North Pacific, the crew of a deep-sea recovery ship, the MV *Challenger*, are mercilessly gunned to death. Only one man survives, adrift in the ocean, and hundreds of miles from land.

In the deserts of Iraq, a clandestine meeting between one of the world's foremost assassins and his ruthless benefactor sets in train a cascade of horrific events that will shape the world for good.

And in America, with two weeks to go before a NATO summit that President Charles Nash hopes will finally bring peace to the long-simmering cold war between Iran and the United States, a network of sleeper agents prepares to bring America to her knees. They are well armed, trained and funded ... and they're prepared to die.

But Jason Trapp is watching.

And he's not done yet.

Head to Amazon to read Depth Charge, book four in the *Jason Trapp* thriller series.

FOR ALL THE LATEST NEWS

I hope you enjoyed Flash Point. If you did, and don't fancy sifting through thousands of books on Amazon and leaving your next great read to chance, then sign up to my mailing list and be the first to hear when I release a new book.

Visit - www.jack-slater.com/updates

Keep reading if you want to learn more about the real-life inspiration that led me to write *Flash Point*...

Thanks so much for reading!

Jack.